The Power and Faith to Maintain Vows Through the Ages

1167 A.D. . . . Nazareth . . .

"The City of Brass" by Deborah Turner Harris and Robert J. Harris: Saladin's forces are poised for Allah's victory over Christ; in a lost temple of magic and horror, the demon Baphomet will defeat all the gods . . .

1314 A.D. . . . Paris . . .

"Obligations" by Katherine Kurtz: Sir Adam Sinclair, the Adept, must travel the Astral Path to _____ and beyond, seeking the fate of a _____ _____-long Templar quest . . .

1746 . . .

"Word of Honor" by _____ hope to reclaim his king _____ magic—but the battle was turne _____ s theft, a wrong that could only be made r _____ om beyond the grave . . .

1952 . . . Texas . . .

"Knight of Other Days" by Elizabeth Moon: In a border hamlet, a *bruja* and a doomed mortal must decide the fate of a Templar stone that stops "the dead who could curse the world" . . .

Forever . . .

"Death and the Knight" by Poul Anderson: At any cost, the Time Patrol must stop a future scientist and his lover from saving the Templars—and destroying history!

TALES OF THE
KNIGHTS TEMPLAR

EDITED BY
KATHERINE KURTZ

ASPECT

WARNER BOOKS

A Time Warner Company

Today, as it has for eight centuries, the Supreme Military Order of the Temple of Jerusalem continues to maintain the Christian presence in the Holy Land. The Grand Magistry resides in Portugal; however, Knights and Dames of the Order are drawn from all over the world. English-speaking readers desiring further information about the ongoing work of the Order may address enquiries to:

Supreme Military Order of the Temple of Jerusalem
P. O. Box 2176
Washington, D.C. 20013-2176

WARNER BOOKS EDITION

Copyright © 1995 by Katherine Kurtz
All rights reserved.

Aspect is a trademark of Warner Books, Inc.

Cover design by Don Puckey
Cover illustration by Gary Ruddell

Warner Books, Inc.
1271 Avenue of the Americas
New York, NY 10020

Visit our web site at
http://pathfinder.com/twep

 A Time Warner Company

Printed in the United States of America

First Printing: June, 1995

10 9 8 7 6 5 4 3

To the Knights of the Order of the Temple of Jerusalem,
Past, Present, and Future

Non nobis, Domine, non nobis,
sed nomini tuo da gloriam.

Table of Contents

Introduction

𝕴n 1118, a French crusader called Hugues de Payens and eight fellow knights founded the Military Order most commonly known as the Knights Templar. During the two centuries that followed, the Templars established a well-deserved reputation as (among other things) superb fighting men and incomparable financiers. In the less than two hundred years the Order formally existed, they also achieved a notoriety unprecedented among other religious or chivalric bodies anywhere in the world.

On October 13, 1307, a day so infamous that Friday the 13th would become a synonym for ill fortune, officers of King Philip IV of France carried out mass arrests in a well-coordinated dawn raid that left several thousand Templars—knights, sergeants, priests, and serving brethren—in chains, charged with heresy, blasphemy, various obscenities, and homosexual practices. None of these charges was ever proven, even in France—and the Order was found innocent elsewhere—but in the seven years following the arrests, hundreds of Templars suffered excruciating tortures intended to force "confessions," and more than a hundred died under torture or were executed by burning at the stake.

The ostensible reason for suppressing the Order of the Temple had been to eradicate heresy; a more pragmatic motive had to do with seizing the vast wealth of the Templars for the King of France—and eliminating a too-powerful Order that answered only to the pope. (The Templars had denied Philip admission to the Order as an honorary lay knight, so personal pique may have been a motive as well.) Neither the Order's champions nor its detractors failed to note that both Philip and the pope, who had abandoned the Order to Philip's avarice, were to die within a year of being cursed by the last Grand Master, Jacques de Molay, as he and his Preceptor for Normandy were burned at the stake on March 14, 1314.

The preceding is a bare-bones synopsis of the Order's rise and fall, but a more detailed look at the Templars' history suggests more complicated circumstances that all added to the legendary stature the Order enjoys today. Historical perspective places the birth of the Order in the immediate aftermath of the Christian capture of Jerusalem in 1099, which led to increasing numbers of pilgrims journeying to the Holy Land to visit Jerusalem and other holy places. Despite the establishment of the Kingdom of Jerusalem, with a royal line of Western kings, travel in the area remained dangerous. Defense of the Christian-held lands was difficult, and men could seldom be spared to patrol the travel routes and protect pilgrims.

The Hospitaller Order, later to become the Knights of the Hospital of St. John of Jerusalem, had been founded in 1113 to house and minister to sick and injured pilgrims, but they did not immediately expand their role to include the protection of these pilgrims. Into this void came a

French nobleman from Champagne called Hugues de Payens, kin to the counts of Troyes, to found a second crusading Order initially calling themselves the Poor Knights of Christ. Tradition preserves the names of the founding nine in a list that probably vacillates between the factual and the mythic: Hugues de Payens, Geoffroy de Saint-Omer, Andre de Montbard, Andre de Gondemare, Payen (or Nivard) de Montdidier, Archambault de Saint-Aignan, Godefroy Bissor, Roffal (or Rossal or Roland), and Hugh Comte de Champagne—though the latter is known to have joined later. Undertaking to guard the pilgrimage routes and live as a religious community of warrior-monks (and under guidance from canons of the Church of the Holy Sepulchre in Jerusalem), they adopted a religious rule based on that of St. Augustine and made vows of poverty, chastity, and obedience before the Patriarch of Jerusalem.

Their offer of assistance was welcomed by King Baldwin II of Jerusalem, who granted them accommodation on the site of King Solomon's Temple, the cellars of which were said to have housed King Solomon's stables. Thus derived their eventual name: Pauperes Commilitones Christi Templique Salomonis—the Poor Fellow-Soldiers of Christ and the Temple of Solomon, later known as the Knights of the Temple, or Knights Templar.

For men vowed to protect pilgrims and holy sites, these first Templars do not seem to have done a great deal of protecting during the first few years of their existence, or to have attracted much interest in East or West. They recruited few, if any, new members. They lived in real poverty, without any distinctive attire or significant military presence. An early seal of the Order shows two knights riding on the same horse, said to be symbolic of their shared poverty and brotherhood. (This does not reflect later reality, for while individual Templars owned nothing, each knight would have required at least two or three horses in order to function in any military capacity—and sergeants and other lay retainers to support him.)

During that first decade of existence, the greater part of the knights' energy seems to have been focused on establishing their headquarters underneath the old Temple. Some later historians, searching for an explanation of the Templars' great eventual wealth, would suggest that the proto-Templars found some fabulous treasure while digging in the old foundations. (At least one esoteric tradition maintains that the real task of Payens and his eight co-founders was to carry out research and excavations that would result in the recovery of certain relics and manuscripts said to preserve mystical and even magical secrets of Judaism and ancient Egypt. According to this tradition, the knowledge thus obtained was transmitted through oral tradition within a secret inner circle whose existence was not even suspected by rank-and-file members of the Order.)

Whatever the true purpose of the founding nine, Hugues de Payens seems to have been ready for the Templars' next phase by 1127, when he embarked for Europe with five of his knights to seek official recognition by the church. Presenting himself and his companions before the Council of Troyes in 1128, he briefly recounted their history and mission, presented their proposed constitutions, and asked that they be given a rule of their own.

Their petition was successful. The future St. Bernard of Clairvaux gave the Templars a rule of seventy-two articles derived partially from his own Cistercian Rule (which had been based on the Rule of St. Benedict), partially from existing practices already adopted from the guidance of the Patriarch of Jerusalem and the Rule of St. Augustine, and in part based on a rule of Essenian origin known as the Rule of the Master of Justice.

In addition, with Bernard's concurrence, the knight brothers adopted the snow-white habit worn by the Cistercians and the canons of the Holy Sepulchre, symbolizing purity, and added to a white mantle the red cross of martyrdom, already long worn by crusaders. In all likelihood, the form of cross first used was a red patriarchal cross, with its double crossbar, since the knights had made their original vows to the Patriarch of Jerusalem and hence were his knights; but other forms became more common following papal recognition, including the more familiar Maltese cross, whose eight points symbolized the Beatitudes. Sergeants and squires wore the red cross on black or brown mantles.

A further distinction of appearance that proved an unexpected advantage in the Holy Land was the rule's requirement that, contrary to European custom of the time, the knights were to crop their hair short but keep their beards long. Since facial hair represented masculinity and virility in Middle Eastern culture, the bearded Templars were regarded by their Muslim foes with far more respect than the long-haired and clean-shaven European crusaders, who were seen as feminine and disgraceful.

By the time of Hugues' death in 1136, the Order was flourishing, with preceptories and commanderies in France, England, Scotland, and Ireland, ever-increasing grants and bequests of lands and revenues, and a growing reputation for ferocity in battle. Hugues had been a pious knight with determination and leadership abilities; his successor as Grand Master was Robert de Craon, or Robert the Burgundian, who brought administrative skills to the office.

By 1139, Robert had gained the unequivocal support of the papacy, when Innocent II created a new category of chaplain brothers for the Templars. Placing the Order under direct papal jurisdiction answerable only to him, Innocent further gave the knights the autonomy to act independently of the ecclesiastical and secular rulers. In addition, he extended their function beyond the mere protection of pilgrims, exhorting them to defend the Catholic church against all enemies of the Cross.

This broadening of their mandate enabled the Order to grow mightily in the decades that followed, rapidly establishing preceptories, commanderies, and other holdings in Spain, Portugal, Germany, and elsewhere in Europe. Fighting under the distinctive black and white battle standard called Beauceant, they soon presented a formidable military presence in the Holy Land.

Single-minded of purpose, their very motto proclaimed their allegiance: *Non nobis, Domine, non nobis sed nomini tuo da gloriam*—"Not to us, Lord, not to us but to Thy Name give the glory." By their vows and their very rule, they must follow orders without question, might not retreat in battle unless outnumbered at least three to one and only then upon direct order, neither gave nor received quarter, could not be ransomed, must stand and die if so ordered. And many of them did.

By the 1170s, the combined strength of the Temple and the Hospital would have made up close to half the effective Christian fighting force in the Holy Land, equally divided, with perhaps three hundred Knights Templar in the Kingdom of Jerusalem (along with their ancillary sergeants, squires, and other functionaries) and probably comparable numbers maintained in Antioch and Tripoli. And as the crusaders gained victories, both the Temple and the Hospital were given castles to garrison, forming a network of strongholds throughout the lands held by the Christians.

It was not to last. Though the Templars had become a powerful and indispensable part of the defense of the Holy Land, Jerusalem fell to the forces of Saladin in the summer of 1187, following the Frankish defeat at the Horns of Hittin.

Whereon hangs our first tale. One of the charges later made against the Templars was that they had consorted too freely with the Saracens, perhaps even taking on religious taints. One of the names ascribed to the idol supposedly worshiped by the Templars was Baphomet, a corruption of the name Muhammad—a particularly specious connection, since the Muslims abhorred physical representations of their Prophet. (Another interpretation renders Baphomet as Sophia, which could link with more esoteric connections.)

Speculations that the Templars allied themselves with the Order of Assassins probably spring, in part, from the fact that many Templars became fluent in Arabic—suspicious in itself, in some minds—and even more apocryphal claims that the Templars refused to let the Assassins convert to Christianity, because that would have ended their payment of tribute to the Temple. (The grain of truth here is that the Templars *were* extremely acquisitive, and jealous of their share of the spoils of war.) During their trial, one imaginative source even claimed that the Templars had done homage to Saladin himself, who later remarked that the Templars met with defeat because of their addiction to the vice of sodomy and their betrayal of their faith and law. (This particular charge seems to have been pure invention, so far as modern historians can ascertain. Small wonder that the Grand Master was said to have been "stupefied" by it.)

Nonetheless, it was inevitable that the Order did come into contact with Saracen influences, and it is certainly possible that individual knights did treat with the enemy. One might speculate whether there was more to this chapter in Templar history than ever came to the attention of the scholarly chroniclers.

The City of Brass

Deborah Turner Harris and Robert J. Harris

The killing began at noon.

As the desert sun approached its zenith, seven battered and bloodstained Templar knights were dragged forth from the back of the covered cart where they had been languishing in chains since their capture. Wrists bound behind them, they moved haltingly, weakened by heat and hunger and the debilitating pain of untended wounds. Last to emerge into the pitiless midday glare, the young knight known to his brothers as Thierry de Challon favored his Mamluk guards with a wordless snarl of defiance. Whatever fate might be in store for his fellow captives, he did not intend to go meekly like a lamb to the slaughter.

He and his six companions were the only survivors, as far as Thierry knew, of the engagement that had taken place two days ago at Cresson, a small natural spring half a day's journey to the east of Nazareth in the sunbaked heart of the Holy Land. One hundred thirty Templar knights, riding out under the command of Gerard de Ridefort, had arrived at the oasis to find the surrounding terrain occupied by a Muslim host numbering several thousand. What insane impulse of vainglory had prompted de Ridefort to hurl his own relatively insignificant force against this mighty contingent of Saladin's army, Thierry could not begin to guess. But de Ridefort was their Grand Master, and when he charged the Saracen lines, they had been compelled to follow.

The ensuing engagement had been a massacre. Many Mamluk warriors had died, cut down in the initial fury of the Frankish charge, but more had surged in to take their places, surrounding the embattled knights like a tide. Exposed to the arrows of the emir's Turkish archers without the shielding support of their own infantry, the Templars had had their horses systematically shot out from under them. Once dismounted, each of them had continued to fight, on foot and in isolation, until the bitter, bloody end.

Thierry had been among the last left standing. He had fought his hardest, until at last his sword had been struck from his hand. Winded and bleeding, he had steeled himself to be hacked to pieces by the bloodstained scimitars of his swarming adversaries. Instead, to his fury and utter humiliation, they had thrown a net over his head, dragging him down into the dust as if he had been some brutish wild beast to be captured and caged for the decadent amusement of Saladin's captains and their languishing concubines.

It was still not clear why he and his fellow captives had been denied the dignity of death on the battlefield. None of them possessed any special advantage of family wealth or influence to make them valuable as hostages, nor were any of them sufficiently highly placed within the Order to have incurred Saladin's personal wrath. Nevertheless, there had to be a reason why their lives so far had been spared. As his guards chivied him along behind the others,

Thierry grimly surmised that they would not have to speculate for very much longer.

The prisoners were hustled uphill toward a crescent-shaped formation of stones that rose up out of the midst of the Saracen encampment like an island from the sea. Waiting for them within this elevated amphitheater of stones was a strange deputation from the crowded encampment below. Foremost among them was an aged *faqir*, a spidery, shriveled figure wearing nothing but a filthy twist of rags wound around his leathery loins. Behind the *faqir*, like a mountain overshadowing a tree, loomed the towering figure of a Mamluk swordsman.

The swordsman was stripped to the waist, the knotty muscles of his arms and chest glistening with sweat in the sweltering heat. His head was bare, clean-shaven except for the obligatory scalplock of hair by which the Prophet would draw him up into heaven. The giant's powerful hands grasped the hilt of a broad-bladed scimitar, its point resting lightly on the ground between his sandaled feet. The singular length and heaviness of the blade identified it as a weapon of execution.

First to face up to the weight of the sword was the English knight Robert of Shrewsbury. Hands tightly trussed behind his back, he was taken to the *faqir*, before whom he stood swaying dizzily in the heat. The *faqir* looked long and hard at the young Englishman for several minutes, searching his face as though looking for some secret, hidden sign. Then he muttered something aside to the headsman in Arabic and gave a curt nod.

A single whistling sweep of the great scimitar sent the Englishman's head flying from his shoulders in a far-flung splatter of blood. The head struck the ground with a dull thud and rolled away among the rocks. As one set of guards heaved the headless trunk to one side, the *faqir* scanned the remaining Templars in search of another victim. This time the choice fell upon a young Burgundian, Reynald d'Arnaux.

Thierry held himself erect, even though his senses were swimming with the blistering heat and the sickly sweet stench of spilled blood. Five years ago, he had gone down on his knees before the wealthy and beautiful Isabeau Vilenoise, begging her to overlook his poverty and marry him. She had spurned him with the cruel reminder that he was only a younger son with no entitlements to his credit. Forced to swallow this bitter humiliation, Thierry had vowed afterward never again to bow his knee in servile petition to any other creature of the earth.

Instead, he had dedicated his life—the life that no one else cared for—to a purpose of his own choosing. Joining the Knights Templar had been a part of that choice, and since then he had lived and worked in expectation of reaping future benefits. If he died now, it would be without fulfilling his sworn promises. Likewise he would never have tasted the rewards of his service.

With this thought in mind, Thierry watched in stony silence as, one by one, the other knights were brought before the *faqir* to be examined and then beheaded. Beside him the Saxon knight Conrad of Bremen was praying in a harsh whisper for the salvation of his immortal soul. He was still praying when the guards hustled him forward, and he died with the words of the Paternoster on his lips.

Then it was Thierry's turn. The *faqir* studied him closely, his black eyes alight with burning intensity, as if their owner were attempting to penetrate the uttermost depths of his soul. In a voice as hot and dry as the desert wind, he inquired, "Why do *you* not pray, infidel?"

The question was posed in Arabic. Thierry summoned a sneer. "I am not like these others," he informed the *faqir* in the same language. "Give me a chance and I will prove it."

The old man grinned malevolently. "If you are speaking the truth, the sword will prove it for you."

Thierry's guards dropped back. The executioner raised the scimitar high, its curved blade still dripping with the blood of its last victim. Thierry's bound hands writhed behind his back, fighting the constraint of the ropes long enough for his fingers to trace an invisible symbol in the air.

Hear me, Master! he urged without speaking, *as I have placed my soul in your hands, I charge you to deliver me from this untimely death.*

With this injunction, he lifted his eyes toward the sky. His defiant, unblinking gaze was drawn through the near-blinding light to a point of darkness at the center of the sun. There was a scintillating flash and a shrill whistling hiss.

"Stop!" called the *faqir*.

Fire scored the underside of Thierry's jaw. He gave an involuntary start, then realized that his head was still attached to his shoulders. He shut his eyes and swallowed, feeling the scimitar quiver against his throat where its edge had gashed the skin. Through a sudden haze of dizziness, he heard the *faqir*'s voice say, "He is the one who will serve. Remove his bonds and let him be taken to the Servant of the Prophet."

Once his hands were free, Thierry was led down off the hill and taken to a tent in a neighboring part of the camp. Here he was provided with food and water and the services of an Arab physician, who bathed and tended his wounds. Thereafter, eased and refreshed, he was given fresh clothes and conducted back through the Saracen lines toward a flourishing grove of greenery which marked the presence of an oasis. Here beneath a cluster of date palms stood a pavilion of striped silk surmounted by the green silk banner of the Prophet.

While the guards stationed themselves on either side of the threshold, a soft-footed servant ushered Thierry into the tent. The abrupt change from light to shade momentarily confounded his sight. As he stood blinking, a steely voice addressed him in Frankish from the cool shadows.

"Welcome, sir knight. Come forward and be seated. You and I have matters of import to discuss."

Thierry knuckled the lingering dazzle from his eyes. Before him, on a pile of variegated cushions, lounged a lean, hawk-faced man clad in the loose, lightweight robes of a desert prince. The dark, intelligent features, surmounted by a jeweled turban of yellow silk, were those of Salah al-Din Yusuf ibn Ayyub himself.

Saladin!

Thierry squared his shoulders. Glaring down at his Order's most formidable adversary, he said coldly, "I was not aware that we had anything to discuss."

"That remains to be seen," said Saladin. "The report of you I have had from my holy man suggests that you might be one to profit from what I have to tell you."

He gestured toward an adjoining spread of rugs and cushions. Warily, Thierry sank down amid the opulent welter of soft fabrics and intricate embroideries. Saladin settled back, languid and feral as a resting lion. Surveying the young knight's scowling, blond-bearded face, he asked, "Have you ever heard of a place called the City of Brass?"

Thierry mutely shook his head.

"Among the legends of my people," Saladin informed him, "are tales concerning an ancient stronghold, built long ago by a race of sorcerers. These stories place that city—the City of Brass—somewhere in the midst of these lands that were once ruled by Solomon the Wise. It is said that in a palace at the heart of the city lies a marvelous relic, the possession of which confers wealth and power.

Some claim it is the head of a sorcerer—or perhaps an afreet which can foretell the future. Many have gone out to look for this city, hoping to lay claim to its secrets, but none has ever yet returned. Certainly this mysterious relic of which we speak is still there for the finding."

He paused. Thierry asked, "What has this to do with me?"

Saladin's chiseled lips framed a thin smile. "It may have everything to do with you, Knight of the Temple. It would be no small help to me if I had the means to foretell the course of future events. What I require is someone to seek out the City of Brass on my behalf, find this head of prophecy, and bring it back to me. You have given indications that you might succeed where others before you have failed."

"A strange compliment," said Thierry with a mirthless grin. "Why do you not send one of the many thousand men under your command?"

"Because the legends assert that any man who enters the City of Brass will surely lose his soul," said Saladin. "As a true servant of the Prophet, I cannot send a believer there. An unbeliever like yourself, however, is another matter. There are some, even among your own people, who claim that you Templars are servants of the demon Baphomet. Perhaps the loss of your soul is not something you have any reason to fear—"

An explosive exclamation from Thierry interrupted him. Blue eyes glittering, the young knight lurched to his feet, his right hand moving toward his hip where the hilt of his sword should have been. Saladin made a gesture of placation.

"Peace!" he exclaimed. "I spoke only in jest. I do not doubt the strength of the Templars' faith, however misguided it may be. Your religious convictions are of less concern to me than your proven fortitude as a fighting man—unless, of course, you would be prepared to for-swear this false god of yours and embrace the true religion of the Prophet?"

Thierry subsided, still bristling. "I could not change my allegiance," he informed Saladin, "even if I wanted to."

The Saracen lord shrugged. "In that case, I offer you this choice. You can return to the hill, where your head will be struck off from your body. Or you can seek out the City of Brass and return with a head with which to ransom your own. Should you manage to discharge this errand and live to tell about it, you will have earned my gratitude and your own freedom."

Thierry considered this proposal in silence. After a long moment, Saladin spoke again.

"My armies are gathering," the Saracen leader said softly. "When they are all assembled, we shall fall upon Jerusalem as a lion falls upon a yearling goat. Undertake this mission for me, and you may ride on before me to render an account of the size of my host and the disposition of my captains to your brother knights and anyone else who will listen to you. Moreover, having done what none of the Faithful have been able to do, you will have proven the superiority of your god. Well?"

Thierry drew himself up. He said roughly, "Tell me how to find this City of Brass."

A look of stern satisfaction passed across Saladin's face. "In good time," he said. "First you must swear by all you hold holy that you will indeed seek out the fabled city and return here to my camp with the prize I seek."

Thierry placed his right hand over his heart. "I do so swear," he said grimly.

The sun was a bowl of molten bronze, so hot that it seemed to have scorched all the color out of the desert sky. Thierry guided his sweating horse at a snail's pace along the uneven floor of a sunbaked valley. The surrounding terrain was a parched wilderness of withered thorn trees and venomous scorpions. But directly in front of him now, towering up a hundred feet into the air on either hand, stood two slender pinnacles of stone: the Horns of the Gazelle—the gateway, so he had been told, to the deserts surrounding the City of Brass.

The Saracen encampment lay four days behind him. The intervening journey had been gruelling, even by the standards Thierry had grown accustomed to since joining the Templar Order. His tongue was thick with thirst, and his eyes stung from the grit being blown up into his face by the capricious desert wind. The longsword strapped in its sheath across his back had worn blisters between his shoulder blades, despite the protective thickness of the quilted acton he was wearing underneath his borrowed desert robes.

The sword was the one he had carried at Cresson. The dagger strapped to his thigh had been salvaged from some brother knight's corpse left lying on the battlefield. The rest of his gear—blankets, waterskins, and provisions— had been supplied by Saladin prior to his departure. The mount he was riding was no heavy-boned Frankish charger but a stunted hill pony, bad-tempered as a camel and hardy as a mountain goat.

Besides these basic necessities for desert travel, Saladin had provided one thing more: a scarab-shaped amulet half the size of a man's palm. Thierry was wearing it openly, suspended around his neck on a stout leather thong. The scarab's body was of polished bronze, its carapace cut from a single piece of dark red carnelian. Boldly stamped upon the underside of the body was Saladin's own seal.

That seal was Thierry's guarantee of safe passage through Saracen territory. He had been assured that while he carried it, no member of the Faithful would venture to harm him. The amulet, however, had another, secret function, one that Saladin had not shared with Thierry until the last moment before he set out. Only then had Thierry learned that concealed beneath the carapace was a hollow compartment containing a small silver key.

The key was intricately made, its metal blackened with antiquity. Framed at the center of the elaborately wrought headpiece was a window of clear rock crystal the size of a man's thumbnail.

"This key was made in the City of Brass," Saladin had informed him in a low voice. "Once you have passed through the Horns of the Gazelle, it will be your guide."

The set of instructions which accompanied this revelation had seemed senseless to Thierry at the time. As he rode forward into the shadow of the twin stone pillars, however, he became conscious of an eerie tingling sensation at the base of his skull. The tingling grew stronger as he approached the gap. Staring up at the slender soaring columns, Thierry felt his skepticism wither away in a sudden shiver of dread.

That very fear, so foreign to his nature and his knightly profession, was the spur that drove him forward. By some strange trick of the desert light, the Horns seemed to lean in toward one another. High overhead, their twin summits seemed for an instant to merge in the illusion of an arch. As Thierry passed between them, a sudden heavy pulse slammed him full in the chest.

Like a hammer striking a gong, the sensation seemed to center on the amulet where it rested against his breastbone. With a choked cry Thierry slumped over his saddlebow. His horse took a skittish forward bound, almost unseating him. The next instant they were through the gap, with the pillar stones behind them.

The sense of vibration abruptly vanished. Recovering, Thierry snatched the reins short. The pony jibbed, throwing its ugly head nervously from side to side. Thierry forced it to a standstill, then whipped around in the saddle to look back the way he had come.

Still breathless with shock, he half expected to see the beginnings of a landslide. Instead, the stone pillars stood firm, pointed like needles toward the sun-bleached sky. The shadows under the rocks were wavering like ghosts in the desert heat. Otherwise everything was preternaturally still.

Thierry drew a deep breath and scanned the prospect in front of him. The terrain on this side of the gateway was much the same as that he had left behind him, an arid panorama of sand, stone, and dry brush, with no visible clues as to which way he should proceed. His gaze dropped to the amulet resting against his chest. Securing the pony's reins to his saddlebow, he took scarab in hand and thumbed the tiny catch at the base of the head.

The carapace sprang open. Thierry removed the key and weighed it thoughtfully in his palm. "The stone is a window on the City of Brass," Saladin had said. "When you are facing the direction in which the city lies, you will find yourself viewing its image in the window before you."

With a humorless shrug, Thierry raised the crystal to his right eye and scanned the landscape in front of him in a wide arc from left to right. Initially the lens showed him nothing that he didn't expect to see. His gaze traveled on past the median. As his vision gravitated toward the northeast, an image suddenly manifested itself on the crystal pane in front of him.

An image of walls and roofs, arches and towers.

Thierry recoiled with a muttered imprecation. A second look, however, confirmed his discovery. There in front of him, reduced to miniature by the size of the crystal, floated the metallic image of a city made of brass.

When he turned aside, the image vanished. When he returned the lens to its previous orientation, the image reappeared.

Thierry lowered his hand, his teeth glinting through his beard in a mirthless smile. "It would seem my course lies in that direction," he muttered to himself aloud. "Very well, so be it."

The decision he had made five years ago—the decision which had set him apart from his fellow Templars—was, he felt sure, the true reason he had been chosen to seek out whatever strange destiny now awaited him. With a renewed sense of purpose, he put the key away for safekeeping and prepared to ride on.

Normally he would have rested through the heat of the afternoon and continued his journey once the sun was down; now, however, it seemed advisable to carry on in broad daylight while the brightness of the sun made the image in the crystal easy to see. For the next several hours he rode north by northeast, pausing every so often to check his bearings. When darkness came on, he found a nest of boulders large enough to shelter him from the wind, and there made camp for the night.

As soon as the sun was up, he rose and carried on his way. After a morning spent toiling through an arid range of foothills, he arrived at the edge of a wide plateau. A hazy line on the opposite horizon hinted at more hills to come. After a brief rest in the meager shade of a tall rock, he took a few sparing sips of water and pressed on again.

The plateau was a dancing floor for whirlwinds. Thierry could see them whipping their way across the landscape, tossing up fierce plumes of sand and loose rock. He began to come across sunken ravines, like the remnants of long-vanished sea caves. The ravines were strewn with monstrous bones—the skeletal remains of strange leviathan creatures left dead and stranded here unimaginable eons ago.

By nightfall he had come no farther than midway. His sleep that night was fitful, tormented by dreams of sparkling fountains that ran dry each time he came to drink. At dawn he gave the pony the last of the water in his waterskin and set out again in a daze of fever and thirst. The image of the city glittered in the crystal before him like a mocking promise of deliverance.

The dark haze he had seen on the horizon the day before assumed the forbidding shape of an unbroken palisade of cliffs. The midday sun showed the faces of the rocks to be as sheer and unscalable as the ramparts of a mighty fortress. Thierry drew rein in the shadow of the walls. Fighting off the blinding stupefaction of thirst, he consulted the key again, and discovered he was being directed toward somewhere off to his left.

Keeping close to the cliff's base, he had covered little more than a furlong when the pony suddenly pricked up its drooping ears. Even as Thierry started up out of his own daze, it gave a wheezing snort and lunged forward.

A vertical rift seemed to open up out of nowhere in front of them. It was narrow and tight as a chimney flue. Nostrils flaring, the pony shot for the gap. When Thierry tried to rein in, he was scraped from the saddle and flung bruisingly to the ground behind.

Cursing, he picked himself up and limped forward. Just beyond the entrance to the gap lay a small enclosure no more than ten feet across. The floor of the enclosure had been hollowed out on one side to form a shallow basin. The basin was brimming with water.

The pony was already drinking noisily. Throwing caution to the winds, Thierry plunged in to do the same. The water was rust brown and had a bitter mineral taste, but he was not disposed to question whether or not it might be poisoned. He slaked his thirst and filled his waterskins, only then pausing to consult the key.

To his puzzlement, it seemed to be pointing him toward the cliff itself. He scrubbed a hand roughly across the lower half of his face and sat back on his haunches to think. As he did so, his ear caught the sluggish trickle of running water. Straightening up, he cast a look around the walls of the enclosure, trying to determine where the sound was coming from.

The rock wall above was broken by a narrow zigzag fault. Half masked by neighboring slabs of stone, the fault seemed to extend all the way to the clifftop. Thierry measured the rift with his eye. It looked difficult, but not impossible to scale.

After hobbling the pony, he stripped the saddle from the animal's back and left it with the rest of his sparse gear in a heap among the rocks. His longsword, however, he retained, along with a gourdful of water and a handful of dry biscuits tied up in a sack at his belt. The key he returned to its compartment inside the amulet bearing Saladin's seal. Tucking the amulet itself inside his robe, he set his gaze on the clifftop and resolutely began to climb.

The rocks were furnace-hot to the touch. Halfway to the top, he was obliged to stop and wrap his hands with rags torn from the hem of his robe. Light-headed from the heat, he forced himself not to look down. After a nerve-wracking struggle up a perpendicular shaft, he at last arrived at the safety of a jutting ledge.

The ledge receded into a dark cave mouth. Left without any visible means to continue his ascent, Thierry sat down to catch his breath and consult the key. It came as no surprise to discover that he could only advance by entering the cave. He put the key back in its place and stepped through the opening.

Having neither torch nor lantern, he could only trust to

luck to prevent him from going astray in the dark. Keeping his right hand in contact with the wall, he began gingerly to advance. The darkness gaped to receive him, cold as the grave after the blazing heat of the sun he was leaving behind. Shivering, he was about to take a last backward look at the doorway when he realized that there was a faint glow emanating from the amulet riding on his chest.

The source of the glow was not the amulet itself, but the key inside. Long past questioning the nature and properties of the key, Thierry dropped down on one knee and carefully thumbed the catch. The blaze of light as he took out the key was strong enough to show him a long tunnel stretching away from him into the distance. Holding the key at arm's length before him, he stood up and set out along the passageway.

The tunnel ran straight. Initially the walls were blank, but after a while Thierry became aware of faint lines of inscription running along beside him on either hand. The inscriptions were disquieting to study too closely. He wrenched his gaze away and pressed on.

It seemed as if he had been walking for hours when his straining eyes spotted a winking pinpoint of light ahead of him. The pinpoint rapidly expanded until he could make out the shape of another opening. His heart beating more quickly, he put the key away and quickened his pace. Hurrying forward, he emerged into strong sunlight on a high balcony of stone overlooking the circular sweep of a broad plain. The plain was entirely encircled by mountains. Seen from above, it was a scorched anvil of hard-baked earth, its surface fissured with cracks. At the center of the plain lay a harshly glittering collection of buildings, littering the parched ground like blocks scattered at random by a giant's hand. The maze of roofs and turrets was enclosed within a metallic ring of high walls.

The City of Brass itself!

Thierry stopped to fortify himself with some biscuit and a drink before making his descent to the valley floor. Not a breath of wind was stirring as he set out across the plain. He had the impression it had not rained here for uncounted centuries. Cut off from the rest of the world, this remote plain was arid and lifeless, a place where the hand of Creation had faltered.

Thierry approached the city from the west. Towering gates of tarnished brass stood ajar like the sagging jaws of a skull. Thierry slipped through the gap and halted. Dwarfed by the surrounding walls, he cast a long look around him at the perfectly preserved structures of a city long dead and all but forgotten.

He was standing on one side of what might once have been a broad marketplace. All the edifices fronting the square, however, had only blank facades, like so many unfinished drawings. Thierry looked in vain for some sign of a door or a window. If there was any way in or out of these buildings, he could not see any.

Crossing the square, he struck a wide avenue that ran eastward through a succession of soaring arches. The buildings lining both sides of the avenue might once have been shops, but again there was no visible means of entry or exit. There was not a sound anywhere. The ground seemed to drink up the sound of Thierry's footbeats, leaving only silence behind.

The shopfronts gave way to houses, some of them three or four floors high, their foundations decorated with tiles, their roofs overlaid with brass. But here again the walls themselves were featureless, blank-sided as a set of child's blocks. Thierry hurried past them, averting his gaze from their blind exteriors. Whatever force or agency had sealed this city up within itself was, he felt, still active, and still present.

At the center of the city lay the palace. Thierry made his way silently through a succession of courtyards mapped out by machicolated walls and overhanging turrets. At the center of the maze stood a great domed edifice flanked on four sides by spires of forge-tempered brass. Here, beneath a colonnaded portico, he at last discovered a doorway.

The doorway was fitted with a set of brass portals half again the height of a tall man. The portals were standing open and the gap between them was wide enough to have admitted a yoke of oxen. The floor beyond the threshold was of smoothly polished brass. At the center of the floor, dimly mirrored in its tarnished surface, stood an elevated dais surmounted by a canopy of brazen filigree.

Mounted on the dais was an altar. It had been made from a great slab of black granite laid across two lesser blocks of the same stone. Harsh light, falling through an unseen opening in the vault above, made a pool of brightness on the altar table. At the center of that circle of light stood an ornately finished casket of pure silver.

Thierry eased his way cautiously across the threshold. When nothing leaped out at him from the shadows, he set out across the floor toward the foot of the dais. As he started up the steps, his eye was drawn toward a dull glimmer of white lurking in the shadows beneath the altar stones. A closer look revealed that it was a human skull.

More bones were lying nearby. Thierry recognized a pelvis and part of an arm among the fragments of a shattered rib cage. The shank bones had been broken open and sucked clean of marrow. The rest of the skeleton showed the hungry marks of carnivore teeth.

Thierry sucked in a soft, hissing breath and cast a wary look around him. His straining senses could detect no other presence besides his own. Only slightly reassured, he slipped his sword from the sheath across his back.

Gripping it firmly by the hilt, he leaned in to inspect the casket.

The casket had the look of a reliquary. The panels that made up its flat sides and peaked lid were densely overlaid with interlocking traceries of some arcane form of script. Peering more closely, Thierry discovered a keyhole concealed among the manifold whorls. Warily laying his sword naked before him on the altar top, he opened the amulet and once again took out the key.

The key fitted smoothly into the lock. Thierry drew a deep breath and gave it a turn. There was a sharp crack and a sudden sulfurous flare. Staggering back a pace, Thierry saw the crystal in the key's headpiece burst explosively into flame.

Biting back a cry, he made a reflexive move to snuff it out. The fierce heat scorched his fingers and made him snatch his hand away. Engulfed in fire, the key began to dissolve. In mere seconds, there was nothing left of it but a puddle of molten slag.

The flame guttered and died. Thin tendrils of evil-smelling smoke leaked from the keyhole. There was a hiss, followed by a thin, metallic chime. As the tone dissipated, the lid of the casket sprang up and the sides fell away to reveal the object locked away inside.

It was a severed human head.

The head was that of a man. It was gaunt and bearded, the eyes closed, the skin sunburned and weathered to the coarseness of leather. Staring hard, Thierry wondered what power or charm could have kept it thus incorrupt. Even as he stared in bemused astonishment, the closed eyelids quivered and retracted.

Dark eyes stared wide, alight with the fires of some remote inner vision. The bearded lips writhed in an effort to speak. Thierry strained forward. A dry whisper made itself heard in the shadows of the vault.

Even now the ax is laid to the roots of the trees, murmured the head, *so that any tree which fails to produce good fruit will be cut down and thrown into the fire.*

It was a passage Thierry knew from Scripture. Hearing the words, he realized the identity of the speaker. He stared in awe, knowing that in this severed head he beheld all that was left on earth of the man once known as John the Baptist.

Even as the prophetic import of this discovery sank into his mind, a huge shadow fell across his shoulder from behind. Thierry seized his sword and spun around. Out of the brazen fabric of the floor a noisome cloud of vapors was rising. Still growing and expanding, the cloud soared toward the roof. Following its progress as it rose, Thierry suddenly found himself gazing up into two compound clusters of hungry, lambent eyes.

Each eye contained a pupil of fire. Faceted one to another, they glittered like jewels of flame. A slot of a mouth gaped open like a furnace door, exposing a long red gullet armored on the inside with grinding scales. A tongue like a scourge flicked in and out between a double row of venom-dripping canine teeth.

The creature's fiery aspect proclaimed it one of the greater *djinn.* Snarling defiance, Thierry planted his feet in a fighter's stance. Out of the depths of the creature's smoldering bulk rose a sibilant peal of laughter that set the air quivering. A deep contralto voice, thick with fulsome melody, spoke from the roof, using a language of darkness that penetrated Thierry's mind with forced comprehension.

"Welcome, son of humankind," it mocked. "Whatever treasure you came here seeking, be sure you've found more than you bargained for."

Thierry left the dais in a single fluid bound. Sword gripped high in both hands, he swung the blade around in a whistling arc aimed at where he thought the creature's underbelly might be.

The *djinn*'s response was a belch of flame and laughter that knocked him back on his haunches like a blast of cannon fire. Still brandishing his sword in front of him, Thierry said harshly, "By the Name that is above all names, I charge you to tell me how so sacred a relic as this comes to be guarded by so damnable a being as you!"

The *djinn*'s glittering eyes burned brighter. "The City of Brass is my fortress. Whatever lies within its walls is mine to do with as I wish."

"Nevertheless," said Thierry, "It was not always so. Answer my question, or I swear to you I will pronounce the Name by which you suffer."

The *djinn* gave a malevolent hiss. "It will take more than the speaking of a name to save you, mortal."

"Perhaps," Thierry agreed stonily, "but it will cost you a painful reminder of the strength of the divine wrath."

The *djinn*'s multifaceted eyes hooded themselves for a moment. There was a bristling pause before it capitulated and began to speak.

"The head of the Baptist was carried off into the desert by some of that prophet's own followers. It was they who used divers mystic arts to keep it incorrupt, in order that it might continue to speak to them in this life. They believed that the Baptist was the One incarnate, and believed that the head itself held power to call down fire upon the world. Seeking refuge from that wrath, they wandered far and wide, and at last found the City of Brass here in the desert, where it had been built by the descendants of Cain in ages past, before the Deluge. Caring nothing for its origins, they occupied the city as their own and caused this temple to be made a shrine to house the object of their veneration.

"Their beliefs concerning the Baptist's head were a

blasphemy," the *djinn* continued, "and for this sin the Almighty cursed them, sealing them up within their homes and leaving the Palace to the servants of His enemy. Thus did I come to make my home here, and here I feed upon the souls of those who come in search of the fabled head."

Sudden hunger quickened the fire in the *djinn*'s jewellike eyes. Swift as an adder, it shot past Thierry, interposing its vaporous bulk between him and the doorway.

The young Templar stood his ground. "You may try to take my soul, demon," he challenged, "if you dare."

The *djinn* belched out another roar of laughter. Quivering with gleeful anticipation, it put out a tentacular arm and plunged it like a dagger into the young knight's breast.

Thierry staggered slightly under the impact. There was a deep-throated sucking sound. Snarling and slavering in sudden bafflement, the *djinn* pressed in closer. Then all at once it recoiled with an anguished, ear-splitting howl.

Still howling, it tried to pull away, only to find itself held fast. As it continued to shriek and struggle, a sudden bolt of black fire billowed up out of Thierry's chest cavity. Corrosive as acid, the flame ate its way up the *djinn*'s outstretched arm. Like some dark leprosy, it overwhelmed the creature's body in a consuming winding sheet.

The *djinn*'s frantic thrashing grew weaker. Wholly enveloped by the black flame, it withered and shrank, dwindling down to human proportions. Thierry watched impassively as the creature writhed and moaned in throes of mortal agony.

"You should not try to take that which has already been bought by one greater than yourself," he observed coldly.

"By Baphomet!" the *djinn* gasped through its agony.

"Aye, by Baphomet," Thierry confirmed grimly. "Damned I may be, but you are twice damned for trying to take what is his."

The *djinn* gave a final piteous wail. The black fire flickered and began to die away. The *djinn*'s ravaged form collapsed to the floor. Thierry came to stand over it, sword in hand.

The words of his demonic master echoed in the depths of his mind. *"The Almighty One has cheated you of earthly happiness. If you will do me service, I will ensure that all you desire is placed within your hands. Among the most militant of my adversaries are the Knights of the Temple, whose appointed mission is to bring a new order to the warring nations of the world. Should these holy knights succeed in uncovering the secrets of the Temple, they will have the means within their grasp to banish the evils upon which I feed: poverty, injustice, cupidity, and despair. Join the fellowship of these Templars, corrupt them with blasphemies, and you will have had your revenge on the One who scorned you and yet would elevate them."*

"My lord Baphomet," he intoned to the surrounding air, "I now see your will in all that has transpired. The Baptist's head, sorcerously preserved, which you have delivered into my hands, will give me the means to bend the Templar Order to your will. Those who submit will reap the world's wealth and the rewards of earthly pride. Those who resist will see their virtues set at nought. So shall the Order become your instrument and devour the very heart of Christendom."

He paused and looked down at the charred, foul-smelling form of the *djinn*. "One more thing remains to be done," he murmured.

So saying, he raised his sword high above his head, and with a single downstroke struck the *djinn*'s head from its still-twitching body.

Dusk was gathering over encampment at Ra's al-Ma' as a tall, robed figure mounted on a ragged hill pony rode slowly through the ranks of the Saracen host and at last drew rein outside the entrance to Saladin's silken pavilion. Thierry de Challon remained seated in the saddle while a servant ran to inform the great commander of his presence. Saladin himself emerged a moment later.

"We meet again, sir knight," he observed, "against all expectations on my part. What news do you bring back from your travels?"

For answer, Thierry thrust a hand into the bag that was hanging from his saddlebow. When he drew it out again he was holding a severed head by a hank of coiled snaky hair. The dead face was a monstrous parody of human features, a swollen tongue protruding from between sharp fangs.

"I have brought you this from the City of Brass," Thierry said, and let the head drop so that it thudded to the ground at Saladin's feet.

Only a visible effort of will prevented the Commander of the Faithful from recoiling before that grotesque, inhuman visage. He gave a slow nod, acknowledging that this was indeed a hideous wonder such as he had dispatched Thierry to bring to him.

"And what is that you are carrying under your cloak?" the Saracen leader asked curiously, indicating the outline of a casketlike object strapped to the back of the Templar's saddle.

"Of what concern is that to you?" Thierry countered. "You swore that when my mission for you was completed, I should return to my Order in Jerusalem unmolested."

Saladin acknowledged the reminder with a shrug. "I did so swear," he agreed, "by the Prophet himself. Do you still have the key I gave you?"

"It perished and cannot be returned," said Thierry. "The amulet I will keep for the time being, as a sign of your protection. Once I rejoin my Order, I will arrange to have it sent back to you."

"There is no need," said Saladin with a fleeting smile of little mirth. "You may leave it for me in the Temple at Jerusalem. Go, then, warrior, and prepare for that battle."

Thierry nodded tersely and reined his horse around. As he did so, the eyes of the *djinn*'s severed head rolled open. The blackened lips writhed. A voice dry as tinder issued from between the creature's carious teeth.

"The fire is waiting, Templar," it hissed after him, "for you and all your brethren. Only time stands between you, and it grows shorter."

Thierry did not look back. His face set toward Jerusalem, he rode steadfastly on, carrying with him the head of John the Baptist and the destiny of the Templars.

INTERLUDE ONE

No evidence has ever been found to suggest that the Templars did, indeed, worship the head of John the Baptist—or, indeed, that they worshiped a head at all—though this was among the variations on the charge of idolatry, which certainly figured in the Templars' downfall. Nonetheless, there still exists today in the regions around Baghdad a remnant of a Gnostic sect known as the Mandaeans, also called Nasoreans or Christians of Saint John, which arose in the first or second century. Their teachings were akin to those of the Manichaeans, and St. John the Baptist figured prominently in their writings. (The original Mandaeans were probably disciples of John the Baptist, who *did* have his head, at least for a time.) Given this factual snippet, we might well postulate that today's Mandaeans represent a splinter group left behind by those heretics who fled to the City of Brass, perhaps taking with them the head of John the Baptist. Such a relic would have been in keeping with what many believed to be part of the Templar treasure.

It is more likely, however, that more conventional treasure occupied the attention of the vast majority of the knights, as their fortunes shifted in the Holy Land following the fall of Jerusalem. Gradually forced to withdraw westward, their energies focused increasingly on trade and financial services.

Templar galleys had long provided secure transport for pilgrims and crusaders as well as the Templars themselves—at a price. Rather than returning empty, Templar captains now began to establish new regular trade routes between their Mediterranean and Atlantic ports.

So secure were the Templar treasuries that they became safe depositories for the wealth of kings as well as their own. Templars often served as advisers, diplomats, ambassadors. Richard Lionheart became almost an honorary Templar. The Master of the English Temple stood at the side of King John when he signed the Magna Carta in 1215, and also signed it. Two knights were requested to serve in the household of Pope Alexander III. So well regarded was the fiscal integrity of the Order that the Temple often became agents for the management of properties and trusts, the negotiation and expediting of ransoms, and even the collection of taxes.

As mortgage bankers, the Templars got around the church's prohibition against usury by taking the revenues of a mortgaged property until it was redeemed. Interest on cash loans was secured by writing the note for more than the actual amount of the loan. Their system of security and verification for written draft demands enabled credit to be moved between Templar establishments with minimal risk of loss, foreshadowing the development of checks and other financial instruments. Such a financial network melded well with the confidentiality required for intelligence gathering, which had been a mainstay of the Templar military presence in the Holy Land.

So the Temple prospered, generating increasing wealth both from financial services and from constant charitable bequests and donations by pious individuals. Rarely was a will of importance drawn that did not include an article in the Temple's favor, and many were the illustrious men who, on their deathbed, took Templar vows so that they might be buried in the habit of the Order and thus accrue benefits in heaven. So great was the power and prestige of the Order that the Grand Master ranked as a sovereign prince among the nobility of Europe, taking precedence over all ambassadors and peers in the general councils of the church. Answering only to the pope, and immune from all lay and ecclesiastical jurisdiction, the Order came to represent a power outside the usual limitations under which lesser mortals were forced to operate.

It was inevitable that this immunity and power should cause resentment, and Philip IV of France was the man who finally decided to do something about it.

He had come to the throne in 1285, at the age of twenty-six. Known as Philip le Bel or Philip the Fair—for his physical appearance, not any appreciation of justice—he found himself frequently bailed out of trouble by the Temple. It was the Temple that advanced him the money for his daughter's dowry, when she was betrothed to the future Edward II of England. The Temple had supported him in his confrontations with Pope Boniface VIII, who would have asserted the superiority of the papacy over any secular ruler. And it was in the Paris Temple that Philip had been forced to take refuge for three days in June 1306, because of the Paris riots. Yet these favors from the Temple seemed to breed only resentment.

Furthermore, Philip was a religious zealot, still fired with hopes of organizing a new Crusade to liberate Jerusalem and the Holy Land. It could not be done without vast financial resources, and it could not be done without the cooperation of the Military Orders.

To secure both, Philip embroidered upon a plan already under consideration by the pope: the amalgamation of the Temple and the Hospital into a single Order to be called the Knights of Jerusalem, with concurrent appointment of a combined European commander of all secular forces, to be known as the Rex Bellator, or "War King." Philip countered with the proposal that *he* should be that Rex Bellator, and further, that the kings of France should become hereditary Grand Masters of the merged Order, with full access to their combined wealth and resources.

The Grand Masters of both the Temple and the Hospital flatly rejected the notion; nor was the pope enthusiastic. Philip was furious. He had all but deposed one pope, Boniface VIII; a second, Benedict IX, had died very conveniently, under somewhat suspicious circumstances; and Philip subsequently had put his own man, Clement V, on the papal throne and moved its seat to Avignon. But now the man who owed him for a papal tiara seemed reluctant to do anything about these troublesome Templars. Fortunately, Philip had a proven weapon at his disposal.

Philip's previous nemesis, Pope Boniface VIII, had been accused of heresy, sodomy, blasphemy, and a variety of magical practices including sexual congress with a pet demon said to dwell in the pontiff's ring. The author of these extraordinary charges—who sought a postmortem trial of the dead pope, with his remains to be exhumed and burned if convicted—was a royal favorite called Guillaume de Nogaret, whose parents (or grandfather, or close relatives) were said to have been burned as heretics during the Albigensian Crusade. Subsequently educated by the church, perhaps in an attempt to stamp out any latent heretical leanings, Nogaret was to use his legal training as a sword to strike back at the church that had burned his relatives.

Undeterred by the excommunication pronounced upon him by the short-lived Pope Benedict IX, and unrepentant regarding his role in the harrying of Boniface VIII, Nogaret had few qualms about taking on the Temple. If the king wanted the Military Orders broken, and their wealth diverted to the royal coffers, Nogaret would do it for him—and destroy whomever stood in his way, especially the arrogant Templars. Perhaps Nogaret might even get his excommunication lifted by the present pope, Clement V.

Eagerly Nogaret set about assembling a suitable list of accusations against the Temple, aided by half a score of infiltrators and disaffected knights who had been expelled, usually for good cause. (In a trial run of the methods that later would be used against the Templars, Nogaret effected the arrest and imprisonment of every Jew in France, on July 22, 1306, and shortly thereafter confiscated their property and expelled them from France.) Meanwhile, under cover of discussing plans for the new Crusade, the Masters of the Temple and the Hospital were summoned to attend the pope in Poitiers.

The Master of the Hospitallers declined, pleading urgent business in Rhodes. Jacques de Molay, the Grand Master of the Temple, was well aware of the merger being considered, but was eager to present his views about how a new Crusade might come about without the merger, confident that the pope would protect the Order. In late 1306 or early 1307, he arrived at Marseilles with an escort of six Templar galleys and proceeded overland to Paris—not incognito as the pope had requested, but accompanied by sixty mounted knights with their accompanying sergeants and squires and servants, and a baggage train of twelve packhorses laden with gold and jewels to the value of 150,000 gold florins. Had he been expecting serious trouble, it is doubtful he would have brought this much of the Order's wealth back into France, though he doubtless thought the treasury of the Paris Temple safe enough.

He went first to see the king, who received him courteously enough, listened to his views about a new Crusade, and gave no hint of the treachery already being set in motion. Reassured that the king's intentions were not so threatening after all, de Molay returned briefly to the Paris Temple before setting out for Poitiers and his papal audience.

But the king was several steps ahead of him. Before de Molay could reach Poitiers, Philip had his own audience with the pope. Feigning dismay and shock that he must be the one to bear such tidings, the king confronted the pontiff with a stunning list of accusations against the Temple, indicating that his agents believed this to be only the surface of the rot. He left the incredulous pope with orders to investigate the allegations—for with all the Temple's immunities, only the pope could do so.

Pope Clement was appalled, and told the Grand Master of the charges upon his arrival, in May 1307. De Molay was aghast at first, but then became more puzzled than alarmed, for the charges seemed so outrageous to him that he could not countenance that anyone would believe them. Nor had any intimation of the charges been conveyed to him in his meeting with the king. Besides, what danger could there be? The Order of the Temple was responsible only to the pope, and could not be disciplined by any secular ruler for any offense; and as a holy Order, they were exempt from torture. Furthermore, the wealth of the Temple was backed by a well-disciplined standing army answerable only to the Grand Master.

Still, the signs were becoming more and more difficult to ignore. Though de Molay continued to maintain the outward conviction that nothing could happen, one must wonder just when he began to see . . . an end in sight.

End in Sight

Lawrence Schimel

ven the Grand Master was not allowed to eat alone. To fast was temptation, to consume a penance, and at dusk a brother knight came and politely broke Jacques de Molay's meditations on the state of the Order. De Molay smiled up at the younger knight, remembering that it was equally his duty to watch and make sure that his companion ate. The Knights Templar had been founded on this system of balances, and of late it seemed the only thing which kept the Order going.

As they walked down the corridor toward the refectory, de Molay could not help continuing his musings, wondering if the Order had become obsolete, if it could survive now that the Crusades were over. They were deprived of their purpose: to protect travelers to the Holy Lands, to fight the Saracens in the name of the Lord. Already, de Molay had noticed among the men a furtive restlessness, for they lacked an outlet for their passions and desires. They were fighting men, and without an enemy to fight, they would turn upon themselves.

The companion system had therefore been more rigorously enforced. Templars went abroad into the world in pairs, lest they find themselves embroiled in a conflict with nonbrothers. With two knights looking out for each other, one could calm the other down should his temper rise too close to boiling over. But the tension within the Order continued to rise, and without release it threatened to disrupt the Order entirely.

De Molay did not yet know what he might do to solve these problems, and in the meantime he clung to the traditions and habits that had been established by wiser men before him. If it had not been for this young knight, he reflected, he would have stayed absorbed in his contemplation all evening, without even noticing the missed meal. He tried to recall the youth's name, but could not; silence was not one of their official vows, but it had become an almost unspoken one within the Order. Too often, too much discussion led the men toward brawls, or the subject of women, while quiet contemplation left them to dwell upon the spirit of the Lord within them and their mission to fight in His name.

De Molay stared down at his bowl of soup, with hardly the appetite for even a spoonful. He stirred its contents, still musing on the dilemmas of the Order. He wondered if things would change, if they would need to change for the Order to survive. And that terrified him. Vegetables swirled within the clear liquid and seemed to form the image of a face, a familiar face, the face of . . . was it his father? De Molay peered more closely. No, it was Hugues de Payens! Not his own father, but father and founder of the Order of the Temple of Jerusalem!

De Molay wondered if he should share his discovery with his companion, or even the hall at large. But he wondered, too, if perhaps the vision was strictly personal, if the first Grand Master was trying to speak to his current successor of grave and important matters concerning the Order.

De Payens did not speak with words, but when de Molay bent his attention to his predecessor's image, intent on fathoming his message, the image in the soup's surface changed. De Molay watched as the familiar stones of the building around him came into view within his bowl, and a feeling of dread began to form in the empty pit of his stomach, gnawing at his soul. As the first pink rays of dawn came arching over the horizon, so, too, came the officers of King Philip IV, hordes upon hordes of armed men, who lay hold of the complex and its inhabitants, throwing them all into chains. The scene again shifted, to King Philip's dungeons, where Templar Knights were being tortured for confessions de Molay imagined were so vile, he was glad that Hugues de Payens's dire forebodings were silent.

When the waters of his bowl cleared of visions, de Molay considered what actions he must now take. He did not know how soon this attack would come, so he must attack swiftly. He would send the fleet immediately away from La Rochelle, of course. It was too powerful a weapon to let fall into King Philip's hands, and as long as it stayed free, there remained hope for the Templars and the fight against the enemies of God. And, of course, he would have to send the Templars' various treasures with the fleet, since they would need the money to rebuild their ranks when it was again time for them to reestablish themselves. Besides, King Philip's attack was no doubt based largely on the rumors that the Templar treasury was vaster than his own, rumors that were not ungrounded in truth.

But what of the men? Certainly, de Molay would not himself be leaving. The Grand Master's place was at the post of highest danger, leading his men to victory from the forefront of the battle.

Would there be a victory for them this time? de Molay wondered. He had seen disaster in de Payens's warning vision, and he did not for a second doubt its validity. His men would be taken by the thousands during King Philip's raid, and many of them would die.

But was there another choice for them? Could he disband the Order, and send them back to their homes, where they would be worse than the Saracens as they crossed over the land like a swarm of locusts, unburdened by any code of restrictions?

No, de Molay decided, though his decision tore at his heart. It was better that they stay and fight, that they be taken fighting, that they die fighting in the name of the Lord.

"Beauceant," de Molay whispered under his breath, as tears fell into his soup. His companion stared at him, looking as if about to comment on the slow pace with which he ate. Jacques de Molay sadly lowered his head toward his bowl and did penance.

INTERLUDE TWO

We probably will never know when de Molay acknowledged the impending fate of the Temple. The meeting with the king surely must have reinforced hints of warning that had been building for some time. Upon his return to Paris, de Molay summoned a general chapter of the Order, which met at the Paris Temple on July 24 in strictest secrecy. Though details of that meeting are unknown, orders shortly went out to every commandery in the kingdom to tighten security, and under no circumstances to reveal anything to anyone about the secret rituals and meetings of the Order—a probable indication that the accusation of idolatry had been discussed. Late that summer, de Molay called in many of the Order's books and extant rules and had them burnt.

On September 23, 1307, Guillaume de Nogaret at last set his long-awaited plans in motion. Having received the royal seals from the king only the day before, he sent out sealed orders to seneschals and baillies all over the kingdom, not to be opened until October 12. And on that day, while the Grand Master walked in the funeral procession of the king's deceased sister-in-law, basking in the great honor done him and the Order by the king, Nogaret's sealed orders were being opened and read.

In the predawn hours of Friday, October 13, 1307, the king's officers made simultaneous raids on nearly every Templar house in France, arresting every member of the Order to be found. Including knights, sergeants, serving brothers, and priests, they numbered several thousand. Strangely enough, there was almost no resistance—which perhaps reflects de Molay's confidence that the pope would protect the Order and that it would be found innocent of any charges. Nogaret himself led the raid on the Paris Temple, and personally saw to the arrest and incarceration of the Grand Master and many of his principal officers.

Though the pope had not authorized the arrests and argued with the king for some time over whether the king had the right to do so, he seems to have decided that Philip was not acting out of greed, since Philip proposed that the riches of the Temple would be placed at the disposal of the church, to finance the next Crusade. (This never happened. Instead, Philip secured a pledge of 200,000 livres from the Hospitallers, for which he was to ensure that the Hospital got the Temple's lands.) Still, the charges were serious and had to be investigated—though only individual Templars might be examined; the pontiff reserved for himself the right to deal with the Order as a whole.

In the months that followed, the Order came under the less than tender attentions of the Holy Office of the Inquisition, established in 1229 to inquire into cases of heresy and prevent its spread by whatever means, including the use of torture to extract confessions. St. Dominic and his followers, the Order of the Friars Preachers or "Black Friars" (so named for the black cowl and cloak worn over their white robes), had been particularly single-minded in attacking heresy, with the result that the Dominican Order—the Domini Canes, the "Hounds of the Lord"— became the principal agents of the Inquisition. More than a hundred Templars died under torture during the first few months of questioning, and many more came to confess nearly anything in the several years that followed, just to stop the pain. A few even took their own lives rather than endure it.

The inquisitors themselves were divided on the question of the Templars. On May 30, 1311, the Master of the Order of Friars Preachers, Aymeric of Piacenza, resigned his office rather than be compelled to attend a church council being convened at Vienne for the purpose of suppressing the Knights Templar. (As a secondary function, Vienne was also expected to deal with the mystical sectarians called Beghards and Beguines, who figure in our next story. One of the latter had been executed the previous year: a woman called Margaret Porete, whose mystical writings had aroused the ire of conventional theologians.) Appalled at the treatment of the Templars, and especially opposed to the use of torture to extract confessions, Aymeric had for several years evaded even direct efforts of King Philip IV and the pope to coerce the Dominicans into harrying the hapless Templars "more efficiently." His dramatic resignation deprived the Templars' enemies of a distinguished presence badly needed to bolster the illusion of legality vital for the success of the king's plan.

The same Chapter that saw Aymeric's resignation also assigned Meister Eckhart, the great German preacher, scholar, and mystic, to return to Saint-Jacques in Paris, the foremost theological school of the Dominican Order, for an almost unprecedented second regency. It is unknown exactly why Eckhart was sent, but on several occasions he had represented Aymeric on missions of supervision and reform.

Resident at that time at Saint-Jacques was Guillaume Imbert, the former Grand Inquisitor of France and Confessor of King Philip, who had been instrumental in drawing up the formal charges against the Knights Templar in 1307. Imbert had personally interrogated more than 140 knights and serving brothers, often subjecting them to torture, and had been temporarily removed from office for flouting papal authority in pursuing the persecution of the Templars on the king's orders, not the pope's. Events at the time of Eckhart's return to Paris could well have transpired as the following story suggests.

Choices

Richard Woods

1

Rain had fallen throughout the sullen day. Although it was early September, a chill had crept up from the Seine during the afternoon, insinuating itself around the youth's spindly legs and seeping into his very bones. Squatting cross-legged near the tavern door, he shivered reflexively when a shadow only slightly darker than the declining daylight passed over him.

"Alms, please! For God's sake, pity a poor student," he wheedled, clutching his ragged cape closer around his thin shoulders and trying to sound even more piteous than he felt.

"Here, scum," the shadow snarled. "Eat this!"

Hearing the man hawking up his phlegm, the boy barely had time to snatch his bowl aside as a thick globule spattered against the muddy pavement where it had just lain.

"May all your wives be bearded," he muttered under his breath, and moved to the other side of the door. "Cretinous wretch!"

The burgher may have heard him, or perhaps belatedly recognized an opportunity to revenge himself on the day. Whatever the provocation, the student heard the heavy steps stop and turn. But he felt too weak to scramble to his feet and run. As the steps grew louder, he steeled himself for the blow, cringing and shielding his head with his arms.

"Filth!" the too-familiar voice growled.

For what seemed an eternity, the boy waited for the blow to fall. Instead came another voice, deeper and oddly clipped.

"Enough. Go."

When he opened his eyes, he first saw two enormous feet in front of him, muddy to the ankles beneath the tattered hem of a gray cloak stained dark by rain and mud. The youth peered beneath his arm, up past the worn scrip and faded cross sewn to the shoulder of the cloak. Still upraised, the portly citizen's wrist was held fast in the grip of a massive figure wearing a round-brimmed, drooping hat. A formidable staff in his intercessor's other hand served as a further barrier between the student and his would-be assailant. The boy noticed that the man's little finger was missing.

For a moment, neither moved. Then the burgher stepped back.

"Release me . . ." he said, eyeing the staff and the worn shoes hung around the man's neck by their cords, "holy pilgrim."

The words sounded sour in his mouth, but the taller man opened his hand, and the burgher vanished quickly. After glancing above him at the streaming sign, shaped like a cockle shell, the traveler pushed open the heavy plank door.

"Sire, my thanks," the student murmured with as much

enthusiasm as he could muster. "You are truly sent from heaven. I'm starving, you see, and—"

Without a word, his rescuer passed inside.

"Wait! Sire *pilgrim*!" The screech echoed harshly against the walls. But to hell with dignity. He *was* starving. . . . "Alms, please! For the love of God!"

The door closed with a definitive thump, and the boy's heart fell like a stone off the ramparts of the Grand Châtelet.

"Saint Severin, help me!" he muttered in desperation. "Saint Julien-the-Poor! Saint Denis the Martyr—"

The door opened and a huge arm shot out and grabbed the boy by the scruff of his threadbare cape and hood. He felt old stitches separating, but before he could protest, he was hoisted off the pavement and hauled into the warm, sticky interior as if he had been a sack of oats. Next, he was planted firmly on the floor beside the pilgrim, who stood hatless in the center of the straw-covered floor like one of the stone saints on the cathedral. His head was framed on top by a shaggy mop of close-cropped, gray-blond hair, and beneath by a short, ill-cut beard of similar hue and texture. The thick, hooked staff was leaning against the doorpost, from which the traveler's battered hat and worn leather shoes now hung by their laces next to the frayed water bottle.

"Go elsewhere!" someone muttered. "No beggars in here!"

The pilgrim glanced around at the tables cluttered with scraps of sodden bread and earthen mugs, the several patrons seated on benches, the fireplace with its rack of roasting meats and collection of tankards, pots, and kettles. Grunting appreciatively, he reached into his scrip and withdrew a small bag.

"Food!" he said, shaking it to make the coins jingle. "I can pay."

A squat man in a leather apron approached from the back.

"There." He gestured to an empty table near the fire. Then his gaze wandered to the student.

"Both," said the pilgrim.

His eyes were blue—or, rather, eye. For the student could see only one. His left eye was half hidden by an irregular white ridge that traversed the man's face vertically. Where the scar passed into his beard, the hair paled, thinned, and disappeared, like weeds parting for one of the old Roman roads.

With another grunt, the pilgrim removed his dripping cloak and hung it on a peg close to the fireplace.

"What are you called?" From his odd, chopped accent, the boy surmised he was Saxon.

"Robert, sire," the student said, following the example of the older man. "From Troyes."

The pilgrim heaved his huge frame onto the bench. A heavyset girl in a stained but respectable smock placed two earthernware mugs on the plank table as Robert joined him. The faintly musty scent of wine made him suddenly light-headed.

"Do they not feed you where you lodge, Robert of Troyes?"

The youth's mouth watered desperately as he waited for the pilgrim to taste his wine first, as courtesy required. The fragrance of beast and fowl spitted over the fire, crocks of stew, and fresh bread was dizzying. He swallowed repeatedly, praying silently to Saint Lazarus to keep him from fainting before he could eat.

"I was beaten and robbed in the forest as I returned to Paris last week. By other students, I think. But that was all I had for my burse—my parents are poor. So, I . . ."

The approach of the tavern-keeper, bearing trenchers

covered with flat loaves soaked in stew, so distracted him that he could not finish.

"*Benedicat Dominum,*" the pilgrim muttered piously, at the same time removing a knife from his belt.

"Amen!" Robert choked out.

The pilgrim grunted and sliced off a morsel of the savory. Lacking a knife, Robert tore nervously at the edge, trying to appear less ravenous than he felt. It was probably civet or squirrel, for all he knew, but as the hot juice touched his tongue, it could have been ambrosia. Tears welled at the corners of his eyes.

"So you beg." The pilgrim reached over the table and turned the boy's face to inspect the bruise still evident on one cheek.

Robert nodded, his mouth crammed too full of the broth-soaked bread to speak.

"Wait, messire!" The tavern-keeper's high-pitched voice cut stridently through the smoke and murmured conversation. "You have not yet paid."

Chewing blissfully, Robert twisted around. A tall figure in an odd, belted tunic, conspicuously patched but not soiled or heavily worn, was poised to leave, his hand on the door latch. The tavern-keeper approached gingerly, wiping his hands on his apron.

"When a man has reached the great and high knowledge, he is no longer bound to pay for food and drink," the man replied in a steady, smooth tone. "For he has become one with God."

"But sire, I have expenses!" the publican objected shrilly. "You have eaten well, and such food is not free!"

Now aware of the other customers' attention, the man pulled himself up to loom even higher over the landlord.

"God created all things to serve those who are free in spirit," he proclaimed. "Everything that God ever created is our property. Others must serve and obey. If they refuse, they alone stand guilty."

"Sire, please—"

Without warning, the man struck the tavern-keeper across the face with the back of his hand. Stunned, the little man staggered back. The serving girl stifled a shriek, and several of the other customers half rose from their benches. None, however, came to the publican's assistance as his attacker pursued and began to kick him.

Robert turned back to the pilgrim. His place was vacant. But the booming voice he heard was familiar enough.

"Libertine dog!"

Snapping around again, Robert saw that the pilgrim had quietly slipped off his seat during the scuffle and had circled the tables. Springing with a deftness and speed that belied his bulk, he grabbed the taller man by the tunic with both hands, spun him around, and shoved him against the door with a force that rattled the hinges. Then, grasping a hank of hair, he pounded the man's head twice sharply against the thick boards.

The man cried out as he was hammered a third time and then shoved against the door while the pilgrim thrust his free hand into the folds of his tunic.

"Ach, you only forgot!" The pilgrim ripped loose a leather pouch and cast it to the floor, where it landed with a heavy, satisfying clank. Several coins escaped and skittered into the straw. "How blessed are the poor in spirit, brother!" the pilgrim observed. "Take what is yours, landlord. Then call for the provost's guards. The Inquisitor of Paris will no doubt find this man of some interest!"

He turned back to his prisoner and stared mercilessly into his face.

"I pray you, pilgrim, let me go!" the man pleaded. "I will pay you!"

"I have no need of your money," the Saxon said coldly.

With a shrug, he tossed the shrinking bully aside and returned to the table, where Robert sat transfixed. The bully abandoned all further thought for his purse and bolted for the door, throwing it open to flee into the deepening gloom.

After retrieving his damages, the tavern-keeper dogged the pilgrim back to the fire with the still-bulging purse in hand.

"Mercy, sire. But what shall I—"

"He was a heretic and a thief," the pilgrim replied. "Give the rest to the poor."

The tavern-keeper stood still, his eyes widening as if he had been struck again.

"No, wait." The pilgrim extended his hand. "Let me see."

Timidly, the tavern-keeper placed the bag in the man's huge paw. The Saxon's one blue eye turned on Robert.

"What are you lacking?"

"More than ten livres," Robert groaned. "My tuition and keep for a year."

Shaking loose the coins, the big man methodically counted out the sum.

"Here. The thief has made good your loss." He slapped the silver, gold, and copper coins onto the plank table. "Be more careful when you travel."

Not waiting to be asked again, Robert raked the money into his wooden bowl, then fished out a ragged kerchief from his sleeve, wrapped the bowl in it, and stuffed the precious bundle into his tunic.

"As for the rest—" the pilgrim turned again to the anxious publican and tossed him the bag, now considerably lighter, "take this to the parish church tomorrow and give it to the poor," he ordered. "Not to the priest!"

"Yes, surely, sire," the short man agreed over the laughter of the other patrons.

"Swear," his benefactor added. "By God's blood."

Glancing around nervously, the tavern-keeper crossed himself.

"I—I swear."

"Now we will eat," the pilgrim concluded, turning to his wide-eyed companion.

For some time, the Saxon silently studied the boy as he wolfed down his supper. Twice he signaled to the publican to refill the trencher.

"No more, sire!" Robert protested as the third steaming loaf was placed before him. "Please! I shall burst," he added, quickly stuffing his mouth.

"How long has it been since you ate?"

"Three days, sire."

The pilgrim grunted and waited patiently as the food disappeared, somewhat less rapidly than had the previous portions. When Robert had mopped up the final drop of juice, he looked up and found the clear blue eye regarding him intently. From the glint in the scar, he suspected the other was, as well.

"Well, young Robert," the pilgrim said. "And what do you make of me?"

"Of you, sire?" Robert said warily. "That you are a brave and generous man. I am greatly in your debt."

The pilgrim leaned closer. "And nothing else?"

"Ah . . . no, sire." Surely discretion was called for. Robert swallowed hard, regretting the last cup of wine, for it had fogged his wits.

"I have a request of you."

Had he been entertained by a sodomite? Robert wondered if he could reach the door before he found himself compromised.

"Sire?"

"Do you know the convent of the Preaching Friars?"

"The Dominicans? Yes, sire. Saint-Jacques is on this very street. Just—"

"Be still!" the Saxon giant hissed, glancing around. "Listen to me." A gold coin appeared between his thumb and forefinger. "You are to go to the Jacobins and ask for one of the masters. His name is Eckhart. Can you remember that?"

"Yes, sire. Eckhart."

"You are to tell him that a penitent pilgrim from Hochheim seeks to make confession. Tell him I will be at the church tomorrow one hour after terce."

"Yes, sire. Hochheim. An hour after terce."

"Do not fail me, Robert." The pilgrim placed his hand palm down on the table. When he lifted it, a grosso gleamed up at the youth.

"By the Virgin's veil, sire. I will tell him."

"Go."

As Robert de Troyes splashed down the Rue de Saint-Jacques, the thought crossed his mind that he might as easily disappear into his lodgings, hide for a day, and be no worse off. On the other hand, there was something about the pilgrim that made him reconsider. And he had sworn. His mother had warned him about swearing. . . .

His reverie was broken by the tramp of mailed feet. Robert dodged into an alley, clutching the bowl through his tunic and sodden cape. But he had been seen.

"You, boy!" shouted the sergeant leading the guards. "Stop! Come here!"

Meekly, Robert approached the squad. Students enjoyed great latitude in the Latin Quarter. Still, it was not wise to antagonize the royal police.

"Surely the bell has not rung?" he asked as amiably as he could. His heart drummed audibly.

"Quiet, brat. Did you see a man on the street clad as a pilgrim? A big fellow, half blind, speaks with a bad accent."

"No, sire, I have seen no one. I have been at vespers myself—"

"Liar," the sergeant snarled, shoving him briskly aside.

Purposefully, Robert slipped and fell backward into a puddle of filthy water. He cried out as if in pain. The guards laughed, especially when he convincingly slipped again as he tried to rise and muddied himself further.

"Come," the sergeant said to his fellows. "The Templar can't have gotten far."

As the squad moved on, Robert scrambled to his feet, pleased with himself. A Templar? Surely not.

Then he noticed someone shadowing the troopers several yards behind. Although now wrapped in a dark mantle, there was no mistaking the bully of earlier in the evening, or the look of scorn and malice as he passed.

2

As it was a festive occasion, the prior had announced a *gaudium* after solemnly reading out the *mandamus,* the letter assigning Master Eckhart to the convent of Saint-Jacques for a second regency. The only other tenant twice to hold the chair for foreigners had died thirty-five years before—the Neapolitan genius and (not to be denied) troublemaker Thomas of Aquino.

Eckhart von Hochheim was no Aquinas. But, as the prior had droned on over the prone, white-robed figure making his *venia* on the floor of the great refectory, built a half century before by the Preachers' sainted patron, King

Louis IX, the assembled friars had had cause to reflect that at fifty-one, Eckhart's career in teaching, administration, and diplomacy was as illustrious in many ways as Thomas's had been. He enjoyed the trust of the Order, having held a host of elective and appointed offices. Twice he had been chosen by his German brethren to be provincial. But the most recent election had been canceled by the General Chapter earlier that year in Naples, when the delegates had chosen instead to return him to Paris.

"You have come back in tumultuous times," said the corpulent friar seated next to him, when Eckhart returned to his place at table.

"All times are tumultuous." Eckhart laughed. "It is good to see you again, old friend. Word came to me in Erfurt that you had preceded me back to Saint-Jacques."

"Five years ago, by the kindness of the brethren at Oxford. I am being allowed to pursue historical quarry."

"The English have evidently been kind to you in other ways as well—you have grown in stature as well as wisdom."

Nicholas Trevet patted his paunch affectionately. "As Thomas properly reminded us, willowy one, *bonum diffusivum sui*— goodness naturally expands."

"Is there no hope for me, then?"

"You walk too much. The administration of regions such as you have had assigned to you is excessively pedestrian. I prefer water voyages, myself."

"But by God's grace, Nicholas, like yourself I will now have the opportunity for study and teaching. It has been too long absent from my life."

Trevet nodded in the direction of a lower table where three young friars were engaged in lively exchange. A fourth sat listening intently. "I understand young Nicholas von Strassburg will be your assistant. He is the dark, quiet one."

"So I'm told. I met him when he was a beginning student at the priory there. He seemed quite bright, so I am not surprised to find him here as lector. But so far I have not had the opportunity to reacquaint myself."

"I will arrest him for you after the meal. He is quite personable despite his reticence and, of course, something of a countryman. But I must confess that his German sounds a bit soft around the edges to my untutored ear."

"We should have no difficulty understanding each other."

"No," Trevet said. "You appear to have much in common."

While the serving brothers loaded the tables with a feast of unusual variety and quality, Trevet took it upon himself to recount the major changes that had occurred at Saint-Jacques after Eckhart had finished his first regency eight years earlier and left to become Provincial of Saxony. Older than the German by a few years and unrepentantly prolix, he was as well versed in rumor, gossip, and speculation as in history. Still, he maintained a critical air that somehow distanced him from the often sordid details of the events that so interested him, an attitude that marked him as unmistakably English and had endeared him to Eckhart when they first met as senior students over a decade earlier.

Trevet's most dramatic revelation concerned Guillaume Imbert, who had been appointed confessor to the king a year after Eckhart left, and shortly afterward was named Inquisitor General of France.

"I remember him well," Eckhart said. "He was very . . . intense. And pious."

Trevet delicately speared a piece of fish with his knife. "At the king's insistence, he is now allowed to have his own apartment here in the priory," he observed with evident distaste. "He conducts business there, takes meals there, and even entertains his friends there."

"Is that why he is not here now?"

"Partly. Brother Guillaume has not been entirely well these last several months, if truth be told."

"From what manner of illness does he suffer?"

Trevet touched his brow with a stubby finger. "Not of the body, my dear man. He rarely sleeps for fear of dreams. When he does sleep, his groans and cries fill the cloister."

"A pity. No doubt the weight of so difficult an office."

Trevet pursed his lips. "Having been raised by the hand of Nogaret, I should not doubt that he has cause for remorse."

"Nogaret? The king's viper? The pope-killer?"

Trevet glanced around warily. "He is truly a dangerous man. But he did not countenance killing Boniface. I am told that at Agnani, he in fact restrained the hand of Sciarra Colonna when he would have stabbed the old man to death."

"Nogaret hardly meant him well," Eckhart said flatly. "He did not prevent the Colonna from striking him in the face with his gauntlet. And what of our brother, Boccasini?"

"Pope Benedict was another matter," Trevet muttered. "Like Gaetani, for whom he named himself, he soon made himself a thorn in Philip's flesh. His death was sudden and unexpected, it is true. But there was no evidence he was poisoned, much less a direct link to Nogaret. Such rumors are untrustworthy."

"Like all rumors," Eckhart said. "I am told he died from eating poisoned figs on the day he was to pronounce against the attackers of Pope Boniface."

Trevet paused, then returned the fig he had been considering to its basket.

"Struck down by the hand of God, according to Nogaret," he said. "So now we have a pliant French pope, the council is about to begin in Vienne, we have no Master, and Friar Guillaume rots away in his private apartment haunted by dreams of burning Templars and that poor Beguine from Hainaut. Times have changed, Eckhart."

He selected a small apple, stunted like most by the unseasonably cold summer, and polished it briefly against his white scapular.

"Is it not true," asked Eckhart, "that Guillaume donated a valuable Hebrew Bible to the brethren at Bologna last February?"

"Oh, indeed. We have several here, too." Trevet expertly split the apple and carved the halves into slices. "Since our good brother supervised the expulsion of the Jews from this wretched kingdom for his royal master, he could have endowed half the priories of Christendom with Hebrew Bibles. And a good deal else, I'll wager, that most likely went into the king's treasury. But it might be wiser not to speak of such things too loudly. To be known as an admirer of the Jews would not serve to endear you to some of the brethren even here."

"But surely, Nicholas, you have read Rabbi Moses yourself."

"Of course, and I know well of your fondness for his teachings. Frater Thomas was also enamored of his speculations. But times have changed, as I said earlier. Did I tell you about the case of the unfortunate bishop of Troyes, Guichard, now languishing in the Louvre? According to the charges, he is the son of a demon and a mortal woman who sold his soul to the devil in exchange for the love of Queen Joanna. That failing, he poisoned Joanna's mother, Queen Blanche, and stuck pins into a waxen image of the queen herself and thus killed her. Nogaret also accused him of blasphemy, sodomy, usury, simony, counterfeiting, and inciting to riot."

"What was his true offense?"

"He seems to have loaned the two queens quite a lot of money which he foolishly wanted back. There was also some unpleasantness about land. The usual, I fear."

"Will he burn?"

"If the king and Nogaret have their way, he will. Thus canceling all debts."

The conversation was interrupted by the prior's bell. Silence returned as the reader mounted the lectern to chant the pericope from the day's Gospel and seek the final blessing. Shortly afterward, Eckhart found himself again in the company of the English friar, now accompanied by a tall, well-built, but much younger brother who smiled shyly at the revered master.

"Come walk with us in the cloister garth, Eckhart," Trevet insisted. "This is Nicholas the Second, who is bachelor this year and your new assistant."

"The students call me Nicholas Minor." the young friar laughed. "To distinguish me from our learned friend here."

"As well as the last pope with that name," Eckhart said, as the white-robed trio began their circuit of the roofed arcade. "I am pleased to see you again, Nicholas."

"Then you remember me?"

"Oh, yes. You were pointed out to me by my former student, Tauler. He thought you showed promise."

Nicholas lowered his eyes modestly. "Father Johannes is a very great preacher."

"And a good judge of character. I am told he now preaches frequently in the Beguine houses."

"The whole region is aflame with the Spirit," Nicholas Minor said, his eyes alight. "Everywhere, people talk of God."

"Not all the flames are metaphorical," Trevet added somberly. "A growing number of bishops are less than pleased that these women and their male counterparts—Beghards, they call them—have taken it upon themselves to preach and teach, as well as to pray and perform their good works."

"There are such controversies in Germany, also," Eckhart said. "And increasing oppression, I fear. Earlier, Nicholas Major, you mentioned a woman from Hainaut. This is the Beguine who was executed here in Paris last year?"

"Ah, yes. That poor woman, Marguerite Porete. Another of Friar's Guillaume's forensic triumphs."

"It was reported that she was convicted by the theological faculty."

"And correctly reported, alas. Some of the brethren here concurred in that vote. Berengar of Landorra, for one."

"He can be severe. But why was there such a process at all? Surely the bishop of Paris—"

"Ah, but you see, the Beguine had previously submitted her little book to several theologians, Godfrey of Fontaines among them, God rest his mischievous soul. And Master Godfrey had approved it. He said her teaching was difficult, perhaps too rigorous for the simple souls for whom it was written, but without heretical intent or matter. In order for Friar Guillaume to obtain a conviction, Godfrey—who was inconveniently dead by then—would have to be overruled. It took twenty-four masters of theology to do it. But our pious brother and, I am told—" Trevet glanced around again and lowered his voice, "Nogaret himself, were able to convince them."

"She never spoke," Nicholas Minor added, "either to admit or to deny."

"Even in the face of torture?"

"Even at the stake."

For a moment Eckhart gazed through the drizzling mist into the garth. "She must have been steadied by God."

"Or by the devil," Trevet said. "Surely you are not a partisan of the Free Spirit, Eckhart."

"Of freedom, yes, and of the Spirit—that, too, Master Nicholas. But not of heresy. Was she a heretic?"

"I have not seen the book. All copies were destroyed, it is said. But Berengar and the others who had been shown the extracts were of one mind in believing so."

"Extracts? Did they not see the whole?"

"It is customary in such matters to prepare only a list of erroneous statements. Theologians are much too preoccupied to sort through hundreds of pages of straw looking for a single turd." The older man winked. "The inquisitors prefer to use their own noses for that."

"I would like to see this book, Nicholas."

"So would I, my friend."

In the brief lull that followed, Eckhart seemed to disappear into himself. Then the younger Nicholas asked, "Is it true that Nogaret is of Cathar stock?"

Trevet nodded. "Rumor has it that his grand-sire was burned in the Carcassonne. But Nogaret himself was reared in the true faith."

A half-smile formed at the corners of Eckhart's wide, generous mouth. "Perhaps. He has not proved himself overly kind to popes."

"And yet he indulges the Inquisition and raises Guillaume to prominence," Nicholas Minor objected. "Is this the act of a secret Cathar?"

"Ah, but consider, my young friend," Trevet said. "How better to exact his revenge? Controlling the Inquisition is far more cunning than destroying such a marvelous weapon."

"But how?"

The older friar smiled enigmatically. "By driving a wedge between the Inquisition and the pope. That would permit the king to dictate its policies and guide its actions through his good friend and confessor. Thanks to Nogaret, the Grand Inquisitor of France is in fact accountable more to the crown than to the weakling pope in his new palace at Avignon. Twice Clement attempted to censure Imbert over the Templar travesty, and even suspended him and everyone else connected with the original process. Nogaret quickly assured that it all came to nothing."

Eckhart's voice was low as he said, "This is distressing news, Nicholas."

"As I said before, things have changed greatly since you were last here, Eckhart. The university has changed. Paris has changed. The world, I fear, has changed. Mostly for the worse."

"What lives, changes, old friend," Eckhart replied.

The gate bell sounded in the distance. A moment later, a lay brother approached.

"Pray forgive my intruding, masters," he said, kissing the hem of his black scapular to ask pardon. "But there is a ragged student at the gate seeking Friar Eckhart. Shall I send him away?"

"No, Brother. Never neglect to show hospitality to strangers—"

"For some have thus entertained angels unawares," Trevet concluded with a sanctimonious wink.

Robert delivered the message while eyeing the spacious interior of the priory grounds through the wicket gate.

"From Hochheim?" Eckhart repeated. "Are you sure?"

"I am sure. Later, a sergeant of the guard said he was a Templar. Could that be true? He has a scar on his face and only one good eye."

Eckhart gazed at the boy stolidly for a moment. "Yes, it could be true. Tell him I will be in the church."

Robert touched his forehead in salute and disappeared into the mist and rain, leaving Eckhart staring after him.

"Graf Friedrich?" he murmured aloud.

The pilgrim was no longer at the Blue Coquille when Robert returned, hurrying so as to reach his lodgings before the Maci bell tolled. The patrons regarded him coolly and the tavern-keeper quickly showed him the door again. He did not linger to inquire further about his benefactor.

3

It took several moments for the shock of recognition to pass.

"We have both grown old," Eckhart said at last, from the relative seclusion of the arched colonnade in the north aisle.

"The years have been kinder to you since we parted at Erfurt—you for the Preaching Friars, I to win my spurs and make a great name for myself."

"I received word in Cologne that you had entered the Poor Knights of Christ," Eckhart said.

"It is a long story."

Eckhart surveyed the merchant's simple but finely tailored clothes.

"Your young messenger said you were a pilgrim."

"The pilgrim went on his way to Compostella. I regret having to shave my beard! But it was no longer safe, thanks to that false Beghard in the tavern. Paris crawls with proponents of the Free Spirit."

"Some say there are Templars about as well. Come."

Eckhart led the way through the church to the chapel of the Passion, where they could speak more freely.

"You are at risk, then?" Eckhart asked.

"I signed no confession, nor renounced my vows." Friedrich gazed up at the outstretched arms of the dying Christ. "In the Rhineland, the Order was declared innocent. But here, my very life is at stake."

"Why have you jeopardized it to visit me, Friedrich? Not out of old friendship, I trust."

"I need your help. I must gain entrance to the Temple. I am sure that Jakob von Molay is imprisoned there. I must see him."

"The Grand Master? He is known to you?"

"We served together in the Holy Land for ten years. But this is not a personal visit, Eckhart."

Years spent negotiating difficult diplomatic assignments alerted the friar to the nuance of mission.

"I am told it is under royal protection. How could I help?"

"The Inquisitor General, Imbert—is he not known to you?"

"He is a son of this priory. We lived here together when I incepted and during my first regency. He was a lector then. Aymeric, too."

"I have heard that your Master Aymeric resigned rather than grace the perfidious council with his presence."

"It was a difficult choice. But the pope had sworn that he would be deposed and penanced if he did not comply."

"A brave man. We will need such in Vienne!" Friedrich crossed himself emphatically. "But this—this dog-hearted son of perdition, Imbert . . . could he grant permission to enter the Temple?"

"Perhaps," Eckhart replied. "If he *would,* which is another matter."

"Will you ask him?"

Eckhart looked long and soberly at his childhood friend. "Very well. But it will not be easy. I shall have to find a cause."

"May God assist you! It was criminal, Eckhart. They put them to the test—knights, priests, serving brothers. . . . Even the pope protested at first—feebly—until his compliance was required by the king. Or should I say 'purchased'?"

"Strong words, Friedrich."

"It is true, Eckhart. By my oath!"

" 'To drink and swear like a Templar,' they say. Very well, come back in two days at this time."

4

"Not many ask to see Guillaume these days," the prior said, as he guided Eckhart to the Inquisitor's apartment. Because of the incessant drizzle, they took the indoor route through the refectory and kitchen. "Nor does he often admit visitors. But he declared interest in seeing you as soon as it was known that you were returning. He seems to set some store by your old friendship."

"I could not claim that we were friends," Eckhart said. "He was always a mystery to me."

"He is a mystery to us all. Without question, his favor with the king has benefited the priory materially. But I fear it has also earned us the fear and enmity of many ordinary people."

The Inquisitor's rooms were situated opposite the School of St. Thomas, across the lower courtyard but near enough to the kitchens to provide easy access, as well as to the service gate and, beyond it, the city gate of Saint-Michel.

" 'Tis an embarrassment and an affront to common life

to have him thus sequestered," the prior complained as they entered a short corridor. "But necessary, all things considered. Guillaume's presence had a chilling effect on the student brothers in particular, when he came to choir or the refectory. Not that we saw much of him in those early years of his appointment. His interrogation of the Templars required extensive travel."

He rapped sharply on a heavy oaken door at the end of the corridor.

"*Entrez!*" cried a thin, metallic voice from within.

"I will leave you now, Eckhart," the prior whispered. "Surely some business must require my attention . . . elsewhere."

Oiled parchment had been placed over the windows as if it were already winter, so that the large anteroom where the aged friar sat hunched over a writing table, wrapped in his cloak and a fur mantle, appeared dark and somber. There was a chill in the close air.

"*Salve, Frater,*" Eckhart said.

Guillaume Imbert lifted his hawklike face and squinted against the light that flooded into the room behind the visitor.

"*Ach, Bruder Eckhart,*" he said in Thuringian. "*Wilkommen.*"

He rose with some difficulty and approached the larger man, with whom he exchanged the ritual *pax*—the embrace of peace. Eckhart noted the deep lines in the old man's face, the red webbing in his eyes, the scaly flush on his throat and jaw.

"It has been a long time," the Grand Inquisitor said, waving Eckhart to a chair and resuming his own perch. "We are honored to have you back with us. Greatly honored."

"It is a pleasure to be relieved of administrative duties even for a while." Eckhart laughed. "Perhaps now I can return to my *magnum opus*. I have only managed to write three introductory passages in three years."

"It is a crucifixion, Eckhart. A bleak, endless martyrdom."

Silence returned to the tomblike chamber. Out of the corner of his eye, Eckhart glimpsed mounds of documents, stacks of books, scrolls, seals, and wax. But no flame.

"Do you lack for fire, Wilhelm?"

"No! No fire!" the old man almost shouted. "I—I dislike fire."

"Friar Nicholas, the Englishman, expressed some concern that you are becoming unwell."

Imbert dismissed the suggestion with a wave of his hand. "Trevet is an old woman. It's only the ravages of age, Eckhart. And work."

"It is very taxing, then, this work of yours."

"I can see that you do not approve. But it was necessary, Eckhart. These are treacherous times. When even the pope . . ." His voice trailed off.

"There is also some concern, Wilhelm, that the Holy Inquisition is being sundered from the arm of the church. Master Aymeric—"

"Aymeric! Mark me, Eckhart—his desperate flight from responsibility will have no effect whatsoever on the outcome of the council. The fate of the Templars is already decided."

"Perhaps. But his resignation will nevertheless have a pronounced effect on our own Order."

"No doubt. But it will not matter much in the end. Nothing, I fear, matters much in the end. And to be honest, I no longer have much to do with the case of the Templars. There have been other . . . matters to attend to."

"Such as the Beguine who was burned last year?"

"Beghards and Beguines! We have had too much of

these sanctimonious packrats who would teach theology to masters and prelates!" The Inquisitor tilted his head back and peered sharply at Eckhart through narrow, reddened eyes.

"But are not the Beguines of Paris under the protection of our own prior and the king himself?"

"Bah. It is not those behind the walls of the great Beguinage that concern me, but the itinerants. Most are no doubt partisans of the Free Spirit. Heretics all."

"How can you be sure? In Cologne and Strassburg—"

"Because it is my *duty!*" Imbert shouted.

Eckhart realized he must have blanched at the outburst, for Imbert lowered his eyes as well as his voice.

"Forgive me—my patience has been strained of late. As for Margaret of Hainaut, she was a poor, deluded pawn in the game of chess between Philip and Clement. Like the Templars themselves. Not that she wasn't dangerous. Those who preach freedom of the spirit are always dangerous. She was also utterly sincere, Eckhart. And such ones are the most dangerous of all."

"Was she truly a heretic?"

"Her writings were judged to be manifestly heretical by the theological faculty of the university. Even Friar Berengar agreed. But what is heresy? If fragments of your teachings were detached from your commentaries and made to stand alone under the scrutiny of men with narrow but penetrating minds, you, too, might be called a heretic. Oh, yes. Writing down your thoughts is dangerous, Eckhart. Even more dangerous is having them written down by others."

"But why her? Were not others more guilty of error?"

"Undoubtedly. But she was there, Eckhart. She wandered into our midst like a fawn among wolves."

"And so deserved to die?"

"Does anyone deserve to die? Did those Poor Knights

of Christ *deserve* to die?" For a moment, the Grand Inquisitor fell silent, his reddened eyes staring into the distance, as if seeing again the flames of the field of Saint-Antoine. "They would not gainsay their retractions, you know. They died protesting their innocence."

"And were they innocent?"

"What is innocence?" Imbert laughed feebly, perhaps aware that his rhetorical question too closely paralleled Pilate's jibe. He coughed, then continued.

"They had to die, Eckhart, as she had to die. They chose to die. Thus the king wins. And the pope wins, also. Philip removes more enemies from the board and again proves himself the church's most loyal son. He acts from the purest of motives. The Templars must be destroyed because they are a threat to the faith, not because they are rich and powerful and accountable only to the pope."

"And Margaret of Hainaut?"

"Her prosecution was an act of selfless concern," Imbert said with a wry smile. "A pruning necessary to save the injured tree."

"And to demonstrate that Philip's prosecution of the Templars was similarly prompted only by disinterested zeal for the faith?"

"But she *was* a heretic, Eckhart! Here—"

Reaching behind him into the shadows, Imbert foraged among the books and parchments.

"Ah! Yes, read it, Eckhart. You are a master of theology. Read it and tell me if she was not deluded herself and dangerous to the simple faithful."

He held out the little book, crudely bound between boards. Eckhart took it and opened the cover.

"*Miroir des simples âmes,*" he read. "It does not sound dangerous, this mirror of simple souls."

"Read it, my friend. Then come back and tell me whether or not it is as harmless as it seems. And then I think I shall have it burned. It needs to be burned. It should have been burned long ago. . . . You had a request?"

"I do, Bruder Wilhelm. I wish to enter the Temple."

Imbert's rheumy eyes darted to meet Eckhart's steady gaze. He seemed alarmed by the mention of the Temple.

"No one is allowed to enter or leave except by special writ of passage. Why would a master of theology want to visit such a place of infamy?"

"I wish to see for myself what has become of the Templars. If possible, I wish to speak to one of those who are held there. It is a matter of conscience, Wilhelm."

The thin eyebrows arched slightly. "Conscience? Yes, I can well imagine you have a conscience, Eckhart. It is part of my work to assess consciences. Did you know that?"

"Of course."

"Nothing is more seductive than freedom of conscience. And nothing is a greater cause of suffering. Who is it you wish to see?"

"It is said that the Grand Master is being held there."

"Is it? Are you sure he is in the Temple itself?"

"I am sure."

"What you ask may be impossible. It will surely be difficult. I have had nothing to do with the case of the Templars for over three years . . . at the pleasure of His Holiness and the consent of the king." This last he said with bitterness. "And the Temple is under royal control."

"But its prisoners remain under the jurisdiction of the Inquisition. Surely it would not be considered strange if representatives of the Inquisitor General of France were to pay an official visit."

Imbert stared at him curiously. "You would need a writ of passage."

"I know that."

"Do you also know what you will find there?" Imbert shook his head disapprovingly. "A foolish old man, failing in mind, broken in spirit, and short of whatever courage he may once have had. He has twice confessed to heresy and blasphemy and tolerating sodomitical acts. He withdrew his confession before the papal commissioners, then found himself retracting his withdrawal. Grand Master, indeed! He wept like a child when shown the *instrumenta*."

"Perhaps I would have wept, too."

"I doubt it. Whom would you take as your companion?"

"Perhaps young Nicholas from Strassburg. He strikes me as perceptive and discreet."

Imbert shrugged. "Your new bachelor? A likely choice. I do not know him. But I have heard that he is circumspect and keeps his own counsel. I suppose it should do no harm so long as you both *remain* discreet."

The old inquisitor paused, then seemed to smile very slightly. "Very well. Come back tomorrow and I will give you a writ of passage."

5

Eckhart explained as much as seemed prudent to the young lector from Strassburg. Hesitant at first, Nicholas Minor nevertheless agreed to allow Friedrich to substitute for him and, as they were almost of a size, to provide him a habit and cloak.

"My second habit was recently washed. I will loan him this one, lest it appear too clean. But you must tell me everything when this is finished."

Eckhart smiled. "A fair bargain. I hope to be able to do so."

When Friedrich appeared the next morning, Eckhart was brief.

"Go to the church of Saint-Jacques-de-la-Boucherie off the Rue des Arsis. I will meet you there within the hour with another friar, whom you will impersonate. The Temple is only half a mile farther, but we must be quick in order to return if possible before sext."

"God grant you a happy and peaceful death, Eckhart!"

"Amen, my friend. Now, go. And be wary crossing the bridge."

The priest of the old church remembered Eckhart from years past, and agreed without hesitation to allow him the use of the sacristy, "for his kindness to the poor." Hidden from view, Eckhart and Nicholas clothed the Saxon knight in the borrowed Dominican robes, which despite Nicholas's own height, fit snugly.

"But it will serve," Eckhart observed as Nicholas placed the black cloak and cowl over the white habit. "I'd prefer to see you tonsured, but there's no helping that for now. Keep your cowl well forward. That will also serve to cover your face."

"I catch your meaning." Friedrich traced the path of the scar with his finger.

"Nicholas, hide yourself here to the extent you are able," Eckhart said as Friedrich secured his disguise. "We should return in two hours."

"I have brought a copy of St. Augustine's *Confessio,* Master. With a candle or two, I should fare well enough."

Eckhart patted a bulge in the side of his own habit. "A book is always a good companion. Even if considered heretical by some. . . ."

Although the streets leading to the Porte-du-Temple were far removed from the ordinary haunts of students, numbers of them clogged the way, some of them more than a little drunk despite the early hour.

"It is still two days until the Feast of the Holy Cross," Eckhart explained, "but the students arrive early to settle into their lodgings and prepare. Much of their money for books and food will be misspent, I fear, on baubles and brothels."

A small flock of young scholars turned suddenly off the Rue Saint-Jehan-en-Grive, singing raucously, only their linked arms keeping some of them on their feet. Finding the narrow street mutually blocked, the friars and the boys all halted abruptly.

"Good morrow, jolly preachers," said one of the students, a robust lad whose hair seemed plastered to his head with vomit. "Join us in a pint!"

"I'd as soon join you in—" Friedrich began.

"Sire!" came a familiar voice as Eckhart laid a restraining hand on the Templar's arm.

A slight youth stepped away from his comrades, none too steadily, and leaned closer to peer at Friedrich's face.

"First a pilgrim, then a Templar, now a Preaching Friar!"

Startled, the ersatz Dominican pulled his cowl farther down over his forehead.

"And the holy Jacobin!" the boy continued amiably. He bowed to Eckhart and, using his arm as a baton, opened a gap in the wall of tipsy students to allow the friars passage.

"Thank you, my son," Eckhart said, as he ushered the growling Templar through their midst. "And good day!"

Robert was not to be put off. Abandoning his friends, who closed ranks and resumed their bawdy song, he came alongside the friars.

"If you are seeking the road to Spain—" he began jovially.

Friedrich's arm shot out like a viper and yanked the startled youth close to his side. He did not break stride as he dragged the boy along.

"There is a dagger in my other hand, Robert of Troyes," he said in a low, menacing voice. "If you say one word more, I shall slit your throat and throw your body into a sewer."

"I—I meant no harm, good Father!" the student yelped, sobering quickly. "Surely I was mistaken. By Jesus' tomb, I have never seen you before in my life!"

Robert attempted to pull free, but Friedrich did not relax his iron grip. The boy had seen too much.

"Walk with us, my son," the Saxon advised in a pious tone. "It will benefit your soul."

"May it save my life!" Robert groaned.

"It may also benefit your purse," Eckhart said. "Friar, ah, Peregrinus, do you have a grosso somewhere on your person?"

Friedrich grunted affirmatively. "This lout has already benefited handsomely from my service. What would you have of him?"

"We will see. Yes, come with us, Robert."

The great preceptory of Paris was built on a marsh northeast of the city and called simply the Temple. Its walls and towers were as secure as those of the Louvre or the Grand Châtelet. There Philip himself had taken refuge from the mob when riots greeted his debasement of the coinage a few years earlier. There much of the royal treasury had been deposited for safekeeping. As many as four thousand knights, priests, and serving brothers had been housed within its precincts. Taken, however, on that fatal Friday in 1307 by royal baillies armed only with writs of arrest and seizure, most of its inmates had been dispersed to other prisons, placed in chains, and its spacious buildings occupied by Philip's troops.

Not all the royal, civic, and episcopal prisons of Paris could hold the number of Templars arrested throughout the Kingdom of France that day. They were assigned even to monasteries and private houses of rich burghers loyal to the king. As time passed, more and more of the Templars signed the confessions required of them, accepted their penances, and obtained their freedom (and pensions).

But not all capitulated. Scores perished in agony when put to the question by Guillaume Imbert and his henchmen. Some were said to have committed suicide to end the torture. Well over a hundred paid for their defense of the Order at the stake.

In the end, only a handful of important prisoners remained to be disposed of, including the Grand Master, the Visitor of Paris, and the Preceptors of Normandy and the Aquitaine. Their places of confinement were secret, but what could have been more appropriate than the vast fortress outside the city walls on the road to Belleville?

"Wait for us here," Eckhart said to Robert, when they stopped near a small grove of willows and scrub oaks opposite the drawbridge and gatehouse. "If we do not return in the space of two hours, hasten to the church of Saint-Jacques-de-la-Boucherie. Tell the friar in the sacristy there to inform the prior at the Jacobin convent to have Friar Guillaume secure our release. He will understand."

"I will, Friar Eckhart," Robert said, more soberly. "I would not detain you, but should I not see you again, I would have you know that as a boy, I always wanted to be a Knight of the Temple. In my heart I already was. To protect pilgrims, to fight the Turk—but I was too small. Since I was good at letters, my parents hoped that I might find a place in the church as a minor clerk or better. Perhaps even a Preaching Friar."

"You could do worse," Eckhart said with a smile. "And so they saved and sent you to the faculty of arts in Paris."

The youth nodded. "After a year, I think I forgot why I had come. It is a dizzying experience, being a student at the university. I never thought there could be so much wine. . . ."

"You may still find yourself serving both God and man, Robert. May we meet again soon."

When the black-cloaked friars reached the sentry, Eckhart displayed the writ of passage with the seal of the Inquisitor General of France prominently displayed. The guard studied it, bowed respectfully, and stepped aside to allow them to enter, although Eckhart did not miss the young man's furtive gesture as they passed him, pressing his crossed thumb and forefinger against his lips to ward off evil.

They were shown to the keep, and there, after passing through more doors and checkpoints, the warder unlocked the thick, reinforced door to the crypt. Again, the writ of passage worked like a magic spell opening a hidden door in some fabled mountainside. Down the narrow stairs, behind yet another door, lay the prison with its cages for men under dark, arched ceilings.

"Here are two friars to see you," the warder announced, banging his keys against the wall.

"I have seen too many friars in my life," replied a deep, sonorous voice. The cell was something like a monk's chamber. Not inhuman, but stark. There was a straw-covered cot, a small table, and a chair on which the prisoner sat, his head buried in his hands. A hole near the peak of one of the thick walls admitted a modicum of air and light. There was another hole in the floor to relieve nature, and below, the sound of flowing water. But where three walls would have stood, rods and bars of iron contained the prisoner and deprived him at the same time of all privacy. There were six such cages, but only one was occupied.

"Leave us," Eckhart said.

Without a word, the warder closed the door behind him. The sounds of the catch falling into place echoed through the crypt. When the old man finally looked up, his eyes grew wide in disbelief.

"Friedrich!" he gasped, struggling to his feet. "*Here!*"

"Quietly," the Templar said, placing his finger to his lips. He took in the details of the old man's appearance—the long, straggly beard and unkempt hair, now gone white, the pallid complexion, the ragged Templar tunic...

"This is Friar Eckhart, my friend from childhood, who obtained passage for us from Imbert himself."

"God bless you, friar. I pray you to forgive my earlier words. But I and my brethren have suffered much from the hands of the Preachers."

"I am well aware, Jakob of Molay. But we are not all of the same mind in this. Be swift. We do not have much time."

With a nod, he withdrew to the farther end of the crypt and, removing a book from within his tunic, began to read. But Friedrich and the old man did not deign to whisper. The Saxon Templar came quickly to the point.

"They put you to the test?"

The old man held up his hands. The fingers were misshapen and gnarled like the exposed roots of an ancient oak. He pulled back the damp, ragged sleeves of his threadbare tunic to reveal withered arms pitted and scarred from cuts and burns the spent force of his body would never heal. Friedrich shook his head.

"At Mainz, I offered to undergo the ordeal to prove my

innocence and that of the Order," he said. "It was not deemed necessary by the bishops."

"Friedrich, we were tortured simply to make us confess, not to establish guilt or innocence," de Molay replied. "Those who confessed were reprimanded and released. Those who did not were tortured until they died— or, when the papal commission intervened, were given over to perpetual imprisonment. In the end, I confessed because I was old and tired and weak. They would not let me die."

"You admitted the charges."

"Not all. I confessed only to those things I considered myself truly capable of. But it went as had been planned. I told them nothing of the movement of the fleet, nor of the treasury. And, of course, I retracted my confession before the papal commissioners. But when they finished and departed, I was again threatened by the king's inquisitor with torture and death as a *relapsus,* so I recanted. I am an old man, no longer strong."

"Strong enough, Jakob. The fleet is safe, under Girard de Villiers, and Hugues de Châlons has so far outfoxed the wolf. Pierre de Boucle is also still at large. Imblanke has been returned to France, but may yet preserve his life. Even here the Order is not destroyed. Nor shall it be."

"*Deo gratias,*" the old man said, and wept.

"Take courage. Your sacrifice has not been in vain. God alone knows when you shall be freed, but the day will come. We must go. Be strong, brother."

"May I have your blessing, Friar?" the old man said, raising his voice.

Eckhart approached. "And more, if I am able. Do you have sufficient light to read?"

"For a few hours a day, but I am not well lettered, and my eyes are now very imperfect."

"Then listen to me as I read. Is your memory good?"

"My pain lies in being unable to forget."

"Then remember this well, as if it were Christ himself speaking." Eckhart broke open the parchment pages of his book and began to read in a low, steady voice.

"The annihilated soul knows only one thing, which is to know that she knows nothing, and wills only one thing, which is that she wills nothing. And this nothing-knowing and this nothing-willing give her everything. No one can find her. She is saved by faith alone. She is alone in love, she does nothing for God, she leaves nothing to God. She cannot be taught, she cannot be robbed, she cannot be given anything. She has no will."

"But what does that mean?" the old man asked, bewildered, as Eckhart closed the book.

"You wished to be a Poor Knight of Christ, Jakob. Someone become truly poor in Christ wants nothing, knows nothing, and has nothing. Anyone who wants nothing has no attachment to life or death, to pain or pleasure. Such a person is so poor that he no longer wills even to fulfill God's will.

"And he should be as free of his own will as when he was nothing. For then he has no God outside himself to want, to know, or to have. Only by such a one is God's will truly done. He finds God everywhere, because all things are full of God."

He stopped. The utter silence in the dim crypt was broken only by the occasional sound of a drop of water falling.

"All things. . . ." de Molay repeated. "Yes, I believe that. I will remember. Go with God, friar."

"As God will go with you."

As they left the dungeon of the Temple, Friedrich's face in the shadow of his cowl was, Eckhart saw, a mask of barely repressed fury. Nor was there any doubt about the reason for that anger. Not for him the words of the dead Beguine which Eckhart had found so compelling, and which he prayed might have begun their work of peace in de Molay's soul.

"Had you not considered a rescue?" the Dominican asked as they left the keep. "Surely there are enough Templars at large and resources at hand to attempt it."

"Of course it was considered," Friedrich snapped. "But it would only confound things. As he well understands, Jakob von Molay is more valuable to us in prison than he would be at liberty."

"Ah."

Leaving the confines of the Temple proved no more difficult than entering. Again, the writ provided by Imbert elicited unhindered passage. But when the friars crossed the drawbridge, they found no sign of Robert of Troyes. Rather, a line of armed horse sergeants faced them from the road.

"By my soul," Friedrich said under his breath, "if that son of perdition has sold us to the provost—"

"Do not be too hasty, Friedrich. And try to appear serene. He may have come to some harm."

One of the horses was spurred forward. "Good morrow, holy friars," said the lieutenant. "We have been cautioned that a renegade Templar heretic is at large. Your lives could be at risk, and therefore the Provost of the City has ordered us to see to your safe return."

Aware of the low growl in Friedrich's throat, Eckhart again placed a cautionary hand on the Templar's arm.

"That is very kind of you, but it will not be necessary."

"We must follow orders, good friar."

With that, he turned his mount and headed it back toward the city. He stopped once and looked back meaningfully.

"Come," Eckhart said to his companion. "It isn't every day we are graced with such courtesy."

Friedrich shot him a look of helpless rage.

The unusual procession returned along the Rue du Temple and passed through the city gate without attracting undue attention, although children and beggars sometimes stopped to gawk.

"I should have cut the boy's throat when I had the chance," the Templar grumbled.

"It is more likely, Friedrich, that my old friend Imbert notified the provost. He probably doubted my reason for wanting to visit the Temple."

"Then where is Robert?"

"He may well have escaped when the mounted guard approached. We may at least hope so."

"Could he have been arrested?"

"Possibly. But university students enjoy many immunities. When even one has suffered maltreatment, the resulting strikes have convulsed the city for months. As a master, I may have sufficient immunity to prevent our arrest as well."

Constrained by the narrower streets near the banks of the Seine, the horsemen were forced to proceed single file. Carts, pedestrians, children, housewives, beggars, and students all mingled freely in parishes such as Saint-Jacques-de-la-Boucherie, where rich and poor lived in close proximity. But the lieutenant led them only across the top of the densely crowded parish, avoiding the Rue des Asis, and crossed to the Rue Saint-Denis.

"This I had not foreseen," Eckhart said as they veered south past the Saints-Innocents with its somber charnel house. "We will not pass the church of Saint-Jacques-de-la-Boucherie. The guards will no doubt escort us directly to the Châtelet. The provost cannot imprison us, but he could detain us if there was reason to suspect that one or both of us were only posing as clerics."

"What then?"

"He would send for the prior to verify our state. I am beginning to regret my plan."

"It was a good plan. We were betrayed. If by Robert of Troyes, I will strangle him with my own hands. In any case, I do not intend to be arrested, Eckhart. I have only a dagger under this cloak, and at best I will be cut down quickly. Or perhaps I could reach the Seine. . . ."

"Either way will probably mean your death. And I would still be left to explain the situation. It will be wiser, I think, to explain first. Failing that, I think the prior can be trusted to be discreet."

"And Imbert?"

"We shall see. . . ."

As the horse sergeants and friars approached the Châtelet and the bridge beyond it, near the Boucherie, where the street narrowed sharply, a farmer's cart laden with vegetables and poultry suddenly jutted out from the line leading to the toll gate. Angry voices erupted in curses. The lieutenant's horse shied and reared. Shouting pedestrians scattered from the ambit of the hooves, disrupting the file even more. Eckhart and Friedrich also ducked aside. At the same moment, a swarm of students appeared from a side street, laughing and singing drunkenly. Somewhere, a fight broke out. Cursing, the sergeants attempted to urge their mounts into the crowd to quell the growing disturbance.

"Is it a riot?" Friedrich shouted as the students plucked up cabbages and turnips and began pelting the guard.

"No!" Eckhart called back. "A rescue!"

"This way!" cried a now-familiar voice.

Wheeling, Friedrich saw Robert beckoning him toward a sudden opening in the wall of students. The Templar threw off his black cloak, which Eckhart caught on the fly. He quickly stripped off Nicholas' habit, bundled it into a ball, and pitched it into Eckhart's open arms. An instant later, both Friedrich and Robert plunged into the throng of students and vanished.

"Quickly!" commanded a voice at Eckhart's ear, as his arm was pulled sharply.

He turned as a white-robed figure plucked the cloak from his arm and began wrapping himself in it.

"Nicholas!"

"If we hurry," the young friar said, tugging at the master's sleeve, "we should reach Saint-Jacques by nones."

"Your visit was rewarding, then?" the prior asked, after granting the blessing sought by Eckhart and Nicholas on their return.

"In a manner of speaking," Eckhart said, rising with more difficulty than he would admit to.

"I'm afraid I must nevertheless assign you a small penance. Frater Guillaume has been asking for you. He seems rather desperate."

"I can well imagine."

When Eckhart went to the Inquisitor's rooms later that afternoon, Imbert made no mention of the visit to the Temple. Nor did Eckhart inquire about the provost's protective gesture during their return. For the old man was clearly shaken, his eyes red-rimmed and staring.

"She was here, Eckhart! Early—just after matins . . . the woman from Hainaut—Porete! In this room. . . . I saw her! Radiant! And she spoke. There were others, many others, with her. . . . Accusing me!"

Eckhart glanced about the dark, sepulchral chamber.

"Calmly, Guillaume," he said in French. "What did she say?"

"She called me a slave of reason, devoid of love, and

wholly lacking in grace. . . . She condemned me, Eckhart—*me*! And the others did as well."

"Possibly. But I do not think you have had a vision,
Guillaume. This was a dream—a waking dream. You saw
only the embodiment of your own fears."

"But what have I to fear?"

"Only one thing is worth fearing—to have fallen away
from truth."

"Have I, Eckhart? Have I fallen away from truth?"

"God alone knows."

6

> The soldiers of Christ wage the battles of their
> Lord in safety. They fear not the sin of killing an
> enemy or the peril of their own death, inasmuch as
> death either inflicted or borne for Christ has no
> taint of crime and rather merits the greater glory.

> St. Bernard of Clairvaux
> "On the Praise of the New Knighthood"

After several delays, the Fifteenth Ecumenical Council
opened in Vienne on October 16, 1311, for the purpose of
condemning and suppressing the Poor Knights of Christ
and the Temple of Jerusalem, and appropriately disposing
of its lands and properties. Reports of the proceedings
trickled back to Saint-Jacques over the autumn and winter.
Nicholas Trevet's sources of information were particularly
helpful. From the beginning, matters did not go smoothly
for the pope and the royal party orchestrating matters
from a distance. The cardinals, patriarchs, abbots, and
bishops from beyond the Kingdom of France were doubt-

ful about the charges and disinclined to credit paid witnesses.

Then, in late October, the first session was temporarily
suspended when seven white-mantled and fully armed
Templar knights rode into the cathedral courtyard to defend the Order, claiming that more than a thousand others
waited near Lyons and its environs prepared to support
them. Although Pope Clement had invited a defense, he
never though it would eventuate. He therefore ordered the
arrest of the seven Templars, but soon had to release them
at the insistence of the council delegates.

Growing impatient, the king himself arrived at the
council in March. Two days later, the pope signed a personal warrant to suppress the Order without condemnation, which on April 3 was read publicly at the second
solemn session. On May 2, the Templars' lands, goods,
and properties were enjoined to the Knights Hospitaller.
In return, the Hospitallers agreed to pay the king over
200,000 livres as compensation. Templars who had confessed their crimes were absolved and freed, but forbidden
under penalty of excommunication to wear the habit ever
again.

Those who refused to confess were sentenced to life imprisonment—if they could be found. The fate of the four
principal leaders was reserved to the pope, who left for
Avignon on May 2. Four days afterward, the Council of
Vienne was solemnly adjourned, the decrees of its third
and final session somehow becoming lost. A week later,
Friar Berengar of Landorra, a lector at the *studium gen-
erale* of Paris, was elected Master of the Dominican Order.

During the whole of Eckhart's second year of regency
at Saint-Jacques, de Molay and the others languished in
their prisons. Friedrich's disappearance was complete. On
occasion, Robert of Troyes came to the priory to attend
lectures and became a great favorite among the younger

student friars, who smuggled him into the external refectory for a proper meal whenever opportunity—and Nicholas Minor, who was student master that year—permitted. That was often enough for the rail-thin youth to begin to add flesh to his bones.

In mid-spring of 1313, on another wet and dreary morning almost a year after the end of the council that had witnessed the suppression of the Order of the Temple, Nicholas Trevet brought surprising news to Eckhart in his study. It was Wednesday of Holy Week, sometimes called Spy Wednesday. But lectures would continue until the Triduum began on Maundy Thursday morning, and with it, more solemn silence in the priory.

"Nogaret is dead."

Eckhart set aside the book he was reading. "When?"

"Yesterday," Trevet said. "Of what the doctors call 'natural causes.' Something about it struck me as unusual, however. It is only rumor, of course, but I thought you might be interested."

"If only one thing bothers you, Nicholas, you will live a long and happy life. What was it?"

"Well, old friend, no one could remember who had brought it, but Nogaret had recently been served a plate of ripe figs."

The Feast of Saints Peter and Paul arrived in due course, ending the academic year and with it Eckhart's second residency at Saint-Jacques. Preparations were already under way for his return to Germany. Both Nicholases were subdued at the farewell gaudy, and Eckhart could cheer them only minimally by persuading the prior to let them accompany him as far as Porte Saint-Antoine in two days' time.

Friar Guillaume was absent, as was expected, but in

truth, it was generally known that his mind had begun to fail him more seriously over the past year. Eckhart had resolved to visit him once again before leaving, but amid the somewhat wistful celebration in the refectory, no one took particular note of a tall, burly lay brother making his way across the lower courtyard toward the Inquisitor's apartment, bearing a plate covered by a fine linen napkin. The sounds of conviviality were audible in the corridor as the brother halted before the door and rapped softly.

"*Entrez*," came a muffled, metallic voice from within.

"A treat has been sent for you, Father," the brother said in halting French, closing the door behind him.

Guillaume Imbert sat hunched in a chair near the empty grate, wrapped in a thick black fur, poring over a book in the dim light. He glanced up as the brother displayed a plate of ripe, succulent fruit.

"Set it there." Imbert pointed a thin, bony finger at the nearby table. "I have not seen you before. Are you new to the priory?"

Towering over the shrunken figure of the Inquisitor, the brother stooped down and set the plate within easy reach.

"I am from Erfurt, Father. I have been sent for helping the Meister Eckhart to return."

"The better for us all," Imbert muttered. "What is your name?"

"You may call me Benedict, Father."

"How were you injured?" Imbert pointed at the brother's eye and hand.

"In the Holy Land. Fighting for Christ."

The Inquisitor peered more closely at the man's face. "Very well, Benedict. Please leave now. My regards to the prior."

"Will you not eat?" the brother asked.

The red-rimmed eyes of the Inquisitor of France flicked over the gift of fruit. A fly buzzed somewhere in the room. Finally, he raised his glance to the grizzled, one-eyed brother who stood over him, unmoving and as large as death, and in whose maimed hand a dagger now gleamed coldly.

"Choose."

As comprehension dawned, an unpleasant smile briefly stretched the pinched features of the old man.

"The fruit, I think."

After a moment's consideration, he chose a moist, perfect fig, slowly brought the dark fruit to his mouth, then bit deeply.

"Sleep well," Brother Benedict grunted, then bowed and departed.

"Thank you," the old man called after him.

When the lay brother ordinarily assigned to wait on the Inquisitor came to his room after compline, he found the old man still hunched in his chair, still wrapped in the fur. The room was dark save for the unexpected light of a candle guttering on the serving table next to the chair. Beside the candle was an empty plate, and in Guillaume's rigid hand was what seemed to be a half-eaten fig. From the temperature of the body, the brother calculated that the old man had been dead for several hours.

Eckhart's departure was delayed for a day by the funeral, which while appropriate for the Royal Confessor, was not observed with much circumstance. The king was away on matters of state and few dignitaries attended. The following morning, Eckhart and the two Nicholases were joined at the gate of Saint-Jacques by a fit young man well known to them. He carried a travel bag and had several books for summer reading tied together with a strap.

"May I walk with you as far as Troyes?" he asked.

"You are welcome to come all the way to Erfurt, if you choose," Eckhart said with a smile.

Nicholas Major and Nicholas Minor accompanied Eck-hart and Robert a mile beyond the city gate, through the hovels and shanties eating their way into the fields that spread eastward toward the forest. There, on a grassy hillock, as they said their farewells, a lone horseman approached at a walk among the occasional farm carts and peddlers coming into the city.

"Good morrow, friars!" he called out.

Startled, the little company of friends turned. The familiar voice belonged to a well-dressed noble astride a powerful-looking warhorse. A scarlet plume swept down from his cap, and a patch covered one eye.

"I seek a young man who once thought to become a Poor Knight of Christ," he said.

"He also wanted to be a Preacher!" Eckhart replied. "You will have to fight for him!"

"Come, boy!" shouted the grizzled Templar. "Choose!"

Without hesitation, Robert handed Eckhart the books. He embraced the friars quickly, then ran to the horseman, who grasped his hand and hoisted him up onto the saddle behind him.

"Can you ride pillion, Robert of Troyes?"

"I can learn!"

"Eckhart—till we meet again!" Friedrich shouted.

He wheeled his mount, then waving his cap, spurred the great charger to gallop.

Eckhart laughed and waved.

"*Auf wiedersehen,*" he called.

INTERLUDE THREE

History has little to say about the specific fates of the individuals mentioned in the previous account. The virtuous Aymeric of Piacenza, who had given up his office rather than allow it to be used in an unjustified persecution, retired to the priory of Bologna after his resignation, honored by his brethren during life and revered after death, which came in 1327.

Little is known of Guillaume Imbert after 1308, save his arrest and prosecution of the Beguine, Margaret Porete, who was executed for heresy in Paris on June 1, 1310, less than a fortnight before fifty-four Templars followed her to the stake, protesting their innocence to the end. The chronicles of the Order are perhaps mercifully silent about his final years and death, which occurred sometime in 1312 or 1313, probably at Saint-Jacques. A plate of poisoned figs would not have been an inappropriate method for sending him to his Maker for judgment.

As for Meister Eckhart—he did, indeed, return to Germany after serving his second regency in Paris, but his distinguished career would end under accusation of heresy for teaching many of the doctrines that led to Margaret Porete's condemnation. His trial, like those of the Templars and Porete, was more an exercise of political expedience than one of religious correction. He died in 1328, probably at Avignon, where he was defending himself against charges brought by the Inquisition of the Archbishop of Cologne.

And what was it all for? Considering how well orchestrated the 1307 swoop had been, surprisingly little of the reputed treasure of the Templars ever came into Philip's hands. Most of the Templar treasuries had already been emptied by the time the king's agents came to collect their ill-gotten loot, and many key Templars likewise had disappeared. Gerard de Villiers, Master of the Paris Temple, is said to have fled Paris with fifty horses and a treasure that included 150,000 gold florins. De Villiers was later captured and brought to trial, but none of the treasure was ever recovered.

Another notable asset of the Order that escaped confiscation by the French was the near-legendary Templar fleet, originally assembled to transport crusaders and their horses and equipment to the Holy Land, later to become an important support of the Templars' vast financial empire. Eighteen of the Order's galleys are said to have sailed from the Templars' principal naval port at La Rochelle just ahead of the mass arrests. Neither they nor any of the rest of the fleet were ever heard from again.

Did the Order's mighty galleys carry away vast treasures, secreting them in other parts of the world? How could several hundred ships simply have disappeared so thoroughly? Their ultimate fate is no mystery, for the life of a wooden ship of that period was only about twenty years; and the entire fleet cannot have been new. Nonetheless, these ships could have represented a formidable force for the first decade or so after the dissolution of the Order.

Some historians speculate that Templar ships might have landed fugitive knights on the Irish and Scottish coasts, or sailed farther north toward Russia, gradually dispersing their passengers and cargo to safe havens. Certainly some Templars found their way to Scotland, where the Order was never officially suppressed (Scotland being under interdict at the time papal legates tried to serve the writs). At the battle of Bannochburn in 1314, shortly after Jacques de Molay was burned, tradition has it that many Templars fought against the English with Robert the Bruce. Some say that the day was saved by the sudden and unexpected appearance of a band of knights wearing the distinctive white mantles and red crosses of the Templars. Their descendants are said to have championed the Stuart cause for at least another four centuries.

In England, Ireland, and Scotland, as well as in France, most of the former Templar lands ended up in the hands of the Knights of St. John, which Order many of the dispersed Templars are known to have joined. On the Iberian Peninsula, the Order simply changed names. In Portugal they became the Knights of Christ; in Spain, the Order of Montesa took up much of the Templar tradition. In Germany, where the Templars were found not guilty of the charges, they were absorbed by the Teutonic Knights. Other Orders in other countries emulated at least some of the Templar ideals.

At some point during this survival transmutation, the history of Freemasonry also becomes inextricably interwoven with that of the Temple. And, of course, spiritual descendants of the Knights Templar, both chivalric and Masonic, flourish today in many parts of the world—though mainline history is hard-pressed to provide a direct link through the centuries.

Here we begin to edge into the mythic. Scholars have long debated the truth or falsehood of the charges against the Templars, and have sought rational explanations for their vast power and influence. Orthodox history suggests partial answers, but there persists the unshakable suspicion on the parts of many that regardless of what the *facts* say, there was something special about the Temple besides its unique attainment of power and influence: something mystical, magical. If so, what was the secret knowledge that they guarded?

Several speculations along these lines became the focus for the book *Adept III: The Templar Treasure,* by myself and Deborah Turner Harris, which developed a scenario involving several of the specifically Scottish manifestations of the Temple after its official suppression in 1314. The fate of the Templar treasure of the title is resolved by the end of the book, partly with the help of a Templar neck cross said to have been found on the body of John Grahame of Claverhouse (Bonnie Dundee), when he fell at Killiecrankie. However, it occurred to me that another Templar question had been left unresolved, for Adam Sinclair does not take the time by the end of the book to return the cross to its present-day keeper, another John Graham (he of *Lammas Night*). We can assume that Adam does so, between this book and the next; but we know that Sir Adam Sinclair has other Templar associations, both in this life and in previous ones.

The two senior Adepts, Adam and Graham, had worked well together in their brief encounter, and genuinely liked and respected one another. It got me to wondering whether, when Adam inevitably returned the cross, it might spark something more than a simple handing over of a piece of ancient regalia. . . .

Obligations

Katherine Kurtz

ain was pelting down in earnest as Sir Adam Sinclair swung his hired car off the M-20 Motorway, skirting Ashford to head south along a single-track road. The Kentish countryside was bleak and cold in the early dusk, a promise of frost hanging in the air. As he adjusted the temperature control on the dash, he reflected that at least he could expect a warm welcome at Oakwood.

Thought of Oakwood recalled the reason for his journey from Scotland. The Templar neck cross resting in a flat jeweler's box beneath his heart had been entrusted to him by Oakwood's master on the occasion of his previous visit two months before. It had stood Adam and his allies in good stead. Now it must be returned, and report made of its part in their success.

Still reviewing what he planned to relate, he turned between the stone lions and wrought-iron gates that marked the entrance to the Oakwood estate, heading up the long, rain-swept drive beneath a skeletal canopy of bare branches. Soon he was easing through the open arch of the Tudor gate lodge and into the graveled forecourt, to pull up gently before the stone steps of the manor house. Before he could get out of the car, a dark figure wielding a large black umbrella emerged from behind the front door and headed down the steps to meet him.

"Good evening, Sir Adam," the man said from beneath the umbrella, bowing slightly as he swung the car door wider.

"Hello, Linton," Adam replied. "You didn't need to come out in the rain."

The older man smiled slightly above his striped waistcoat and black coat. "Sir John told me to expect you. I prefer not to present him with soggy guests. Please come in."

"Thank you. I have one bag in the boot."

"I'll see to it, sir. This way, please."

With a gravity appropriate to a longtime retainer, the elderly butler led him through the entryway and a lofty vestibule passage, then along a dimly lit portrait gallery, pausing at length before a familiar door carved with oak leaves and acorns. Opening it softly, the man stepped inside with his back to it and announced, "Sir Adam Sinclair, Sir John."

"Adam!" said the room's occupant, putting aside a book and reading glasses as he rose to meet his guest.

At ninety-two, Brigadier General Sir John Graham could have passed for a man at least twenty years younger. Tall, lean, and handsome still, unbowed by age, he possessed a full head of silvered hair and a sharp hazel gaze that Adam knew missed little. He was an even more senior Adept than Adam, of a different tradition, but unquestionably in the service of the Light. Attired tonight in an open-necked white shirt with black trousers and a baggy black cardigan, he strode forward without recourse to the silver-headed walking stick lying beside his wing chair, taking Adam's handshake with a firm grip.

"Adam, it's wonderful to see you. Come and sit by the fire. Linton, we'll have drinks in here before dinner."

"Very good, Sir John."

Over crystal tumblers of The Macallan, Adam related further details of the case that had brought him to Oakwood the previous September, along with its successful conclusion at Fyvie Castle in the distant north of Scotland. The general listened intently, interjecting the occasional probing question or succinct observation with a deftness that recalled his many years of intelligence work for the government. He had not lost his touch, and Adam found himself wondering whether ex-intelligence officers ever really retired. On his first visit to Oakwood, Sir John had even revealed a hitherto unknown working relationship with Adam's mother during World War II—though Adam had yet to pry the story from either of them.

"So I don't suppose we'll ever know the identity of Gerard's accomplice," Adam said in conclusion. "There wasn't enough left to identify, even before we closed up the old cellars. Other than that, and the consequences to Henri Gerard—which he brought on himself—I don't suppose any real harm was done in the final analysis. Other than Nathan Fiennes' death, of course. I shall miss him."

"I expect you shall. He sounds a remarkable man," the general said. "What about Gerard? Do you think he can be cured?"

"I don't know. As a psychiatrist, I'd like to hope he can be returned to at least a degree of normal functioning; but from an esoteric point of view, I think it's highly doubtful. One doesn't often see a case where elements of a previous life come through so strongly that they almost completely overshadow the present persona. Barring some unforeseen breakthrough, I'm less than optimistic about any meaningful resolution—which is a tragic waste. I'm told he was quite a competent scholar in his field, even if single-minded to the point of obsession."

"Unfortunate," Graham replied. "Have you seen him since the incident?"

"Not yet—though I've kept tabs on his progress through the health services. We dumped him near a hospital on the outskirts of Edinburgh. Eventually, I expect I'll be called in on the case. For now, he's at least receiving kindness and concern. That can go a long way in cases like this."

"True enough," Graham agreed. "But as you said, he largely brought his fate upon himself."

Grimacing for answer, Adam set down his empty tumbler on an occasional table between them, then reached into the inside breast pocket of his suit coat and produced a flat black jeweler's box familiar to both of them.

"Thank you for the loan of this," he said, handing it over.

"Not at all," the general replied as he opened the box to expose what lay within.

The cross inside lay atop a coiled skein of silky black cord, scarlet enamel and gold against a bed of black velvet. About three inches long, it was of a shape called a cross *formée,* with arms slightly flared at the ends—one of the earlier types of cross worn by the Knights Templar during the Crusades.

This particular item, sometimes known as the Dundee Cross, had been in the hereditary keepership of Grahams since the time of another John Grahame, Viscount Dundee, known to Scottish history as Claverhouse or Clavers, Dark John of the Battles, and "Bonnie Dundee." Tradition declared that Dundee had been grand prior of a preserved or reconstituted order of Templars in Scotland at the time of the Jacobite Wars, and that he had been wearing the cross of his rank when he fell at Killiecrankie, his greatest and last victory. As its present keeper gently set its box on the polished rosewood table, the firelight reflecting off Adam's discarded tumbler cast a glitter of fiery sparkles across the rich enamel and gold.

"It's quite a potent symbol, isn't it?" Graham said.

Adam nodded distractedly, letting his gaze be ensnared amid the dazzle of cut crystal. The Templar relic beckoned to a deeply buried part of his being that he rarely chose to face—though he had resolved to do so tonight, if the redoubtable John Graham agreed.

"More potent than perhaps you realize," Adam replied. "If you're willing, I'm hopeful that it might provide one more useful service before I leave it totally in your keeping again."

As he leaned forward to pluck the cross from its box, letting the silken cord dangle free as he cupped the cross in his left palm, the general carefully set down his glass and sat back with fingers steepled before him, elbows resting on the arms of his wing chair.

"What did you have in mind?" he asked.

Adam drew a careful breath.

"You'll recall the working we did the last time I was here."

"Of course."

"Quite apart from the work regarding Dundee, we—touched on a past life I hadn't encountered before. You guided me deeper into trance and helped me make the necessary connection. That was a relatively new experience; I'm usually the one who does the guiding."

Graham inclined his head but did not speak.

"You're very good, Gray—extremely good," Adam said, choosing his words carefully. "I don't think I've ever let anyone take me that deep, even during my psychiatric training."

"I had remarkable teachers," Graham said quietly. A nostalgic sadness touched his voice as he added, "Some of my best students were quite remarkable, too."

"I ask you as a student seeking teaching, then," Adam replied, his hand closing resolutely around the Dundee cross. "When we worked together before, you asked me whether I was aware of a past life pertinent to Dundee and that situation. I *wasn't* aware of the one we eventually explored, but there's another persona who's also somewhat related to this, that I *am* aware of." He opened his hand to display the Templar cross. "It's part of what enabled me to claim authority as a member of the Temple when Dundee's shade confronted me. At the time of the suppression of the Order, I was a Templar knight called Jauffre de Saint Clair, and I died at the stake."

Graham raised an eyebrow.

"That's all I know about him," Adam went on, aware of Graham's discerning gaze upon him as he gently laid the cross back on the table. "I need to find out what transpired before Jauffre met his fate—what led him to that death. I've been aware of a personal connection to the Templars for some time, ancestral as well as spiritual. My estate has a Templar castle that I'm restoring, and I've had occasional dealings with the shade of a previous Templar tenant there.

"But flashes of Jauffre's death seem to crop up at inconvenient times, and I haven't been able to work past it, only around it. At times, it's been almost incapacitating."

He found he had begun absently tracing patterns with his fingertip among the coils of the cross's silken cord, and made himself sit back in his chair as he looked up somewhat sheepishly.

"I think you'll understand that this isn't the sort of thing for which I can ask help from a professional colleague," he said with a wan smile. "I'm afraid orthodox psychiatry views past life regression as trendy at best, and certainly questionable in a reputable psychiatrist. Until I worked with you, I had about resigned myself to never quite resolving the issue."

"Are you asking me to take you back to the time of Jauffre, so that you can work out that death?" the general asked.

"I am," Adam said. "I'll understand if you feel you can't or shouldn't, but I can think of no one I would sooner trust to do it."

"What about Philippa?" Graham asked, referring to Adam's mother. "Surely she's one psychiatrist who wouldn't scoff."

"No, but you're here, and she's in the States. Besides, you have the warrior's perspective; Philippa's experience has been focused on priesthood and healing. They aren't incompatible, or you and I should not be having this discussion, but I think you might bring unique insights to the exercise."

"Very well." The two simple words caught Adam off guard; he had expected more of an argument. "There's time before dinner, I think. I'd already ordered something that would hold, in case your plane was delayed."

"That's fine," Adam found himself saying, despite an uncharacteristic twinge of apprehension that briefly made his stomach queasy.

"So be it, then." Graham retrieved the stick beside his chair, though he stood without using it. "Linton will show you to your room; it's the same one you had last time. Make yourself comfortable, and I'll join you directly. Take the cross with you. I want to get a few things and make certain we won't be disturbed."

A quarter hour later, Adam was ensconced in a snug,

light-paneled room overlooking the entry court, trying not to think too much about what lay ahead. It was already well dark outside, rain still pelting down, and Linton had pulled the heavy drapes across the bow window. A cheery fire burned in the cut-stone fireplace, and a tiny bedside lamp provided a second source of light.

Adam removed his coat and tie and pulled on a pale blue cashmere sweater, for he knew from past experience that the faint chill not dispelled by the fire would soon turn to bone-chilling cold once he began working in trance. He had slipped off his shoes and was looking for an extra blanket when a faint tap at the door announced the arrival of his host.

"It occurred to me after I'd sent you up," Graham said, closing the door behind him, "that we probably shouldn't have had those drinks." He had a heavy-looking green and blue tartan lap rug over one arm, with his stick and a gold-framed print cradled atop it. "Some people prefer not to work with alcohol in their systems. Will that be a problem?"

Adam shook his head and managed a faint smile as Graham deposited the stick just inside the door.

"Not at all. I'd regard one drink as medicinal, in a case like this. It will probably help me to relax."

The general snorted. "I hope you don't find *me* daunting. Anyway, I've brought you an old print of a Knight Templar," he went on, handing the print to Adam. "I'm sure you've seen similar drawings, but I thought it might provide an additional focus."

"Thank you."

Sitting on the edge of the bed, Adam tilted the print to the light. It was a fairly typical etching of a Templar of the time of the Crusades, with the cross of the Order tipped in in red on mantle and surcoat. As the general began shaking out the tartan over his arm, Adam set the print aside and hurriedly adjusted the bed's pillows to his liking.

"I see you've anticipated another need," he said, swinging his feet up so he could help Graham spread the rug over his feet and legs. "I was just looking for another blanket when you came in. I know how cold it can get on the Astral."

"Here at Oakwood, we speak of going on the Second Road," Graham replied, a faint smile quirking at his mouth as he pulled a straight-backed chair closer and sat. "You *are* nervous about this, aren't you?"

It was more a statement than a question, and Adam had to draw a deep breath before he could bring himself to nod agreement.

"You needn't be," Graham said, "though I won't pretend that it's likely to be pleasant. You've already told me that Jauffre burned at the stake—and he probably was tortured to extract a confession; a great many Templars were."

"I'm prepared for that," Adam replied. "That was the only way the inquisitors were able to obtain so many confessions. And only those who confessed and then recanted were executed. Maybe what I have to find out is whether Jauffre kept faith with the Order. I think he must have done, knowing something of the other lives I've led; but I have to know."

"Fair enough." Graham cocked his head at him thoughtfully. "You do realize that you're apt to find out whether at least some of the charges against the Templars were true? Mere torture and burning at the stake may not be the worst you'll have to deal with, at least in psychological terms."

"I've thought about that possibility."

Graham smiled faintly. "I expect you have. Lie back,

then, and we'll get started. I'll do my best to make the process as painless as possible."

Though reason gave Adam no cause to doubt his host's reassurance, apprehension stirred less biddable emotion as he lay back and set about relaxing, drawing a deep breath and exhaling slowly. He had put on the ring of his Adeptship while he waited for the general to join him, symbol of office borne and oaths freely given elsewhere; its sapphire caught the firelight as he tucked the tartan rug more closely around his waist and chest—visual reassurance that he was not going into this totally unprepared.

Close beside him, Graham set a tiny pocket tape recorder on the nightstand and turned it on, then picked up the Templar cross Adam had laid there earlier and slipped it into a jacket pocket with the cord trailing outside. From deeper in the pocket he produced a bright red disposable lighter.

"Let's take a few minutes to relax and center first," the senior Adept said, setting flame to a candle on the nightstand before turning off the bedside lamp. "Close your eyes and concentrate on your breathing: a deep breath in ... and out. Use your own methods to begin settling into trance, the way you did the last time we worked together. We'll use your usual cues to help you go deeper. Another deep breath, now, and let yourself drift slowly deeper ... and deeper ..."

Adam followed the direction willingly, letting the sweet, familiar focus of trancing take him into comfortable realms in which the room and all but Graham's voice softly receded. For a while he was aware of the flicker of firelight and candlelight on his closed eyelids, of the rough texture of wool beneath his fingertips, with his arms stretched relaxed at his sides; but gradually the awareness of even possessing a body began to recede.

"Go deeper now," he heard Graham say as a hand

touched his left wrist and the familiar cue lent impetus to the command. "Go twice as deep as you were before . . . deeper still . . . and now begin casting back in time. Go beyond the level of mind to the level of soul, of spirit—to remembrance of other times, other lives . . . and of one life in particular. The name you bore then was Jauffre de Saint Clair.

"Look for him now; seek him out. The place is Paris; the time is some point between 1307, when the Templars were arrested, and 1314, when Jacques de Molay and Geoffroi de Charney died at the stake, the last to be so executed. To fix on Jauffre's life, you must return briefly to his death, but we shan't stay there long—just long enough to be sure we've found the right time and place."

"Be one with him now, and prepare to face his death, knowing that your present body is safe, your present existence anchored here by my hand on your wrist and the sound of my voice, knowing that memory cannot hurt you. Whatever may happen to Jauffre, know that the part of you that is Adam Sinclair remains detached, a neutral observer, above any pain. Your name is Jauffre de Saint Clair, Knight of the Temple of Jerusalem; and as I place this symbol of that Order on your forehead, its touch will send you fully into that other life."

Even without physical vision, Adam could see the pulsing beacon of the Templar cross approaching, and knew that its touch would produce exactly the result Graham had suggested. A part of him shrank from that certainty, well knowing what lay ahead, glimpsed in nightmare flashes; but another part welcomed the resolution, almost made him lift his head to receive it. However horribly Jauffre de Saint Clair had died, his experiences were part of what made Adam Sinclair what he was today. To achieve his fullest potential in the present, he must understand and accept those experiences of the past.

The touch of cool metal and enamel against his forehead was like an electric shock, even though expected, plunging him fully into Jauffre. All at once he found himself on his knees amid rough kindling, chained to a stake between two ragged, struggling men who were his brethren, as flames began to crackle amid the bundles of faggots piled close around. To either side, dozens more of his fellow knights were chained like him, several to a stake, some of them already screaming as flames enveloped them, though many went passive to their deaths, and some made not a sound.

An ugly murmur of approval swelled upward from the watching crowd as the executioners spread the flames and the shrieks of the victims mounted. Though the fire had not yet touched him, the heat and ash began to choke him, and he shouted out his defiance while he could still speak, with clenched fists raised heavenward: *"Le Temple, c'est pûr! Le Temple se survivra!"*

The executioners paid no heed, and the fire licked higher. He stifled a gasp at the flames' first caress, suddenly aware that he was, indeed, going to die without knowing. He writhed against the unyielding chains, shrinking in vain from the consuming fire, yet the unanswered question remained: Had he succeeded or had he failed?

But he would never know the answer in this life, for no escape now was possible save through the gates of Death. As the flames leaped higher and the true agony began, he forced his blurring gaze above the fire and crossed trembling arms on his breast—for no other expression of faith remained for men condemned as heretics and abandoned by the church. All too soon his gasps turned to cries that he could not stop while still he drew breath, as the fire took its sacrifice of living flesh.

Yet even in those final, interminable seconds, as the fire

seared nerves almost beyond the perception of pain, he
was able to lift despairing hands in final entreaty, his up-
turned face still seeking an answer. But the pain, the
pain. . . .

"That's enough now," said a voice both familiar and
strange, as cool hands pressed his arms back to his sides,
their touch draining away all vestige of the anguish of
charred flesh. "Let go the pain. Retain the thread binding
you to Jauffre, but follow it backward in time now. Find
the moment that made Jauffre something different from
any other Templar martyr. Find the moment for which a
future Adept was set to play a Templar knight. There *was*
such a moment, else Adam Sinclair would not be who he
is today. Find that moment . . . and tell me what you see."

More than eager to comply, Adam/Jauffre cast himself
backward from the fire, past the lesser agonies of torture—sometimes his own, sometimes observed—torture
that only confession could stop—never mind whether the
confessions were true. . . .

Hot irons applied to cringing flesh . . . the lash . . . the
strappado, which could rip a man's arms from his shoulders . . . greased feet held to flames until the flesh sizzled
and the charred bones dropped out . . . if a man could
stand that much. Many died under such torture.

The boot and the thumbscrew . . . teeth yanked from
bleeding gums so the sockets could then be probed to pro-
long and intensify the agony . . . starvation and imprisonment in unspeakable conditions. . . .

But all at once Adam found himself beyond all that,
whole and uninjured, a decade before his ending, kneeling
white-robed and ardent before a bearded, battle-hardened
man with the red cross of the Order on the shoulder of his
white Templar mantle. Half a dozen other white-mantled
knights were ranged to either side of the man, one of them

a cousin. The man presiding, deputizing for the Master of the Paris Temple, was unknown to Jauffre.

"Three times have you asked us for the bread and water and companionship of the Order," the unknown knight was saying in an archaic French that Adam/Jauffre understood. *"If we grant what you desire, will you henceforth put aside all thought of your own will? For when you wish to sleep, you will be made to wake, and when you wish to wake, you will be made to sleep—"*

"Adam, what are you seeing?" asked an insistent voice, overlaying the words Jauffre heard. "Adam, a part of you remains detached and can report what Jauffre is experiencing. Tell me what you see."

It cost him some effort, but Adam somehow found the volition to stir his parched throat to words.

"It's my—Jauffre's—reception as a Templar," he whispered, seeing the scene still through that other's eyes, as a priest of the Order brought forward an open book and Jauffre set his joined hands between those of the unknown Master.

"Swear and promise to God and the Blessed Mary that you will always be obedient to the Master of the Temple, and to whichever brother of the said Order is put above you," the Master commanded. *"That you will preserve chastity, the good usages and the good customs of the Order, and you will live without property, except that it may be conceded to you by your superior. . . ."*

"Adam, stay in contact," Graham's voice urged.

"Yes . . ." Adam murmured, trying to distill Jauffre's experience as he reported it to Graham. "I make vows of obedience and chastity and poverty . . . protection of the holy places, wherever I shall be sent . . . to preserve the statutes and secrets of the Order . . . other things. My— cousin is there," he added, because it seemed important.

"His name?"

"Arnault."

"And where are you?"

"The Temple in Paris . . . a smaller chapel. The doors are closed. Only other Templars are present—maybe ten of them."

"By our Lady's grace, may you persevere henceforth in this high resolve," the Templar priest declared.

As he presented the book he held, Jauffre laid both hands upon it in affirmation of the oath he had just sworn. Gracing the page he bent to kiss was a painting of the Crucifixion, rich with vermilion and cobalt-blue and gold leaf. Unlike most Templars, Jauffre could read the words on the opposite page. The priest spoke those words in blessing as Jauffre's cousin laid the white mantle around his shoulders, with the red cross of the Order bold on the left shoulder.

"Ecce quam bonum et quam jocundum habitare fratres in unum"—How good and happy a thing it is for brethren to dwell together in unity. . . .

The presiding knight raised him up by both hands and kissed him on the mouth, instructing him then to greet his new brethren in like fashion. A part of Adam was aware of later charges against the Temple involving less chaste kissing, and worse, but Jauffre hardly remarked the exchange, for the bestowal of a ritual kiss of peace was common practice throughout France, both in the reception into religious orders and in the sealing of any lay feudal relationship.

"Tell me what you see," Graham's voice intruded. "Describe what's happening."

"The knight receiving me raises me up by both hands and kisses me on the mouth. It isn't what later accusers alleged—certainly nothing at all obscene. My cousin kisses me, the other knights kiss me—nothing to even raise an eyebrow at the time. . . ."

He was briefly aware of further instruction regarding the basic conduct expected of a Knight of the Temple—and then, some time later, other instruction of a more private and secret nature from his cousin Arnault and certain others. Not the clandestine improprieties alleged in later charges against the Order, but examination before a secret Master, and eventual induction into an inner circle of knights who were charged with guarding and protecting certain treasures, certain secrets. . . .

"Speak to me, Adam," came Graham's low-voiced command, as Adam stiffened in surprise and wonder.

But though Adam knew that Jauffre de Saint Clair had lived and died centuries before, and long since expiated any errors committed in that life, he yet was aware of certain bindings that forbade him to speak of what now came before his inner vision.

"Many secrets do we guard," the secret Master told him, once he had passed his probation for the inner circle. *"Not all are for thee to know at this time. But this one shalt thou guard with thy life, and see that it come to no harm."*

He was still a fairly junior knight, and very junior in the inner circle, but he was vouchsafed a glimpse of it. It was Easter, the last but one before the arrests began, and with others of the inner circle he had been summoned by the secret Master to attend in a hidden chapel underneath the treasury room of the Paris Temple.

The new fire was blessed and the Paschal candle lit, as was appropriate for the Easter Vigil. And then, as the night faded into dawning of that joyous Easter morn, priests of the inner circle briefly had displayed a treasured hallow for the veneration of those few privileged to be present.

Jauffre had been kneeling far back, and the lighting had been poor, but for a breathless, spellbound moment for-

ever etched in memory, it seemed that the priests held up
the ghostly apparition of a head. A part of Adam, watching, knew of *that* charge later leveled against the Order—
of worshiping a head, an idol—but in that timeless instant,
though Jauffre did not know precisely *what* it was, he had
no doubt that it was holy, and worth dying for.

"Adam?" Graham murmured from very far away.

"Not now," he managed to whisper, for an urgency now
attended the unfolding of Jauffre's memories.

Sustained by the memory of what he had glimpsed and
felt, his zeal had persisted through the year that followed.
Obedient to the orders of both king and pope, he was
among the hand-picked party of knights sent to Outremer
to escort the Grand Master back to France—not incognito
and with a small retinue, as the pope had requested, but
with sixty knights as escort and a baggage train of gold
and jewels, all of which were installed in the assumed
safety of the Paris Temple.

It was a confusing time. Grand Master Jacques de
Molay was not a learned man—not even literate—but his
faith burned with a passion that awed Jauffre at first, then
frustrated him. For under the guise of talks about a new
Crusade, and negotiations to merge the two great Military
Orders, it was clear to many of de Molay's officers—but
not to him—that the Temple was in grave danger. For if
the king could not force his will on the Order by law—it
being under papal protection that the Grand Master believed to be inviolable—such allegations would be manu-
factured as could not be ignored by the pontiff.

Yet the Grand Master seemed unwilling to believe the
conclusions being drawn by nearly everyone except himself. Jauffre was not privy to what was discussed in the
general chapter that the Grand Master called in July 1307,
but he saw the results in the weeks that followed. By the
beginning of autumn, orders had gone out to every com-

mandery in France to tighten security, and under no circumstances to reveal anything to anyone about the secret rituals and meetings of the Order. To reinforce this instruction, many of the Order's books and extant rules were called in and burned—a distasteful business for Jauffre, who was one of the knights assigned to see the orders carried out, but he obeyed.

Early October found him seated apprehensively among a score of his brethren in a dim-lit chamber hung with tapestries. It was the private sanctum of the secret Master, next to the hidden chapel beneath the Paris treasury. All present were members of the Temple's inner circle, and mostly far senior to Jauffre. Their immediate concern was that earlier that day, in stubborn denial that anything was amiss, Grand Master de Molay had served as an honorary pallbearer in the funeral procession of the Princess Catherine, wife of Charles of Valois, the king's brother. When questioned by one of his officers about the wisdom of such participation, de Molay had declared that surely the king would not show him this honor while simultaneously plotting the Order's destruction.

"I tell you, we must move, and move soon, or it will be too late," a knight called Oliver de Penne was saying. "The Grand Master is an old man and has been too long in the Holy Land. He does not know Nogaret the way we do, the poison he promulgates. Any day now, on the pretext of corruption, the king will seize the treasures of the Temple, its wealth, its fleet, and every one of us that his men can find."

"But the charges are specious, contrived out of whole cloth," another knight objected. "Avarice I could concede, from the king's perspective; 'tis no secret that he covets our wealth, since he cannot have the power that we wield. But heresy, idolatry, blasphemy, obscenity—who would believe such things?"

"Never forget that Guillaume de Nogaret brought down a pope with charges of magical attacks," Jauffre's cousin retorted. "Excommunicated by that pope's successor, and not yet absolved of that excommunication by the present pope, he also seeks to bring down an archbishop and a count's son on similar charges. Do you think he will hesitate to bring down the Temple in the same way, if he can—especially if our destruction will fill the king's coffers? Such attack has worked before—and merely to discredit us is not enough. He must render us so low that we lie beyond any court of appeal save Heaven's."

"But, surely the present pope will not allow—" one of the older knights began.

"Hugues, this is not the papacy of our fathers' times," a new voice interjected, softly but tinged with quiet power. "This pope is the king's creature, as is Nogaret. Clement owes his papal tiara to Philip; he mouths the platitudes he thinks we wish to hear, but he will not lift a finger to save us."

All eyes turned toward the new speaker, for it was the secret Master who had spoken at last. He was not physically imposing—just another white-robed figure among many, beginning to stoop a little with the weight of his years, a white beard spilling down his chest—but the psychic impact of his presence bespoke a vitality and puissance belied by any apparent physical decline.

"It thus behooves us to take measures to save what we may, of what we guard," the Master went on. "Certain temporal treasures already have been moved to places of safety, and I am reliably informed that the Master of the Paris Temple departs this very night to take away the contents of this treasury with the fleet at La Rochelle— though of other precious things he knows nothing. These I may only entrust to you, my brothers."

He had then proceeded to make assignments of certain

relics and hallows to such of his inner circle as seemed appropriate, parceling out the precious secrets of the Order garnered over more than two centuries of acquisition and careful guardianship. As most junior of those present, Jauffre knew few details of what particular items his brother knights received in trust, but all swore fervent and unfailing faith upon a long, flat object wrapped in swaths of padded linen, perhaps half the size of the table behind which the Master sat.

When only that remained, Jauffre still had not been called forward. Nor had the most senior knight besides the Master, a tall, light-haired knight called Frère Christoph, who came now to kneel opposite the Master, the veiled hallow between them, beckoning Jauffre to join him.

Jauffre still could not see what it was that lay within the swaddling linens, but he did not hesitate to follow the older knight's example, touching reverent fingertips to the wrappings as the Master enjoined them upon life and soul and hopes for their future salvation to guard one another and their charge unceasingly. Somehow Jauffre sensed that what lay within the padded linen had something to do with the holy thing that had been shown that Easter morn; and he gave the Master his promise with tears in his eyes and a surge of joy in his heart.

It was a promise Jauffre did not know whether he had kept. For when he and Frère Christoph set out within the hour to spirit the hallow to safety, the king's officers were already beginning their mass arrests of every Templar to be found in France. Jauffre had been ordered to guard the hallow and his fellow guardian with life and soul, but suddenly the best way to do that seemed to be to separate, to entice would-be pursuers astray and even let himself be taken so that Frère Christoph could win free.

"Adam, don't lose touch," Graham said softly. "I know

you're working on this, but you need to tell me what you can."

"Captured," Adam murmured, grimacing as the memories ran faster, more an observer now, only glimpsing snatches of those next two years of torture, deprivation, and pain.

"I had a task to perform . . . don't know whether I succeeded. Torture to extract confessions. . . . I tell them some of what they want to hear."

"Is it true?"

"No. But it stops the torture, after a while . . . and it keeps them from asking other questions that I *may* not answer, on peril of my soul."

"What happens then?" Graham asked. "Only relapsed heretics were burned."

The end was fast approaching again. Adam could almost smell the smoke, and cringed from the mere memory of the fire now looming once more.

"Many die unjustly," Adam whispered. "Some perish from the torture, a few take their own lives. I will not give them that satisfaction, but I cling to the hope that one day I may learn whether or not I failed—whether Christoph won safety with the hallow—until finally comes the opportunity to defend the Order. I am one of many who come forward, hopeful of proving the Order's purity, its innocence of the charges.

"But the church betrays us. They fear we defend ourselves too well, that if we are allowed to speak, the charges will fail. An archbishop convenes a church provincial council outside Paris and lets it be known that he is about to proceed to final judgment against certain relapsed heretics in his keeping. Angrily many of us recant, for surely we cannot be bound over for retracting confessions taken under duress.

"But the pope lifts not a finger to save us. As they chain

us to the stakes, my chief regret is never knowing my success or failure, never knowing what it is I die for."

The flames loomed once again in his inner vision. Adam sensed them, but recovering Jauffre's memory of what brought him to the flames had absolved him of the need to repeat that death again.

Yet there was something remaining to be done, an insistent urge to go beyond trance and onto the Astral—the Second Road, as Graham had termed it. From the depths of trance, still keeping his soul anchored in that profound centeredness that now allowed him to forestall repetition of Jauffre's passing, he slowly opened his eyes to look up at his mentor. Graham was watching him intently and seemed aware that their work was not yet done.

"Are you Jauffre or are you Adam?" he asked softly.

"Neither," Adam said thickly, "and both. I am Master of the Hunt, and the quarry I seek has eluded me for nearly seven hundred years."

"The quarry?" Graham said.

Slowly Adam closed his right hand in a fist, lifting it to press the stone of his ring to his lips before drawing cautious breath, careful not to disturb the balance.

"I need your help on this," he murmured. "There was something Jauffre was charged to protect, to make sure it was taken to a place of safety, so that it wouldn't fall into the hands of the king or the pope—something the Order had been guarding for centuries, something holy."

"What happened to it? What was it?" Graham asked.

Adam slowly shook his head, dipping back into Jauffre. "I do not know. 'Twas entrusted to Frère Christoph and me, but the king's officers pursued us. I led them away so that Christoph could make his escape. But I never did learn his fate . . . or that of the hallow." He closed his eyes briefly, unbidden tears stinging at his lids, then turned his tear-blurred gaze to Graham once again.

"Can you help me find it?" he whispered.

Slowly the general nodded. "There may be a way," he said. "I'm not certain its whereabouts can be brought all the way to the present, but you may be able to discover its immediate fate, within say, a few years of Jauffre's death. Would that satisfy you?"

"Yes!" Adam whispered fiercely, seizing the general's hand.

"Very well. Close your eyes and relax. Go back to the last time you saw it—the 'hallow,' did you call it?"

"Yes."

"See the hallow, then, and recall as much detail as you can. And now come slowly forward, until Jauffre is discarnate. See the image of the hallow still before your inner vision. And now begin to visualize a golden light growing within it, growing brighter and brighter, until suddenly it flares up—too bright to gaze upon. When the light subsides, the hallow is gone, but a golden net persists in afterimage. Do you see it?"

"Yes," Adam whispered.

"Good. Now see yourself reaching out to grasp the edges of the net nearest you. Know that what you seek occupies a unique place on that net, as do all things, all souls. Tense the net slightly. Feel the subtle vibration that leads down one of the strands toward what you seek. And now follow that strand. . . "

Smiling faintly at the imagery, Adam obeyed, his accustomed self-image on the Astral taking on familiar raiment of sapphire blue such as he customarily wore during ritual. The stone in his ring echoed that blue, glowing like a star on his right hand as he set out along a shimmering strand of golden light set with jewels that were souls. The nearest, he knew, was Graham, holding steady Adam's lifeline as he ventured forth.

The velvety ink-black of the cosmos throbbed with the

heartbeat of the universe as his feet flew along the golden strand—more akin to walking a ribbon than a tightrope. His speed increased, sweetly giddying, until suddenly he was brought up short by a starburst of silvery light that made him fling up both hands to shield his eyes.

When he could see again, he was standing in an unfamiliar place, though he sensed it to be part of the vast vaults of the Akashic Records, immortal and imperishable archives of all lives for all time. The softly glowing corridor in which he found himself seemed to stretch to infinity in both directions. Before him, however, hung a shimmering spindle of brilliance that immediately flared and then resolved to the towering column of light he had come to associate with the Masters to whom he answered on the Inner Planes, souls advanced beyond the need to take physical form.

What is it you seek, Master of the Hunt? came the wordless query in the stillness of his mind. *Your purpose in this life lies not in this temple. Do you weary of your burden?*

Nay, Master, Adam replied, *but there is that which remained unfinished in another life and time—not the doing, but the knowing. As Jauffre de Saint Clair, I was set a task to perform—to guard a sacred thing. Since no reproach has befallen me, I must trust that I gave satisfaction. Only—*

Only? came the almost amused reply.

Meekly Adam bowed his head before the shining presence, knowing he must ask; the Master would not volunteer.

I would know what it was I guarded, Master, Adam murmured. *Forgive my mortal curiosity, but I would attain some glimpse of it, some intimation of what Jauffre gave his life to preserve. Do I ask too much, that his sacrifice should be resolved?*

No, Master of the Hunt, you do not ask too much, came the reply, tinged with compassion. *Through the door which yields to the symbol Jauffre served, you shall gaze upon That which bore the Light—though where it now lies, you may not know. This portion of your path lies behind you. Still, may its vision bring peace to Jauffre.*

The shimmering pillar was dissolving even as it bade him wordless farewell, but Adam was already turning to behold a polished silver door behind him, which reflected back not the blue of his soutane but the image of the white-robed and bearded Jauffre. Overlaying that reflection, exactly as tall as he, a scarlet Templar cross blazed across the full height and width of the mirrored surface. The level of the horizontal arms was exactly even with his own when he stretched them to either side in a gesture of entreaty; their breadth was exactly the width of his embrace.

Stepping closer, he laid his arms along that scarlet crossbar in oblation, bowing his forehead to Jauffre's—and to the glyph that symbolized the faith he upheld both as Jauffre and as Adam Sinclair. The door parted down the center at that touch, opening wide to admit him, now clothed as Jauffre, with Jauffre's memories, Jauffre's yearnings.

The faint, heady sweetness of incense softly surrounded him, underlaid with the more delicate scent of beeswax. Far at the opposite end of a narrow, dim-lit nave, he could see the backs of white-clad worshipers bowed before a distant altar, and a priest presiding beyond them.

He paused to reverence the Presence permeating the place, then started forward. The others in the church were robed much as he, Templars all, but neither they nor the priest seemed aware of his approach.

Thus emboldened, he dared to mount the altar steps, heartened to see that it was Frère Christoph who served the altar, raising a silver chalice in the minor elevation of the Mass, the Host held slightly above it, shining like a sun. The words of consecration had brought down Spirit, focusing Divinity in the elements of bread and wine; and normally, Adam would have deemed that Presence enough for any need. But what lay on the altar beneath the chalice breathed its own echo of Divinity.

For now he could see what he had only glimpsed on that long-ago Easter in the chapel beneath the Paris Temple—and what he could only guess at, in its swathing of padded linen, when the Master had given it into the care of Frère Christoph and himself. The long, shallow box was perhaps four feet long by two feet wide, and perhaps a hand's breadth deep, the top covered by a silver interlace of metal wrought like saltires set side by side. And set into that meshlike interlace toward one end, protected by an oval piece of crystal as big as his two hands, he could see the faint, brownish features of a face etched on a lighter cloth. The eyes were closed, an arc above the eyes marked with darker stains, as if of wounds. And in that instant, Adam knew what it was that those long-ago Templars had guarded—what *he* had guarded, as Jauffre de Saint Clair.

That knowledge sent him plummeting back into his own body, his own time. He was trembling as he surfaced, his heart pounding not with fear but with awe. Seeing his apparent distress, Graham set both hands to his temples and ordered him back down into trance, bidding him center and still.

"You're all right; you've just come back too quickly," Graham said, though that was *not* what was causing his agitation. "Draw a deep breath and let it out. Take time to stabilize and recenter, to regain your perspective. And then, in your own good time, come slowly back to normal waking consciousness. Another deep breath . . . that's right . . ."

Adam obeyed, though he found he did not want to speak when he came back this time, and lay there for several seconds with his eyes still closed.

"Adam?" Graham said softly, when his subject did not rouse. "Adam, what did you see?"

Adam opened his eyes, his gaze still half-focused otherwhen as he heaved a heavy sigh. Then he slowly brought his Adept ring to his lips in salute to what he had witnessed. His labored swallow seemed to shatter the silence.

"I think—it was the holy Shroud," he said.

Graham's face went very still.

"You mean—the Shroud that wrapped Jesus in his tomb?"

Adam nodded, the image still before his inner Sight.

"What—did it look like?" Graham asked hesitantly.

Briefly Adam began describing what he had seen, a little surprised that he could, some of the wonder returning as he spoke. When he had finished, his voice trailing into silence, Graham was sitting with his elbows resting on his knees, steepled fingertips pressed lightly to his lips in thought, his gaze fixed unfocused before him. Only when Adam eased cautiously to a sitting position, elbowing the pillows to support him, did the older man look up, a faint smile curving his lips.

"Robert de Boron wrote of 'the great secret uttered at the great sacrament performed *over* the Grail,' " he said softly, obviously quoting. "It's also interesting to note that the earliest Grail romances don't appear in the West until about the twelfth century, soon after the founding of the Temple in Jerusalem. Suddenly one has to wonder whether the early sources were talking about a cup or a chalice at all."

"I don't think I follow you," Adam said.

"Bear with me. We usually think of the Grail as a cup—and maybe it is—though Wolfram von Eschenbach also described it as a stone, and pre-Christian traditions spoke of a cauldron of plenty or regeneration. I'm sure you've heard those theories."

"Yes."

"But you've described something different," Graham continued. "There's a cup or chalice in the equation, but that isn't the true focus. The name of the other guardian was the first clue: Christoph—Christopher—'Christ-Bearer'—how did we miss *that?* It may have been an office, not a name. You even said that the design on top of the box resembled saltire crosses set side by side. A saltire equates with the letter *Chi,* which also stands for *Christos.* That would produce the lattice or trellis effect you described, but it also describes a grille—a *greille*—*gradalis*—*grasal*—which came to mean a bowl or platter—and perhaps a grail."

The implication struck Adam nearly speechless. "Are you suggesting that—the Templars had the Holy Grail?" he whispered.

"Not—exactly. But suppose that the Grail were a container for the Sacred Blood in a different sense than we usually suppose. Not the cup of the Last Supper—and hence the vessel for containing the wine that becomes the Christian sacrament, the Blood of Christ—but the container for the burial cloth that also bore the Sacred Blood. . . . "

"That which bore the Light," Adam murmured, recalling the Master's words. "Then—the Grail could have been a—a reliquary for the Shroud."

"That would tally with what you saw," Graham agreed. "Think about that crystal-covered oval you mentioned, set into the lid of the casket. Suppose that the shroud was kept folded so that the face showed through the crystal.

For that matter, there could have been paintings done of the face, like icons, and dispersed to selected commanderies, only to be displayed on special occasions. If *that* was the basis of the so-called 'head' that the Templars were accused of worshiping, it would explain a lot: secret, inner tradition devotions not understood by some of the brethren themselves, and misinterpreted by their inquisitors."

Adam nodded. "That could certainly account for the proliferation of confessions about a 'head.' And paintings would have been easy to destroy, when the end came."

"Except for the original," Graham said with a smile. "That was entrusted to the 'Christ-Bearer' and a young knight called Jauffre de Saint Clair, who did not fail in his sacred duty."

Adam glanced at his hands, which in the guise of other flesh had borne the Holy. The details of his vision were fading, as they always did once he fully returned from the Inner Planes, but he knew that the essence of Jauffre's sacrifice would remain with him.

"No, that part of Jauffre is resolved, thanks to you," he said. "I can't say that Adam Sinclair is entirely satisfied— even the answers only raise new questions—but there's nothing new on that score. What an irony, though, if the most holy treasure of the Templars became their downfall, because they dared not reveal it, lest they risk it falling into profane hands."

"*Did* it fall into profane hands?" Graham asked. "What became of it? And perhaps more to the point, is what you saw the same as what now resides at Turin? Or if not Turin, there are several other places that claim to possess the True Shroud."

Adam smiled faintly, for the Master had been quite clear that the vision granted Jauffre had told only of the hallow's location *then*, as confirmation that Jauffre had not failed in his task. He had no idea of its present whereabouts; nor could he have spoken of it if he had.

"I don't know," he replied truthfully. "And if I did, I couldn't tell you. Does it matter?"

"Probably not," Graham conceded, "though humankind has always yearned for tangible evidence that the gods do take an active interest in us. What more poignant evidence of the Great Sacrifice than the preservation of the very cloth in which a slain god was wrapped while his spirit descended to the Underworld?"

Adam raised an eyebrow, slightly amused. "I know you aren't a Christian, Gray. How is it that you manage to reduce Christianity to mythology without conveying the slightest disrespect?"

Smiling, Graham gave a wistful shrug of his shoulders. "Some things are universal," he replied. "How should I not respect Divinity, however It chooses to manifest Itself? And how incredibly arrogant I should be if I tried to claim that my view of Divinity was the only valid one."

"You wouldn't be the first," Adam said archly.

"Unfortunately, no. And if you'll indulge me, I'll carry our speculation one step further," Graham went on. "If the Grail *was* a container for the holy Shroud, it would explain why women were always prominent in descriptions of Grail rituals. Orthodox tradition has it that no women were present at the Last Supper—though I've always doubted that—but they certainly played an important part in the burial of Jesus. What more fitting than that they should be depicted as the bearers of the Grail, even as they bore the burial cloths?"

"That would certainly follow," Adam agreed.

"Going beyond Christian symbolism," Graham continued, "we could liken the three Marys of the Crucifixion to aspects of the Triple Goddess, and connect them to Isis, who also gathered up the body—or the parts of it—of a slain priest-king to give it proper burial. . . .

"But I digress," he said, as he noted Adam starting to go a little glassy-eyed at the transition. "And I can see I'm about to overload you, on top of everything that's already happened tonight. Returning to the point, one has to wonder whether what you helped protect as Jauffre de Saint Clair *was* the Shroud of Jesus, bearing the image of another slain priest-king. There's no question that it would have been a potent relic for the Knights of the Temple— well worth risking everything to save it from the avarice of the King of France—well worth dying for."

"Yes," Adam murmured, recalling the fire, but now able to set aside the horror of that death. "Some things *are* worth dying for—and it seems Jauffre didn't fail after all."

"No, he didn't. Knowing that, can you now accept the manner of Jauffre's passing, and let it cease to trouble you in this life?"

"Yes, I can," Adam said with a faint smile. "In fact, dealing with Jauffre enables me to hope that now I may be able to help Henri Gerard, who apparently was Nogaret. I have to wonder whether he had any suspicion about the Shroud's existence, or whether he was simply obsessed with attaining the power he believed the Templars to wield—what was bound up by the Seal of Solomon and the other hallows."

"The latter, I would guess," Graham said. "What you've told me suggests that Nogaret had little awareness of the power generated by that pure faith espoused by most of the Knights of the Temple. But you must be the judge of that. It was you who saw the relic of the Shroud—not I."

"True enough," Adam agreed. "And now that I understand my own part in that time, I think I begin to see an approach that might help Gerard resolve his unfinished business with Nogaret. That's assuming, of course, that I can get him to resume touch with reality. I'll have to get him assigned to my public caseload first."

"Will that be difficult, without arousing suspicion?"

"No. There's nothing to connect me with what happened to him. He brought his fate on himself. Still, a physician doesn't abandon a sick patient—especially if one was witness to what drove him over the edge."

"You saved his life," Graham said, "and quite possibly his soul. Do you think you can restore his sanity as well?"

Adam shrugged. "I'll do my best. I don't entertain much hope for any speedy resolution—perhaps not even entirely in this lifetime—but with luck, and perhaps some eventual healing from the Grail, maybe he can at least start the next time 'round with a clean slate."

Graham chuckled and retrieved the Templar cross from where it had fallen amid the bedclothes, laying it back into its box.

"I wonder if you realize," he said, switching off the tape recorder, "how refreshing it is to talk to a professional like yourself who accepts all of this as a given."

As he popped out the little cassette and handed it to Adam, Adam grinned, then pointedly rose to tuck the cassette into a pocket of his suit coat, draped across the back of a nearby chair.

"Careful where you say that," he replied lightly, "or you might get me stricken off the medical register. There aren't many psychiatrists who believe in reincarnation—at least not publicly."

"Do *you?*"

"Not publicly," Adam replied with a smile, as Graham rose. "But in private, at least after sessions like tonight, I would have to give you an unqualified yes. I sometimes become less certain once the immediacy fades, but even then it seems useful to act as if it were true. And you?"

As Adam slipped back into his shoes, Graham smiled wistfully, briefly glancing away as he fingered a silver chain at the open collar of his shirt.

"Oh, yes," he said softly, drawing up what dangled from the chain, though Adam could not see what it was. "I believe in reincarnation. Perhaps one day I'll tell you about the man who gave me this." His hand closed briefly around whatever was on the chain before dropping it back inside his shirt.

"But enough of this. I think we both could use some supper. Shall we see what Linton's left us? And you must tell me how Philippa fares."

INTERLUDE FOUR

Thanks to Jauffre de Saint Clair, we have touched on several of the specific charges alleged against the Templars. Some had made appearances in allegations of heresy and witchcraft for years, and would continue to do so for centuries to come. It may be useful, at this point, to examine the charges in slightly more detail, along with possible explanations for certain kinds of charges. Though many of the charges are contradictory, the Templars were expected to admit:

- That at their reception into the Order, postulants were required to deny God, Christ, the Apostles, and/or the Virgin Mary, by word and/or by spitting or trampling or urinating on the Cross. (This charge makes little sense, given that the knights routinely laid down their lives for the God they supposedly denied. Some who confessed to this charge qualified their answers, saying that they denied only on their lips, not in their hearts, or that they spat—or trampled, or urinated—*beside* the Cross. Some claimed that the denial was meant to symbolize Saint Peter's denial of Christ, with the intention that the knight would not emulate Peter if captured by Saracens—and, in fact, many knights perished at the hands of Saracen executioners rather than deny their faith. Others justified the admission by claiming the denial was a test of the unquestioning obedience required of all Templars.)

- That postulants were then required to bestow the Osculum Infame, the "kiss of shame," on their receptor, by kissing him on the mouth, navel, penis, or buttocks. (Sometimes the roles are reversed, with the postulant receiving the kisses. Such charges were common enough in allegations of devil worship, but no evidence of such behavior by the Templars was ever brought forward.)

- That the Order not only permitted but encouraged homosexual practices among its members. (Only two brethren confessed to availing themselves of this alleged instruction—somewhat remarkable in an all-male enclave, where such behavior might have been not unexpected.)

- That they worshiped idols in their secret ceremonies. (No evidence of this was ever produced.)

- That a cord "blessed" by contact with an idol was issued to new postulants at their reception, to be worn always next to the shirt or the flesh as a sign of chastity. (Though several men admitted to this, or said they had heard of it, no cord was ever produced. The charge harks back to one made against the Cathars, who wore a cord—unconnected with idols—as a sign of their chastity. This charge also totally ignores the fact that most Christian religious orders regarded the cincture or girdle as a symbol of chastity—including the Templars' Dominican inquisitors.)

- That the Order's priests did not consecrate the Host;

and, related, that the Host was spat into a latrine; (If the Host was not consecrated, then spitting it into a latrine would not have been an offense. There is no evidence that either was done.)

- That the Order permitted lay absolution. (The officer presiding at a chapter meeting had the authority to absolve brethren from infractions of the rule, *to the extent to which he was empowered,* but absolution from actual sin was reserved to a priest.)

- That the business of the Order was conducted in secret. (Of course. This was common practice in all religious Orders, as regards their internal workings; and since the Templars often were concerned with security regarding their military operations, secrecy was especially appropriate in these instances.)

The all-encompassing charge was heresy, defined as denial or doubt by any baptized person of any accepted and authoritative teaching of the Roman Catholic faith, proof of which would permit confiscation of property and suppression. A penitent who confessed his errors and denounced them could be absolved, assigned a suitable penance, and perhaps even hope for eventual release to join another religious Order.

The catch was that confession under torture was deemed valid and irrevocable, and anyone who later retracted a confession thus obtained became a relapsed heretic. Such apostasy merited only one fate: to be abandoned by the church and turned over to the secular arm for immediate execution at the stake.

Of course, to escape torture, most victims eventually confessed to at least some of the charges—anything to stop the pain. The Preceptor of Paris later stated that he would have confessed to killing God Himself, if that would stop the torture.

Nonetheless, the charges were compiled—without a shred of evidence being produced other than hearsay. At least the charge of idolatry should have produced some item of physical evidence, if it were true. The idol was alleged to be the head of a bearded man—some said John the Baptist, some said Hugues de Payens, some claimed it was a woman's head, some had no idea who it might be. It had two faces—no, one face—no, three; it had but one face, but legs varying in number. It was gold, silver, wood, copper—an actual mummified head. Occasionally it was described as a painting. Sometimes it was a cat that was adored—black, white, brown, or red—and that must be kissed beneath the tail.

Interestingly enough, despite the enormous amount of attention given to the allegation of idolatry, and the extensive search of every available Templar location, no evidence was found. Indeed, the only item even resembling a head was a silver-gilt reliquary shaped like a woman's head, containing the bones of a single skull and an inscription reading *caput LVIII*. It was said by some to be a genuine relic of one of the eleven thousand virgin martyrs venerated as saints by the early Christians, and was never considered seriously as evidence of idolatry. If there had been another head, it would have become a potent Templar relic in the years after the suppression.

The relics and increasingly mythic lore of the Temple have continued to inspire speculation in certain quarters. Particularly potent are the aspects that connect survival of the Temple, in some form, with the survival of the Kingdom of Scots, especially as the Scottish struggle to maintain independence becomes increasingly romanticized in the period of the later Stuart kings and the Jacobite Rebellion of 1745. (*Jacobite* refers to supporters of James II of England—VII of Scotland—and his descendants.)

In September 1745, half a century after Bonnie Dundee

fell at Killiecrankie, and more than two hundred years after exiled Templar Knights came to the aid of Robert the Bruce at Bannochburn, Prince Charles Edward Stuart (better known as Bonnie Prince Charlie) is said to have received Scottish Templars in private audience at Holyrood Palace, and to have accepted the office of Grand Master of the Temple as it then existed. And after the disaster of Culloden—which pretty much ended serious Jacobite pretensions in Scotland—the Brotherhood of Freemasonry took up the Templar cause (and, some say, the Jacobite cause as well), melding together the Solomonic origins of the original Temple in Jerusalem, the mythical mission of the original knights to protect that holy place, and other esoteric material that may or may not have originated in biblical times.

Part of that synthesis took place or was furthered in the New World, where the American colonies were forging a new form of government never seen before in the Old World. The North American continent would provide a haven for many folk of Scottish descent, most of them little aware how deeply their roots extended back to Scotland, and a romantic war fought centuries before.

Word of Honor

Tanya Huff

The prayer became a background drone without
words, without meaning; holding no relevance to
her life even had she bothered to listen.

Pat Tarrill shoved her hands deep in her jacket pockets
and wondered why she'd come. The moment she'd read
about it in the paper, attending the Culloden Memorial
Ceremony had become like an itch she had to scratch—although it wasn't the sort of thing she'd normally waste her
time at. *And that's exactly what I'm doing. Wasting time.*
Sometimes she felt like that was all she'd been doing the
entire twenty-five years of her life. Wasting time.

The prayer ended. Pat looked up, squinted against the
wind blowing in off Northumberland Strait, and locked
eyes with a wizened old man in a wheelchair. She scowled
and stepped forward but lost sight of him as the bodies
around the cairn shifted position.

Probably just a dirty old man, she thought as she closed
her eyes and lost herself in the wail of the pipes.

Later, while everyone else hurried off to the banquet

laid out in St. Mary's Church hall, Pat walked slowly to the cairn and lightly touched the damp stain. Raising her fingers to her face she sniffed the residue and smiled. Once again she heard her grandfather grumble that "no true Scot would waste whiskey on a rock." But her grandfather had been dead for years and the family had left old Scotland for Nova Scotia in 1770.

Wiping her fingers on her jeans, Pat headed for her car. She hadn't been able to afford a ticket to the banquet and wouldn't have gone even if she could have. All that *Scots wha hae* stuff made her nauseous.

"Especially," she muttered, digging for her keys, "since most of this lot has been no closer to Scotland than Glace Bay."

With one hand on the pitted handle of her car door, she slowly turned, pulled around by the certain knowledge that she was being observed. It was the old man again, sitting in his chair at the edge of the churchyard and staring in her direction. This time, a tall, pale man in a tan overcoat stood behind him—also staring. *Staring down his nose,* Pat corrected, for even at that distance the younger man's attitude was blatantly obvious. Flipping the two of them the finger, she slid into her car.

She caught one last glimpse of them in the rearview mirror as she peeled out of the gravel parking lot. Tall and pale appeared to be arguing with the old man.

"Patricia Tarrill?"

"Pat Tarrill. Yeah."

"I'm Harris MacClery, Mr. Hardie's solicitor."

Tucking the receiver between ear and shoulder, Pat forced her right foot into a cowboy boot. "So, should I know you?"

"I'm Mr. *Chalmer* Hardie's solicitor."

"Oh." Everyone in Atlantic Canada knew of Chalmer

Hardie. He owned . . . well, he owned a good chunk of Atlantic Canada.

"Mr. Hardie would like to speak with you."

"With me?" Her voice rose to an undignified squeak. "What about?"

"A job."

Pat's gaze pivoted toward the stack of unpaid bills threatening to bury the phone. She'd been unemployed for a month, and the job hadn't lasted long enough for her to qualify for unemployment insurance. "I'll take it."

"Don't you want to know what it's about?"

She could hear his disapproval, and frankly, she didn't give two shits. Anything would be better than yet another visit to the welfare office. "No," she told him, "I don't."

As she scribbled directions on the back of an envelope, she wondered if her luck had finally changed.

Chalmer Hardie lived in Dunmaglass, a hamlet tucked between Baileys Brook and Lismore—the village where the Culloden Memorial had taken place. More specifically, Chalmer Hardie *was* Dunmaglass. Tucked up against the road was a gas station/general store/post office and then up a long lane was the biggest house Pat had ever seen.

She swore softly in awe as she parked the car, then swore again as a tall, pale man came out of the house to meet her.

"Ms. Tarrill." It wasn't a question, but then, he knew what she looked like. "Mr. Hardie is waiting."

"Ms. Tarrill." The old man in the wheelchair held out his hand. "I'm very happy to meet you."

"Um, me, too. That is, I'm happy to meet you." His hand felt dry and soft, and although his fingers curved around hers, they didn't grip. Up close, his skin was pale yellow and it hung off his skull in loose folds, falling into accordion pleats around his neck.

"Please forgive me if we go directly to business." He waved her toward a brocade wing chair. "I dislike wasting the little time I have left."

Pat lowered herself into the chair feeling as if she should've worn a skirt and resenting the feeling.

"I have a commission I wish you to fulfill for me, Ms. Tarrill." Eyes locked on hers, Chalmer Hardie folded his hands over a small wooden box resting on his lap. "In return, you will receive ten thousand dollars and a position in one of my companies."

"A position?"

"A job, Ms. Tarrill."

"And ten thousand dollars?"

"That is correct."

"So, who do you want me to kill?" She regretted it almost instantly, but the richest man in the Maritimes merely shook his head.

"I'm afraid he's already dead." The old man's fingers tightened around the box. "I want you to return something to him."

"Him who?"

"Alexander MacGillivray. He led Clan Chattan at Culloden, as the chief was, at the time, a member of the Black Watch and thus not in a position to support the prince."

"I know."

Sparse white eyebrows rose. "You know?"

Pat shrugged. "My grandfather was big into all that . . ." she paused and searched for an alternative to *Scottish history crap,* "heritage stuff."

"I see. Would it be too much to ask that he ever mentioned the Knights Templar?"

She frowned and recalled that he'd once gotten into a

drunken fight with a Knight of Columbus. "Yeah, it would."

"Then I'm afraid we'll have to include a short history lesson, or none of this will make sense."

For ten thousand bucks and a job, Pat could care less if it made sense, but she arranged her face into what she hoped was an interested expression and waited.

Frowning slightly, Hardie thought for a moment. When he began to speak, his voice took on the cadences of a lecture hall.

"The Knights Templar were a brotherhood of fighting monks sworn to defend the Holy Land of the Bible from the infidel. In 1132, the Patriarch of Jerusalem gave Hugues de Payens, the first Master of the Knights, a relic, a splinter of the True Cross sealed into a small crystal orb that could be worn like a medallion. This medallion was to protect the Master and, through his leadership, the holy knights.

"In 1307, King Philip IV of France, for reasons we haven't time to go into, decided to destroy the Templars. He convinced the current Grand Master, Jacques de Molay, to come to France, planning to arrest him and all the Templars in the country in one fell swoop. Which he did. They were tortured and many of them, including their Master, were burned alive as heretics."

"Wait a minute," Pat protested, leaning forward. "I thought the medallion thing was supposed to protect them."

Hardie grimaced. "Yes, well, a very short time before they were arrested, de Molay was warned. He sent a messenger with the medallion to the Templar fleet with orders for them to put out to sea."

"If he was warned, why didn't he run himself?"

"Because that would not have been the honorable thing to do."

"Like, dying's so honorable." She bit her lip and wished just once that her brain would work before her mouth.

The old man stared at her for a long moment, then continued as though she hadn't expressed an opinion.

"While de Molay believed that nothing would happen to him personally, he had a strong and accurate suspicion that King Philip was after the Templars' not inconsiderable treasure. Much of that treasure had already been loaded onto the ships of the fleet.

"The fleet landed in Scotland. Maintaining their tradition of service, the knights became a secular organization and married into the existing Scottish nobility. The treasure the fleet carried was divided amongst the knights for safekeeping and, as the centuries passed, many pieces became family heirlooms and were passed from father to son.

"Now, then, Culloden . . . In 1745 Bonnie Prince Charlie returned from exile to Scotland and suffered a final defeat at Culloden. The clans supporting him were slaughtered. Among the dead were many men of the old Templar families."

He opened the box on his lap and beckoned Pat closer. Resting on a padded red velvet lining was probably the ugliest piece of jewelry she'd ever seen—and as a fan of the Home Shopping Network, she'd seen some ugly jewelry. In the center of a gold disk about two inches across, patterned with what looked like little specks of gold, was a yellowish and uneven crystal sphere about the size of a marble. A modern gold chain filled the rest of the box.

"An ancestor of mine stole that before the battle from Alexander MacGillivray. You, Ms. Tarrill, are looking at an actual sliver of the True Cross."

Squinting, Pat could just barely make out a black speck

in the center of the crystal. *Sliver of the True Cross my aunt fanny.*

"This is what . . ." she searched her memory for the name and couldn't find it, "that Templar guy sent out of France?"

"Yes."

"How do you know?"

"Trust me, Ms. Tarrill. I know. I want you to take this holy relic and place it in the grave of Alexander MacGillivray."

"In Scotland?"

"That is correct. Mr. MacClery will give you details. I will, of course, pay all expenses."

Pat studied the medallion, lips pursed. "I have another question."

"Perfectly understandable."

"Why me?"

"Because I am too sick to make the journey and because I had a dream." His lips twitched into a half smile as though he realized how ridiculous he sounded but didn't care. "I dreamt about a young woman beside the cairn at the Culloden Memorial Service—you, Ms. Tarrill."

"You're going to trust me with this, give me ten thousand bucks and a job, based on a dream?"

"You don't understand." One finger lightly touched the crystal. "But you will."

As crazy as it sounded, he seemed to believe it.

"Did the dream give you my name?"

"No. Mr. MacClery had your license plate traced."

Her eyes narrowed. Lawyers! "So, why do you want this thing returned? I mean, if it was supposed to protect MacGillivray and Clan Chattan at Culloden, giving it back isn't going to change the fact that the Duke of Cumberland kicked butt."

"I don't want to change things, Ms. Tarrill. I want to do what's right." His chin lifted, and she saw the effort that small movement needed. "I have been dying for a long time; time enough to develop a conscience, if you will. I want the Cross of Christ back where it belongs, and I want you to take it there." His shoulders slumped. "I would rather go myself, but I left it too long."

Pat glanced toward the door and wondered if lawyers listened through keyholes. "Is Mr. MacClery going with me?"

"No. You'll go alone."

"Well, what proof do you want that I actually put it in the grave?"

"Your word will be sufficient."

"My word? That's it?"

"Yes."

She could tell from his expression that he truly believed her word would be enough. Wondering how anyone so gullible had gotten so rich, she gave it.

Pat had never been up in a plane before and, as much as she'd intended to be cool about it, she kept her face pressed against the window until the lights of St. John's were replaced by the featureless black of the North Atlantic. In her purse, safe under her left arm, she carried the boxed medallion and a hefty packet of money MacClery had given her just before she boarded.

Although it was an overnight flight, Pat didn't expect to sleep; she was too excited. But the food was awful and she'd seen the movie, and soon staying awake became more trouble than it was worth.

A few moments later, wondering grumpily who'd play the bagpipes on an airplane, she opened her eyes.

Instead of the blue tweed of the seat in front of her, she was looking down at an attractive young man—tall and muscular, red-gold hair above delicate dark brows and long, thick lashes. At the moment he needed a shave and a bath, but she still wouldn't kick him out of bed for eating crackers.

A hand, with rather a great quantity of black hair growing across the back of it, reached down and shook the young man's shoulder. With a bit of a shock, she realized the hand was hers.

Well, this dream obviously isn't heading where I'd like it to. . . .

"Alex! Get your great lazy carcass on its feet. There's a battle to be fought." Her mouth formed the words, but she had no control over either content or delivery. It appeared she was merely a passenger.

Gray eyes snapped open. "Davie? I must've dozed off."

"You fell asleep, but there's no crime in that. Lord John is with His Highness in Culloden House, and Cumberland's men are up and about."

"Aye, then so should I be." Shaking his head to clear the sleep from it, Alexander MacGillivray, lieutenant colonel of Clan Chattan, heaved himself up onto his feet, his right hand moving to touch his breast as he stood. His fair skin went paler still, and his eyes widened so far they must've hurt. He dug under his clothing then whirled about to search the place he'd lain.

"What is it, Alex? Have you lost something?" Pat felt Davie's heart begin to race and over it, pressed hard against his skin, she felt a warm weight hanging. All at once, she knew it had to be the medallion.

That son of a bitch!

Stuffed into Davie Hardie's head, she could access what it held; he'd known the medallion had been in the MacGillivray family for a very long time, but had only recently discovered what it was. More a scholar than a soldier, he'd found a reference to it in an old manuscript, had tracked it back to the Templar landing in Argyll where the MacGillivrays originated, had combed the scraps of Templar history that remained, and had discovered what it held and the power attributed to it. He hadn't intended to take advantage of what he'd found—but then Charles Edward Stewart and war had come to Scotland.

Pat could feel Davie Hardie's fear of facing Cumberland's army, and touched the memory of how he'd stolen the medallion's protection for himself—even though he'd known that if it were worn by one with the right, it could very well protect the entire clan. *That cowardly son of a bitch!*

When Alexander MacGillivray straightened, Pat could read his thoughts off his face. By losing the medallion, he'd betrayed a sacred trust. There was only one thing he could do.

"Alex?"

The young commander squared his shoulders, faced his own death, and tugged on his bonnet. "Come along, Davie. I need to talk to the chiefs before we take our place in line."

You need to talk to your pal Davie, that's what you need to do! Then the dream twisted sideways and Pat winced as a gust of sleet and rain whipped into her face. The duke of Cumberland's army was a red blot on the moor no more than five hundred yards away. When Hardie turned, she saw MacGillivray. When he turned a little farther, she could see the companies in line.

Then the first gun boomed across the moor and Hardie whirled in time to see the smoke. A heartbeat later, there was nothing to see but smoke and nothing to hear but screaming.

I don't want to be here! Pat struggled to free herself from the dream. Her terror and Hardie's became one terror. Dream or not, she wanted to die no less than he did.

The cannonade went on. And on.

Through it all, she saw MacGillivray, striding up and down the ranks of his men, giving them courage to stand. Sons were blown to bits beside their fathers, brothers beside brothers. The shot killed chief and humblie indiscriminately, but the line held.

And the cannonade went on.

The clansmen were yelling for the order to charge so they could bring their broadswords into play. The order never came.

And the cannonade went on.

"Sword out, Davie. We've taken as much of this as we're going to."

Hardie grabbed his colonel's arm. "Are you mad?" he yelled over the roar of the guns and shrieks of the dying. "It's not your place to give the order!"

"It's not my place to stand here and watch my people slaughtered!"

"Then why fight at all? Even Lord Murray says we're likely to lose!"

All at once, Pat realized why a man only twenty-five had been chosen to lead the clan in the absence of its chief. Something in his expression spoke quietly of strength and courage and responsibility. "We took an oath to fight for the prince."

"We'll all be killed!"

MacGillivray's eyes narrowed. "Then we'll die with honor."

Pat felt Hardie tremble and wonder how much his colonel suspected. "But the prince!"

"This isn't his doing, it's that damned Irishman, O'Sullivan." Spinning on one heel, he scrugged his bonnet down over his brow and made his way back to the center of the line.

A moment later, Clan Chattan charged forward into the

smoke hoarsely yelling "Loch Moy!" and "Dunmaglass!" The pipes screamed the rant until they were handed to a boy and the piper pulled his sword and charged forward with the rest.

Davie Hardie charged because he had no choice. Pat caught only glimpses of the faces that ran by, faces that wore rage and despair equally mixed. Then she realized that there seemed to be a great many running by as Hardie stumbled and slowed and made a show of advancing without moving forward.

Cumberland's artillery had switched to grape shot. Faintly, over the roar of the big guns, Pat heard the drum roll firing of muskets. Men fell all around him, whole families died, but nothing touched Davie Hardie.

Then, through a break in the smoke and the dying, Pat saw a red-gold head reach the front line of English infantry. Swinging his broadsword, MacGillivray plunged through, leapt over the bodies he'd cut down, and was lost in the scarlet coats.

With his cry of "Dunmaglass" ringing in her ears, Pat woke. She was clutching her purse so tightly that the edges of the box cut into her hands through the vinyl.

"Death before dishonor, my butt," she muttered as she pushed up the window's stiff plastic shade and blinked in the sudden glare of morning sun. That philosophy had got Alexander MacGillivray dead and buried. Davie Hardie had turned dishonor into a long life in the New World. So he'd had to live knowing that his theft had been responsible for the death of his friend; at least he was alive.

Chill out, Pat. It was only a dream.

She accepted a cup of coffee from the stewardess and stirred in double sugar, the spoon rattling against the side of the cup.

Dreams don't mean shit.

But she could still feel Hardie's willingness to do anything rather than die, and it left a bad taste in her mouth.

Customs at Glasgow airport passed her through with a cheery good morning and instructions on where to wait for her connecting flight north to Inverness. At Inverness airport, she was met by a ruddy young man who introduced himself as Gordon Ritchie, Mr. Hardie's driver. After a few moments of exhausted confusion while they settled *which* Mr. Hardie, he retrieved her suitcase and bundled her into a discreet black sedan.

"It was all arranged over the phone," Gordon explained as he drove toward A96 and Inverness. "Here I am, at your beck and call until you head back across the pond."

Pat smiled sleepily. "I love the way you talk."

"Beg your pardon, Ms. Tarrill?"

"Never mind, it's a Canadian thing, you wouldn't understand." A large truck passed the car on the wrong side of the road. Heart in her throat, Pat closed her eyes. Although she hadn't intended to sleep, she remembered nothing more until Gordon called out, "We're here, Ms. Tarrill."

Yawning, she peered out the window. "Call me Pat, and where's here?"

"Station Hotel, Academy Street. Mr. Hardie—Mr. Chalmer Hardie, that is—booked you a room here. It's not the best hotel in town . . ."

He sounded so apologetic that she laughed. "Trust me, Mr. Hardie knows what he's doing." She could just see herself in some swanky Scottish hotel. *Likely get tossed out for not rolling my r's.*

Her room held a double bed, an overstuffed chair, a small desk spread with tourist brochures, and a chest of drawers. It had a color TV bolted to its stand and a bathroom with a tub and shower.

"Looks like Mr. Hardie blew the wad." Pat dragged herself as far as the bed and collapsed. After a moment, she pulled the box out of her purse, flipped it open, and stared down at the medallion. It looked the same as it had on the other side of the Atlantic.

"Well, why wouldn't it?" Setting the open box on the bedside table, she stripped and crawled between the sheets. Although it was still early, she'd been traveling for twenty-four hours and was ready to call it a night.

"Bernard? Is that you?"

Who the hell is Bernard? Yanked back to consciousness, Pat opened her eyes and found herself peering down into the bearded face of a burly man standing in the center of a small boat. The combination of dead fish, salt water, and rotting sewage smelled a lot like Halifax harbor.

"Quiet, Robert," she heard herself say. "Do you want to wake all of Harfleur?"

I guess I'm *Bernard.* She felt the familiar weight resting on his chest. *Oh, no, what now?* She searched through the young man's memories and found enough references to hear Chalmer Hardie's voice say, *"In 1307 King Philip IV of France decided to destroy the Templars."*

Pat tried unsuccessfully to wake up. *First Culloden, now this! Why can't I dream about sex, like a normal person?*

The wooden rungs damp and punky under callused palms, Bernard scrambled down a rickety ladder and joined the man in the boat. Both wore the red Templar cross on a dark brown mantle. They were sergeants, men-at-arms, Pat discovered, delving into Bernard's memories again, permitted to serve the Order though they weren't nobly born. Bernard had served for only a few short months, and his oaths still burned brightly behind every conscious thought.

"I will suffer all that is pleasing to God."

How do I come up with this stuff? She looked over Robert's shoulder and saw, in the gray light of predawn, the eighteen galleys of the Templar fleet riding at anchor in the harbor.

Covered in road dirt and breathing heavily, Bernard grabbed for support as the boat rocked beneath the two men. "I've come from the Grand Master himself. He said to tell the Preceptor of France that it is time and that he gives this holy relic into his charge."

As he raised it, the crystal orb in the center of the medallion seemed to gather up what little light there was, and Pat could feel the young man's astonished pride at being chosen to bear it.

Over the soft slap, slap of the water against the pilings came the heavy tread of armed men.

Scrambling back up the ladder, Bernard peered over the edge of the dock and muttered "The seneschal!" in such a tone that Pat heard, *"The cops!"*

Right, let's get out of here.

Chalmer Hardie's voice murmured, *". . . burned alive as heretics."*

To her surprise, Bernard raised the medallion to his lips, kissed it devoutly, turned, and dropped the heavy chain over Robert's head.

Pat's point of view shifted radically, and her stomach shifted with it.

"Row like you've never rowed before," Bernard told Robert. "I'll delay them as long as I can."

If they close the harbor, the fleet will be trapped. It was Robert's thought, not hers. Hers went more like: *He's going to get himself killed! There's five guys on that wharf! Bernard, get in the damned boat!*

Deftly sliding the oars into the locks, Robert echoed her cry. "Get in the boat. We can both—"

"No." Bernard's gaze measured the distance from the dock to the fleet and the fleet to the harbor mouth. "Wait until I engage before moving clear. They'll have crossbows."

Then Pat remembered Davie Hardie. *Put the medallion back on, you idiot. It'll protect you!*

But this time Robert said only, "Go with God, Brother."

A calm smile flashed in the depths of the young Templar's beard.

You know what the medallion can do! she screamed at him. *So the fleet leaves without it; so what? Is getting it on that boat more important than your life?*

Apparently it was.

When the shouting began, followed quickly by the clash of steel against steel, Robert pulled away from the dock with long, silent strokes. As he rowed, he prayed and tried not to envy the other man's opportunity to prove his devotion to the Lord in battle.

The sun had risen and there was light enough to see Bernard keep all five at bay. Every blow he struck, every blow he took, moved the boat and the holy relic that much closer to the Templar flagship. With his blood, with his life, Bernard bought the safety of the fleet.

A ray of sunlight touched his sword and the entire dockside disappeared in a brilliant flash of white-gold light.

Pat threw up an arm to protect her eyes. When the afterimages faded, she discovered that the sun had, indeed, risen and that she'd forgotten to close the blinds before she went to bed.

"Shit."

Something cold slithered across her cheek. Her reaction flung her halfway across the room before she realized it was the chain of the medallion. During the night, she'd taken it from its box and returned to sleep with it cupped in her hand.

Moving slowly, she set it carefully back against the red velvet and sank down on the edge of the bed. Wiping damp palms on the sheets, she sucked in a deep breath.

"Look, I'm grateful that you seem to be translating these violent little highlights into modern English and all, so that I understand what's going on, but . . .

"But I'm losing my mind." Scowling, she stomped into the bathroom. "I'm talking to an ugly piece of jewelry. Obviously, Chalmer Hardie's history lesson made an impression. I'm not stupid," she reminded her reflection. "I could take what he told me and fill in the pieces. I mean, I could be making all that stuff up out of old movies, couldn't I?" She closed her eyes for a moment. "And now I'm talking to a mirror. What next, the toilet?"

She went back into the bedroom and flicked the box shut. "You," she told it, "are more trouble than you're worth."

Worth . . .

In a country where the biggest tourist draw was history, there had to be a store that sold pieces of the past. Even back in Halifax, there were places where a person could buy anything from old family silver to eighteenth century admiral's insignia.

Gordon assumed jet lag when she called to say she wouldn't need him, and Pat didn't bother to correct his assumption.

"Mr. Hardie said you might want to rest before you went off to do whatever it is you're doing for him."

"You don't know?"

He laughed. "I assumed you would."

So Chalmer Hardie hadn't set up the driver to spy on her. Why settle for ten thousand and a job when she could have ten thousand, a job, and whatever the medallion would bring? No one would ever know, and Mr. Hardie could die happy, believing she'd been fool enough to stuff it into MacGillivray's grave. With the medallion shoved into the bottom of her purse, Pat headed out into Inverness.

She found what she was searching for in the High Street, where shops ranged from authentic Highland to blatant kitsch, all determined to separate tourists from their money. The crowded window of Neal's Curios held several World War II medals, a tea set that was obviously regimental silver, although Pat couldn't read the engraving under the raised crest, and an ornate chalice that she'd seen a twin of in *Indiana Jones and the Last Crusade*.

An old ship's bell rang as she pushed open the door and went into the shop. The middle-aged woman behind the counter put down her book and favored her with a dazzling smile. "And how may we help you taday, lassie?"

"Are you the owner?"

"Aye. Mrs. Neal, that's me."

"Do you buy old things?"

The smile faded and most of the accent went with it. "Sometimes."

"How much would you give me for this?" Pat dug the box out of her purse and opened it on the scratched glass counter.

Mrs. Neal's pale eyes widened as she peered at the medallion.

"There's a piece of the True Cross in the crystal," Pat added.

The older woman recovered her poise. "Dearie, if you laid all the so-called pieces of the True Cross end to end, you could circle the earth at the equator. Twice."

"But this piece comes with a history. . . ."

"Have you any proof?" Mrs. Neal asked when Pat finished embroidering the story Chalmer Hardie had told her.

Both her hands were flat on the counter and she leaned forward expectantly.

"Trust me," the old man had said. *"I know."*

Pat sighed. "No. No proof."

It wasn't exactly a snort of disbelief. "Then I'll give you five hundred pounds for it, but that's mostly for the gold. I can't pay for the fairy tale."

At the current exchange rate, five hundred pounds came to over a thousand dollars Canadian. Pat drummed her fingers lightly on the counter while she thought about it. It was less than what she'd expected to get, but she could use the money, and Alexander MacGillivray certainly couldn't use the medallion.

She opened her mouth to agree to the sale and closed it on air. In the glass cabinet directly below her fingertips was a red-enameled cross with flared ends, about three inches long. Except for the size, it could have been the cross on the mantle of a Templar sergeant who'd fought and died to protect the medallion she was about to sell.

Unable to stop her hand from shaking, she picked up the box and shoved it back into her purse. She managed to stammer out that she'd like to think about the offer, then turned and nearly ran from the shop.

Before the door had fully closed, Mrs. Neal half turned and bellowed, "Andrew!"

The scrawny young man who hurried in from the storeroom looked annoyed about the summons. "What is it, Gran? I was having a bit of a kip."

"You can sleep later. I have a job for you." She grabbed his elbow and hustled him over to the door. "See that gray jacket scurrying away? Follow the young woman wearing it and, when you're sure you won't be caught, grab her purse."

"What's in it?"

"A piece of very old jewelry your gran took a liking to. Now go."

She pushed him out onto the sidewalk and watched while he slouched up the street. When both her grandson and the young woman disappeared from sight, she returned to her place behind the counter and slid a box of papers off an overloaded shelf. After a moment's search, she smoothed a faint photocopy of a magazine article out on the counter. The article had speculated about the possibility of the Templar fleet having landed in Argyll, and had then gone on to list some of the treasure it might have carried. One page held a sketch of a gold medallion that surrounded a marble-sized piece of crystal that was reputed to contain a sliver of the True Cross.

Mrs. Neal smiled happily. She knew any number of people who would pay a great deal of money for such a relic without asking uncomfortable questions about how she'd found it.

"I don't believe in signs." Pat threw the box down onto the bed and the medallion spilled out. She paced across the room and back. "I don't believe in you, either. You're a fairy tale, just like Mrs. Neal said. The delusions of a dying old man. I should have sold you. I *will* sell you."

But she left both box and medallion on the bed and spent the afternoon staring at soccer on television. When the game ended, she ordered room service and spent the evening watching programs she didn't understand.

At eleven, Pat put the medallion back in the box, wrapped the box in a shirt, and stuffed the bundle into the deepest corner of her suitcase.

"I'm going back there tomorrow," she announced defiantly as she turned off the light.

"Tomorrow, His Majesty intends to arrest the entire Order."

What's going on? I don't even remember going to sleep!
Pat fought against opening her eyes but they opened anyway. *Bernard?*

The young sergeant was on one knee at her feet, his expression anger, disbelief, and awe about equally mixed.

I don't want any part of this! Pat could feel the weight of the medallion and knew the old man who wore it as Jacques de Molay, the Grand Master of the Knights Templar.

Last Grand Master, she corrected, but like all the others, he couldn't hear her. She could feel his anger as he told Bernard what would happen at dawn and gave him the message to pass on to the Preceptor of France—who with fifty knights had all but emptied the Paris Temple five days before. She touched de Molay's decision to stay behind lest the king be warned by his absence.

"There will be horses for you between Paris and Harfleur. You *must* arrive before dawn, do you understand?"

"Yes, Worshipful Master."

De Molay's hands went to the chain about his neck and he lifted the medallion over his head. He closed his eyes and raised it to his lips, much as Bernard had done— *would do,* Pat amended.

"Take this also to the Preceptor; tell him I give it into his charge." He gazed down into the young sergeant's eyes. "In the crystal is a sliver from the Cross of our Lord. I would not have it fall into the hands of that *jackal*—" Biting off what would have become an extensive tirade against the king, he held out the medallion. "It will protect you as you ride."

Bernard leaned forward and pressed his lips against the gold. As the Grand Master settled the chain over his head, Pat—who settled into his head—thought he was going to pass out. "Worshipful Master, I am not worthy—"

"*I* will say who is worthy," de Molay snapped.

"Yes, Worshipful Master." Looking up into de Molay's face, Pat was reminded of her grandfather.

He's a stubborn old man: certain he's right, regardless of the evidence. And he was going to die. And there was nothing she could do about it. *Because he died over six hundred years ago,* she told herself. *Get a grip.*

Given the way Bernard had died—would die—Pat expected to hear him declare that he would guard the medallion with his life, but then she realized there was no need, that it was understood.

I don't believe these guys. One of them's staying behind to die, and one of them's riding off to die, and neither of them has to!

If de Molay had left Paris with the rest . . .

If Bernard had got in the boat . . .

If MacGillivray had refused to charge . . .

She woke up furious at the world.

A long, hot shower did little to help, and breakfast sat like a rock in her stomach.

"You're worth five hundred pounds to me," she snarled as she crammed shirt, box, and medallion into her purse. "That's all. Five hundred pounds. One thousand—"

Her heart slammed up into her throat as the phone shattered the morning into little pieces. "What?"

"It's Gordon Ritchie, Ms. Tarrill—Pat. I'm in the lobby. If you're feeling better, I thought I might show you around . . ." His voice trailed off. "Is this a bad time?"

"No. No, it's not." This was exactly what she needed. Something to take her mind off the medallion.

"So, where are we going?"

"Well, when he hired me, Mr. Hardie suggested I might take you to Culloden Moor." Gordon held open the lobby door. "The National Trust for Scotland's visitor's center just reopened for the season."

Culloden? Pat ground her teeth. *Been there. Done that.*

Catching a glimpse of her expression, Gordon frowned. "I could take you somewhere else—"

"No." She cut him off. "Might just as well go along with Mr. Hardie's suggestion. He's paying the bills." Although she was beginning to believe he might not be calling the tune. *Yeah, right. As I've said before, Pat, get a grip.*

Swearing under his breath, Andrew ran for his car.

A cold wind was blowing across the moor when they reached the visitor's center. Pat hunched her shoulders, shoved her hands deep into her pockets, and tried not to remember her dream of the slaughter. She watched the audiovisual presentation, poked around old Leanach Cottage, then started down the path that ran out onto the battlefield, Gordon trailing along behind. She passed the English Stone without pausing, continued west, and came to a roughly triangular, weather-beaten monument.

" 'Well of the Dead.' " Her fingers traced the inscription as she read. " 'Here the Chief of the MacGillivrays fell.' "

The wind slapped rain into her face. Over the call of the pipes, Pat heard the guns and men screaming and one voice gathering up the clan to aim it at the enemy.

"Dunmaglass!"

"Pat? Are you all right?"

At Gordon's touch, she shook free of the memory and straightened. "I'd like to go back to the hotel now." He looked so worried that she snarled, "I'm tired, okay?"

He stepped back, quickly masking his reaction, and she wished that just once she'd learn to think before she spoke. He only wanted to help. . . . But she couldn't seem to find the apology she knew he deserved.

"But Gran!" Andrew protested, raising a hand to protect his head. "The first time she even left the bloody hotel, she had this guy driving her around. He never left her."

Mrs. Neal threw the rolled magazine aside and grabbed her grandson's shirtfront. "Then get a couple of your friends and, if you have to, take care of the guy driving her around."

"I could get Colin and Tony. They helped with that bit of silver—"

"I don't care *who* you get," the old lady spat. "Just bring me that medallion!"

On the way back to the hotel, Pat had Gordon stop and buy her two bottles of cheap scotch. He hadn't approved—she saw it in the set of his shoulders and the thin line of his mouth—but he took the money and came back with the bottles. When she tried to explain, the words got stuck.

Better he thinks I'm a bitch than a lunatic.

She couldn't remember where she'd read that alcohol prevented dreaming, and after the first couple of glasses, she didn't care. As afternoon darkened into evening, she curled up in the overstuffed chair and drank herself into a stupor.

"You don't understand, Ms. Tarrill." The old man had stroked the crystal lightly with one swollen finger. *"But you will."*

Before Pat could speak, Chalmer Hardie whirled away, replaced by a progression of scowling old men in offices, shipyards, and mills, all working as though work was all they had. Clothing and surroundings became more and more old-fashioned, and by the time she touched a mind she knew, she realized she was tracing the trail of the medallion back through time.

"Dunmaglass!"

Once again, she watched Alexander MacGillivray lead the charge across Culloden Moor. Then she watched as the MacGillivrays, son to father, returned the clan to Argyll. There were more young men than old in this group, for these were men willing to take a stand in a dark time. There were MacGillivrays on the shore when the Templar fleet sailed into Loch Caignish.

"Go with God, Brother."

Bernard smiled and climbed to his death.

"In this crystal is a sliver of the Cross of our Lord. I would not have it fall into the hands of that jackal—"

The Masters of the Knights Templar had not lived an easy life. In spite of the protection of the Cross, many of them died in battle. She saw William de Beaujey, the last Master of the Temple before the Moslems regained the Holy Land, fall defending a breach in the wall of Acre. She saw de Sonnac blinded at Mansourah and de Peragors dying on the sands of Gaza. Master, before Master, before Master, until an old man slipped a medallion over the head of Hugues de Payens.

All at once, Pat could hear pounding and jeers and was suddenly lifted into dim light under an overcast sky. She could see a crowd gathered and a city in the distance, but she could feel no one except herself. Then she looked down. The sliver had been taken from near the top of the cross. She saw a crown of thorns, dark hair matted with blood, and the top curve of shoulders marked by a whip.

NO!

For the first time, someone heard her.

Yes.

*   *   *

Tears streaming down her face, Pat woke, still curled in the chair, still clutching the second bottle. When she leapt to her feet, the bottle fell and rolled beneath the bed. She didn't notice. She clawed the box out of her purse, clawed the medallion out of the box, and stared at the crystal.

"All right. That's it. You win." Dragging her nose over her sleeve, she shoved the medallion into one pocket of her jacket, shoved her wallet in the other, and grabbed the phone.

"Gordon? I'm doing what Mr. Hardie wants me to do, now, tonight."

"Ms. Tarrill?"

"Pat. Do you know where the church is in Petty?"

"Sure, my uncle has the parish, but—"

"I'm not drunk." In fact, she'd never felt more sober. "I need to do this." She checked her watch. "It's only just past ten. I'll meet you out front."

She heard him sigh. "I'll be right there."

The car barely had a chance to slow before she flung open the door and threw herself into the passenger seat.

"Ms. Tarrill, I—" He broke off as he caught sight of her face. "Good God, you look terrified. What's wrong?"

Pat found a laugh that didn't mean much. "Good God indeed. I'll tell you later. If I can. Right now, I have something to get rid of."

"And you wanted to call it a night." Andrew let the car get two blocks away, then pulled out after it. The large man crammed into the passenger seat of the mini said nothing, and the larger man folded into the back merely grunted.

The church in Petty stood alone on a hill about seven miles east of Inverness, just off the A96. A three-quarter moon and a sky bright with stars sketched out the surrounding graveyard in stark silver and black. Gordon pulled into the driveway and killed the motor.

"At least it's stopped raining," Pat muttered, getting out of the car. "No, you wait here," she added, when Gordon attempted to follow. "I have to do this alone."

Lips pressed into a thin line, he dropped into the driver's seat, reclined it back, and pointedly closed his eyes.

Chalmer Hardie's instructions had been clear. *"The MacKintosh mausoleum is against the west side of the church. Close by it, you'll find a gravestone with only a sword cut into the face. MacGillivray's fiancée managed to bury him, but with Cumberland's army squatting in Inverness, she could find no one who dared put his name on the stone. There are MacGillivrays buried in Kilmartin graveyard under similar stones—Templar stones. Put the medallion in the grave."*

Keeping a tight grip on her imagination, Pat found the ancient mausoleum, skirted it, and stared down at the grave of Alexander MacGillivray. Then suddenly realized what *put the medallion in the grave* meant.

"And me without a shovel." Swallowing hard, she managed to get her stomach under control, although at the moment, the possibility of spending another night with the medallion frightened her more than a bit of gravedigging. She pulled it out of her pocket and glared down at it. All she wanted to do was get rid of it. Why did it have to be so difficult?

"Hand over the jewelry and nobody gets hurt."

Fear clamped both hands around her throat and squeezed her scream into a breathy squeak. When she turned, she saw three substantial shadows between her and the lights that lined Moray Firth. If they were ghosts, hell provided a pungent aftershave. Two of them were huge. The third was a weaselly looking fellow no bigger than she was.

The weaselly fellow smiled. "I won't say we don't want to hurt you, because me pals here rather like a bit of rough stuff. Be a smart lady; give it here." While he spoke, the other two closed in.

Pat laughed a bit hysterically. "Look, you have no idea how much I want to get rid of this. Go ahead and—"

Then she stopped. All she could think of was how Davie Hardie had been willing to do anything rather than die.

"Your word will be sufficient."

"My word? That's it?"

"Yes."

She'd given her word that she'd put the medallion in Alexander MacGillivray's grave. Her chin rose and she placed it carefully back in her pocket. "If you want it, you'll have to take it from me."

"You're being stupid."

"Up yours." Pat took a deep breath and was surprised by how calm she felt.

The man on her left jerked forward and she dove to the right. Fingers tangled in her hair but she twisted free, fell, and scrambled back to her feet. *If I can just get to the car . . .*

Her ears rang as a fist slid off the side of her head. A hand clutched the shoulder of her jacket. If she slid out of it, they'd have the medallion, so she stepped back, driving her heel down onto an instep.

One of them swore and let go. The other wrapped his arm around her neck and hung on. When she struggled, he tightened his grip.

"Right, then." The weaselly fellow pinched her cheek, hard.

Pat tried to bite him.

"That'll be enough of tha—ahhhhhhhhh!"

He sounded terrified.

The arm released her neck and Pat dropped to her knees. Gasping for breath, she watched all three of her assailants race away, tripping and stumbling over the gravestones.

"Good . . . timing . . . Gordon," she panted, and turned.

It wasn't Gordon.

Alexander MacGillivray had been a tall man, and although it was possible to see the church and the mausoleum through him, death hadn't made him any shorter. Pat looked up. Way up. This time the scream made it through the fear. She stood, stumbled backward into a gravestone, and fell. Ghostly fingers reached out toward her. . . .

When she opened her eyes, Pat discovered there was no significant difference between a hospital room in Scotland and one in Canada. They even smelled the same. Ignoring the pain in her head, she pushed herself up onto her elbows and discovered her clothes neatly folded on a chair by the bed.

Teeth clenched, she managed to snag her jacket. Although she half expected the ghost of Alexander MacGillivray to have claimed the medallion, it was still in her pocket. Closing her fingers around it, she stared at the ceiling and thought about what had happened in the graveyard. About what she'd done. About what she hadn't done. About what had sent her there. About the medallion. By the time the nurse came in to check on her, she'd made a decision.

When she fell asleep, she didn't dream.

They'd just cleared the breakfast dishes away—she'd been allowed a glass of juice and hadn't wanted much more—when Gordon, looking as though he'd spent a sleepless night, stuck his head into the room. When he saw she was awake, he walked over to the bed. "I'm not a relative," he explained self-consciously. "They made me go home."

"The nurse said you nearly drove through the doors at emergency."

"It seemed the least I could do." His expression shifted through worry, relief, and anger. "I came running when I heard the screams. When I saw you on the ground . . ."

"You didn't see anyone else?"

"No." He frowned. "Should I have?"

If she said she'd been attacked, the police would have to be involved, and what would be the point?

"Pat, what happened?"

"I saw a ghost." She shrugged and wished she hadn't, as little explosions went off inside her skull. "I guess I tripped and hit my head."

Scooping her clothes off the chair, he sat down. "I guess you did. The nurse at the desk told me that if you'd hit it two inches lower, you'd be dead." He colored as she winced. "Sorry."

"S'okay. Gordon, last night you said your uncle had the parish of Petty. Does that mean he's the minister there?"

It took him a moment to get around the sudden change of topic. "Uh, yes."

"Is he a good man?"

"He's a minister!"

"You know what I mean."

Gordon considered it. "Yes," he said after a moment, "he's a good man."

"Could you call him?" Pat lightly stroked the crystal with one finger. "And ask him to come and see me."

Sunlight brushed the hard angles off the graveyard and softened both the gray of the stones and the red brick of Petty church. Released from the hospital that morning, Pat looked out over the water of Moray Firth, then down at the grave of Alexander MacGillivray.

"I gave my word to Chalmer Hardie that I'd put the medallion in your grave." She sighed and spread her hands. "I don't have it anymore. I tried to call him, but he's in the hospital and MacClery won't let me talk to him. Anyway, I'm going home tomorrow and I thought you deserved an explanation."

When she paused, the silence waited for her to continue. "So many of the Templars died violently that I was confused for a while about the medallion's power to protect. You gave me the clue. If you'd thought it could stop shot, you'd have torn the country apart to find it before you sacrificed the lives of your people. Davie Hardie wanted the medallion to protect him from dying in battle, so that's what it did—but the Templars *expected* to die in battle, so they wanted protection against the things that would cause them to break their vows."

Her cheeks grew hot as she remembered how close to betrayal she personally had come, and how much five hundred pounds sounded like thirty pieces of silver. "Chalmer Hardie wanted me to right the wrong his ancestor did you by having the medallion returned where he thought it belonged. But I don't think it belongs with the dead. I think we could really use that kind of protection active in the world right now.

"Gordon's uncle says there's still Templar organizations in Scotland, even after all this time. I thought you'd like to know that." The gravestone was warm under her fingertips as she traced the shallow carving of the sword. "He gave me his word that he'll give it to the person in charge.

"So I'm bringing you his promise in place of the medallion."

Shoving her hands into her pockets, she turned to go.

Then she remembered one more thing. "I could still lie to Mr. Hardie. Tell him you got the medallion back, pick up that ten grand and the job—but I won't. Because it isn't dying honorably that counts, is it? It's living honorably, right to the end."

As she reached the corner of the church and could see Gordon waiting by the car, the hair lifted off the back of her neck. The silence pulled her around.

Standing on the grave was a tall young man with red-gold hair and pale skin in the clothing of the Jacobite army. Pat forgot to breathe. He hadn't been wearing the medallion the night he'd driven off the three thugs, but today it hung gleaming against his chest.

The air shimmered and she saw a line of men stretch into the distance behind him. They all wore the medallion. Many wore the white mantle and red cross of a Templar Knight. For an instant, she felt a familiar weight around her neck, then both the weight and all the shades but Alexander MacGillivray's disappeared.

Tell Chalmer Hardie, he said to her heart as he faded, *that you kept your word.*

INTERLUDE FIVE

As suggested in the previous story, one of the relics possessed by the Templars *was* a splinter of the True Cross. Described as being encased in gold and jewels, it was one of the few Templar "hallows" actually to fall into the hands of Philip of France. For the injustice he had visited upon the Order (and perhaps for profaning so holy a relic), Philip was to pay a heavy price—and ensure both for himself and for the Order a somewhat different place in history than he had reckoned.

The Temple had been officially suppressed in April 1312, by the bull *Vox in excelso,* which disbanded the Order in the sense of revoking its charter, but made no determination of guilt. In May, the bull *Ad providam* gave all the former properties of the Temple except those in Spain and Portugal to the Knights Hospitaller. The bull *Considerantes,* which followed four days later, reserved to the pope himself the fate of several named Templars: Jacques de Molay, the Grand Master; Geoffroi de Charney, the Preceptor of Normandy; Geoffrey de Goneville, Preceptor of

Poitou; Hugh de Paraud, the Visitor of France and former Treasurer of the Paris Temple; and a Knight referred to as Frère Oliver de Penne, who appears in no other written record, and whose function and fate are unknown. The remaining Templars still in prison were to be dealt with by local provincial councils convened by the archbishops.

During the two years that followed, such councils quickly disposed of their prisoners, usually with notable leniency. Those who had made no confession, continuing to protest the innocence of the Order, were sentenced to life imprisonment, as were those who had confessed and then retracted their confessions. Those who had confessed and stood by their confessions were penanced, absolved, and released, some of them joining other orders that would take them.

But not de Molay and his officers. Denied a personal appeal to the pope, and forced to confirm their previous confessions before a tribunal of three cardinals, the four were then sentenced to life imprisonment. Furthermore, they would be required to repeat their confessions in public.

On March 14, 1314, in a spectacle calculated to convince the people that the persecution of the Order had been just, the four were brought to a specially constructed platform before the Cathedral of Notre Dame, garbed in their Templar robes for certain identification and laden with chains to underline their guilt. But instead of reciting the expected confession, the aged Grand Master, now well past seventy and physically broken by his ordeal, stepped forward and made the following statement, quoted in translation in John J. Robinson's *Dungeon, Fire, and Sword,* pp. 467–8:

> I think it only right that at so solemn a moment, when my life has so little time to run, I should

reveal the deception which has been practiced and speak up for the truth. Before heaven and earth and all of you here as my witnesses, I admit that I am guilty of the grossest iniquity. But the iniquity is that I have lied in admitting the disgusting charges laid against the Order. I declare that the Order is innocent. Its purity and saintliness are beyond question. I have indeed confessed that the Order is guilty, but I have done so only to save myself from terrible tortures by saying what my enemies wished me to say. Other knights who have retracted their confessions have been led to the stake, yet the thought of dying is not so awful that I shall confess foul crimes which have never been committed. Life is offered to me, but at the price of infamy. At such a price, life is not worth having. I do not grieve that I must die if life can be bought only by piling one lie upon another.

De Molay's declaration brought a roar of anger from the crowd, all but drowning out Geoffroi de Charney's similar statement of retraction. Before the situation could get totally out of hand, the king's officers hustled the four off the platform and ordered the crowd to disperse.

Later that very afternoon, de Molay and de Charney were brought back to the Île de la Cité in the Seine, not far from Notre Dame Cathedral, where two stakes had been prepared. Stripped of their Templar robes, the pair were chained to the stakes, then surrounded with seasoned wood and charcoal selected to produce a slow, hot fire that would literally roast the victims alive before it consumed them.

As the fires were lit, both de Molay and de Charney continued to shout out their innocence and that of the Order, calling upon heaven for justice. Many citizens of Paris watched from tiny boats, now uncertain what to believe, for a man's dying declaration carried considerable weight. It is said that de Molay, as the heat blistered and contorted his flesh, called both the pope and the king to appear with him before the Seat of God before the year was out. He is further said to have cursed the king and his family to the thirteenth generation.

Pope Clement V died the following month, in the early morning hours of April 20, of a sudden onslaught of dysentery. Philip le Bel was taken with a seizure while hunting, on November 29, and survived only long enough to be carried back to his palace to die. Whether from supernatural causes or from the actions of fugitive Templars or their sympathizers employing their knowledge of subtle poisons, de Molay's curse was fulfilled.

Nor did it end with Philip's death. His heart was cut out and sent to a monastery near Paris with the relic of the True Cross he had stolen from the Templars, but the curse extended at least into the next generation, for the direct Capetian royal line ended with Philip's three sons, all of whom died without heirs—Louis X in 1316, Philip V in 1322, and Charles IV in 1328.

After that the French crown passed to the Valois line—for thirteen generations—and then to the ill-fated Bourbons. Legend has it that when the last Bourbon king, Louis XVI, was guillotined in 1793, a man leaped onto the platform (some say he was a Freemason), dipped his hand into the dead king's blood, flicked it out over the crowd, and cried, "Jacques de Molay, thou art avenged!"

Almost certainly, this dramatic reference to the Templars reflects the preservation of Templar lore and tradition that had carried through the various Jacobite rebellions and then into the American and French Revolutions, much of it preserved alongside and within Freemasonry. The name Alexander Deuchar surfaces frequently in the decades that followed, especially in connection with various Templar factions that rose and fell, mostly in a Masonic or quasi-Masonic context, mostly in Scotland, though France and Germany had their share of others calling themselves Templars. Even princes and royal dukes came to be patrons and members of these reconstituted Templar organizations.

Whatever Deuchar's legacy—and modern incarnations of the Order often are sharply divided in their opinions—tradition persisted that the Templars once had been guardians not only of temporal treasures but of secret and mystical knowledge and power, at least some of it somehow connected with the Temple of Solomon. The general occult revival that swept through late Victorian and Edwardian Europe brought to light such diverse phenomena as the Rosicrucians, Spiritualism, Theosophy, Anthroposophy, and the Order of the Golden Dawn. It also reawakened interest in the Temple. Germany of the 1920s and 1930s was to prove a breeding ground for investigation of these and other, even further-ranging esoteric subjects, many of which also attracted the interest of rising members of the National Socialist movement, including a failed painter called Adolph Hitler.

The extent of German interest in the occult is perhaps only slightly exaggerated in such popular films as Stephen Spielberg's *Raiders of the Lost Ark* and its sequel, *Indiana Jones and the Last Crusade.* Such legendary items as the Holy Grail and the Spear of Longinus (said to have pierced Jesus' side at the Crucifixion) were sought in deadly earnest by agents of the Third Reich, and organizations believed to have access to mystical powers—occult lodges, Freemasons, astrologers, Gypsies—were ruthlessly exterminated if they could not be turned to the service of the state.

It was only a matter of time before the Nazis sought out the Knights Templar, whom both Wolfram von Eschenbach and Richard Wagner had identified as Guardians of the Grail and possessors of mystical powers. Drawing inspiration from the discipline and focus of both the Templar and Jesuit Orders, Heinrich Himmler was to fashion his SS as a new order of black knighthood, basing it at Wewelsberg Castle near Paderborn. Meanwhile, if spiritual inheritors of the historical Knights Templar still existed, might their powers not be enlisted in the service of the Reich?

1941

Scott MacMillan

ans Becker stood comfortably at ease in the light mist that swirled around the courtyard in front of Wewelsburg Castle. Small droplets of water formed on the edge of the visor of his coal-scuttle helmet, and by tilting his head slightly forward he could peer through them at the sentry box that guarded the approach to the drawbridge. The droplets formed a string of transparent pearls that distorted and diffused the dark green of the oaks that formed a canopy over the road. The effect rendered the atmosphere of the afternoon even more surreal than it was.

But then, Becker thought to himself, *any meeting with Reichsführer Himmler is a surreal experience.*

Still, these last two days at the castle had been all Becker had hoped for, and more. He had spent three years in the SS, and only recently had managed to get himself assigned permanently to the assortment of crackpots who formed the Ahnenerbe, just before Himmler decided to commit the SS to the role of frontline troops. Although he had to put up with the petty insults of his so-called superiors at the Ahnenerbe, Becker at least had managed to place himself out of the line of fire.

Becker gave an inward smile. For all their smart uniforms and rigid, heel-clicking salutes, the SS weren't as clever as they were cracked up to be. A second-rate assistant director in films, he had found it easy to insinuate his way into the officer corps of the SS, landing a cushy assignment with a film crew preparing a documentary on the search for the lost Ark of the Covenant. This had brought him into contact with Wilhelm Teudt, the chief of the Ahnenerbe. It was Teudt's middle-aged secretary, besotted with Becker's casting-couch athletics, who had contrived to have her boss secure Becker's services on a permanent basis when the Ahnenerbe was absorbed into the SS in 1939.

The Ahnenerbe's headquarters was in Berlin—which, given Becker's social appetite, suited him just fine. The work—he snorted to himself when he thought of what the Ahnenerbe did—was classified, and small wonder. Under Himmler's direction, the Ahnenerbe indulged Hitler's fascination with the occult.

Astrology, voodoo, ESP—they all came in for study at the small gray office block in a quiet suburb of Berlin. Most of the SS officers assigned to the Ahnenerbe were retired university professors who were potty on one or another odd subject. Colorless individuals, they were totally lost in their studies, their books, and their quest for hidden knowledge. They tended to distrust Becker, who quite obviously enjoyed swanning around Berlin in his convertible BMW and pearl-gray SS uniform far more than he did sitting behind a desk wrapped in deep, esoteric studies. As a result, and given his lack of a university degree, Becker was relegated to two rather minor assignments: collecting information on Freemasons and compiling even more information on the Templars.

Considering that they were supposed to be a secret society, the Freemasons had been remarkably easy to track down. They held regular meetings in buildings plainly marked as FREEMASON'S HALL, and virtually anyone who cared to apply for membership was admitted to their ranks. To be sure, they went through a pretty bizarre initiation, but they were admitted nonetheless.

As far as secrecy was concerned, virtually the whole of their dogma was published, and available to anyone who might care to learn their secrets without having to go through the bother of being blindfolded, led into a room with a rope around one's neck, and taking an oath of dubious antiquity. Their purpose was charitable: aid to widows, orphans, and distressed fellow Freemasons. Having spent the better part of a year sifting through all of the documents published by the Brethren, as they styled themselves, Becker decided that Freemasons were about as benign a group of individuals as anyone could hope to find.

Still, their ideas of universal equality of man, as well as their recognition of a higher natural law, did put them beyond the pale as far as the Nazi party was concerned. And since the party was the state, it was inevitable that the Freemasons would sooner or later have to be swept up by the Gestapo. According to rumors—and they could usually be relied upon—the Freemasons were due for the chop sometime early next year.

The Templars, on the other hand, had proved far more difficult to track down. Ostensibly they had been suppressed in 1307, and their hierarchy executed or imprisoned by 1314. Since that time they had sprung up time and time again, in so many places and under such odd circumstances that Becker had formed the view that, while

King Philip le Bel might have cut the head from the serpent, he certainly hadn't killed it. It was obvious that the Order of the Temple had survived and continued to exist right down to the present time.

Not, of course, that Becker's superiors at the Ahnenerbe shared his views. Not that Becker cared. He had collected enough information in the past year to make a spectacular film about the Templars; in fact, for the past four months he had done little else other than work on the treatment for that film. The war wouldn't last forever, and when it was over, he intended to produce and direct *The Secret of the Templars,* and he was counting on some mightily placed patronage to get the picture off the ground.

Becker allowed himself the luxury of a small grin as his thoughts tracked back to that moment four months ago when he had discovered a memo from the Reichsführer SS to one of his predecessors requesting a priority report on the Templars. The memo was nearly a year old, but Becker saw it as his golden opportunity.

Carefully he doctored his treatment, placing a copy of Himmler's memo on top. Then—and he nearly chuckled at his own audacity—Becker had a special rubber stamp made up:

TOP SECRET

FOR REICHSFÜHRER SS

EYES ONLY

His film treatment carefully typed and bound, he had telephoned SS headquarters and requested an armed guard to come and deliver this "secret report" to Himmler's office. Two days later his telephone rang, and within an hour he was on his way to his first meeting with Himmler.

Becker's reminiscences were cut short by a sound drifting up to the castle. Far below, in the valley that Schloss Wewelsburg guarded, he could hear the whine of the supercharged Mercedes limousine as it made its way up the switchback road that led to the fortress. As the minutes dragged on, the phone in the guard box rang; Himmler's car had passed the last checkpoint.

Knowing that the car would arrive within the next two or three minutes, Becker discarded his helmet for the steel-gray peaked cap of an SS officer; no point in giving Himmler any ideas about transfers to the Waffen-SS, he decided. He paused for a moment longer, then shrugged off the black vulcanized poncho that had kept his leather greatcoat from getting too wet, and stepped out from under the protective cover of the castle gates just as Himmler's car halted at the foot of the drawbridge. An SS man in full dress uniform raced out of the guard room and stood to attention at the rear door of the big Mercedes, ready to open it the moment Himmler stepped onto the bridge.

"Heil Hitler!" rang through the castle courtyard, and better than thirty hands shot upward in stiff-armed salute as Heinrich Himmler, Reichsführer SS, arguably the most powerful man in Germany, emerged from the castle and made his way toward the waiting car. Just before the gate that led to the drawbridge, SS General Taubert stood at attention in the misting rain, his right arm rigid as he offered the Nazi salute.

Himmler enthusiastically returned the salute, smiled at Taubert, and shook his hand.

"It has been an honor to have you visit again, Reichsführer," Taubert said, a smile of genuine hospitality beaming out from his friendly face.

Himmler gave Taubert an enigmatic smile in return. "Thank you, General Taubert. It is always a pleasure to visit the spiritual home of our beloved SS." As if on cue, the rain stopped and a feeble ray of sunlight edged its way through the clouds.

From near the car, Becker watched as the two men shook hands and took their leave of one another, Himmler then marching quickly down the drawbridge toward his car.

"Captain Becker," Himmler called out as he walked past.

"Yes, Reichsführer?" Becker trotted over to where Himmler had stopped beside the Mercedes.

"I want to speak to you in Berlin. My office. Tuesday." Himmler gave Becker a crinkly smile. "You've done good work, *Major.*"

Becker stammered out his thanks as the door to Himmler's car slammed shut and the Reichsführer SS was chauffeured back down the mountain.

Within an hour Becker was in his own car, headed toward Berlin, 450 kilometers distant. The scarlet and black BMW 328 cabriolet chewed its way across the near-deserted German countryside until it reached the autobahn, where Becker was able to push the car to a steady 150 kph until, sometime after midnight, he reached the outskirts of Berlin.

Pulling off the autobahn, he threaded his way through the blacked-out streets of the capital, grateful that the RAF hadn't picked this particular night to bomb the city. After a few minutes of dead-slow driving, he turned down a small alley and, half a block farther on, parked in the garage of a large house in one of Berlin's more affluent suburbs.

Like his car, the house had once belonged to a moderately successful film producer, Emil Staubberberg. What had become of Staubberberg rarely crossed Becker's mind. What mattered—to Becker, at any rate—was that he had been fortunate enough to buy the house, its contents, and the car for a song. Becker had met Staubberberg on the lot at UFA, the big film studios on the eastern edge of Berlin. He had gone to see him about a directing job, and when he arrived in Staubberberg's office, found him packing a few possessions into a cardboard box.

"What do you want?" Staubberberg asked as Becker breezed into his office.

"I heard you were looking for someone to replace Victor Lazlo on your next picture," Becker answered.

"Well, I was until about half an hour ago," Staubberberg said, stuffing a pile of scripts into the box. "Then I got this memo from the front office saying that as and from nine AM tomorrow, the studio would be controlled by Dr. Goebbels and the Ministry of Propaganda."

"So what's that got to do with anything?" Becker asked.

Staubberberg turned around and looked at Becker for the first time since he had walked into the office.

"Are you from the dark side of the moon or something?" he asked, then continued without waiting for a reply. "Look, I produce movies—not great ones, but ones people like to see. Dr. Goebbels also produces movies—not great ones, but ones that he can force people to see." Staubberberg sat on the edge of his desk and stared out the window.

"Did you ever watch the crap the Nazis are producing? Well, I have, and it scares the shit out of me. But what really scares the shit out of me are the people who watch these films. They are capable of anything.

"The Nazis are out to get rid of all the intellectuals, the homosexuals, and the Jews, not only in the motion picture business, but everywhere else as well. So, speaking as a closet queer with more than one Jewish granny, I'm headed for the door." Staubberberg lit a cigarette, inhaled deeply, and blew a long plume of smoke into the air.

"You rich?" he finally asked Becker.

"Not on what they pay assistant directors," Becker replied.

"Good. Then you can be my business partner for the next few months." Staubberberg handed Becker the box on his desk. "These are your assets. Now we're going to the bank."

Staubberberg's films might have been second-rate, but his business deals were triple-A rated. At the bank he signed over the rights to all of his films to his "partner," Becker. Using these as collateral, Becker borrowed enough money to buy Staubberberg's house, furniture, and car. Staubberberg used the same money to guarantee that he would buy back the assets of his company from the bank, should Becker default on the loan. He then assigned the buy-back contract to a film distribution company in Sweden in which he was a partner.

As they walked out of the bank, Staubberberg handed Becker his key ring.

"Here," he said. "These are yours now. This one is the front door, the flat silver one is the key to my—your— BMW, and these other two are for the garage in the alley. Oh, and that long skeleton key opens the family crypt in the Jewish cemetery in Worms. If you ever go there, put a pebble on my granny's grave, huh?" With that Staubberberg turned and walked off down the street.

As he locked the BMW in the garage, Becker wondered what had become of Staubberberg; then, with a shrug of his shoulders, he crossed the alley and passed through the gate that led into the back garden of his home. Whistling slightly off key, Becker bounded up the stairs to his back door and let himself in, dumped his hat and overcoat on a chair in the kitchen, and headed upstairs to his bedroom for some much-needed sleep.

*   *   *

"Maria," Becker spoke into the Bakelite intercom on the corner of his desk. "Would you please call signals and tell them that I need to speak to Gestapo headquarters in Brussels?" He released the button on the top of the intercom and returned his attention to the file in front of him.

Through the greatest of good fortune, an insignificant Nazi informer in Switzerland had told the Gestapo that the Order of the Temple was trying to smuggle its archives into that country. The Gestapo, in turn, had managed to bungle the arrest of the smugglers, and in an attempt to scrape the problem off the bottom of their shoe, had sent the file on the case to the Ahnenerbe.

For a moment Becker scowled; the Ahnenerbe was becoming a dump for any project that didn't fit neatly into a National Socialist pigeonhole in any other department, branch, or bureau of the Nazi government. In the last two weeks alone, Admiral Canaris, Chief of Abwehr—German military intelligence—had sent nearly a ton of files to his office, the fruit of having conquered France. The files contained everything the *Sûreté* had gathered on secret societies operating in France between the Franco-Prussian War and World War I.

Becker shook his head and continued to run his finger down the three-page report from the Gestapo, looking for the name of the Swiss informant. The soft purr of his telephone halted his search.

"Becker here," he said as he brought the phone to his ear.

"Gestapo HQ Belguim is on the line, sir." There was a crackle, and then Becker was connected with a faceless voice in Brussels.

"Geheim Staatspolizei, Brussels. May I help you?"

"This is Major Hans Becker, Office Five of the Ahnenerbe, calling. Would you please connect me with . . ." Becker quickly flipped to the back of the file and read the name of the senior investigating officer, "Sergeant Adolf Lindt."

"One moment, please." The voice put Becker on hold, but not for long.

"Hello, this is Lindt. What do you want?" Lindt's voice had a gravelly edge to it, and Becker sensed that the man was probably more at home kicking someone to death in a stinking little cell than he was dealing with the SS in Berlin.

"I am inquiring about an interrogation." Becker could imagine Lindt tensing on the other end of the line.

"Yes?" Lindt's voice was padded in caution.

"The name is . . ." Becker looked again at the file, "Vandenburgh. Clement Isaac Vandenburgh. Is he still in custody?"

"Just a minute. I'll have to check," Lindt said.

Becker winced as the other man dropped the phone on his desk. In the background he could hear indistinct swearing as Lindt dug through rustling paper.

"Hello, Becker? You still there?" Lindt sounded first impatient and then annoyed when Becker replied that he was still there. "Your Vandenburgh was here, but he was released a couple of days ago. Why?"

"I need to talk to him." Becker was irritated by the man's demeanor. "Can you rearrest him?"

"Not without authority," Lindt said. "And certainly not on the authority of the Ahnenerbe."

"Sergeant Lindt—" Becker glanced at his watch, "I am going to have lunch in twenty-five minutes with Deputy Reichsführer Heydrich. Shall I ask him to call you?"

Lindt's voice didn't change. "Only if you want this guy Vandenburgh shot. Otherwise I'll hold him here until you arrive."

"Good." Becker knew he had won. "Call me back when Vandenburgh is in custody."

Placing his phone back on its cradle, Becker smiled slightly. The bluff about lunch with Heydrich always worked. Invoking the name of the most sinister figure in the hierarchy of the Third Reich inevitably provoked full and unquestioning compliance. Becker tidied the papers on his desk, then stood up and crossed over to where he had tossed his hat and greatcoat on a chair. Putting them on, he adjusted his tie so that his Nazi party pin was just visible, then headed out the door to meet with Himmler.

As happened to virtually all of the Reichsführer's visitors, Becker was kept waiting for more than an hour outside Himmler's office. Finally the polished mahogany doors opened and he was ushered into the very center of the spider's web.

"Welcome, Major." Himmler smiled as he came around his massive desk and took Becker by the arm. "You're just in time for coffee." The Reichsführer led him toward the corner of the room where two leather armchairs were drawn intimately together. Flanked by the dark green chairs was a small table set with an elegant porcelain coffee service, the black cups and saucers monogramed with the silver lightning flashes of the SS. As Becker and Himmler settled into the deep leather cushions, an orderly in a white mess jacket appeared with a steaming silver pot filled with dark, rich coffee. Having carefully placed it on the table, he withdrew.

"I must say," Himmler began, once they were alone, "that I have been rather impressed with your work on the Templars." He interrupted himself as he poured the coffee into the small cups. "One lump or two?"

Becker was slightly amused at the way Himmler fussed over the coffee.

"Two, please," he replied.

Silver tongs gripped in spidery fingers carefully lowered two small white cubes of sugar into Becker's cup.

"Milk, Major Becker?"

"Thank you." *What does he want?* Becker wondered as he took the black and silver cup and saucer from Himmler's outstretched hand.

"You see, Major," Himmler continued as if their meeting concerned some mundane matter of administration, "I am creating a new Order of Knighthood. One that will resurrect the ideals of the old Teutonic knights; an order that will send a shiver of revitalization through the spine of all Germans."

"I see," said Becker, hoping that he had chosen the right response.

"I know you do," said Himmler. "I could tell it in your reports. The detail, the depth of research. It's all there. Especially your most recent report. Some would say that it reads like fiction, like some sort of high adventure." Himmler allowed himself a high-pitched, nervous chuckle. "That's because you understand, the same way I understand, the importance of the Templars." He set his cup down on the table and leaned forward, coming closer to Becker, his voice dropping to a whisper. "And you understand the importance of their ancient secret powers."

I may be producing The Secret of the Templars *before the war is over,* Becker thought as the Reichsführer SS continued.

"Major Becker." Himmler regarded Becker over the rim of his cup. "You are to find the Grand Master of the Knight Templars before the twenty-first of June. Once you have him, you are to convince him to come to Berlin, and to resign his office in my favor."

Becker nearly choked on his coffee. Himmler wanted to be the Grand Master of the Templars.

"So," Himmler went on, "I have appointed you to my

personal staff." He reached over to the table and picked up a small black leather folder embossed with a silver SS eagle.

"Here, take this," he said, handing the folder to Becker. "Open it."

Becker did as he was told. Inside, on the personal letter paper of the Reichsführer SS, and above his spidery signature, was a single typewritten paragraph:

> ATTENTION! The bearer of this document is traveling under my personal orders on a matter of the utmost urgency to the SS and the Greater German Reich. He is to be given every assistance in the execution of his duty, and any request that he may make is to be considered as having the full effect of a direct order issued by me. HEIL HITLER!

Becker slowly closed the folder and allowed it to rest on his lap. A more intelligent man would have trembled in fear at the mere thought of the wide-ranging powers conferred by the document he had been handed by Himmler. But Becker wasn't intelligent. Cunning, yes. Smart, certainly. But he lacked the depth of insight necessary to recognize the little black leather folder for what it might be: his death warrant.

Himmler suddenly stood up. "Well, Major Becker," he said, "thank you for coming to my office."

For a brief moment Becker was afraid to stand. Afraid that the trembling excitement that ran through his body at that moment would cause his legs to buckle under him and send him crashing to the floor. But he did stand up.

"Thank you, Reichsführer, for the great trust you have put in me and my abilities." Becker gave a curt bow.

"I know you won't fail me," Himmler said through an enigmatic smile. "Will you, Becker?"

The taxi that took Becker back to his office at the Ahnenerbe had to detour around a section of the city that had been bombed the night before, and this gave him time to focus his thoughts on the task that lay before him. Himmler had told him what he wanted, and had set a definite deadline: June 21, less than ten days away. He had also given Becker carte blanche to do whatever was necessary to accomplish his mission. That much was clear.

What wasn't clear—and this was beginning to bother Becker—was what would happen if he failed in this assignment. At the very least, it would mean a transfer to a combat unit, and at the worst . . . By the time his taxi rolled to a stop in front of the Ahnenerbe headquarters, Becker had resolved on his course of action.

Waiting on Becker's desk when he returned to his office was the message that Gestapo Sergeant Lindt had telephoned to inform him that Vandenburgh was once again in custody. Becker pressed the "talk" button on his intercom.

"Maria, call the transportation office and get me on the first train to Brussels." As an afterthought he added, "And have them book me into a suite at the best hotel in town."

Berlin's central train station was packed with military personnel in transit to the eastern front. Becker pushed his way through the steel-helmeted mob on the platform and eventually made his way to the westbound train that was to take him to Brussels. Once in his compartment, he tossed his suitcase and leather greatcoat onto the rack above the seats and then settled down to gaze out the window at the soldiers crowding the station.

A light rain began to fall, making the steel helmets of the soldiers glisten like mushrooms covered with dew.

The breeze on the platform shifted slightly, blowing a light coating of mist across Becker's window and turning the scene outside his carriage into an impressionist painting done in muddy greens and grays. Becker was trying to imagine how he would capture the color and movement on the platform in a film when the door slid open and three regular army officers piled into the compartment.

A quick glance told Becker that all three were combat veterans. All had been decorated with the Iron Cross, and the youngest-looking of the three—a cavalry captain— had the first-class Iron Cross pinned to his field-green tunic. Becker could almost feel the eyes of the three combat officers scanning across his own gray uniform, devoid of any decorations save his Nazi party membership pin.

"Heading out west?" the cavalry captain asked.

"Yes," Becker replied. "Brussels." The captain's tone of voice and disregard for Becker's superior rank in the SS made him feel slightly uneasy.

"Expect to see much action?" The question came from an infantry major whose silver badge on his tunic indicated that he had sustained at least three wounds in combat.

"No," Becker said. "I'm on the Reichsführer's personal staff. I'm traveling on SS business." He hoped that the icy tone of his voice would cause the three soldiers to stop their line of questioning.

The third officer farted raucously.

"Something in here smells as if it is rotting to death," the major said. "Would you be a good chap and open the window?" His smile and silky voice merely served to underscore the insult that wafted up to assault Becker's nose.

Becker was on the verge of saying something when the railway police managed to shove their way through the crowded corridor and squeeze into the compartment.

"Travel orders, please," a thick-necked bull of a police-man demanded.

As the three soldiers dug in their pockets for their travel papers, Becker produced the black leather folder that contained his orders from Himmler and handed it to the policeman.

The policeman read over Becker's "orders" twice before handing him back the folder with an awkward click of his heels.

The cavalry officer snickered at the policeman's attempted deference to Becker's orders. Becker, sensing that the policeman would jump out of the window if asked, fixed him with a level stare.

"I would appreciate it, Corporal, if you could find these gentlemen"—he waved a gray-gloved hand in the direction of the three army officers—"other accommodations."

"Yes, sir!" The policeman saluted and turned to face the three officers. "You heard the Sturmbannführer. You have to leave."

A moment of stunned silence was shattered by the major's curse.

"Just one goddamned minute . . ." The major's voice trailed off as the metallic crack of a rifle bolt being shoved home cut across the tension in the train compartment.

"Now, you can either leave the compartment, or I can put you off this train." The policeman's neck was red with anger. "What's it going to be?"

The three officers stared at the big policeman, and at the other policeman behind him, his Mauser carbine held snug against his shoulder. Jaws clenched, they stood up and silently pulled their kits from the overhead racks. As they shoved their way past the police, the last officer paused long enough to fart again.

"Have a nice war," he said over his shoulder, before

shrugging his way past the police to move off down the crowded corridor after his friends.

"Post a guard outside my compartment, Corporal," Becker said, then turned to stare out the window at the crowded station platform.

After what seemed to be an endless delay, the train finally jerked to life and steamed its way out of the Bahnhof. As Becker headed west, the weather worsened, the heavy splat of summer rain turning into a thunderstorm that rocked the train with the rumble of distant thunder. As the miles wore on under darkened skies, Becker nodded off to sleep.

The camera slowly tracked down the long corridor of the castle dungeon until it stopped in front of an iron-studded oak door. Slowly the door swung open, and the camera moved into the dark, dank cell. Dimly visible in the background, a hooded figure sat motionless in an ornately carved chair. The camera moved in closer, revealing the figure to be wearing the robes of the Grand Master of the Templars. Slowly, the figure raised his skeletal hands and pulled back the hood covering his face. . . .

At first Becker thought it was just another crash of thunder that jolted him awake, but the screech of the train's brakes on the iron tracks brought him fully conscious, aware that something horribly wrong had happened. Before he could drop to the floor of his compartment, he heard the overhead roar of an aircraft engine, followed moments later by a second, deafening blast.

The train had ground to a halt, and the second bomb had found its target—a carriage filled for the most part with new recruits moving west to replace combat soldiers stationed in France. For just a moment Becker was caught up in the absolute silence that followed in the wake of the bomb blast. Then, like a radio suddenly switched on at full volume, the sounds of the aftermath assailed him.

Behind him, in the carriage that had taken the hit from the enemy bomb, the strangled curses of wounded and trapped soldiers provided a bass chorus for the mangled, shrill screams of the dying. As his eyes focused, Becker saw small shafts of light splashing pools on the floor. Following the shafts upward, he could see patches of sky through the bullet holes in the roof of his railway carriage, oblong evidence of the enemy pilot's skill in strafing the train. It was only when he tried to stand that Becker realized he was wounded, a neat graze along the side of his head.

For a moment he was distracted by the black stain on his gray sleeve. Staring at it, he tried hard to imagine what it was. Then he knew: blood. His blood. Somewhere, deep down inside, Becker was disappointed that the stain wasn't a bright, glorious, Technicolor red. Somehow, the sight of his own blood, black on the sleeve of his uniform, made him feel cheated. It lacked the cinematic impact that he had always imagined spilled blood would have. It was as if his sacrifice for the Fatherland wasn't regarded as worthy by the gods of war.

Struggling to his feet, Becker shoved open the door of the compartment and had to step over the body of the railway policeman who had been enforcing his demanded privacy. His first instinct had been to bend down to see if the man needed help, but the large hole in the top of the guard's steel helmet dissuaded Becker from any closer examination. A single round from a .50-caliber machine gun would finish most men and, judging from the ragged shreds of the dead policeman's uniform, he had taken half a dozen hits. Stumbling over the corpse, Becker lurched his way to the end of the car and dropped to the ground outside.

In the chaos surrounding the bombed train, Becker

managed to make his way forward toward the engine. The front railway carriages, farthest from the actual bomb damage, were virtually deserted, the occupants having gone back to assist in the rescue of those who were wounded or trapped in the wreckage. After a few hundred meters, Becker—his head throbbing from his wound— reached the still puffing locomotive.

The engineer was laid out on the gravel next to the tracks, hands folded neatly across his chest, his cap covering his face. On the step-plate of the engine, the fireman, brakeman, and conductor were shouting and gesturing, plainly engaged in an argument of "Who's in charge here." As Becker climbed up onto the locomotive, the conductor rounded on him.

"What the hell do you think you're doing up here?" the man demanded. "Get the hell back to the train. *NOW!*"

Becker looked at the other two men. "Which one of you is in charge?"

"I am," shouted the chubby conductor. "Now get the fu—"

Becker jerked his pistol from its holster and tapped its muzzle on the conductor's sweaty forehead. "Since you are in charge, you are the first one I'll shoot if you don't all do exactly as I order."

The conductor's eyes bulged, and the brakeman and fireman moved to the far side of the locomotive's cab.

"First, I want one of you to go back and uncouple the front of this train from the wreck. Then I want us to steam as fast as possible to the next town. Understand?" Becker pointed his pistol at the two men in the cab. "I said: Do— you—under—stand?"

The two men nodded vigorously and started to climb down.

"Hold on," said the conductor. "Just what, besides that pistol, gives you the authority to take over this train?"

"This," Becker said, producing the black folder with the silver lightning flashes on its cover. "Direct orders from the Reichsführer."

The conductor didn't bother to look at Becker's orders. Instead he let out a long, exhausted sigh and turned to his two colleagues hanging on the step-plate of the locomotive.

"You heard the man." There was total surrender in his voice. "Uncouple the train."

It took Becker three days to reach Brussels, as much the result of having his head wound attended to as the enemy bombing of the German rail centers. When he finally did alight at the main train station in Brussels, he was tired and anxious to get to Gestapo headquarters. An hour and a half later a staff car delivered him to the squat red brick building that housed the machinery of the dreaded Nazi Secret Police. After passing through the usual security checkpoint, Becker was shown to Sergeant Lindt's office.

"Heil Hitler." Lindt stood up as Becker entered his office, bringing his right arm up in the obligatory Nazi party salute.

"Heil." Becker returned the salute and let his eyes sweep around Lindt's cramped office. Three battered oak filing cabinets lined one of the nicotine-stained ivory walls. Lindt's desk was in the center of the room, and behind it, under a grimy window, was a table with four neatly stacked piles of file folders. There was a swivel chair behind the desk, and against the opposite wall was another chair next to a hat stand. There was also a photograph of Lindt, showing him standing slightly behind the Führer, glaring out from under a coal scuttle helmet.

"So where's Vandenburgh?" Becker asked without any preamble.

"Downstairs. Cell thirty-seven." Lindt's voice matched

his broken nose and pockmarked face. "You want him brought up to the office?"

"Is that where interviews are usually held?" Becker asked.

"Not if you want to keep the carpet clean." Lindt snorted. "We usually deal with them in the basement or in their cells."

Becker paused for a moment, then asked, "Where did you last interrogate him?"

"The basement," was Lindt's curt reply.

"Then in that instance, have him brought to your office."

Lindt picked up the phone on his desk and spoke briefly to someone on the other end of the line.

"The prisoner will be here in a few minutes," he said, replacing the handset on the cradle. "You want a coffee?"

The coffee was stale, with the scorched taste that comes from one too many attempts to reheat it. After his first swallow, Becker ran his tongue over his teeth, hoping he could somehow get the scummy taste out of his mouth.

Maybe, he thought, *I can give this to Vandenburgh to make him talk.*

That was going to be a problem. Getting Vandenburgh to lead him to the Grand Master of the Order of the Temple probably wouldn't be easy. Against his better judgment, Becker was about to try another swallow of coffee when there was a knock at the office door.

"Come in." Lindt's voice was matter-of-fact.

Two uniformed security policemen entered the office with Vandenburgh, his hands manacled behind him. Becker was surprised at the prisoner's condition. Even though it was obvious that he hadn't shaved or bathed since his arrest five days earlier, Vandenburgh still had an air of dignity about him. Six feet tall, silver-haired, with an aristocratic, hawk-nosed face and piercing grey eyes, it was obvious at a glance that he was an absolute gentleman. Like all prisoners, his shoes, belt, and jacket had been taken away when he was incarcerated.

"Uncuff him," Lindt said, shoving a chair into the center of the room.

The guards did as they were told, and Vandenburgh used his freedom to hitch up his trousers.

"Sit!" Lindt barked at the prisoner. Vandenburgh paused for a moment, just long enough to make it clear that it was *his* decision to sit down, before lowering himself into the chair.

"Now, then." Becker cleared his throat. "Herr Vandenburgh . . ."

"7128," Lindt interrupted. "Call the prisoner by his number: 7128. We don't use names."

Becker looked up at Lindt. "Thank you, Sergeant. But the gentleman is no longer a prisoner."

Lindt shot Becker a "who-died-and-made-you-king" look. "Then in that case, perhaps you'll excuse me." Lindt turned on his heel and walked out of the office.

"Now, Herr Vandenburgh—"

"Chevalier," the older man interrupted. "If you please."

Becker had to check his temper. "Certainly, *Chevalier.*" *God,* he thought, *this guy is either a complete fool or the most cool-headed man on earth.* "Now, my office in Berlin is trying to track down certain Templar items, and we were hoping you would be able to assist us."

"Excuse me," Vandenburgh said, "but is that a bloodstain on your sleeve?"

Becker was momentarily distracted by the question. "Uh, yes. I was wounded in an enemy attack on my way here from Berlin."

"Ah, then it was you who ordered my rearrest." Vandenburgh fixed Becker with a sliver of a smile.

"No," Becker lied. "I merely asked the Gestapo to keep

you under surveillance until I could come to Brussels and meet with you."

Vandenburgh's smile hardened, and Becker had a feeling in the pit of his stomach that the man's gray eyes saw right through him.

"As is so often the case, someone overreacted." Now Becker tried a smile of his own. "I am sorry for any inconvenience or hardship this may have caused."

"It doesn't matter," Vandenburgh replied. "You're too late."

"Too late for what?" Becker asked.

"The archives, if that's what you've come about," Vandenburgh said.

"In a manner of speaking, that's one of the things I'd like to discuss with you," Becker replied, slightly annoyed that the unshaven man seated opposite him managed to stay one step ahead of the interrogation. "I need to know where those records are."

"In the Ecuadorian Embassy, Major." Vandenburgh's smile broadened. "They are under diplomatic seal, awaiting transfer to Portugal."

"We could ask for their surrender," Becker said.

"You'll never get it," Vandenburgh replied, his voice hard-edged. "Ribbentrop won't violate diplomatic protocol, especially for Herr Himmler."

Becker was surprised that Vandenburgh was aware of the rift between the Reichsführer and the German foreign minister. The party went to great pains—quite often other people's pains—to prevent the rivalries of Hitler's inner circle from becoming public knowledge. He looked away from Vandenburgh and stared out the window, deciding how next to proceed. After several seconds, he turned back to the prisoner.

"There's something I want to show you," Becker said. He reached into his pocket and produced the small leather folder containing his special orders from Himmler. "Open it," he said, and slid the folder across the desk.

The old man reached over to the desk and picked up the folder.

"As you can see," Becker said as Vandenburgh read the orders, "I have been given extreme powers by the Reichsführer. Would you like to know why?"

"To prevent the archives of the Templars from leaving Belgium?" Vandenburgh ventured, replacing the black leather folder on the desk.

"No," said Becker, leaning forward in his chair. "Because I am Himmler's personal envoy to the Grand Master of the Order of the Templars."

The older man made no immediate reply, but merely sat opposite Becker, his head tilted back, staring at the fly-blown ceiling. In the silence that ensued, Becker imagined that he could hear a muffled scream drift up from deep within the building. The thought made him shiver.

"There is no 'Grand Master,'" Vandenburgh said at last. "The Order is governed by a Regent working with a Supreme Council."

"That's as may be," Becker said, toying with a letter opener on the desk. "But we believe otherwise. That's why Himmler wants to meet with *your* Grand Master."

"Supposing for a moment that there was a Grand Master." Vandenburgh looked down at the floor as he spoke, careful to give nothing away by even the slightest change of expression. "What could the Order possibly gain by a meeting with Himmler?"

Becker sensed he was onto a winning streak. "The two things your Order most wants to achieve," he said, balancing the letter opener on the palm of his hand.

"And those are?" Vandenburgh asked, looking Becker straight in the eye.

"Recognition"—Becker pointed the letter opener at Vandenburgh—"and your own sovereign territory."

"And how will you accomplish that, may I ask?" Vandenburgh's voice remained calm, but his fists betrayed his inner excitement at the prospect set before him.

"I need hardly remind you of Germany's success in North Africa. In a short time General Rommel will have captured Cairo. From there it will be but a short drive across the desert to Jerusalem." Becker had hoped for some sign of reaction at the mention of Jerusalem, but Vandenburgh remained impassive as he spoke.

"That assumes much, Major," he said, leaning forward and placing his hands flat on the desk. "The Libyan desert is far enough from Cairo, let alone Jerusalem."

"It can also be very far from this office to the street outside. But I know that if I let you go, we will meet again tomorrow." Becker smiled. "Won't we?"

"It will take three days, at least," Vandenburgh said.

"Day after tomorrow, at the latest," Becker said. "Or you're a dead man."

Vandenburgh nodded.

"Then you are free to go," Becker said as he rose from behind the desk and walked across the office. "Only don't try to escape. I've arranged for a Gestapo agent to follow your every move." He opened the door and motioned for Sergeant Lindt to come in. "Will you please find Chevalier Vandenburgh's things and arrange for a car to take him to his home?"

Lindt grunted, then went over to Vandenburgh and clapped a heavy hand on his shoulder. "Come on," he said. "You're leaving."

Vandenburgh rose unhurriedly to his feet and, clutching his beltless trousers, followed Lindt from the room. In the doorway he paused and turned to face Becker.

"I shall meet you at noon in the lobby of the Excelsior Hotel," he said. "The day after tomorrow."

After leaving Gestapo headquarters, Becker went next to SS headquarters to report his arrival in the city. There he was told to return for a meeting with SS General Heinz Lammerding in the afternoon. A staff car from the SS motor pool drove him across town to his hotel—which turned out to be the Excelsior. He no longer wondered at Vandenburgh's choice of meeting place. Luxurious, the Excelsior had been commandeered by the Nazi top brass.

Despite Becker's special orders from Himmler, the hotel manager refused to allocate him anything other than a private room on the third floor, the top three floors being reserved for generals and colonels. But the room was well appointed, with a dresser, a desk, two chairs, and a single bed with an ornate gilt headboard. A rococo wardrobe stood in one corner next to the window, and beside it was a door leading to a bathroom shared with the adjoining room.

Becker dumped his case on the bed and set about unpacking. He had brought some civilian clothes—a tweed jacket, corduroy trousers, and a pair of stout brogues— and these went into the wardrobe. He made a small pile of socks and underwear to be sent down to the hotel laundry and then set out his shaving kit on the small dresser under the window. Satisfied with his unpacking, he checked his watch and then headed down to the lobby.

Out front his car was still waiting, and as Becker approached, the driver got out and opened the rear door of the big Minerva sedan.

The driver closed the door and then slid behind the large white steering wheel.

"Where to, sir?" he asked.

"SS headquarters," Becker replied. "I have a meeting with General Lammerding in half an hour."

Unlike the meeting with Himmler, General Lammerding did not keep Becker waiting. Instead, the moment he arrived at SS headquarters, Becker was taken immediately to the general's office.

Lammerding was by the windows, bent over a table covered with maps. As Becker was ushered in, the general stood up and crossed to the center of the room.

"Ah, Major Becker." The general extended his hand. "It is a pleasure to meet you."

"The honor is mine, General," Becker said, shaking Lammerding's hand.

"So, I hear from Berlin that you were something of a hero a few days ago," Lammerding said, guiding Becker closer to his desk.

"Oh," Becker said. "You mean the train. I'm afraid that what I did was pragmatic, not heroic."

"You saved a train from certain destruction by enemy aircraft," the general said with a smile. "That action certainly merits the admiration of us all." He picked up a small box from the corner of his desk and opened it, removing a medal.

"Therefore, it gives me great pleasure to present you with the War Merit Cross, with swords." He pinned the decoration on Becker's chest.

"*Heil Hitler!*" The general's hand shot up in a stiff-armed salute.

"*Heil Hitler!*" Becker responded, returning the general's salute.

"Congratulations, Major," the general said, shaking his hand again. "Now, if you will excuse me—Fritz will show you out. Fritz!"

An orderly opened the door. "Yes, General?"

"The major is leaving. Please show him to his car." Lammerding turned to Becker. "Good-bye, Major. And good luck."

"Congratulations, Major," Fritz said as he escorted Becker down the stairs that led to the parking structure. "If I may suggest something?" The question hung in the air.

"Certainly," Becker said, hoping that it would be the name of one of the better-looking typists in the building.

"Don't wear that medal out of the building. It's a target." Fritz pulled open the door. "Just wrap the ribbon through your top button hole, and hope no one mistakes it for the Iron Cross."

Becker slipped the medal off his tunic and dropped it into his pocket. "Thanks for the advice, Corporal," he said.

"There's your car, sir." Fritz motioned for Becker's Minerva to be brought forward. "Enjoy your stay in Belgium."

Becker climbed into the back of his car and in a few minutes was heading back to his hotel.

A Wehrmacht signals private was waiting by the reception desk in the lobby of the Excelsior Hotel when Becker walked up and asked for his key.

"Major Becker?" the private asked, his right hand touching the rim of his helmet.

"Yes?" Becker said, nodding in recognition of the salute.

"I have a message for you from the Reichsführer's office." The signals private dug through the leather dispatch case hanging from his hip. "I will have to see your ID and ask you to sign for this," he said, pulling a gray envelope with a red stripe down its center from his case.

Becker produced his SS identity card and handed it to the soldier. Satisfied that the photo matched Becker's face, the man handed him the envelope and a receipt book.

"Sign here," he said, indicating the line next to

Becker's name. When Becker had done so, the man took back the receipt book, saluted again, and left the hotel.

Up in his room, Becker opened the gray and red envelope and removed the telegram from Himmler. The buff-colored page contained a single line of pasted teletype:

THIS IS TO CONFIRM MEETING WITH
RfSS 21 JUNE 1941, 2130 HRS.

There was no signature, but the terse style told Becker that it was sent from Hedwig Pottast, Himmler's private secretary, who set all of the Reichsführer's personal appointments. So now he not only knew the date of his possible execution, he also knew the time. As he undressed for bed, Becker hoped that Vandenburgh wouldn't miss their luncheon meeting.

The next day and a half were the longest that Becker could ever remember spending, anywhere. Brussels was, under the best of circumstances, a second-rate city compared to any other European capital. Under the heel of German occupation, it took on a drabness that Becker found totally stultifying. After a brief stab at sightseeing, he gave up and returned to his hotel, immersing himself in his notes on the Order of the Temple.

The ancient history of the Order, its official demise, and its continuation through the next four centuries as a quasi-secret order of chivalry were of little interest to Becker. The real key to the Order, he decided, was the events of 1847. In that year the Order of the Holy Sepulchre was reorganized, placed under papal control, and allegiance to the Catholic faith was demanded of all its members. This caused many of its knights to leave the Holy Sepulchre and to seek admission in the Order of the Temple.

Both the Order of the Temple and the Holy Sepulchre

had, since 1704, at least, the restoration of "Christian Jerusalem" as their main stated goal. In 1847, when the Holy Sepulchre declared that its main purpose was the support of the papacy and the propagation of the Roman Catholic religion, the Templars stood alone in their desire to see Jerusalem restored as the center of faith for all Christians. Toward that end, the Templars had repeatedly entered into negotiations—and conspiracies—to regain the holiest of cities.

Of course, the various popes had been in complete opposition to the Templars; Templar success would mean a shift in spiritual power from the Vatican to Jerusalem, and the beginning of the ascendancy of Orthodox Christianity over Roman Catholicism. Not surprisingly, the Templars had found their greatest allies in Northern and Eastern Europe, as well as in Scotland and England. The Ottoman Empire had also been quietly supportive of the Templars, hoping that by allowing them to re-form a tiny remnant of the Kingdom of Jerusalem, they would be rid of the constant bickering of the many Christian faiths that jostled and fought for privilege in that city. Even the Kaiser had agreed to the establishment of a Templar city-state if Germany had won the first World War. After that war, the British and the French had seen that turmoil, not stability, in the Middle East was to their advantage, and had destroyed any hopes the Templars had of regaining the city of Jerusalem.

Becker rubbed his eyes and checked the time on his watch: 2:25 in the morning. Setting aside his notes on the Order of the Temple, he stretched and decided to call it a night. He had a plan, and now all he needed was Vandenburgh's cooperation. He had to meet with the Grand Master and convince him to resign in favor of Himmler. Once that was done, the Reichsführer would create a special Templar state in the Holy Land, with the former Grand

Master installed as—what was the term Vandenburgh had used?—Regent. And if that plan failed—well, Becker had another scenario already laid out.

Becker picked up his Walther automatic pistol and sighted down its slide at one of the bedposts. Grand Masters, he decided, could be replaced, and he had just the man in mind for the job, should it become necessary to fill an immediate vacancy in the office. Looking through his notes one last time, he came across a single name: Leuprecht. According to the files, this Swiss Templar seemed to be something of a troublemaker in the Order and would be the ideal candidate to replace whoever might be the existing Grand Master, if push came to shove. Judging by Leuprecht's record, he'd jump at the chance to be the head of the Order of the Temple. Climbing into bed, Becker switched off the bedside lamp, satisfied that, whatever the outcome of his meeting with Vandenburgh, he'd be back in Berlin by the twenty-first.

In the morning Becker bathed and shaved, but wasn't in the mood for breakfast. Instead he had coffee in his room and waited patiently for Vandenburgh to arrive at noon. At five minutes before the appointed hour, Becker shrugged into his uniform tunic, carefully adjusting the black wound badge on his pocket and the ribbon of his War Merit Cross in his top button hole. Satisfied with his appearance in the mirror on the back of his door, he headed downstairs to meet with Vandenburgh.

In the lobby, Vandenburgh was already waiting for Becker, virtually the only civilian in a sea of green and gray uniforms. Becker noticed him immediately in his dark blue pinstripe suit, pearl-gray homberg, and spats. Tall and aristocratic, Vandenburgh stood casually by a potted palm, elegantly resting on a rosewood walking stick with a gold handle. In his buttonhole was a tiny red patriarchal cross resting discreetly in the center of a black silk rosette, edged with two tiny gold flashes: the subtle insignia of a knight grand cross of the Order of the Temple.

At Becker's approach, Vandenburgh inclined his head slightly, touching the brim of his hat with the first two fingers of his right hand.

"Good afternoon, Major Becker," Vandenburgh said when the other man was within speaking distance.

"Chevalier," Becker replied. "I trust you will be able to join me for an early lunch?"

"Sadly, no," Vandenburgh said. "I doubt that you will have time for lunch yourself, once we have spoken." He glanced around the room before he continued. "Perhaps we could speak somewhere more private?"

"Certainly," Becker said. In the corner he saw an empty table with two leather armchairs drawn up next to it. Indicating the table with a gesture of his hand, he said, "Will that do?"

"Perfectly," said Vandenburgh as he followed Becker over to the table.

"Now," Becker said, once they were seated. "When do I meet with your Grand Master?"

"Tonight," Vandenburgh replied. "At the castle of Gisors."

"Gisors?" Becker asked. "Where's that?"

"In France, my dear Major." Vandenburgh smiled at Becker. "Northwest of Paris, about two hundred kilometers south of Brussels."

Becker looked at his watch. It was 12:20. That meant he could be in Gisors by six in the evening. Even if it took all night to convince the Grand Master to come to Berlin, they would still be back in the capital of the Greater German Reich with a day to spare. If the Grand Master was implacable, then Becker still had more than forty-eight hours in which to contact Leuprecht and persuade him to assume the office of Grand Master.

"So when do we leave?" Becker asked.

"We don't," Vandenburgh said. "The Grand Master will send an envoy to meet you here at the hotel in one hour. Please be ready, as the car and driver will wait only five minutes."

"Forgive my sense of the melodramatic, Chevalier, but how do I know this isn't a trap?" Becker kept his face impassive.

"The driver is a member of our Order, as you would expect," Vandenburgh said.

"Of course," Becker replied.

"He is also with the Swiss Embassy here in Brussels." Vandenburgh crossed his legs and tugged momentarily at the crease in his trousers. "He will be in an embassy car. That, together with your 'special pass,' should prevent any problems. But if you are still concerned, you can give his name to the Gestapo, just in case. Or"—he smiled again—"you can cancel the trip."

Becker returned Vandenburgh's smile. "No, I'll be ready," he said, taking a small notebook and gold pencil from his pocket. "What did you say is the name of the driver?"

"Leuprecht. Anton Leuprecht." Vandenburgh's face remained impassive. "Now, if you'll excuse me, I must be going." He rose from his seat and turned to leave, then stopped and turned to face Becker again.

"You must forgive me," he said. "I nearly forgot to congratulate you on your decoration." He nodded toward the ribbon wrapped through the buttonhole of Becker's tunic. "The War Merit Cross, is it not?"

"Yes."

"Well, congratulations." Vandenburgh turned and walked across the lobby of the Excelsior, disappearing through the revolving doors that led out onto the broad boulevards of Brussels.

Becker sat at his table for some moments, considering his immediate good fortune. To have Leuprecht drive him to his meeting with the Grand Master was a stroke of luck that ranked right up there with his discovery of Himmler's memo about the Templars four months ago. To have the Grand Master *and* the potential successor to that office both in his grasp at the same time meant that his plan would succeed without fail.

Looking at his watch, he saw that he had less than thirty minutes before Leuprecht would arrive at the hotel to take him to Gisors. Standing, Becker looked around the lobby for a telephone. Spotting one in a small kiosk partially hidden by a potted palm, he walked over and placed a call to Gestapo headquarters.

Yes, Becker thought, as he waited for his call to be put through, *in less than twenty-four hours I will have the Grand Master in Berlin.*

"Hello, Sergeant Lindt?" Becker said when at last his call was answered. "This is Major Becker. I want you to prepare an arrest warrant for Anton Leuprecht, a Swiss national resident in Belgium."

"Sorry, Major, can't do it," was Lindt's reply.

"What do you mean, can't do it?" Becker asked. "I have express orders from Himmler that say you'd better do it."

"I know all about your orders, but I still can't arrest Luprecht." Lindt's voice sounded strained.

"I'm not asking you to arrest him, Lindt. Just prepare the warrant, that's all." Becker was becoming irritated.

"Look, Major," Lindt said. "Even issuing a warrant for this guy Leuprecht can't be done. It's impossible."

"Why?" Becker asked, wondering for a moment if he should threaten to have Lindt shot.

"Because," Lindt slowly replied, "Leuprecht works for the SD—the Sicherheitsdienst. And you know how Deputy Reichsführer Heydrich reacts to anyone interfering with *his* Secret Police."

"I see," Becker said, a cold knot forming in his stomach. "In that case, I'll call you back tomorrow." He replaced the telephone on the cradle and leaned against the glass door of the kiosk, staring out across the lobby and wondering if, after all, Leuprecht could be convinced to work for Himmler, if it came to the crunch.

A loud rapping on the side of the kiosk derailed Becker's train of thought.

"Do you mind doing your thinking elsewhere?" The voice belonged to a Wehrmacht general. "I need to make a call."

"Certainly, General," Becker replied. And then, with a nod toward the senior officer, he went up to his room to change into his civilian clothes.

Becker carefully hung his gray uniform in the wardrobe and placed his military shirt over the back of a chair. From his bag he removed a tattersall shirt made of thick cotton, and a dark green knit tie. Slipping on the shirt, he pulled on his corduroy trousers and then stepped into his dark brown brogues. He quickly knotted his tie and then shrugged on his tweed jacket. His SS identity card went in the left pocket, and the leather folder containing Himmler's special orders was tucked into one of the inner pockets of the jacket. Becker then picked up his pistol and, checking that the magazine was full and that there was a round in the chamber, dropped it into the right-hand pocket of his jacket. A soft brown hat with a coffee-colored silk band completed the transformation from SS officer to civilian. Becker gave himself an approving glance in the mirror, then went down to the lobby to meet Leuprecht.

The Swiss was dressed much like Becker, but despite his civilian clothes, seemed to almost blend into the background of German uniforms swirling their way through the lobby. He was smoking a cigarette, gazing out a window at the passersby. As Becker approached, he had time to study his quarry.

He decided that Leuprecht had a mean, almost cruel mouth, and eyes that could only be described as reptilian. He was about average height, and without any remarkable features other than his mouth and eyes. He looked exactly like a Gestapo informant. In an instant, Becker knew that the man would sell out the Grand Master at the first opportunity. He also knew that Leuprecht wouldn't hesitate to sell him out, if it came to that. The weight of the loaded Walther in his pocket gave Becker added self-assurance about dealing with him.

"Herr Leuprecht?" Becker said as he approached the man.

"No," said a voice from behind a pillar. "I'm over here."

Becker was surprised, and turned to face the speaker. Unlike the man Becker had mistaken for Leuprecht, the man who was now staring at him had the bland, passive look of a schoolteacher.

Becker tried to recover his poise. "Are you ready to go?" he asked.

"Certainly, Major." Leuprecht's voice was cultured, but he spoke with the slow deliberation of the Swiss. "My car is outside."

In front of the hotel Becker climbed into the front seat of Leuprecht's car, a big American Buick. Before starting the engine, Leuprecht turned to Becker.

"Do you have an overcoat?" he asked.

"No," Becker said. "Will I need one?"

"Only if it gets cold." Leuprecht gave a slight chuckle. "This car doesn't have a heater."

"I'll do all right as I am," Becker replied. "How long to Gisors?"

"About five hours under the present conditions," Leuprecht answered. "They expect you to arrive at eight o'clock."

It took a little over an hour to reach the French border. The first two army checkpoints that Becker and Leuprecht encountered showed no real interest in the dark green Buick, and they were perfunctorily waved through without the need to produce any sort of identity papers.

The French frontier was another matter altogether, the traffic queue reaching back into Belgium for more than a kilometer. After fifteen minutes without moving, Becker left the car and walked forward to the German roadblock. Leuprecht watched from the running board of the Buick as Becker handed his identity card to one of the soldiers directing traffic. The soldier saluted, then led Becker to a small hut beside the road.

Becker entered the hut, emerging a few minutes later with an officer, who gave several quick commands to the men guarding the checkpoint. Instantly they began directing traffic to pull over to the side of the road, and Leuprecht found himself being waved forward. At the checkpoint Becker climbed back into the Buick.

"There's another checkpoint up ahead about two kilometers," Becker said. "I've asked that they call ahead and alert them that we're coming."

Leuprecht slipped the gear lever down into first and eased the Buick quietly past the tangle of barbed wire and machine gun nests and headed on toward Gisors. The second checkpoint was open when Leuprecht and Becker arrived, and they only paused long enough for Becker to show his identity card before they were on their way again.

"You must have some very powerful connections," Leuprecht said as they pulled away from the checkpoint.

"I'm on the Reichsführer's personal staff," Becker replied.

"So I was told," Leuprecht said. "Vandenburgh said you were. He also said that you were wounded a few days ago, and that you had the War Merit Cross."

"What else did Vandenburgh tell you?" Becker asked.

"Just that I was supposed to do whatever you asked, and see to it that you were returned safely to your hotel in the morning." Leuprecht shifted the car into top gear and settled down to a steady seventy-five kilometers per hour.

"Did he tell you the purpose of our trip to Gisors?" Becker asked.

"No, only that you were going to meet with one of the higher-ups in the Order." Leuprecht slowed for a sharp curve in the road, shifting down into second gear.

"What sort of place are we going to in Gisors?" Becker asked.

"The castle, that's where," Leuprecht replied.

"Yes, Vandenburgh mentioned that," Becker said. He stared out over the hood of the Buick, watching the countryside roll past. "What sort of a castle? Ruined?"

"Pretty much," Leuprecht said. "It was built between 1097 and 1184. Off and on—mostly on—it belonged to the English, finally becoming French in 1449. Its connection with the Order of the Temple dates from 1158, when command of the castle was handed over to three high ranking Templars."

Becker yawned. "So it was in Templar hands until the suppression of the Order in 1307?"

"A bit longer than that," Leuprecht replied. "The Castle of Gisors has remained an important part of the Order down to this very day."

"Then you claim an unbroken succession from the original Knights Templar?" Becker asked.

"We must," Leuprecht said. "Or else you wouldn't be here tonight. Would you?"

Before Becker could answer, Leuprecht pulled the car over to the side of the road and got out, walking to the woods a few meters from the road to relieve himself. As Becker waited in the car, he made up his mind about how to proceed with Leuprecht. When the Swiss returned to the car, Becker was ready for him.

"Tell me," Becker said as they pulled back onto the road, "have you ever considered the possibility of becoming the Grand Master of the Order?"

Leuprecht's answer betrayed nothing. "If asked, of course I would serve."

"And who would ask you?" Becker asked.

"The Regent and the Supreme Council have the combined power to select a new Grand Master," Leuprecht said. "They would be the ones doing the asking."

"That sounds like a very powerful group of gentlemen," Becker said.

"That, Major Becker, is an understatement if ever there was one. I don't think you realize the absolute power the Grand Master of the Templars possesses," Leuprecht said. "It is a power that reaches back for centuries and extends forward into the next millennium."

"And the Regent?" Becker asked.

"Second in power only to the Grand Master, and in some ways more to be feared," was Leuprecht's answer.

Well, Becker thought, *there's my answer. Leuprecht will take the job if I have to kill the present Grand Master. And there's no doubt but that he'd cooperate to stay in power. Yes, he'd be willing to be Grand Master for a few days in exchange for being Regent for life.*

It was nearly eight o'clock at night, and Leuprecht had

switched on the headlights of the Buick. Slowing to a walking pace, he carefully turned the car off the main road and proceeded for some minutes along a narrow path that wound its way through the woods and up a gently rising hill until, at last, he came to a stop in the darkening shadow of the Castle of Gisors.

Becker started to leave the car, but stopped halfway out the door. The velvet-blue sky, the first stars beginning to shine through like small diamonds in a jeweler's tray, provided the perfect backdrop for the massive tower and slighted walls of the castle, their black silhouette still crisp in the softly fading twilight. Becker drank it in, impressing it on his mind, knowing that it would be a key shot when he made his film about the Templars.

The slamming of Leuprecht's door brought him back to the present reality.

"Come on," Leuprecht said. "It's just eight, and you don't want to keep anyone waiting." Having spoken, he headed into the dark ruins of the castle.

Becker quickly followed, scrambling over the rubble of one of the walls and crossing to the donjon tower in the corner.

"Give me a hand," Leuprecht said, crouching down and shoving against a large stone slab.

Becker did as asked and put his shoulder to the stone, shoving with all of his strength. With a dry grating sound the stone moved, revealing a small opening and a flight of stairs leading down.

Leuprecht reached into his pocket and produced a thick white candle and a match case. Striking one of the matches on the stone slab, he lit the candle and passed it over to Becker.

"Take this," he said, handing Becker the candle. "Follow the steps down to the bottom. There you will find a lamp. Light it and follow the passage to the end."

"Are you coming?" asked Becker, not sure that he could trust Leuprecht to remain behind.

"No," Leuprecht replied. "My orders are to stay up here until you have concluded your meeting, then drive you back to Brussels."

Becker didn't like it, but he had no choice. "All right," he said after a moment's hesitation. "I should be back within an hour." Holding the candle high and in front of him, Becker crouched down and went through the opening.

Inside the passageway, Becker was relieved to discover that there was room enough to stand up as he carefully made his way down the stone stairs. With his left hand resting on the wall, he slowly took each step, testing it first to be certain it would hold his weight. The candle threw off barely enough light for him to see more than a few feet in front of him, and it seemed like hours before he finally reached the chamber at the bottom of the stairs.

Dropping to his knees, Becker held the candle high over his head, searching in the flickering shadows for the lamp Leuprecht told him he would find. Finally, after more than a minute, he found an old oil lamp with a glass chimney. Carefully he raised the chimney and touched the flame of the candle to the wick. A dull yellow flame licked up, and Becker lowered the chimney, then turned up the wick. Pale ivory light forced back the darkness, showing Becker that he was at the end of a long corridor. Blowing out the candle, he placed it in his jacket pocket, then proceeded slowly down the corridor until he came to an iron-studded oak door.

Pressing against the door, Becker was surprised when it swung easily on its hinges, revealing an octagonal room beyond. The ceiling was high and elaborately vaulted. Shadows cast upward by his lamp darted and flickered around intricately carved gargoyles and found hiding places behind ornately wrought corbels. Arranged around the room were large coffers and heavy stone sarcophagi, and set into niches in the wall were pale white statues, indistinct in the feeble light of Becker's oil lamp.

As he moved across the wide expanse of the room, Becker became aware of another presence. Of someone watching him. Finally, as the shadows retreated in the advance of his lamp, he could make out the dim outline of an ornate chair, a throne where sat a motionless hooded and white-robed figure.

For an instant Becker froze in his tracks, raw terror gripping his heart. One hand instinctively went to his pocket. The figure did not move. Reassured by the presence of his weapon, Becker advanced a few more paces toward the chair.

"Set down the lamp," a voice commanded.

Becker nearly jumped out of his skin as the hooded figure spoke. With trembling hands he set the lamp on one of the coffers. Gulping hard, he tried to focus his eyes in the semidarkness to get a better look at the figure before him.

Peering past the dazzle of the lamplight, Becker now could make out the red patriarchal cross emblazoned on the front of the hooded figure's white robe, tied at the neck with a heavy golden silk cord. As he watched, the figure raised parchment-colored hands and slowly drew back its hood, revealing an ancient face crowned with the crimson cap of the Grand Master of the Order of the Temple.

For a moment Becker thought he would faint. Then the silence was broken by the Grand Master.

"What is it you have been sent here to offer the Order?" The voice betrayed the age of centuries, but carried with it an authority that was not to be questioned. Soft, it pierced through to the very center of Becker's being as if it were a spear hurtled by a champion.

Becker cleared his throat before speaking. "Heinrich Himmler, Reichsführer, commands me to inform you that, in exchange for your resigning as Grand Master of the Order of the Temple, he will return to the Order of the Temple the city of Jerusalem and create a new kingdom in the Holy Land, over which you shall reign as Regent."

The Grand Master stared at Becker with glowing eyes, as though he could see through him and look into his very soul.

"And by what authority does your Reichsführer make such an offer?" The eyes burned into Becker. "Germany has yet to enter the Holy Land."

Becker's tongue seemed to thicken and stick to the roof of his mouth. He swallowed twice before he was able to reply. "The German army is virtually invincible. Within a week Cairo will fall, and then we shall push on to Jerusalem." A burst of inspiration flashed across Becker's mind as he spoke. "The *Beauceant* shall lead us into your kingdom."

"So you propose a crusade?" the Grand Master asked.

"The crusade is begun already," Becker said. "We offer you the honor of leading it."

"Indeed," came the quiet reply. "And what sort of crusade is it? Let me tell you. Yours is a crusade of the blackest evil imaginable. You enslave nations, not liberate them. You destroy whole races and in their place breed the spawn of terror. And now you wish to enlist my connivance in handing over the Order of the Temple so that your petty Reichsführer can challenge the power of the dark one who now leads Germany into a maelstrom of destruction.

"You represent *everything* our Order has opposed for the last six hundred years. Are you really so naive as to think that we would shatter our knightly vows for the dusty streets of Jerusalem?" The Grand Master leaned forward, canting his head slightly to one side. "God will deliver us the Holy City in His own good time." He then leaned back in his throne, his pale hands pulling his hood over his head.

Becker was rooted to the spot by the sheer power of the Grand Master's voice, and for several heartbeats was unable even to breathe.

"Tell your Reichsführer that I choose to decline his offer," the Grand Master said after several seconds of silence.

"With the greatest respect, sir, I think—" Becker began, once his voice had returned.

"Silence!" commanded the Grand Master. "I would no more trust your Reichsführer than I would trust any other godless pagan. Go from here, and go at once!"

So, Becker thought to himself, *it's time for Leuprecht to become Grand Master of the Templars.* The thought of killing the Grand Master caused his stomach to knot and his mouth to go dry as he reached into his pocket for his pistol. But as his fingers closed around the grip, the gun suddenly became burning hot.

Jerking his hand out of his pocket, he could just smell the stench of scorched wool. As the first wafts of smoke reached his nostrils, the gun burned its way through his pocket and fell to the ground, where it glowed cherry-red. Its grips turned into pools of liquid brown plastic moments before the gun melted into a puddle of silvery metal on the cold stone floor.

Becker tried to take a step back, but found himself immobilized by fear. Perspiration poured down his face like drops of rain, stinging his eyes. Nervously he licked his lips, the salty taste of his sweat burning his tongue and mouth. His skin prickled with the heat, drawing itself tight across his body. As he stood rooted to the ground in front of the Grand Master, he realized that his clothes were be-

ginning to disintegrate, as if rotted by some kind of acid.
Raglike, they began to drop at his feet.

The Grand Master watched as Becker, terrified and bewildered, began to desiccate before him. Impassive, he
slowly raised his left hand and began an ancient incanta-
tion.

"Non nobis, Domine, non nobis . . ."

A shaft of pale blue light streamed out of the palm of
the Grand Master's hand, turning to an oily smoke as it
enveloped Becker's body and ever so slowly wound its
way around him. A wraithlike shroud, its color changed
from a pale electric blue to silvery white, glowing brighter
as it constricted around Becker's body.

Becker tried to scream, but his lungs had become dry as
leather and could not force the air past his throat. He felt
his eyes turn gritty, stinging, burning as if his eye sockets
had been packed with rock salt. His vision blurred and
faded, and he could feel himself growing smaller, shrinking as his body transformed into some other substance,
the smokelike shroud wrapping ever tighter around him.
The last thing Becker heard was a deep-throated chorus
slowly intoning the Grand Master's chant: *". . . sed nomini tuo da gloriam. . . ."*

Suddenly the cloud enveloping Becker darkened, turning black, drawing into it all of the light in the octagonal
chamber. Then the sound began, the horrible screeching
as Becker's soul was pressed from him and consumed by
the vapor that had changed him from man to thing. As the
wail of Becker's last torment receded to another plane, his
shroud slowly vanished.

The Grand Master was silent. In front of him, Becker's
oil lamp guttered and went out, returning the chamber to
its age-old darkness. Outside, in the courtyard of the ruined castle, Leuprecht struggled for more than an hour
until he finally succeeded in replacing the stone slab over

the entrance to the passageway that led down under the castle tower. Then, making his way to where he had parked the dark green Buick, he began his lone journey back to Brussels.

*   *   *

Vandenburgh did, indeed, succeed in transferring the archives of the Order of the Temple to safety in Portugal under diplomatic seal, where they remain to this day, under the care of the present Regent and Grand Master of the Order. Anton Leuprecht remained in Switzerland after the war and was involved in Templar intrigues until his death in the 1980s.

In 1946 French esotericist Roger Lhomoy discovered a hidden entrance to the crypt under the donjon at the castle of Gisors. Deep beneath the castle he found a large chamber that contained thirty coffers, nineteen sarcophagi, and twelve statues of knights carved from chalk, set in niches in the granite walls of the crypt. On the floor, in front of a crumbling ornate wooden chair, were the remains of another statue. The statue, which had been smashed to pieces, was unlike all of the others. When examined, it was determined that this statue had been made of salt.

INTERLUDE SIX

The end of World War II did not put an end to speculation about the Templars, any more than previous wars had done. Protection of the secrets of the Temple is a theme that has run through Templar lore continuously in the centuries following their official demise. Carrying the mythology forward, out of their own time and place, can produce some intriguing quantum leaps of speculation, especially when the stories cross the Atlantic to lands where no historic Templar ever set foot.

Knight of Other Days

Elizabeth Moon

Xavier saw him arrive: an old man, sitting upright on his scrawny old horse the way old men did. A real caballero, then, and not one of the touristas his uncle had told him about, who slouched in the saddle as if it were a chair. Man enough to ride across the big ranchos and not fall prey to the fence riders. Though perhaps he was a Kiñero. It was said they never left the vast spread, but it was also said they sometimes took their own way back to Mexico on family business. It might be such a one here, who would ride through town and find the ford across the river by night.

Xavier himself was evading his older brothers and his mother. His brothers had promised him a beating for what he had said about Juanito's behavior during Mass. His mother had a list of chores that would keep him in range of his brothers all day. He had taken off with the goats at daybreak and now lay in the hot shade off a huisache.

The stranger would pass him only a length away, if he stayed to the obvious path. Xavier watched the horse pick its way down the gravelly slope. Bigger than it looked, that horse. Not a King Ranch horse, though a man returning to Mexico on business might not want one of the sorrel horses anyone in South Texas could recognize. And the man didn't wear a *vaquero's* dress, and the saddle—

It was at that moment that Xavier saw the stranger's eyes and felt his own mouth gape open to the heat. Blue. Very blue, and very clear, beneath gray-white hair. The stranger smiled and said something Xavier didn't understand. Xavier felt his heart racing in his chest, felt himself collapsing inside, and wondered frantically if the stranger had cursed him so quickly. Evil eye? *Susto?*

He blinked, gasped, fought for steadier breath, and looked again. Now the stranger's hair was not gray, but the pale yellow of cornmeal. He sat erect, tall, with a shining around him that Xavier was quite ready to take for a sign, whether from God or someone else he was not sure. The horse—tall, gleaming now, prancing under its arched neck and flowing mane—the horse was like no horse he had ever seen. Perhaps the charros he had heard about?

Dazed, Xavier crept out from under the huisache into the full light of an August midmorning. He glanced around and saw what he had seen every day of his life: Roma, Texas, and its surroundings. Brush-covered gravel hills capped with crumbling, cobbly stone; the straggle of little houses, some of old stone and adobe; the church, the school, the two-lane highway passing through from Rio Grande City to Guerrero and on to Laredo. The dirt road that straggled out northward, up into the ranches where bony cattle survived on manos with the thorns burned off. At the south end of the town, the rugged bluff above the Rio Grande—the Rio Bravo to those on the other side, in Mexico.

"Roma?" the stranger asked now, in an accent Xavier could not identify.

"*Aya*," Xavier said, pointing. "There—Roma."

The stranger stared, then shook his head. The horse pawed the path with one great hoof . . . bigger, Xavier, realized, than the plates in their kitchen.

"Roma is bigger than that, fool of a boy," the stranger said. Then, as Xavier stared, uncertain, he seemed to shrink into himself, becoming once again the old, shrunken man Xavier had first seen. And the horse, too, now looked like any hard-ridden beast of no particular breeding—too shaggy for quality, too heavy of neck and head. The old man muttered something Xavier could not understand at all, then smiled. A surprisingly sweet smile, it was, but Xavier was not fooled. A true vision could come to anyone, even small boys—an angel or a devil in some unexpected guise. Father Patrick was always saying you could not trust the sweet words of men, only the justice of God.

So Xavier crossed himself and muttered a paternoster. And when the stranger joined in, both with the crossing and the Latin, Xavier was sure it must be an angel. Certainly not a devil. None of them could make the sign of the cross. Still, he did not come any closer, and he watched as the old man shifted his weight and the horse went on down the trail to the first street.

The old man glared down the slope at the little clutter of low houses, the slick ribbon of heated asphalt running east and west, the lazy brown river sleeping in the hot sun below a rock ledge. Roma, indeed! So this was how the magic dwindled. Fury and despair warred in him; he could almost feel their clawed feet on either rib, their teeth locked in his heart. No time, no time. Whatever this was, this place called Roma by a river—the wrong Roma, the wrong river—he would have to finish his work here. He had chanced it all, and lost. He would never see the

seven hills again, the Tiber's flow; he would never feel a
Mediterranean breeze on his cheek.

Beneath him, the horse shifted impatiently. He flexed
his back, releasing, and it paced forward. The hill behind
him wasn't much of a hill, and the town ahead looked to
fit its hill. Only the hot wind, hot already this early, blowing out of the scrubby waste across the river, felt familiar.
It had been many years—more than he could readily
count—since he had felt that heat. Then, he had flinched
from its blast, but now, he accepted gratefully the ease it
promised his joints.

It was a good sign that the boy had crossed himself, had
known his paternoster. If it should be a region of
Catholics, he might yet find a successor. The power
weighed on him. He had sought it, to be sure, in those
days when he had been young and foolish. He had been
glad to take up the burden, before he knew what it
weighed.

Slowly, as slowly as if his horse were the rack-boned,
spavined creature it appeared to the outer eyes, the old
man rode down into the town. His gaze missed nothing.
Not the pig in its narrow sty, not the little gardens protected by wattle or stone wall from drying winds. Not the
bare-bottomed babies playing in the yards, the girls hanging out wash, the quick slap of palms indoors shaping tor-
tillas, the boys quarreling, the smells of cooking, of
chickens and pigs and goats and humans. He rode past the
little store and post office on the highway, past a pink
house with a washing machine on the front porch, past a
gas station. He could feel the eyes on him, though no one
spoke. He saw the cross on the church, nearer the river,
and when he came closer he saw that it stood on a stony
prominence.

Now what? He dismounted and opened the door. A
faint ecclesiastical odor seeped out along with a cool

breath. But no one was within, though a light glimmered at the altar. He cleared his throat; no one answered. The priest—surely there was a priest—must be away. For long? He had no idea.

The horse pulled away, straining toward a tuft of grass burnt brown as old hay. It was hungry, and no wonder. So was he. He would have to find out when the priest might return; he would have to find food and shelter. The words of the Rule came back to him, as so often, in mockery. " . . . Shall have meat but three times a week." In the camps he had not seen meat for years on end. "Shall eat in common." That he had done, when he had eaten at all. Poverty had been the easiest part of his vow to keep, all down the years. Chastity . . . well, easier now, in age. Obedience, that was the difficulty.

He touched his chest, where beneath his clothes the sliver of bone rested. He had vowed obedience to God, of course, but also another, more immediate obedience, to the Master. He had no Master now, but that bit of bone; and in the years he had carried it, it had ceased to speak in his inner ear. He had no one now to follow, and for a soldier this was a greater burden than his age. How could he follow orders if none were given?

Esperanza had wakened before dawn with the memory of many screams ringing in her ears. Again. Each time closer . . . and unlike her old teacher, she took no pleasure in that knowledge. She lay straight, arms at her sides, and let herself feel the pull of the earth, the sea, the sun still below the rim of the world, the four winds. Through her narrow window, a trickle of predawn coolness roughed her skin like a cat's tongue. She heard the thin *skreek* of a gate hinge, and the clatter of little hooves. So. That little scamp Xavier, Pico's son, was off with the goats before dawn again. He must have angered his brothers again; this was his favorite escape.

She rose from her narrow bed, touching without thinking the charms she wore, the charms of the bed itself. *For a safe night, I thank you,* she said without sound, and felt the darkness accept her thanks. She murmured a little in her throat, something no skulking thief could hear and use against her, then looked sideways out her window. There, to the east, the vague blurred streak of coming dawn. A truck went by on the road, its tires whining. The truck was no concern of hers, but the street was. She had her ways of knowing what she needed to know, night and day.

She stretched out on her bed again, riding the sense of power that knowledge gave her, until something jolted the inside of her head. Something more powerful . . . something dangerous . . . some great change . . . coming soon. Coming today.

She went into the kitchen. Something hissed at her from the floor, and her blood went cold. Then she felt the fur on her ankles, the twining of the kitten around her feet. *Fool,* she said to herself. *Fool. Go and look. Find out.*

Thus Esperanza was the second person in Roma to see the old man. She had gone up to the store for nothing but the chance to look at the charms she had put beneath certain windows, above certain doors. Had they been moved? Had the persons involved done what they'd been told to do? She was eyeing the cards of lace and ribbons, well aware of the sidelong looks she herself got from the children who hung around the candy rack, when she heard the hoofbeats.

Not that hoofbeats themselves were that unusual. But this sounded like a monster of a horse, and with the hoofbeats came that tightening of her skin that told her great magic was near. She edged up the aisle with the bread, the baked goods (inferior store-bought cookies, cinnamon rolls, fried pies) and peeked out the front window. And blinked. The old man in ragged white garments that belonged on the poorest peon off some ranch in the Mexican hinterlands . . . the old man on the scrawny dark horse . . . that was the source of the power she felt. It threw back her probing touch as if a horse shook a fly off its hide. She had never felt anything like it.

She reached again, and again her curiosity, her intuition, slid off that old man as if he were not human. For she had power over men as well as women: She had never met a man she could not understand, not even that silly foreign priest. She prided herself on that; she knew things about the priest he did not know about himself, and she knew things about every man in the town: who would sire only daughters, who had no eggs at all, who wore the horns, and worse. There was always worse; that was the secret depth of her knowledge.

But this man—if man he was—bewildered her questing intelligence. And he carried—it was not himself, but in his possession—magic of such power that she could almost weep to think of it. Almost—but weeping, which was most women's useful tool, could not be hers. She never wept true tears, to give power to those who would drink them. No, she would not weep. She would find out what it was, and gain that power for herself.

Father Patrick Dougherty would have worried, except that Xavier said the old man was a knight. Of course he wasn't really a knight; that was only the boy's imagination, or the old man's fairy tales, but if Xavier's interest was in stories of mounted heroes, he hadn't been hurt. Yet.

"But he don't speak no *Español*, not really, so I can't understand all he say. His *Ingles* ain't so good, either."

The priest spoke Spanish, but the boys laughed at his

accent and replied only in their fractured English, liberally laced with Border idiom.

"I should go see him, perhaps," he said, half to himself. He knew he should go see the old man, but he also knew Alfonso Gutierrez was dying, and he was on his way out to the ranch.

"He'll be all right," Xavier said, scratching one foot as he stood on the other. "He's a good man."

The priest doubted that. Why would a good white man come to Roma, Texas, and live in a single back room by himself and give candy to boys like Xavier? He himself had come because he was sent; he would have chosen a greener land and people who spoke English with his own lilt, if he'd had the choice. Old men giving candy to boys was bad enough, but the strange stories— he didn't fit, the old man. But Alfonso was dying, and it was time for his regular call.

Xavier grinned, the urchin grin that the priest found strikingly similar to the urchins of his homeland. Boys were boys anywhere, he thought. In spite of changes in the world, in spite of movies and that new distraction, television, boys still made mischief and still grinned dimpled, gap-toothed grins.

Men, however . . . men changed in ways the priest didn't entirely understand. Oh, they had the same lusts as always—Xavier the boy would become Xavier the young man, risking his immortal soul, not to mention his life, with the plump whores behind the tavern. He would stand before the altar to marry some shy girl; he would father a stair-step gaggle of dark-eyed children and get fat and old. . . .

The priest yanked his mind back to the immediate problem, and thought about it all the way out to the ranch and all the way back. This stranger, now, this white man from far away, who spoke no Spanish and bad English, who gave candy to boys and told them romantic stories . . . he would not let such a man harm his boys, the boys whose souls he was here at the end of the world to save. When he got back, he would ask Xavier to show him where the old man lived.

"He live here," Xavier said. "He pay Miz Rosales five dollar—" The priest glanced at the rickety lean-to room held onto the back of the Rosales house by nothing more than faith and a coat of pink paint. It had been built for the older Rosales boys, before they and their father died of fever. Now the Widow Rosales rented it out when she could. A shed roof; a door with its blue-painted frame open to the yard and close to the back gate into the alley. Not really an alley, more of a public footpath, wide enough for two or three to walk together, to drive a pig along, to lead a donkey. Not wide enough for a car.

"He has a car?" the priest asked. He had to have a car. How else could a white man, a stranger, have come here? But Father Patrick saw no car—indeed, had seen no car he did not know in the past year, except on the highway itself.

"No *carro*," Xavier said. He was almost dancing with glee; he had interested the priest, and he would have something to brag about. "He come on horse."

"On a horse!" The priest stared at him, suspecting a child's romantic fabrication. No one traveled by horse anymore, not in the 1950s. Not here, where straying off the public roads could be quick cause for a quick shot and no inquest at all. Some few people had a horse, and the men who worked on those dangerous ranches—but . . .

"A *real* horse," Xavier insisted. The priest thought about that. In Xavier's world, a real horse might be not only an actual horse, but a horse unknown in this town—a cavalry mount, a horse from the movies, something new.

"What did it look like? The horse?"

The boy spread out his arms. "Oh, *muy grande*—much big, very tall. Shiny, like oil. Like a charro horse, in Mexico."

A showy horse, then, big and shiny. Here? He saw no sign of a horse in that silent, bare yard. Only the Rosales dog, lean and yellow, tied with a thick rope to the pole of the clothesline. Only the retama tree casting its threadbare shade over a wooden table . . . a corona vine, almost indecently lush at this season, sprawled over the little wooden shack in the yard's corner.

"Not here," the boy said, unnecessarily. "The horse went away."

Went away. Like something in the boy's imagination, when he opened his eyes. The priest, confused and stifled in the heat, let his eyes drift around the yard. Bare dirt, a tire planted with verbena so bright a red it hurt the eye, blue—those blue-painted door and window frames. At once he felt a surge of anger. These people! They would not give up their ridiculous superstitions. . . .

"He let it go," the boy went on, eagerly. "He sent it away—my cousin Miguelito saw it. Into the river."

Blue around the doors and windows to keep the evil spirits out, and charms besides . . . not even Christian charms, a crucifix or Madonna or St. Christopher medal, but little knots of this or that, twigs and leaves, feathers and shells. The Widow Rosales, who came to Mass faithfully, and whose front door was innocently blank except for the blue paint, had nailed something like a birds' nest above the rear.

Xavier followed his glance and scowled. "You don' wanna bother with that," he said. "That's the—" and he glanced aside, made the sign and spit over his shoulder.

"I know who that is," Father Patrick said. He knew, and he didn't know. He had been warned about these people and their witches, their *curanderos* and *curanderas,* rarely openly called *brujos* or *brujas,* who pretended to be healers but were dabbling in far blacker arts than healing. Powerless, of course, except to the superstitious. He knew a *curandera* practiced in this town. But he didn't know who she was. Xavier did—they all did—but they all pretended not to understand his question.

"Bruja? No!" they said, making the sign of the cross, pulling their children close. *"No curandero aqui!"* they would say, men and women and children, when he asked. *"No curandera."*

But the blue windows and doors, the obvious charms the babies wore . . . One of these women, who came to Mass and knelt passively before him, who slurred the clean Latin of the liturgy into soft Spanish . . . one of these women was the devil's personal agent. *Curandera.* Witch.

He dragged his gaze back to the lean-to. Xavier had already darted forward to knock on the doorpost. No one answered. The old man should be there; Xavier said he sat or lay in the room all day. That he did his meager shopping early or late. Perhaps he was ill? Father Patrick came forward and peeked through the half-open door.

The little room lay bare to his eyes. A metal-framed cot, with a thin mattress wrapped in sheets and a coarse gray blanket. Who needed a blanket in this heat? A crucifix on the wall—proper, but it surprised him. Probably Señora Rosales had put it there. A three-drawer chest, tilting to the side, with skewed drawers that wouldn't quite shut. It had been painted dark red by an unskilled hand, and across the top lay an ornate doily crocheted in yellow cotton yarn. On the doily, a blue enameled washbasin and pitcher. A single box of unpainted wood with a plain metal clasp.

"His books," Xavier said, waving at the box. "He got

books, old books. And the shirt with the cross, under his bed—"

"We can't go in," Father Patrick said. "He's not here; it's not right. I'll come back."

"He won't mind." Xavier had pushed the door all the way open and now posed in the middle of the room graceful as a dancer, a bullfighter.

Across the yard, the yellow dog lifted its head and ran out a long red tongue.

"Eh!" It was an old man's voice, but one with power in it nonetheless. Father Patrick turned and watched him come in the gate.

The old man wore *huaraches* and white cotton pants and shirt, just like the poorest Mexican peon. He had gray hair straggling around his ears, and a short gray beard, but he did not manage to look Mexican at all. The priest had met Mexicans of European descent, even Northern European descent. He knew about the Irish mercenary who had married into the famous Garcia family; he knew about the elegant blonde women who shopped in Paris and Milan and laughed at the stupid gringos across the river in Texas who couldn't even speak Spanish. But the old man here did not fool him an instant. Those flame-blue eyes, those cheekbones, that set of jaw—that had come from very far away a long time ago.

"Pah-dray," the old man said, politely enough, but with no softness in his voice where the Spanish word rolled over from a *d* to an *r*. A voice like iron, cold iron with a little rust on it. The priest saw the rust like a cross on the man's body, and shivered in spite of himself.

"I'm Father Patrick Dougherty," the priest said. He was conscious of slowing his voice, making allowances for someone who might not understand English that well.

"Ah. Father Patrick. The local priest?"

What was that accent? Not German, not French, and

certainly not British. But better English than Xavier's, for all that. He knew immediately that this man had some education, that he would know and understand things Xavier never could.

"Yes, I am," Father Patrick said. Then, on an impulse, "*Dominus vobiscum.*"

The old man smiled at him and answered in Latin less accented than his English. "*Et cum spiritu tuo.*" He continued then in rapid Latin that strained Father Patrick's understanding. "I greet you with relief, good priest. We must talk, seriously and privately. I have important tidings for you. Can you tell me where we are?"

Perhaps the old man had a touch of sun. Father Patrick answered the question simply, almost gently, but in English. "Roma, my son. In Texas, near Mexico. You have come far?"

"Very far." The old man grimaced and shook his head as if to clear his ears. He, too, returned to English, but haltingly. "It is not like the old Roma, this place. I thought— But that matters not. You have not enough Latin for conversation?"

"No," Father Patrick said. "I know the liturgy, of course, and read it fair enough, but not to speak, to chat in. You, sir, must have had a Catholic education."

"Yes." When the old man did not go on, Father Patrick asked directly.

"Where?"

"Cracow."

Cracow? Poland? That could almost make sense. Since the war, all sorts of refugees had ended up along the border. His fellow priests in South Texas had found before now people for whom the only common language was the Latin liturgy. They heard in confession stories which no one had yet mentioned in the press. Remote as it was, this region shivered to the stamp of arms across half the world.

"You are Polish, then?" Father Patrick asked. He had known a few Poles in seminary; he struggled to remember any words of Polish he might have heard and came up empty.

"Not Polish," the old man said with a grin. "Latvian."

Odder and odder, but still understandable. At least the man was a Christian, not a Communist or something. And Catholic—that was good, although Father Patrick thought he remembered that Latvians were Protestants. Perhaps he had chosen this remote village just because of its name.

"Come to Mass," Father Patrick said. "And confession," he added. He told himself that he cared only about the old man's soul and the children's welfare, but he was uneasily conscious that he felt a certain relief in the presence of another set of blue eyes.

"Buggery? Of course there was buggery. Always is, when you have men priding themselves on not being attracted by women."

The old man gulped at the beer Father Patrick had brought, and set the dark bottle down with a solid clunk. He had been to Mass; he had not appeared to notice the careful space around him in the church. Now, in the hot afternoon, they sat talking at the table in the Widow Rosales' backyard, and the old man had begun with the sort of stories he told Xavier. Stories of knights, of Crusaders in the Holy Land and in Spain, of El Cid and Saladin. Of quarrels and treasures, of secrets and conspiracies, and finally of Philip the Fair, the grandson of the sainted Louis, of whom the old man had no great opinion. Father Patrick had let him ramble on. It was the best way with strangers, to let them fill the silence with more than they knew.

"The question is, whose buggery was at issue? That fool Philip's or the Order's?"

"Philip?" Father Patrick had lost track of the tale; he was more interested in the teller. A real historian, or a fervent amateur? He seemed to know a lot of unsavory details; if he'd been telling all this to Xavier and the other boys, it would have to stop.

"Oh, come now, Father. You know the story, I'm sure. Probably still taught as an example of what happens when pride overrules common sense."

"You're ... ah ... talking about some ... church organization?"

The blue eyes blazed. "I am talking about the Knights of the Temple of Solomon. Our Order."

A crazy, then, who had read too deeply, too intensely, escaping into imagination. The Templars had been one of the Militant Orders; he knew that much. A picture he had seen in a history book swam before his mental eye: a great castle, brooding over a caravan route. Another: knights in white, with red crosses on breast and back, swinging swords in a battle against Islamic warriors with scimitars. The Order had been suppressed after the Crusades, but he didn't remember the details.

"You're a ... uh ... historian? I don't know much about it."

The look he got he remembered from catechism classes, when it was meant to intimidate and humiliate. It still worked.

"I am no historian; I am a soldier." Another pull at the beer. "I remember ... remember being told, that is." That sounded as if he'd changed his direction in midword. He still had that much grip on reality. "Admittedly, the Order made mistakes. One is not supposed to criticize one's elders, but everyone knows the ripest fruit begs to be plucked. We were too rich, too powerful; too many favors owed to us, and too many who could profit by our loss. The Hospitallers, for instance."

"But . . . er . . . immorality?" The priest could not bring himself to use the coarse term. He had heard it often enough, in all its many variations, but to use it . . . no.

"Buggery," the old man said firmly. "That and other abominations. Magery, repudiating Christ, spitting on the cross, all the usual things—the same list they charged witches with." Another gulp of beer, this one emptying the bottle. "Supposedly we seduced choirboys, pages, the young men who worked on our estates, as well as spending our own time arse-kissing—well, Philip should have been an expert in *that*, so it was said. And I suppose some did. I knew a sergeant who'd been shifted from house to house to break off what his superiors called particular friendships. When he was with us, he couldn't keep his eyes off one of the grooms."

"And you yourself?" the priest asked.

The old man looked at him, the blue eyes suddenly cold as northern ice. "It interests you?" Father Patrick felt himself going hot, hotter than the late afternoon glare of sun—but the old man had already turned away. "No, of course not. Your care for these poor ones is all pure, eh?" Was that sarcasm in his voice?

"I am sworn to chastity," Father Patrick said. It was all he dared to say.

"Oh, so were we. Poverty, chastity, obedience. Military obedience, not some silly girls' school notion of it—obedience that counted when the dust rose up and the arrows flew and the Turks or the Arabs came with flashing blades—" He broke off suddenly, shaking his head.

Father Patrick made another attempt to edge him toward reality. "But that was long ago—centuries—"

"Aye, centuries." A long, rattling sigh that might have been dragged up from his feet with a chain. "And centuries since that cold day in Paris, aye. And the night after, too, in the icy river."

"It must be difficult, when you know so much and the past is so vivid to you, to deal with the daily life here and now," Father Patrick said. "This little town . . . isolation . . ."

"Father, you haven't heard me," the old man said. He glared, his eyes as full of light as a hawk's. "You aren't really listening."

"Oh, I am. I am indeed." Father Patrick knew he was listening to more than the words. An old man, a refugee; God only knew what he had endured to come this far. More than age could shake loose reason. "You're telling me wonderful things about the knights of God in the Crusades, to be sure. Great saints and great sinners in those days; sometimes I think now we have only the great sinners. Xavier has told me about your stories; he said—and truly—that you make them seem very real.

"But you told me you are preparing for death. You must realize that what we need to deal with is the state of your soul *now,* not the accusations made against these knights five hundred years ago?"

"Six hundred," the old man said. "And you're wrong— you need to know about them—you need to understand what I am. What I have, and what you must guard with your life—" But his voice broke in a fit of coughing, and Father Patrick held water to his lips and tried to calm him.

"Later," he said. "Now you must rest; whatever you have to tell me about your—" he almost said hobbyhorse, and stopped himself. "About your specialty, that can come later."

Without intending to do so, Father Patrick found himself at his next visit explaining his dilemma to the old man. Better that, he told himself, than encouraging the old man in his delusion that he was a member of an extinct militant order. Such delusions could be the reasonable result of surviving the unmentionable horrors of the recent war in Europe, but to make a final confession and die well, the old man would have to regain his sanity, his connection to the real world. And for that purpose, Father Patrick told himself, even the banal struggle between himself and the *curandera* might be a blessed intervention.

"I do not know her name," he said. "But she terrifies these people. She sells charms, tells fortunes. I've explained repeatedly, exhorted them . . . and I still find babies with those disgusting little strings around their necks, windows with bundles of herbs—probably poisonous—over them."

"They don't respect you?"

"I wouldn't say that, exactly. They come to Mass regularly; they are generous in their gifts, considering their poverty. Barring an occasional drunken knife fight or a little wife-beating, I could not fault their charity. They are quick to take in the widow and orphan; they love their families. But they do not trust God's power to overcome evil. They will dodge behind His back, so to speak, and try to make their own bargain with the devil."

"An evil woman, you say. A witch. To tell you the truth, Father, I am less eager to condemn witches after what happened to our own illustrious and courageous Master. . . . "

"But my problem," said Father Patrick firmly, before the old man could start in again, "my problem is that I cannot seem to loosen her grip on them. In this day and age—with the new dam, the international dam, being built only upstream from here, a new era—it is ridiculous. You have a Catholic education; you come from Europe. You will perhaps have met ignorant peasants in your day?"

"Mmm, yes. Superstitious, greedy, sly. Easy to frighten,

and difficult to calm. Once Philip convinced even the bourgeoisie, let alone the peasants—"

"So you see my problem," Father Patrick interrupted firmly. "Perhaps you have more experience. What can I do, as a priest, to . . . to work around her, to displace her?"

The look he got this time was contemptuous. "You do not think like a soldier." So the old man had been one, and more than a conscript from that tone of pride. In what war, though? And was that soldierly heritage the reason for his choice of delusions? Father Patrick shook his head and answered mildly.

"I'm not a soldier; I'm a priest."

"I see." A long pause, during which the old man traced a design on the tabletop with a wet finger. "Do you know that?"

Father Patrick looked, and saw nothing but the last angle and curve; the rest dried quickly in the heat. Even that much tickled his mind with a memory, but he couldn't grasp it. A letter? And not in the Roman alphabet? But the old man had swiped his hand quickly across the rest. When he picked it up, a brown coin lay there, a Mexican piece probably. Father Patrick pushed it back. "No—the beer is my treat. It's little enough I can do for you—"

"Just pick it up," the old man said. "Just touch it." Father Patrick shook his head.

"No . . . please. I don't want it. I won't take your money."

"You haven't listened to a word I've said," the old man said. He sat back and glared, and said something in a foreign tongue which Father Patrick was sure would require a penance if translated. "You don't believe me," the old man said, as if it were a repetition.

Father Patrick felt his own neck getting hotter than even the August sun could make it. He had listened by the hour; he had tried to help the old man come to grips with reality. "I believe in God the Father," he began, in the Latin they both knew. "And in Jesus Christ His only Son. . . . " He paused, for effect. "It is not part of my duty to believe in *you,* only to pray for your soul."

The blue eyes dimmed. "As I for yours, Father Patrick. Go in peace."

Esperanza chose her time carefully. The Widow Rosales had gone to the post office window in the store to pick up her monthly check. She would gossip awhile with the others who had come for the same purpose. And she, Esperanza, could enter the Rosales yard on the pretext of bringing a gift. And she would see the stranger up close, and then she would know what she would know.

She opened the gate, as if it were her own, and padded up across the yard to the table under the retama tree. "Lupe!" she called, as if expecting the Widow Rosales to be home. "Lupe, I brought you some tomatoes from the Escobar's—"

"You," said a quiet voice at her elbow.

"Ey," she said, dropping an onion. It was only half a pretense; she had not sensed him until he spoke. It was like the great storms which could come out of a calm, in one sudden blast of wind.

"You are the witch," he said in English. She knew that much English, but she knew better than to show it. No man minds a silent woman, her father had said. She stood silent, hands folded, waiting. "*Bruja. Curandera,*" the old man said. He didn't have the accent right, but she could understand that. A quick glance at him—yes, the blue eyes she had heard of, a different blue than she had ever seen. And very old, and dying . . . she could tell that, this close to him. Yet he had with him, on his person, in his hand, very close—such power as ought to keep him young forever. She could feel it rumbling in her bones. "You speak no English?" he asked. "*Ingles?*" So, he had learned that much Spanish.

"*Nada,*" she said. "*No Ingles.*" Of course she knew some English, but she wasn't about to say so. She looked politely away from those eyes again.

"You know about power," he said. He spoke slowly, so slowly that Esperanza had time to think each word to its Spanish equivalent. She did not look up; she dared not. How did he know? Could he sense her power as she sensed his? "You frighten the priest," he went on. "Are you an evil woman?"

When she understood that, she gave him a quick glare, intended to pierce and wound. Evil! They were always so quick to accuse, the men in general, and the men of power in particular. Let a woman do anything wise or strong, and they said she was evil. But his answering look was mild.

"Show me your power," he said. He held out his hand; even looking down, she saw it. "Please."

She could not tell it if was his courtesy or her own desire for that power, but she found herself holding his hand as if he were any husband come to find out if the baby was his, if his son would return from the army, if the lost cow would be found. She felt the age of it, the fragility of approaching death in the looseness of its skin, the slackness of tendon and muscle. In the sunlight, the lines on his palm showed clearly.

"You have come from far away," she said in Spanish. It didn't occur to her that he might not understand. "You have crossed the water . . . a great water . . . more than one. You have fought many battles." She had been saying that to the men who came to her since the war, and it was always true. But this man's battles . . . they felt different. And that line—she hated to speak of it. "You were in hiding a long time. And your son—no, not your son, but

someone you thought of as your son—died, and you felt
you had outlived yourself. You came seeking death, and
you bear a great wound that must be healed."

She felt the air around her pulsing in a vast heartbeat,
and then she had to let go of his hand, feeling the sting of
tears in her eyes. She squeezed her eyes shut: *Do not cry,
Esperanza. Not now, of all times.*

"More," he said softly. "There is more. Tell me."

She did not need to look at his hand again. She could
feel directly what he bore, and to her surprise there were
two foci, both upon him, but different. "Your power," she
said. "It seeks a home, for when you die." That was true
of both. One she recognized . . . a bit of someone's body, a
tooth or bone or fingernail. It had the power of all such
relics. The other, the more powerful, lay outside her experience.

"Yes," he breathed. "I know . . . it should go to the
priest. But he won't believe me."

"No," she said. "Not our padre. If it is to rest here, it
must be with me." She had surprised herself; she felt her
mouth hanging open and covered it quickly with her hand
and shawl.

"It is a man's power," the old man said firmly. "A
king's wisdom. It is not for a woman."

"Pardon me, *jefe,*" she said, looking away. Why had she
let her tongue run loose? Now he knew she wanted it;
now he would guard it more closely.

"Only God can pardon you," he said. He said it not in
English, but in a language near enough Spanish that she
could make out the meaning. It sounded like the priest's
talk in Mass, but the accent was different. Secret laughter
shivered in her bones. His God need not pardon her; his
God had never condemned her, except in the mouth of
that priest.

"You laugh at God?" he asked.

"God laughs in me," she said, not entirely sure what she meant by that, only knowing it was true.

"I . . . see." She could feel those skylit eyes on her skin as if they were flames. His interest hurt, pulled her tight against her own assumptions. At last she had to look up, and meet that piercing blue gaze. No wonder gringos were insane, so many of them had those pale eyes. No decency at all; no veils between the soul and the world.

"If only you were . . . " he murmured. Then: "You keep many secrets, I daresay."

She did not answer that; she knew she didn't have to. He had a secret, and it weighed on him, as secrets always did weigh on good people. Only the greediest, most evil, truly delighted in an unshared secret. He wanted to tell her, and he would if she did nothing to impede him.

"What do you think of this?" he asked. On the hand he held out was a small brown object the size of a fifty-centavo piece, incised with a design unlike anything she had ever seen. Beside it another, a sliver of obvious bone, darkened with age. Power blazed from his hand.

Esperanza extended a trembling forefinger. "That—" she pointed to the bone, the more familiar, "is the bone of someone you loved. It is the unhealed wound of your sorrow." She would not tell a man, a gringo, a friend of the priest, what else it was, what could be done with such a bone, cherished so long. Its thin voice piped vengeance in her ear. "This—" she pointed at the rounded brown shape, "is another power, but it is not a power I know."

"And yet you attend Mass," the old man said. "You should know this power, if you know good and evil. Tell me, do you know what it does?"

That was obvious. Behind it, in some other place, voices roared curses. She did not know the language, but she knew the tone of cursing. It held them back, from whatever mischief they would do. But how to say that?

"It is the stone that stops the mouth of the dead who would curse the world," she said finally.

"Close enough," the old man said. "And you, witch, would you see the world cursed?"

For a moment the old vision wavered in her sight, the vision given by the old woman who had taught her the arts, who had demanded those years of service. Terrible lights, terrible winds, great deaths, so terrible even the vultures died after gorging. A foretelling which had made her teacher cackle in glee, knowing she would not live to suffer in it but those who had tormented her might. Or their grandchildren, she didn't care. Esperanza had burst into tears that first time, and the old woman had tasted her tears and scolded her. *You are too soft. You must learn.* She had not cried again, but she had never enjoyed her own visions of coming doom.

"No," she said. "But it is cursed, whether or not I wish it."

"Not utterly, not so long as this is safe. Will you keep it so?"

"I?" Surprise drew her eyes back to him. "I am a woman, sir, and you said—"

"I have kept my vows these many years, and found no solution. . . . I will try breaking them at last, and risk a little." He smiled at her; she felt her heart skip a beat. "Open your hand, witch."

She opened her hand, and he turned his over. For a moment they stood, hand clasped to hand, with the power burning between them. The bone pricked her palm; the other thing, whatever it was, felt like warm clay asking to be molded. Then the old man pulled his hand back, and she had to close her fist to keep from dropping the things.

"Now look," he said. She looked. The bone was unchanged; the other could have been any fifty-centavo piece, an unremarkable coin not worth stealing. "Don't spend it," he said lightly. Then, more seriously, "Except for the right things."

When the old man died, after coming to his senses and making a proper confession, Father Patrick Dougherty saw him decently buried and said Mass for him. He would miss their talks; the old man had finally revealed that he had studied history in Cracow and Vilnius, that he had fought "in the forests" of Latvia and Lithuania, which Father Patrick took to mean in irregular forces. He said nothing more about relics.

Under his thin mattress the priest found a flat leather wallet with twenty American dollars. He gave the money to the Widow Rosales. He took the books in the box for himself. He did not find what Xavier took.

Two days after the burial, Xavier slipped away from his home with the worn cloth bundled under his arm and climbed into the back of a truck filling with laborers for the new dam. His father explained that "*mi hijo*" wanted to see the dam for himself. The men chuckled and knuckled his head gently. The truck lurched ahead, bouncing along the spur road that led from the highway to the river. Xavier squeezed himself into the front corner and peered out between the panels. Although they had explained the dam, what he saw made no sense. Open pits, rows of huge pipes big enough to live in, a line of growling concrete mixers with the first already letting its gray load rasp down the ramp into a hole.

"You will know the place," the old man had said. "It is important that this last remnant of our Order be buried safely."

"You will know the place," the *curandera* had said. "The old man was right, and here is a charm that will bind the waters."

So far he had no idea what that meant. Once off the

truck, he was ordered this way and that by foremen who didn't want a small boy anywhere around. "Away from the trucks, boy. Away from those pipes, boy. None of your mischief, boy." His father had disappeared into a swarm of workmen shoveling sand and gravel; his father had warned him to stay out of trouble.

He was hot and thirsty. The old man had told him about that, about being hot and thirsty on the battlefield. About the sting of sweat in a swordcut, about the stench of blood and filth. *If only you were older,* the old man had said, *what a crusader you would make.* Thinking of that, Xavier hitched up his bundle and kept skulking from shade to shade, from cover to cover. The gringo foremen, huge and hulking with their red sunburned faces, were the Infidel; he was a knight on a secret mission for the Order.

He knew the place when he found it. One of a row of deep pits, wood-lined now, waiting for its filling of concrete. No one was near enough to notice. He fished the fifty-cent piece out of his pocket and wondered about the *curandera.* Why would she give money for this burial? Or was it about something else? His fingers lingered on the coin. Fifty centavos. He shook his head. He was a Knight of the Cross, a holy warrior; he had his orders.

Xavier slid the coin into the folded cloth under his arm and very carefully climbed down into the pit, down the rough wood forms, from brace to brace. It was cool and shadowy here, smelling of raw wood, damp gravel, stone. The growling machines seemed far away; in the close stillness he could hear his own breath again. He raked out a little hole in the gravel, laid the cloth and the coin it wrapped into it, and pushed the gravel back over it, Then he climbed out, into the glaring sunlight, the heat, the noise.

He believed in visions as he believed in *susto* and the evil eye and the terrible things the *curandera* kept in her back room. (He had once peeked and seen the eggs rolling in their jar, the dangling bundles of pungent herbs and various feathers.) Now he had no reason to find answers for the figure that wavered in the air above him, the tall warrior on the great horse, the shining white surcoat with a broad red cross on breast and back. And no reason at all to doubt the twinkling flight of something toward his hand, which when he opened it was a silver dollar, American.

As a grown man, he nailed it over his bed, and never wondered whence came his ten strong sons.

And Esperanza put the sliver of bone with her other bones and sang it to sleep.

INTERLUDE SEVEN

A last Templar turning up in Roma, Texas, may seem far-fetched, but as we have seen, speculation about the survival of the Templars, in some form, has been with us since 1314. What if it all *were* true, and the Temple was possessed of some secret knowledge, some potent legacy of mystical power passed through an inner circle of initiates down through the ages, with the mandate to protect the weak, right wrongs, restore what was lost, make whole the broken?

Dion Fortune, a British occultist writing between the two world wars, spoke of the Astral Police, whose agents could be summoned in one's hour of need by visualizing a red cross on a black background. Some have chosen to visualize that cross as a Templar cross. At least one modern author has asserted, perhaps not at all facetiously, that "The Templars are everywhere." The thought is somewhat comforting—that spiritual descendants of the Knights Templar might function as crack special forces operatives on the Astral, continuing to guard certain hallows entrusted to them all those centuries ago. Maybe Wolfram von Eschenbach and others had it right when they portrayed the Grail Knights as Templars.

Stealing God

Debra Doyle and James D. Macdonald

Jwas working the security leak at Rennes-le-Château when the word came down. The Rennes flub was over a hundred years old, but the situation needed constant tending to keep people off the scent. That's the thing about botches. They never go away.

Now I had new orders. Drop whatever I was doing and get my young ass over to New York mosh-gosh. Roger that, color me gone. I was on the Concorde out of Paris before the hole in the air finished closing behind me in Languedoc.

With the Temple paying my way, cost wasn't a worry. I had enough other things to think about. The masters weren't bringing me across the Atlantic just to chew the fat. We had plenty of secure links. Whatever this was, it required my presence.

Sherlock Holmes said that it was a capital mistake to theorize before one had information. My old sergeant, back when I was learning the trade, told me to catch some sleep whenever I could. I dozed my way over the Atlantic and didn't wake up until we hit JFK.

Customs inspection was smooth and uneventful—I had only one piece of carry-on luggage, with nothing in it that the customs people might recognize as a weapon. I took the third cab in the rank outside the terminal and was on my way. First stop was at The Cloisters in Fort Tryon Park, to pay my respects to the Magdalene Chalice. My arrival would be noted there, and the contact would come soon.

Outside the museum I got another cab to Central Park West. I made my way to the Rambles, that part of the park where the city can't be seen and you can almost imagine yourself in the wilderness.

Sure enough, a man was waiting. He wore the signs, the air, and the majesty. I made a quiet obeisance, just to go by the book, and he responded. But I didn't need any of the signals in order to recognize one of the two masters.

There are only three and thirty of us in the inner Temple, plus the masters. We're the part of the Temple that's hidden from all the other Knights Templar: the secret from the holders of the secrets, the ace up the sleeve. All of us warriors, all of us priests. We serve, we obey. When needed, we kick ass.

"Hello," he said. "It's been years."

"Sure has, John," I replied. "What's up?"

We spoke in Latin, for the same reason the Church does. No matter where you are or where you're from, you can communicate.

"There's a problem," he said. "Over on the East Side."

The Grail. It had to be. "Instructions?"

"Go in, check it out, report back."

"Anything special I'm looking for?"

"No," he said. "Just be aware that the last three people who got those same orders haven't reported in yet."

We nodded to each other and parted. I walked south. There are a bunch of hotels along Central Park South, and I wanted to hit the bar in one of them and do some thinking. For Prester John to be away from Chatillon meant that things were more serious than I'd suspected.

I sat in the bar at the Saint Moritz, drinking Laphroaig neat the way God and Scotland made it, while I wondered what in the name of King Anfortas could be going on over at the UN, and how I was going to check. Halfway down the bar another man sat playing with the little puddle of water that had collected around the base of his frosty mug of beer. He was drinking one of those watery American brews with no flavor, no body, and no strength to recommend it, though it had apparently gotten him half plowed regardless. After a minute or two I realized what had drawn my attention: He was tracing designs in the water on the bar.

Designs I recognized. Runes.

Did they think I was blind, I wondered, or so ignorant that I wouldn't notice? But I didn't perceive any immediate danger, and a sudden departure would tip my hand to whoever was watching. Maybe this guy was just a random drunk who happened to know his mystic symbols.

Sure, and maybe random drunks had nailed three other knights.

No, more likely he was a Golden Dawner or a Luciferian. Probably a Luciferian. Lucies have a special relationship with the Grail, or they think they do. I tipped up the last drops of Laphroaig, harsh on my tongue like a slurry of ground glass and peat moss, called for another shot, and drank half of it. The money lying by the shot glass would pay for my drink. I left the bar, left the hotel, turned east, and started walking. Leaving good booze unfinished is a venial sin, but that way it'd look like I'd just stepped over to the men's room and was coming back soon—good for a head start.

Halfway down the block I spotted a convenient bunch of construction barriers. I ducked behind them, and as soon as I was out of sight from the street, my left hand darted into my bag. A couple of seconds to work the charm and I stepped out onto the sidewalk, Tarnkappe fully charged and ready in my hand. My bag remained behind, looking for anyone without True Sight like a rotting sack of garbage.

There are only three Tarnkappen in the world, and I had one of them. Something like that can come in handy in my line of work, and it was about to come in handy again. I walked slowly until I was sure that anyone following me from the Saint Moritz was on my tail. Then I cruised eastward, window-shopping. Windows make great mirrors to show what's behind you—and sure enough, here came my runic friend, Mr. Beer.

I turned a few random corners to make certain he was following, then got into a crowd and slipped on the Kappe. A few seconds later, after a bit of fancy footwork to make sure that my location and method weren't revealed by a trail of people tripping over nothing, I leaned against the side of a building and watched to see what would happen next.

Mr. Beer was confused, all right. He cast up and down the street a bit, but pretty soon he figured out that he'd botched the job. He stepped into a phone booth, then punched in a string and spoke a couple of words. His face was at the wrong angle for lipreading, but I could guess what he was saying: "I lost him."

Maybe I couldn't see what he was saying, but I'd managed to get the number he'd dialed. The whole time he was on the phone, I was on the other side of the street with a small pair of binoculars. He hadn't shielded the button pad with his hand. Half trained—a Lucie, for sure.

I trailed him until he went into a hotel and up to a room. Then I slipped the Kappe into my back pocket and followed that up by slipping a few quick questions to people who didn't even know afterward that they'd been questioned. Before long I knew that Beer's name was Max Lang, that he spoke with a foreign accent, that he'd been there for one week and planned to stay for another, and that he tipped well.

I left him in the hotel. The trail had taken me to the Waldorf-Astoria in midtown. Might as well head over to the United Nations building. It was still early, with lots of light in the sky and lots of people on the sidewalk. I kept my eyes open, but I didn't pick up a tail.

I turned the problem over in my mind. Max Lang couldn't have found his way out of a paper bag if you gave him a map and printed instructions. So how did he find me in the bar? And how did he come to know the Therion rune sequence?

The UN building stands towering over FDR Drive, along the East River. Security there is tight by American standards, which means laughable for anyplace else in the world. Inside the building I knew which way to go, and I had passes that were as good as genuine to get me anywhere I needed.

I stood for a moment just inside the metal detectors at the front doors, feeling with my senses. Was there something wrong in the building? Nothing big enough to show up without a divination, and I doubted that the guards would let me get away with performing one here, even if they weren't bent to the left—and with three knights missing already, only a fool wouldn't assume that the guards were bent. Prester John doesn't use fools. I headed for the Meditation Room.

The Meditation Room was right where I'd left it last time I'd been in town. No obvious problems. I went in. Everything was still in place. There was the mural in the front of the room, with its abstract picture of the sun, half dark, and half light. Cathar symbolism, and Manichean before that. We kept the picture up there to remind the Cathars how wrong they'd been. And there was the Grail—a natural lodestone, cut and polished into a gleaming rectangular block.

Wolfram von Eschenbach let the cat out of the bag when he wrote *Parzival,* back in the twelve hundreds. Somehow he'd gotten the straight word on what the Grail looked like. According to the Luciferians, who claim to know the inside story, the Grail had been the central stone in Lucifer's crown, back before he had a couple of really bad days and got his dumb ass tossed out of Heaven. When Lucifer landed in Hell, they say, the Grail landed on Earth.

What *was* true was that the Grail had banged around the Middle East for quite a while—capstone of the Great Pyramid, cornerstone of the Temple of Solomon, that sort of thing. Back during the Crusades we'd been given the keeping of it. We never could hide the fact that there was a Grail, or that it was holy, but for a long time we tried to get people to go looking for dinnerware. Then someone talked. Somewhere, somehow, there was a leak. And blunders, like I said, never go away.

So far, though, everything looked all peachy-keen and peaceful at the United Nations. The room, the mural, the big chunk of polished rock. I pulled out a little pocket compass. Yep, that was still a lodestone over there.

One more test. I opened the little gold case in my pants pocket and slipped out a consecrated Host. I palmed it, then walked past the Grail on my way out of the room. My hand brushed the polished stone as I went by. Then I was out of the room, heading for the main doors and the street.

I raised my hand to straighten my hair, and as my hand passed my lips, I took the Host. Then I knew there was something really, desperately wrong. No taste of blood.

Hosts bleed when they touch the Holy Grail. Don't ask me how; I'm not enough of a mystic to answer. But I do know why—Godhood in the presence of Itself makes for interesting physical manifestations.

There was a stone back there in the meditation room. But either it wasn't the real Grail, or it wasn't holy anymore.

Whoever did this was far more powerful than I'd imagined. They either had to smuggle a six-and-a-half-ton block of rock into the UN, and smuggle another six-and-a-half-ton block of rock out of there without anyone noticing, or they had to defile something that had never been defiled—not even on Friday the 13th, when some men with real power and knowledge had given it their best shot and come away with nothing but their own sins to show for the effort.

I had to report back. Prester John needed to know about this as soon as possible.

That was when they hit me, just as I stepped out onto the street. I felt a light impact on the side of my neck, like a mosquito. I slapped at it by reflex, but before my hand got there, my knees were already buckling. Two men moved in on either side of me, supporting me. My eyes were open, and I could see and remember, but my arms and legs weren't responding anymore.

"Come on," the man on my right said. "You're going for a little ride."

They walked me across the plaza, three men holding hands. No one looked twice. You see some funny things in New York.

They put me in the back of a limo. Another man was behind the wheel, waiting for them. The door shut and we pulled away from the curb. The guy on my right pushed my head down so I wasn't visible from outside, which meant I couldn't see where they were taking me, either.

We crossed a bridge—I could hear it humming in the tires—then slowed to join other traffic. I pulled inside myself and looked for where the poison was in my body. It was potent, but there couldn't be much of it. I could handle not-much.

With enough concentration some people can slow their heartbeat down to where doctors can't detect it. Other people can slow their breathing to where they can make a coffinful of air last a week. I concentrated on finding all the molecules of poison in my bloodstream and making Maxwell's Demon shunt them off to somewhere harmless.

Little finger of my left hand, say. Let it concentrate there and not get out.

The car was slowing again. Stopping. Too soon. I hadn't gotten all the poison localized yet.

They pulled me out of the backseat. We were on a dock, probably on Long Island. No one else was in sight. I could see now what was going to happen: Into the water, the current carries me away, I'm too weak to swim, I drown. The poison is too dilute, or it breaks down, or it's masked by the by-products of decomposition and the toxicological examination doesn't find it at the autopsy.

They weren't asking any questions. Instead, we went out to the end of the pier, them walking and me being walked. Two of them held me out over the water while the third—the one who'd been the driver—spoke.

"We do not slay thee. Thy blood is not on us. We desire no earthly thing: Go to God with all ye possess. Sink ye or swim ye, thou art nothing more to us."

A roaring sounded in my ears, and I was falling forward. Water, cold and salt, rushed into my nose and mouth.

Human bodies float in salt water. *Concentrate on moving the poison. Give me enough control that I can float on my back* . . . I was sinking. The light was growing dim. I concentrated on lowering my need for oxygen, lowering my heartbeat, lowering everything.

Move the poison. Don't use air. Float.

Then it was working. I could feel strength and control return to my arms and legs. I was deep underwater. I opened my eyes and looked around. I saw shadow and pilings not too far away: the bottom of the pier.

Swim that way—slowly—keep the poison in the left little finger. Don't use air. Then float up.

I didn't dare gasp for breath when I got to the surface. For all I knew, my assailants were still up there waiting. Slowly, quietly, I allowed my lungs to empty, then fill again. I hooked my left arm around the nearest piling, then reached down with my right hand and undid a shoelace. I hoped I wouldn't lose the shoe.

Using the lace, I tied a tourniquet around my left little finger—now the drug couldn't get out—and reached down again to my belt. The buckle hid a small push-dagger, made of carbonite so metal detectors wouldn't pick it up. Don't let the material fool you; it's hard and sharp. I cut the end of my little finger, held the knife between my teeth, and squeezed out the poisoned blood. The blood came out thick and dark, trailing away in the water like a streamer of red. Then I unloosed the tourniquet and it was time to go.

The foot of the pier was set in a cement wall about seven feet high, but the wall was old and crumbling. I got a fingerhold, then a foothold. At last I was out of the water. I crawled up until I was lying on top of the wall, under the decking of the pier. Anyone looking for me would have to be in the water to see me. I stayed there, waiting and listening, for a hundred heartbeats, then two hundred, and heard nothing but waves lapping up against the wall.

A sound. A board creaked on the dock. They'd left someone behind, all right—someone waiting like I was, only not so quietly.

But those cowboys had been a little slack. Either they'd trusted their drug too much, or else it was really important to their ritual that I keep all my possessions. The end result was the same: I hadn't been searched. When I reached a hand down to my pocket, the Tarnkappe was still where I'd stuffed it when I'd gotten done with Max Lang.

A visit to Lang looked like it was in the cards. Later. There were other things to do first.

I put on the Kappe, then crawled out of my hiding place and up onto the shore. There he was, out on the pier: a man in a business suit, carrying a Ruger mini-14 at high port. I sat on the shore, hoping I'd dry out enough so that water drops splashing on the pavement wouldn't give me away. Or chattering teeth—the sun was heading down and it was going to get cold pretty soon for a man in wet clothes.

Whatever those lads had hit me with, it'd left me with the beginning of a king-of-hell headache. I ignored the discomfort and concentrated on the man on the pier. Who was he? I'd never seen him before.

I heard the second man coming before I saw him, tramping heavy-footed down the road to the pier. He walked out and greeted the first. This time I could read their lips: "Time to go . . . there's a meeting . . . yes, we both have to be there . . . forget him, he's gone."

They walked back off the pier and I swung in behind them, letting the sound of their footfalls cover mine.

They had a car parked up the way—not the one that had

brought me here. This one had two bucket seats up in front and nothing behind. They got inside; I got up on the back bumper and leaned forward across the trunk, holding on with arms spread wide. The car pulled away. All I had to do now was stay on board until they got to wherever they were going. That, and hope the Tarnkappe didn't come off at highway speeds.

The first sign we came to told me that I was NOW LEAVING BABYLON, NEW YORK. Babylon. Figures. Nothing happens by chance, not when you have the Grail involved. It all means something. The trick is finding out what.

This pair wasn't real gabby. I'd hoped to do some more lipreading in the rearview mirror, but as far as I could tell they drove back to the Big Apple in stony silence. They took the Midtown Tunnel back in, then local streets to somewhere on the East Side around 70th street. That was where I had my next bit of bad luck.

Out on the highway, the Tarnkappe had stuck on my head like glue. But here in the concrete canyons, a side gust took it away and there I was in plain view on the back deck. All I could do was roll off and scuttle for safety between the rushing cars, while taxis screamed at me and bicycle messengers tried to leave tire stripes up my back.

I made it to the other side of the street. The Tarnkappe was gone, blown who-knows-where by the wind, and I couldn't make myself conspicuous by doubling back to look for it. A quick stroll around the corner, down one subway entrance and up another, and I was as safe as I could hope to be with my shoes squishing seawater.

I started out at a New Yorker's street pace for the spot where I'd ditched my bag. By now the sun was down for real and the neon darkness was coming up: a bad time of day for strangers to go wandering around Central Park. Me, I kind of hoped someone would try for a mugging. I had a foul mood to work off, and smashing someone's face in the name of righteousness would just about do the trick.

Nobody tried anything, and my bag was waiting where I'd left it. I changed clothes right there in the alley, and debated reporting in. But someone had gone to a lot of trouble to make me vanish, and I wanted the secret of my survival to be shared by the minimum number.

Sure, I had my orders. But blind obedience isn't what the Temple needs from the thirty and three. Distasteful as I found the possibility, I had to consider whether I'd been sold out from inside. If so, then reporting in would be a very bad idea.

Maybe those other three knights had figured things out the same way. They could be lying low and saying nothing until the situation clarified. But I didn't think it was likely. Odds were that they were sweating it out in Purgatory right now—like I'd be, if I didn't start taking precautions.

I began by using the kit in my bag to make a few changes to my appearance. No sense having everyone who'd already seen me recognize me the next time I showed up. Meanwhile, it was dinner time, which meant there was a good chance that my Mr. Lang would be away from his room. A search might show me something useful. And when he got back from dinner, I wanted to ask him some questions.

The rooms at his hotel had those new-style keycards with the magnetic strip. Some people think the keycards are secure, and they'll probably stop the teenagers who bought a Teach Yourself Locksmithing course out of the back of a comic book. The one on Lang's room didn't even slow me down.

Lang wasn't out, after all. He was in the room, but I wasn't going to get any answers out of him without a

Ouija board. He was naked, lying on his back in the bathtub. Someone had been there before me—someone with a sharp knife and a sick imagination.

I dipped my finger in the little bottle of chrism I carry in my tote and made a quick cross on his forehead.

"For thy sins I grant thee absolution," I muttered—wherever he'd gone, he needed all the help he could get. Lucies aren't famed for their high salvation rate.

Then I searched the room, even though whoever had taken care of Lang would have done that job once already. Aside from the mess in the bathtub, the contents of the hotel room didn't have much to say about anything, except maybe the banality of evil: no address books; no letters or memos; no telltale impressions on the memo pad. Nothing of any interest at all.

Then I found something, taped to the back of a drawer. My unknown searcher had missed it. Or maybe he'd left it behind, having no use for it—he hadn't used bullets on Lang, only the knife. But there it was, a Colt Commander, a big mean .45 automatic.

I checked it over. Five rounds in the magazine, one up the spout. Weapon cocked, safety off. I lowered the hammer to half-cock and took the Colt with me, stuffing it in my waistband in the back, under the sport coat I was wearing. That lump of cold metal made me feel a lot better about the rest of the evening.

One more thing to do: I picked up the room phone, got an outside line, and punched in the number Lang had called that afternoon. After two rings, someone picked it up.

"International Research," said a female voice.

"This is Max," I said, my voice as muffled as I could make it. "I'm in trouble."

Then I hung up.

Before I left the room, I opened the curtains all the way.

Then I eased myself out of the hotel and over to a vantage point across the street, where a water tower on a lower building gave me a view of the room I'd just left. The bad guys who'd tried to drown me hadn't taken my pocket binoculars, either. Those were good optics—when I used the binocs to look across the street, it was like I was standing in the hotel room.

I waited. The wind was cold, and a little after one in the morning it started to rain. It was just past 4 A.M., at that hour before dawn when sick men die, when I spotted something happening.

Across the street the door eased open, then drifted shut. A woman walked into the room. She was tall, slender, and stacked. Black lace-up boots, tight black jeans, tight black sweater. Single strand of pearls. Red hair, long enough to sit on, loose down her back. A black raincoat hung over her right arm. She was wearing black leather gloves. In her left hand she had a H&K nine-millimeter. Color coordinated: The artillery was black, too.

She did a walk-through of the room. Nothing hurried. I watched her long enough that I could recognize her again, and then I was sliding down from my perch. The lady had carried a raincoat. If she planned to go out into the weather, I was going to find out where she was headed. My guess was that she was from International Research, whoever they really were.

I was betting that she'd come out the main door. So I did a slow walk up and down the street, one sidewalk and then the other, before I spotted her through the glass in the lobby, putting on that coat. Then she was out the revolving door and away.

One nice thing about New York is that it's possible to follow someone on foot. The car situation is so crazy that no one brings a private vehicle onto the island if they can help it. She might still call a cab, but if she did, so could I.

I've never yet in my career told a cabbie to "Follow that car," but there's a first time for everything.

I wasn't going to get the chance tonight. A limo was cruising up the street at walking speed, coming up behind the lady in black. I recognized it. The boys who'd grabbed me yesterday had used that car or one just like it to carry me out to Babylon for sacrifice.

The car stopped and the two clowns in the back got out. They looked like the same pair of devout souls who'd invited me to a total-immersion baptism. It was time for me to join the fun. I angled across the rain-soaked street, pulling that big-ass Colt into my hand as I went.

The two goons had caught up with the lady, but she wasn't going as quietly as I had the day before. Maybe they'd missed with their drugged dart—she was muffled to the nose in her raincoat, with the collar turned up. Or maybe they wanted her talkative when they got wherever they were going. No matter. They were distracted, and the driver was watching the show.

I came up beside the window out of his blind spot. Using the .45 as a pair of knucks, I punched right through the glass into the back of his head. Then I pulled the door open and him out with it, spilling him onto his back in the street. I kicked him once on the point of the chin while he lay there.

"For these and all thy sins I absolve thee," I muttered, making a cross over him with the Colt.

The whole thing hadn't taken more than a couple of seconds, and now it was time to go help the lady. Generally speaking I'm not the kind of knight who goes around rescuing damsels in distress—but I wanted to talk with this one, and keeping her alive was the only way to go.

I used the roof of the car as a vaulting horse and landed feet first on top of one of the goons, bringing him down with me in a tangle of arms and legs. It took me a second to extricate myself, with elbows, knees, and the heavy automatic smashing into my man along the way. He got in a couple of good licks, then gave up all interest and started holding what was left of his nuts.

Meanwhile the lady in black was doing the best she could. But her little nine-millimeter was caught under the raincoat, and the man who had her was too strong. He'd thrown an arm around her neck in the classic choke come-along and was dragging her into the backseat. Maybe he hadn't noticed that the driver wasn't there anymore.

I took him in the back of the skull with the butt of the Colt Commander. He slipped to the ground to join his moaning pal.

"Come on!" I yelled at the lady. "Let's get out of here!"

"Where to?" she gasped.

"Into the car."

I slid behind the wheel—the keys were still in the ignition and the engine was turning over—and slammed the driver's-side door. The lady didn't argue. She got in beside me and closed the other door, and I took off from the curb.

I made a left turn across traffic into a side street, and said, "Where to, sister?"

"Who are you?"

Rather than give her an answer, I said, "The cops are gonna be all over this block in a couple of minutes—I saw the doorman go running inside like a man with 911 on his mind. You got a safe place to go?"

She gave an address down in SoHo. I drove to the address, ditched the car, and went with her up to an apartment: third floor of a brownstone, three rooms and a kitchen. I hoped she was in a rent-controlled building, or this place would be costing her a pretty.

The apartment was almost empty: nothing but a coffeemaker in the kitchen, a couple of sofas, and a bed, all visible from right inside the front door.

"Take a seat," she said. "I'll make coffee."

She stripped off her coat and turned to hang it on a peg by the door. When she turned back, the little nine-millimeter was pointing right between my eyes. I'd stuffed the .45 into my waistband in back again, to keep her from getting nervous. Her get nervous? That was a laugh.

"You've missed three recognition signals," she said. "You aren't from Section. So how's about you tell me who you are?"

"People call me Crossman," I said. "Peter Crossman."

"Is that your real name?"

"No, but it'll do. I'm the connection for midtown. You want coke, you call me."

"Your kind isn't known for making citizen arrests," she said. The muzzle of the nine-millimeter never wavered, even though from the way her chest was going up and down she had to be nervous about something. "What did you think you were up to tonight?"

"Someone who doesn't work for me using muscle in my territory, that interests me. Let one bunch get away with it, pretty soon it's all over town that Crossman's gone soft, and they're all trying to move in. Can't let that happen."

"So—" she started, but never finished. A knock sounded on the door.

"Maggie," came a voice from outside. "Maggie, I know you're in there. Open up."

She made the little pistol vanish. "Come on in—it isn't locked."

The door swung open, and I got a sinking feeling in my guts. The Mutt and Jeff act waiting on the landing were the same pair who'd given me the ride back to town the day before. The watchers from the dock in Babylon. I didn't think they recognized me—the Tarnkappe had kept me invisible at first, and then I'd changed my face. I was glad now that I'd taken the precaution.

They came in. They were wrapped in dripping raincoats—no way of telling what kind of firepower they were carrying underneath, but it would take 'em a while to pull anything clear. The first guy, the short one, nodded over at me. "Who's the meat?"

"A guy named Crossman," Maggie said. "He's some kind of drug lord. Showed up tonight and pulled my buns out of a bad situation while you two were sucking down cold ones in some bar."

"Get rid of him," the second guy said.

"No, I think I want him to stay." She looked at me. "You do want to stay, don't you? I'll let you buy me a drink after all this is over."

"Yeah," I said. "I want to stay."

That was the truth. This whole affair was getting more interesting by the minute. And as for buying that drink—I couldn't help wondering what sort of temptation she had in mind for me to resist.

She started to say something else, and that was when the door to the apartment flew open again. This time it was the two guys from the street—the ones who had tried to stuff Maggie into their car, the same ones who'd grabbed me outside the UN. One of them was carrying a Remington Model 870. The other was lugging a Stoner. They both looked pissed off.

They didn't bother with the formalities.

"One of you bastards," the guy with the Stoner said, "knows something we want to know. So we aren't going to kill you now. But we have other ways of finding out, so don't think we'll hesitate to shoot you if we have to. So. Who's going to tell me: Where's the Holy Grail?"

"It's in Logres, asshole," said Maggie's shorter guy.

The new arrival with the riot gun butt-stroked him across the room. He went down hard.

"I sure hope he wasn't the only guy who knew," Remington said, "or the rest of you are going to have a really rough time. Who wants to give us a serious answer?"

Maggie was standing beside and a little behind me. I felt something soft and warm pressing into my hand while everyone else was looking at the guy on the floor. It felt like a leather bag with marbles inside. I took it and made it vanish into my front pants pocket.

Stoner looked at me—maybe he'd seen me move. "Don't I know you from somewhere?"

I shook my head a fraction of an inch one way and then the other. "I don't think so."

I wasn't as scared as I hoped I looked, but things weren't shaping up too good. The new guys hadn't disarmed anyone yet, and neither weapon was pointing right at me, but with my piece tucked into my waistband in back, I wouldn't have put a lot of money on getting it clear before they could turn me into Swiss cheese with ketchup. Besides, I wanted these gents alive. Someone knew where the Grail was, and all of these jokers looked like they knew more than I did.

"Lay off," Maggie said. "This one's your basic crook I picked up. You don't want him, you want me."

Whatever they were after, odds were it was in that little sack—at least Maggie thought it was. But I knew better. You don't carry a six-point-five-ton block of lodestone around in a leather drawstring bag.

"Yeah, sister, we want you," Remington said. "What were you doing at the Waldorf tonight?"

"Visiting a friend. Got a problem with that?" She'd drifted a little away from me. Maybe no one remembered she'd ever gotten close.

"Do you have it?"

"No. It isn't here."

Even the guys with the long guns were treating Maggie with respect—she must rate in someone's organization, I thought. Meanwhile, she was getting close to the light switch. I kept watch out of the corner of my eye, ready to make my move when she made hers.

"Where is it?" Remington said again.

She drifted another step sideways. "Do you know the stoneyard for St. John the Divine?"

Then her elbow smashed backward against the switch and the lights went out. I leaped over the sofa in a flat dive, rolled, and came up crouching in the corner near the window, with my back to the wall and the .45 in a two-hand grip in front of me.

I heard a nine-millimeter go popping off where Maggie had been standing, and an answering roar from the Remington—both of them laid over the stitching sound of the Stoner firing full auto.

That about did it for my ears. Too much gunfire and you're hearing bells ring an hour later. Of course, now the bad guys couldn't hear me, either. But my eyes were adjusting to the dark, and anyone standing up in front of the windows would be silhouetted against the skyglow.

I started duckwalking in the direction of the door, keeping my head low. My foot hit something hard. I reached down with my right hand, my left holding the .45 steady in front of me. It was the Stoner. The barrel was warm, which was more than you could say about the hand that held it. No pulse in the radial artery. I mouthed an absolution and continued moving along the wall.

Over by the window, another shadow was moving—a male, standing, with the distinctive shape of a pump-action in his hands. The weapon was swinging in slow arcs across the room. It stopped—he'd seen something. He started raising the shotgun to his shoulder.

I drew a careful bead on him. "Go in peace to love and serve the Lord," I muttered, and pulled the trigger.

Then I was rolling away, because a scattergun like the Remington doesn't need much aiming. But I needn't have worried—I saw his shadow drop in that boneless way people get when they're shot. A .45 yields a 98 percent one-shot kill rate. If I hit him . . . well, I don't miss often.

I fetched up against someone very soft and very warm—Maggie, waiting in the shadows by the other corner. She reached up and flipped the lights back on.

I stood flattened against the wall and looked around. Stoner and Remington had both bought their parts of the farm. Maggie's two prettyboys were hugging the carpet and playing possum—at least they'd been smart enough not to be targets.

The tall one got to his feet.

"You found it?" he said to Maggie. "Come on, let's get over there."

"It isn't so far," Maggie said. "In fact it's—"

"Shut up," I said. "These two jokers aren't on your team."

"What do you mean?"

She was bringing the nine-mike-mike to bear on me. I pointed my own weapon at the floor, so she wouldn't get the wrong idea and make a hasty move, and nodded at the pair of corpses.

"How do you think the Bobbsey Twins over there found this place?" I asked. "They sure didn't follow us. I bet these two guys brought 'em along, and were going to play good cop/bad cop with us."

"But—" Maggie began.

"He's right, you know," the shorter one said. He produced an Uzi and brought it up to cover us. "Put down your weapons."

There comes a time when you know you've lost. I

dropped my piece. Maggie did the same. The guy with the Uzi nodded at his buddy.

"Fred, pick them up."

The tall one—Fred, I guess his name was—stepped forward and bent over to pick up the handguns.

Shorty was still talking to Maggie. "The Grail isn't at St. John the Divine. We already checked. So I'm afraid I'll have to search you—several times, in a variety of positions. Unless you tell me where the Grail is right now. The truth and no tricks."

Maggie shook her head. "I don't think so."

"A pity," said Shorty. "You'll still be a Bride of Christ—you just won't be a virgin Bride of Christ—and you'll wind up telling me anyway."

"I don't know where it is," Maggie said.

"Then all my work will be for nothing," Shorty said, but he was grinning as he said it.

"Please," I said, trying to make my voice sound like I was scared witless. "I don't know what any of this is about. Please let me go—"

"Shut him up," Shorty said.

At least I'd gotten his eyes on me instead of Maggie. And Fred was coming up, his pistol in one hand, mine in the other. That's when I kicked him, a reaping circular kick, taking him in the throat. It raised him to his feet and set him stumbling backward.

Shorty fired—but someone should have taught him how to shoot. His round missed me, thought I could feel the wind of it past my cheek and the answering spatter of plaster from the wall. I dove forward, spearing Fred in the belly with my head. Shorty's second shot took his partner between the shoulder blades as Fred was driven backward into him.

Then all three of us went down, and a moment later it

was over. I rolled onto my back. Maggie was standing over me.

"You've been hit."

"I don't think so." But when I looked down at myself, sure enough there was blood pouring out, soaking the pocket where I'd put her bag—and where I kept my supply of Hosts. The Hosts were bleeding.

At that moment I knew. And looking into her eyes, I could tell she knew, too.

"It really was the Grail," she said.

"Looks like. Let's get out of here before the cops show up."

"Where to?"

"I'll introduce you to a man," I said. "You'll like him."

We left. The first police car arrived, lights flashing, when we were halfway down the block.

As dawn was breaking over a soggy New York morning, I was in the Rambles again. Prester John was waiting.

"Here it is," I said, tossing the sack to him. He opened the bag and rolled out the gemstones inside it.

"Yes," he said. "The substance is here, though the accidents have changed." The accidents. I should have thought of that back at the UN, when the Host that touched the meditation stone didn't bleed. A wafer, when it's transubstantiated, still has the outward appearance—the accidents—of a flat bit of unleavened bread, while its substance is the body of Christ. In the same way, the Grail's substance—whatever it is that makes it truly the Grail—now had the accidents of a handful of precious stones.

John looked back up at me, his hand clenching around the Grail. "Who's your friend?"

"Sister Mary Magdalene," she said. "From the Special Action Executive of the Poor Clares. I presume you're with the Temple?"

Prester John inclined his head.

"Pleased to meet you," she said. "We'd heard that there was some hanky-panky going on, especially when the Cathar Liberation Army started moving people into town."

"I can fill in the rest," I said. "Maggie's group was infiltrated by the Cathars, just before they got sold out themselves by the Luciferians. That's where Max Lang fits in. The Lucies had been contracted to grab the Grail because they were the only ones besides us who could handle it. Lang carried a bag of jewels in—swapped the substance of the jewels into the lodestone and the substance of the Grail into the jewels—and walked out. That gave them the Grail, but once the Lucies had it, they didn't want to turn it over, at least not to the Cathars. You remember what kind of mess there was last time *they* owned it."

"As if you can speak of anyone owning the Grail," Prester John said. "You're right: Lang must have transubstantiated the Grail into this little sack of jewels, and left the stone in the Meditation Room transubstantiated into a hunk of rock."

It all made sense. It also explained how the Lucies had smuggled six and a half tons of lodestone into and out of the UN—they hadn't. Nobody had carried anything through security that was bigger and heavier than a bag of marbles.

Prester John was shaking his head thoughtfully. "I wonder what made them think they could get away with it?"

"Maybe there's some truth to those stories about Lucifer's crown," I said. "The Lucies sure think so. And the Cathars knew they'd never get close working on their own, so they hired the Luciferians to do the dirty work for them. Then Lang got cold feet. Maybe he saw a vision or something. It's been known to happen. He was working up his nerve to return the Grail when he got hit."

"Lang had swallowed the stones," Maggie said. "I got 'em back. We'd been running electronic intelligence ops on the Lucies for a while. We intercepted one call yesterday afternoon that alerted us, and another call last evening from the hotel. That's when I got sent in. He was messed up enough when I got there that nobody's going to notice a few cuts more."

"Who was it who nailed him?" Prester John said.

"The Cathars," I said. "They'd figured out by then that he was trying to double-cross them."

"Any thoughts on how to get the Grail back to its rightful shape and rightful place?" John said. "We'll have to set new wards, too, so this won't happen again."

"That's your problem," I said. "Maybe you could hire the Lucies yourself. Me, I've got a social engagement. I promised Maggie a drink and I'm going to find her one."

"Hang on," Prester John said. "You're a priest. She's a nun. You can't go on a date."

"Don't worry," I said. "I won't get into the habit."

INTERLUDE EIGHT

It becomes clear, as we explore the maybes and what-ifs of speculation about the Templars, that their legend speaks to some deep-seated part of many people, who will not let the legend die. Even those who have little admiration for the Templars—and in many ways, they were as violent and brutish as any other fighting men of their time—will concede that the Order got a raw deal.

But perhaps that, too, was part of some vast cosmic plan. It is just possible that if the history of the Order of the Temple had not unfolded as we know it did, in our received history, we might be living in an altogether different world. Our knowledge of the nature of time is still in its infancy; but if time should prove fluid and mutable, then we must all hope that Time Lords do or will exist, performing policing tasks of a very special sort: to make certain that crucial aspects of our past are not changed, so that all our yesterdays will unfold into our desired tomorrows. . . .

Poul Anderson writes of the Time Lords thus:

"What is truth? said jesting Pilate, and would
not stay for an answer." What is real, what is
might-be or might-have-been? The quantum
universe flickers to and fro on the edge of the
knowable. There is no way to foretell the destiny of a single particle; and in a chaotic world,
larger destinies may turn on it. St. Thomas
Aquinas declared that God Himself cannot
change the past, because to hold otherwise
would be a contradiction in terms; but St.
Thomas was limited to the logic of Aristotle. Go
into that past, and you are as free as ever you
have been in your own day, free to create or destroy, guide or misguide, stride or stumble. If
thereby you change the course of events that
was in the history you learned, you will abide
untouched, but the future that brought you into
being will have gone, will never have been; it
will be a reality different from what you remember. Perhaps the difference will be slight, even
insignificant. Perhaps it will be monstrous.
Those humans who first mastered the means of
traveling through time created this danger.
Therefore the superhumans who dwell in the
ages beyond them returned to their era to ordain
and establish the Time Patrol.

Death and the Knight

Poul Anderson

Paris, Tuesday, 10 October 1307

Clouds raced low, the hue of iron, on a wind that boomed through the streets and whined in the galleries overhanging them. Dust whirled aloft. Though the chill lessened stenches—offal, horse droppings, privies, graves, smoke ripped ragged out of flues— the city din seemed louder than erstwhile: footfalls, hoofbeats, wheels creaking, hammers thudding, voices raised in chatter, anger, plea, pitch, song, sometimes prayer. Folk surged on their manifold ways, a housewife bound for market, an artisan bound for a task, a priest bound for a deathbed, a mountebank in his shabby finery, a blind beggar, a merchant escorted by two apprentices, a drunken man-at-arms, a begowned student from the university, a wondering visitor from foreign parts, a carter driving his load through the crowd with whip and oaths, others and others and others in their hundreds. Church bells had lately rung tierce and the work of the day was fully acourse.

All made way for Hugues Marot. That was less because

of his height, towering over most men, than his garb. Tunic, hose, and shoes were of good stuff, severe cut, subdued color, and the mantle over them was plain brown; but upon it stood the red cross that signed him a Templar. Likewise did the short black hair and rough beard. Whether or no the rumors were true that the Order was in disfavor with the king, one did not wish to offend such a power. The grimness on his lean features gave urgency to deference. At his heels trotted the boy who had brought his summons to him.

They kept close to the housefronts, avoiding as much as possible the muck in the middle of the street. Presently they came to a building somewhat bigger than its similar and substantial neighbors. Beyond its stableyard, now vacant and with the gate shut, was an oaken door set in half-timbered walls that rose three stories. This had been the home and business place of a well-to-do draper. He fell in debt to the Templars, who seized the property. It was some distance from the Paris Temple, but upon occasion could accommodate a high-born visitor or a confidential meeting.

Hugues stopped at the front door and struck it with his knuckles. A panel slid back from an opening. Someone peered through, then slowly the door swung aside. Two men gave him salutation as befitted his rank. Their faces and stances were taut, and halberds lifted in their fists— not ceremonial, but working weapons. Hugues stared.

"Do you await attack already, brothers, that you go armed indoors?" he asked.

"It is by command of the Knight Companion Fulk," replied the larger. His tone rasped.

Hugues glanced from side to side. As if to forestall any retreat, the second man added, "We are to bring you to him straightway, brother. Pray come." To the messenger: "Back to your quarters, you." The lad sped off.

Flanked by the warrior monks, Hugues entered a vestibule from which a stairway ascended. A door on his right, to the stableyard, was barred. A door on his left stood open on a flagged space filling most of the ground floor. Formerly used for work, sales, and storage, this echoed empty around wooden pillars supporting the ceiling beams. The stair went up over an equally deserted strongroom. The men climbed to the second story, where were the rooms meant for family and guests; underlings slept in the attic. Hugues was ushered to the parlor. It was still darkly wainscoted and richly furnished. A charcoal brazier made the air warm and close.

Fulk de Buchy stood waiting. He was tall, only two inches less than Hugues, hooknosed, grizzled, but as yet lithe and possessing most of his teeth. His mantle was white, as befitted a celibate knight bound by lifelong vows. At his hip hung a sword.

Hugues stopped. "In God's name . . . greeting," he faltered.

Fulk signed to his men, who took positions outside in the corridor, and beckoned. Hughes trod closer.

"In what may I serve you, Master?" he asked. Formality could be a fragile armor. The word conveyed by the boy had been just that he come at once and discreetly.

Fulk sighed. After their years together, Hugues knew that seldom-heard sound. An inward sadness had whispered past the stern mask.

"We may speak freely," Fulk said. "These are trusty men, who will keep silence. I have dismissed everyone else."

"Could we not always speak our minds, you and I?" Hugues blurted.

"Of late, I wonder," Fulk answered. "But we shall see." After a moment: "At last, we shall see."

Hugues clenched his fists, forced them open again, and

said as levelly as he was able, "Never did I lie to you. I looked on you as not only my superior, not only my brother in the Order, but my—" His voice broke. "My friend," he finished.

The knight bit his lip. Blood trickled forth into the beard.

"Why else would I warn you of danger afoot?" Hugues pleaded. "I could have departed and saved myself. But I warn you anew, Fulk, and beg you to escape while time remains. In less than three days now, the ax falls."

"You were not so exact before," the other man said without tone.

"The hour was not so nigh. And I hoped—"

Fulk's hand chopped the protest short. "Have done!" he cried.

Hugues stiffened. Fulk began pacing, back and forth, like one in a cage. He bit off his words, each by each.

"Yes, you claimed a certain foresight, and what you said came to pass. Minor though those things were, they impressed me enough that when you hinted at a terrible morrow, I passed it on in a letter to my kinsman—after all, we know charges are being raised against us. But you were never clear about how you got your power. Only in these past few days, thinking, have I seen how obscure was your talk of Moorish astrologic lore and prophetic dreams." He halted, confronting his suspect, and flung, "The Devil can say truth when it fits his purposes. Whence comes your knowledge, you who call yourself Hugues Marot?"

The younger man made the sign of the cross. "Lawful, Christian—"

"Then why did you not tell me more, tell me fully what to await, that I might go to the Grand Master and all our brothers have time to make ready?"

Hugues lifted his hands to his face. "I could not. Oh,

Fulk, dear friend, I cannot, even now. My tongue is locked. What I—I could utter—that little was forbidden— But you *know* me!"

Starkness responded. "I know you would have me flee, saying naught to anyone. At what peril to my soul, that I break every pledge I ever swore and abandon my brethren in Christ?" Fulk drew breath. "No, brother, if brother you be, no. I have arranged that you are under my command for the next several days. You shall remain here, sequestered, secret from all but myself and these your warders. Then, if indeed the king strikes at us, I can perhaps give you over to the Inquisition—a sorcerer, a fountainhead of evil, whom the Knights of the Temple have discovered among themselves and cast from them—"

The breath sobbed. Pain stretched the face out of shape. "But meanwhile, Hugues, I will hourly pray, with great vows, pray that you prove innocent—merely mistaken, and innocent of all save love. And can you then forgive me?"

He stood for a moment. When he spoke again, the words tolled. "It is for the Order, which we have plighted our loyalty under God. Raoul, Jehan, take him away."

Tears glistened on Hugues' cheekbones. The guards entered. He had no weapon but a knife. With a convulsive movement, he drew it and offered it hilt foremost to Fulk. The knight kept his hands back and it dropped on the floor. Mute, Hugues went off between the men. As he walked, he gripped a small crucifix that hung about his neck, symbol and source of help from beyond this world.

San Francisco, Thursday, 8 March 1990

Manse Everard returned to Wanda Tamberly near sunset. Light streamed through the Golden Gate. From their suite they saw cable cars go clanging down toward the waterfront, islands and the farther shore rising steep from a silver-blue bay, sails like wings of some wandering flock. They had hoped to be out there themselves.

When he came in, she read his battered face and said quietly, "You're on a new mission, aren't you?"

He nodded. "It was pretty clear that was what HQ had in mind when Nick phoned."

She could not keep all resentment out of her voice. Their time together had been less than two months. "They never leave you alone, do they? How many other Unattached agents has the Patrol got, anyway?"

"Nowhere near enough. I didn't have to accept, you know. But after studying the report, I did have to agree I'm probably the best man available for this job." That was what had kept him since morning. The report was the equivalent of a library, most of it not text or audiovisual but direct brain input—history, language, law, customs, dangers.

"Ol' noblesse oblige." Wanda sighed. She met him, laid her cheek on his breast, pressed close against the big body. "Well, it was bound to happen sooner or later. Get it done and pop back to the same hour you tell me goodbye, you hear?"

He grinned. "My idea exactly." He stroked the blond hair. "But look, I don't have to leave right away. I would like to get it behind me"—on his intricately looping world line—"but let's first make whoopee from now through tomorrow night."

"Best offer I've had all day." She raised her lips toward his and for a while the only sound in the room was murmurs.

Stepping back at last, she said, "Hey, that was fine, but before we get down to serious business, suppose you explain what the hell your assignment is." Her voice did not sound altogether steady.

"Sure," he answered. "Over beer?" When she nodded, he fetched two Sierra Nevada Pale. She settled down on the couch with hers. Restless, he kept his feet and loaded his pipe.

"Paris, early fourteenth century," he began. "A field scientist, Hugh Marlow by name, has gotten himself in deep yogurt and we need to haul him out." Speaking English rather than Temporal, he perforce used tenses and moods ill-suited to chronokinetics. "I've had medieval European experience." She shivered slightly. They had shared a part of it. "Also, he's my contemporary by birth—not American: British, but a twentieth-century Western man who must think pretty much like me. That might help a bit." A few generations can make aliens of ancestor and descendant.

"What kind of trouble?" she asked.

"He was studying the Templars, there in France where they were centered at the time, thought they had chapters all over. You remember who they were?"

"Just vaguely, I'm afraid."

Everard struck fire to tobacco, drank smoke, and followed it with ale. "One of the military religious orders founded during the Crusades. After those failed, the Templars continued to be a power, almost sovereign, in fact. Besides war, they went in for banking, and ended up mainly doing that. The outfit got hog-rich. Apparently, though, most of its members stayed pretty austere, and many remained soldiers or sailors. They made themselves unpopular, being a hard and overbearing lot even by the standards of that era, but they seem to have been essentially innocent of the charges that were finally brought against them. You see, among other things King Philip the Fair wanted their treasury. He'd wrung all the gold he could out of the Jews and Lombards, and his ambitions were huge. The Pope, Clement V, was his creature and would back him up. On October thirteenth, 1307, every Templar in France who didn't manage a getaway was arrested in a set of very well-organized surprise raids. The accusations included idolatry, blasphemy, sodomy, you name it. Torture produced the confessions the king wanted. What followed is a long and complicated story. The upshot was that the Templar organization was destroyed and a number of its members, including Grand Master Jacques de Molay, were burned at the stake."

Wanda grimaced. "Poor bastards. Why'd anybody want to research them?"

"Well, they were important." Everard left unspoken that the Time Patrol required full and accurate information on the ages it guarded. She knew. Oh, but she knew! "They did keep certain of their rites and gatherings secret, for more than a century—quite a feat, huh? Of course, in the end that proved helpful to getting them railroaded.

"But what really went on? The chronicles don't say anything reliable. It'd be interesting to know, and the data might be significant. For instance, could surviving Templars, scattered across Europe, North Africa, and the Near East, have influenced, underground, the development of Christian heresies and Muslim sects? Quite a few of them joined the Moors."

Everard puffed for a minute and admired Wanda's head, bright against the deepening sky, before he proceeded.

"Marlow established an identity and enlisted in the Order. He spent a dozen years working his way up in it, till he became a close companion of a ranking knight and was let into the secrets. Then, on the eve of Philip's hit, that knight seized him and confined him incommunicado in a house. Marlow'd talked too much."

"What?" she wondered, puzzled. "He was—is—conditioned, isn't he?"

"Sure. Incapable of telling any unauthorized person he's from the future. But you have to give operatives plenty of leeway, let 'em use their own judgment as situations arise, and—" Everard shrugged. "Marlow's a scientist, an academic type, not a cop. Softhearted, maybe."

"Still, he'd have to be tough and smart to survive in that filthy period, wouldn't he?" she said.

"Uh-huh. I'll be downright eager to quiz him and learn what beans he did spill, and how." Everard paused. "To be quite fair, he did have to show a bit of occult power—forecasting events now and then, that kind of thing, if he was to advance within the Templars in anything like a reasonable time. Similar claims were common throughout the Middle Ages, and winked at if a blueblood thought they were genuine and useful to him. Marlow had permission to do it. Probably he overdid it.

"Anyhow, he got this knight, one Fulk de Buchy, believing that disaster with the king and the Inquisition was imminent. The conditioning wouldn't let him go into detail, and my guess is that Fulk realized it'd take impossibly long to get the ear of the Grand Master and convince him, if it could be done at all. However that is, what happened was that Fulk nabbed Marlow, with the idea of turning him over to the authorities as a sorcerer if the dire prediction came true. He could hope it'd count in the Templars' favor, show they actually were good Christians and so on."

"Hmm." Wanda frowned. "How does the Patrol know this?"

"Why, naturally, Marlow has a miniature radiophone in a crucifix he always carries. Nobody would take that away from him. Once he was locked up alone, he called the milieu base and told them his problem."

"Sorry. I'm being stupid."

"Nonsense." Everard strode across to lay a hand on her shoulder. She smiled at him. "You're simply not accustomed to the devious ways of the Patrol, even after the experiences you've had."

Her smile vanished. "I hope this operation of yours will be . . . devious, not dangerous," she said slowly.

"Aw, now, don't worry. You don't get paid for it. All I have to do is snatch Marlow out of his room."

"Then why do they want *you* to do it?" she challenged. "Any officer could hop a timecycle into there, take him aboard, and hop back out."

"Um-m, the situation is a bit delicate."

"How?"

Everard sought his drink again and paced as he talked. "That's a critical point in a critical timespan. Philip isn't simply wrecking the Templars, he's undermining his feudal lords, drawing more and more power to himself. The Church, too. I said he has Pope Clement in his pocket. The Babylonian Captivity of the Popes in Avignon begins during Philip's reign. They'll return to Rome eventually, but they'll never be the same. In other words, what's in embryo there is the modern, almighty state, Louis XIV, Napoleon, Stalin, IRS." Everard considered. "I don't say that aborting it might not be a nice idea in principle, but it's part of our history, the one the Patrol is here to preserve."

"I see," Wanda replied low. "This calls for a top-notch operator. All kinds of hysteria about the Templars, fanned by the king's party. Any incident that looked like sorcery in action—or divine intervention, for that matter, I suppose—it could make the whole scene explode. With unforeseeable consequences to later events. We can't afford to blunder."

"Yeah. You are a smart girl. At the same time, you understand, we've got to rescue Marlow. He's one of ours. Besides, if he gets questioned under torture . . . he can't admit to the fact of time travel, but what the Inquisition can wring out of him could lead it to our other agents. They'd skip, sure, but that would be the end of our presence in Philip's France. And it is, I repeat, a milieu we need to keep a close eye on."

"We did remain there, though. Didn't we?"

"Yes. In our history. That doesn't mean we inevitably did. I have to make certain."

Wanda shuddered. Then she rose, went to him, took his pipe from him and laid it in an ashtray, caught both his hands in hers, and said almost calmly, "You'll come home safe and successful, Manse. I know you."

She did not know that he would. The hazards of paradox and the wounds to the soul would be overmuch, did Time Patrol people go back to visit their beloved dead or forward to see what was to become of their beloved living.

Harfleur, Wednesday, 11 October 1307

The chief seaport of northwestern France was a logical site for operations headquarters. Where men and cargoes arrived from many different lands and internationally ranging bargains were struck, occasional strange features, manners, or doings drew relatively scant attention. Inland, all except criminals lived in a tightly pulled net of regulations, duties, social standing, tax collection, expectations of how to act and speak and think—"sort of like late twentieth century USA," Everard grumbled to himself. It made discretion difficult, often precarious.

Not that it was ever easy, even in Harfleur. Since first Boniface Reynaud came here from his birthtime nine hundred years futureward, he had spent two decades creating the career of Reinault Bodel, who worked his way from youthful obscurity to the status of a respectable dealer in wool. He did it so well that nobody wondered much about a dockside shed that he kept locked. Suffice it that he had freely shown the proper officials it was empty; if it stood idle, that was his affair, and indeed he talked about someday expanding his business. Nor did anybody grow unduly suspicious of the outsiders who came and went, conferring alone with him. He had chosen his servants, laborers, apprentices, and wife most carefully. To his children he was a kindly father, as medieval fathers went.

Everard's timecycle appeared in the secret space about 9 A.M. He let himself out with a Patrol key and walked to the merchant's place. Big in his own era, gigantic in this, he left a wake of stares. However, his rough garb suggested he was a mariner, likeliest English, not one to mess with. He had sent a dispatch capsule ahead and was admitted immediately to Maistre Bodel's upstairs parlor. Its door closed behind him.

In one corner were a high stool and a table cluttered with things pertaining to business and religion or personal items—ledgers, quills, an inkwell, assorted knives, a fanciful map, a small image of the Virgin, on and on. Otherwise the chamber was rather stately. A single window admitted sufficient light but no real view of the outside, for the glass in the cames, although reasonably clear, was blurringly wavy. It was noise that seeped through, Asianlike clamor of the street below, mumble and bustle of work within, once bell-thunder from the cathedral nearby. Smells were of wool, smoke, bodies and clothes not washed very often. Yet, beneath everything, Everard had a sense of crackling energy. Harfleur—Hareflot, they still called it, as had its Norman founders—was a rookery of

merchant adventurers. From harbors like this, a few life-
times hence, men would set sail for the New World.

He took a chair across the table from Reynaud's. They
had backs, armrests, and cushions, an unusual luxury.
After a few hasty courtesies, he snapped in Temporal,
"What can you tell me about Marlow and his situation?"

"When last he called, the situation appeared unchanged," replied the portly man in the fur-timmed robe.
"He is confined to the strongroom. It has a pallet for him
to sleep on. His guards bring him food and water twice a
day, and at such times a boy empties his chamber pot for
him. They speak to him no more than is barely necessary.
I think my message described the neighbors as being wary
of the Templars and therefore leaving them strictly alone."

"M-hm. But what about Marlow? Has he told you how
much information he let slip, and in what style he did it?"

"That is our main concern, of course. Correct?" Reynaud rubbed his chin. Everard heard the bristles scratching; contemporary razors didn't shave smooth. "He dares
not speak to us at length or often. A listener at the door
could too easily realize that he isn't actually at prayer, and
so may be talking to a familiar spirit or casting a spell or
the like. From what he has said, and what he earlier entered in his periodic reports—until recently, he was careful. You know he had leave to make a few predictions,
describe a few events in distant places, et cetera. He explained this to the Templars partly as dreams and visions,
partly as astrology. Both are everywhere taken seriously;
and the Templars are especially disposed to occultism."

Everard raised his brows. "You mean they are, in fact,
doing forbidden things?"

Reynaud shook his head. "No. At least, not to any great
degree. Everybody nowadays is superstitious. Heresy is
widespread, if mostly covert; likewise witchcraft and
other pagan survivals. Heterodoxy in a thousand different

forms is almost universal among the illiterate majority, ignorant of orthodox theology. The Templars have long been exposed to Islam, not always in a hostile fashion, and the Muslim world is full of magicians. It is no surprise that their leaders, their intellectuals, developed certain ideas and practices that they feel are legitimate but had better not be made public. Marlow's accounts of these are fascinating."

Everard couldn't resist. "Okay"—American word—"what *is* this idol Baphomet they'll be accused of worshiping?"

"'Baphomet' is merely a corruption of 'Mahomet,' a smear by their enemies. It's true that the object has the shape of a head, but it is a reliquary. The relic, acquired long ago in the Holy Land, is believed to be the jawbone of Abraham."

Everard whistled. "Heterodox for sure. Dangerous. Inquisitors might recall that the ancient Greeks kept the jawbones of heroes for oracles. But still, yes, inner-circle Templars could well imagine they can venerate this while staying Christian. . . .

He sat straight. "Let's stick to our work." Wincing, he muttered out of an irrational need, "Sure, it's unpleasant. A lot of men, mostly simple, harmless rank-and-file, are going to be jailed, terrorized, tortured, some burned, the rest left with their lives wrecked, just to glut that son-of-a-bitch Philip. But he *is* the government, and governments are like that, and this is the history that produced us"—and everybody and everything they cared for. Their task was to safeguard it. Louder, harshly: "What did Marlow tell his knightly friend, and why?"

"More than a friend," Reynaud said. "They became lovers. He admits now, he could no longer endure the thought of what would happen to Fulk de Buchy."

"Hmm! So the allegations of homosexuality aren't false?"

"Not entirely." Reynaud shrugged. "What do you expect in an organization supposed to be celibate? I don't imagine more goes on than does in the average monastery. And how many kings and nobles keep favorites?"

"Oh, I'm not passing moral judgments. On the contrary." Everard thought of the lengths to which he might go were Wanda so threatened. "People's bedrooms are none of my business. But hereabouts, the state makes them its business, and may put you to the stake because you loved the wrong person." He scowled. "I'm just trying to understand what we're up against. How much did Marlow let out, and how convinced is Fulk?"

"Marlow told him in general terms that the king plans an attack on the Templars and it will be soon. He begged Fulk to make an excuse to leave France. Kings elsewhere won't follow suit at once, and in such countries as Scotland and Portugal the Templars never will be persecuted. The warning was plausible. As you doubtless know, accusations have been circulating for several years, and an investigation, officially impartial, is in progress. Fulk took Marlow seriously enough to send a letter to a cousin of his, who commands the Templar fleet, urging him to keep his crews alert for trouble."

"Hey!" Everard exclaimed. "I remember—but my briefing only said it's a historical mystery what became of the fleet. It was never seized, nor heard of again, as far as the chronicles go. . . . What will happen?"

Reynaud was, naturally, kept informed about future developments, as the Patrol's field scientists traced them out. "When the arrests begin, the ships will put to sea," he answered. "Most will go to the Moors, like many individual Templars ashore, the men feeling betrayed and disgusted. The Moors will, quite wisely, disperse them among the naval forces of various emirs."

"So already Marlow has had a real impact," said Everard bleakly. "What else might Fulk do, even at this late hour? Once we've rescued Marlow, we'll have to deal with that gentleman . . . somehow."

"What is your plan for Marlow?" Reynaud asked.

"That's what I'm here to discuss and arrange," Everard replied. "We'll have to work out fail-safe tactics. Nothing that'll smack of the supernatural or anything else extraordinary. God knows what that could lead to."

"I expect you have ideas," Reynaud said. An Unattached agent was bound to.

Everard nodded. "Can you find me a few bully boys who know their way around? My notion is that, tonight, we break into the house in Paris. Evidently nobody's staying there but the prisoner, two guards, and a scullion—a novice, I suppose. A robber gang could hear about that and decide to take advantage of it. We'll steal whatever portable goods we find and carry Marlow off with us, presumably to hold him for ransom. What with everything that's about to take place, who'll give him further thought? The robbers figured they couldn't get a ransom after all, cut his throat, and dumped him in the Seine." He paused. "I hope we won't hurt any innocent bystanders too badly."

Sometimes the Patrol must be as ruthless as history itself.

Paris, Wednesday, 11 October 1307

After curfew, when the city gates had closed, none went abroad without necessity, save for the watch and the underworld. The timecycle appeared in a street wholly deserted. An outsize machine bearing saddles for eight, it settled onto the cobblestones with a squelp of mire that seemed loud in the silence.

Everard and his men sprang off. Narrow between high walls and elevated galleries, the street lay blacker than any open field, its air foul and cold. Glow from two small windows well up in one housefront merely deepened the dark. The raiders saw clearly. Their light-amplifying goggles ought to be taken for grotesque masks. Otherwise they wore the patched and dirty garments of the poor. All bore knives; two carried hatchets, one a cudgel, one a quarterstaff; Everard's belt upheld a falchion, short, its blade broad and curved—plausible weapons for bandits.

He squinted at the dim windows. "Damn!" he growled in English. "Somebody awake in there? Maybe just a night lamp. Well, in we go." He switched to Temporal. His team had birthdays scattered through several future centuries and around the globe. "All right, Yan, shoot."

Marlow had described the front door as massive. It would be barred on the inside. Speed was vital. When the racket began, neighbors probably wouldn't dare come to help, but they might send someone looking for a squad of the watch, or by itself it might attract that primitive constabulary. Everard's men must be gone before then, leaving no trace that lacked an ordinary explanation.

Yan, who would stand by at the transporter, saluted and swiveled around a mortar mounted on the frame. Everard had suggested the design, after which its forging and testing had taken many man-hours. It boomed. A balk of hardwood sprang out. A crash resounded. The front door sagged, splinterful, half torn from its hinges, the bar snapped. The timber could be left behind, evidence that the marauders had used a battering ram. That they must have been incommonly strong men would be cause for alarm, but the Templar sensation ought to take minds off it.

Everard was already running. Tabarin, Rosny, Hyman, and Uhl came after. Over the threshold, through the gap and the vestibule—its own inner door open—into the workroom! There they deployed in a line, their leader at the middle, and peered about them.

Pillared and stone-floored, the chamber reached hollow. The kitchen entrance at the far end was shut for the night. The furniture remaining here was an iron coffer, three stools, and the big sales counter, on which four tallow candles in sticks made a wavery dusk to see by. They stank. In the right wall was the door to a separate room below the stairs from the vestibule, formerly for storing valuables, now secured by an ornate built-in lock. A tough-looking man in the brown habit of the Order crouched before it, gripping a halberd and yelling.

"Hold!" Everard cried in the Parisian gutter dialect he had acquired. "Lay down your pole and we'll spare you."

"God's bones, no!" the Templar clamored. Had he been a common soldier before he took his vows? "Jehan! My lord! Help!"

Everard signaled his followers. They dashed for either side of the guard.

They didn't want to kill. Sonic stun guns were nested inside their weapons. Let them close in, distract him, give him a jolt. He'd wake up supposing he'd been whacked from behind—yes, it'd be needful to bang his head with the club, but cautiously.

Two more men sprang out of the vestibule. They were naked, as folk wontedly slept, but armed. The shorter, grubby one likewise carried a halberd. The tall one lifted a long, straight sword. Its blade caught the wan light in a ripple as of fire. Its wielder—

Everard knew that aquiline face. Marlow had often surreptitiously recorded it with a microscanner, to put in his reports along with other views. Did he mean to look at it, over and over, when his mission was done and he must return home?

Fulk de Buchy, Knight of the Temple.

"Ho!" he bayed. "Go for the watch, someone!" Laughter gibed at Everard. "They'll cart away your corpses, swine."

Others clustered in the entry, half a dozen men and boys, unarmed, dismayed, imploring the saints, but witnesses.

Goddamn it, Everard groaned inwardly, *Fulk's spending the night, and he's recalled the household staff.*

"Careful with the stunners!" he barked in Temporal. Don't strike the opposition down with an invisible, sorcerous blow. Maybe he needn't have warned. These were Patrolmen he commanded. They weren't cops like him, though, they were simply the most promising he'd found among personnel familiar with this milieu, hastily briefed and drilled.

They mixed it up with the halberdiers. Fulk was plunging at him.

Too flinking much visibility here. I can't stun him unless we get so close I can fake something—or I can maneuver him in back of a pillar—and his sword's got the reach of mine, and chances are he's better. I know fencing techniques that haven't been invented yet, but they aren't a lot of use when blades like these play. Not for the first time, Everard saw that he might get killed.

As always, he was too busy to feel scared. It was as if his inner self stood aside, watching, interested in a detached fashion, now and then offering advice. The rest of him was in action.

The longsword flashed at his skull. He blocked with his falchion. Metal rang. Everard shoved. His was the advantage in mass and muscle. He forced Fulk's weapon up. His free fist doubled. No knight would expect an uppercut. Fulk disengaged with feline smoothness and flowed out of range.

For an instant they glared across two yards of stone. Everard realized how the posts hemmed him in. It could prove fatal. Almost, he reversed his sword to use the gun in the pommel. He could then move quickly enough that none would notice his enemy had fallen before being struck. But while others rioted around this chamber, Fulk stepped forward. His glaive leaped.

Everard was in karate stance. Reflex eased the tension he kept on one knee and swung him aside from the slash. It passed within an inch. Everard struck for the wrist.

Again Fulk was too swift. Rising, his blade nearly tore the Patrolman's hilt loose from the hand. He kept his left side half toward the foe, arm slanted over breast. It was as if he bore a phantom crusader shield, cross-emblazoned. Above, he grinned with battle glee. His steel snaked forth.

Everard had already cast himself downward. The sword whined barely above his head. He hit the floor in full control. Such martial arts were unknown here. Fulk would have slain a man who flopped while he tried to scramble erect. Everard was coiled, his torso up. He had perhaps half a second until the knight hewed. His falchion smote the thigh.

It bit to the bone. Blood spouted. Fulk howled. He went to his sound knee. Once more he raised his sword. Once more Everard had time only to strike. Now the metal caught the belly. Momentum drove it deep and across. A loop of gut slipped out through a red torrent.

Fulk crumpled. Everard jumped back to his feet. Both swords lay unheeded. He bent over the sprawled man. Blood had splashed him. It dripped down into what was pumping forth and spreading wide. Even as he stood, the spurt lessened, the strong heart failed.

Teeth gleamed in Fulk's beard. A last snarl at his slayer? His right hand lifted. Shakily, he drew the Christian sign. But the words he gasped were *"Hugues, O Hugues—"*

The hand fell. Eyes rolled back, mouth gaped, torn bowels went slack. Everard caught the reek of death.

"I'm sorry," he croaked. "I didn't want that."

But he had work to do. He looked around him. Both pikemen were down, unconscious but apparently not seriously hurt. It must have happened seconds ago, or his squad would have come to his aid. *Those Templars put up a good fight, they did.* Seeing him hale, the Patrolmen turned their attention to the help huddled in the entry.

"Be off or we'll kill you, too!" they bawled.

The attendants weren't schooled in battle. They bolted in abrupt, trampling panic, with a backwash of moans and screams, out the vestibule and the broken door beyond.

Stumbling through the night, they might nonetheless find city guards. "Get busy," Everard ordered. "Collect an armful of loot apiece and we'll clear out. That's as much as a gang who'd raised this kind of ruckus would stop to take." His mind couldn't keep from adding in English, *If they hung around, they'd assuredly hang.* A thought more real nudged him. "Try for well-made things, and handle with care if you can. They're going to museums uptime, you know."

And so a few bits of loveliness would be saved from oblivion, for the enjoyment of a world that, possibly, this operation had also saved. He couldn't be sure. The Patrol might have managed some different corrective action. Or events might have shaped themselves to restore their long-term course; the continuum has considerable resilience. He had merely done what seemed best.

He glanced downward at the dead man. "We had our duty," he whispered. "I think you'd've understood."

While his team hastened upstairs, he sought the strongroom. The clumsy lock would have yielded to almost any burglar tools, but those in his pouch were special and it clicked directly over. He swung the door aside.

Hugh Marlow lurched out of lightlessness. "Who're you?" he choked in English. "I heard— Oh, the Patrol." His gaze found the knight. He forced back a shriek. Then he went to the body and knelt beside it, heedless of the blood, shuddering with the effort not to weep. Everard came after and loomed above him. Marlow looked up.

"Did—did you have to do this?" he stammered.

Everard nodded. "Things happened too fast. We didn't expect we'd find him here."

"No. He . . . returned. To me. He said he could not leave me alone to face . . . whatever was on the way. I hoped . . . against hope . . . I could talk him into flee-ing . . . but he wouldn't desert his brothers, either—"

"He was a man," Everard said. "At least he—I'm not cheerful about this, no, but at least he's been spared tor-ture." Bones crushed in the boot or hauled apart on the rack or the wheel. Flesh pulled off them by red-hot pin-cers. Clamps on the testicles. Needles— Never mind. Governments are ingenious. If, afterward, Fulk had re-canted the confession twisted out of him and denied the dishonor in it, they would have burned him alive.

Marlow nodded. "That's some consolation, isn't it?" He leaned over his friend. "Adieu, Fulk de Buchy, Knight of the Temple." Reaching out, he closed the eyes and held the jaw shut while he kissed the lips.

Everard help him rise, for the floor had gone slippery.

"I'll cooperate fully and freely," Marlow said, flat-voiced, "and I won't ask for clemency."

"You did get reckless," Everard answered, "and it'll lead to the fleet escaping. But that was 'always' in history. It just turns out that this was how it came about. Other-wise, no harm done." Aside from a death. But all men die. "I don't think the Patrol court will be too hard on you. No more field assignments, obviously. However, you can still do useful work in compilation and analysis, and that way redeem yourself."

How smug it sounded.

Well, love doesn't excuse everything by a long shot. But is love in itself ever a sin?

The men were descending with their plunder. "Let's go," Everard said, and led them away.

Epilogue

The Templar legend lives on, still inspiring speculation and an aspiration to many of the higher ideals
the historic knights espoused. A number of modern
chivalric Orders strive to preserve the humanitarian
legacy of their crusader forebears. The Order of Malta and
the Sovereign Military and Hospitaller Order of St. John
of Jerusalem continue some of the work of the original
Hospitallers, carrying out disaster relief and other charitable works and providing ambulance services in a number
of countries, under a number of different names. The Military and Hospitaller Order of St. Lazarus of Jerusalem,
which was founded to care for crusaders who contracted
leprosy, gradually expanded its focus to the plight of lep-
ers the world around and now engages in disaster relief as
well. The Supreme Military Order of the Temple of
Jerusalem, inheritor of the archives spirited out of occupied Belgium under diplomatic seal half a century ago, is
one of several modern-day organizations carrying forward
the Templar name, promoting philanthropic works and the

preservation of heritage. Often the chivalric Orders work together.

We have mentioned the Masonic link to the Temple and perhaps should elaborate briefly on this connection. No Masonic organization claims direct descent from the Temple—to the contrary, Freemasonry traditionally claims to predate the founding of the Temple—but a great deal of Templar symbolism and history is intertwined with Masonic tradition.

Freemasons, who comprise the oldest and largest fraternal organization in the world, progress through three degrees to attain the rank of Master Mason; much of the symbolism of the degree work alludes to the Temple of Solomon. (The last Grand Master of the historic Temple is remembered in the name and many of the rituals of the Order of De Molay, a Masonic organization for building the character of young men between the ages of thirteen and twenty-one.)

Master Masons have the option to continue through one of two associated degree systems generally known as Scottish Rite and York Rite Masonry. Those working in the latter tradition progress through a series of orders or ranks leading to initiation as a Masonic Knight Templar— no merely grandiose title, for the Masonic Templars carry forward part of the Hospitaller tradition of their historic crusader forebears by funding cataract surgery for those who otherwise could not afford it and by maintaining a research facility dedicated to children's eye diseases. Templar imagery appears in numerous other aspects of Masonic work as well.

Outside of Freemasonry, however, perhaps the most poignant tribute to the Templars in this century occurred in London at the end of World War I. To appreciate it, a bit of background is in order.

Most readers of this book will be aware that in England, trial attorneys are called barristers; not everyone will know why. When Pope Clement V gave over the majority of Templar properties to the Knights Hospitaller in 1312, one of the most valuable locations they acquired was the former Templar headquarters in London, sited between Fleet Street and the Thames—an area still called the Temple.

The only Templar structure still surviving there is Temple Church, built of stone brought from Normandy as ballast in Templar ships and consecrated by the Patriarch of Jerusalem in 1185. The original church is round, as were many Templar churches, and contains the effigies of several Templar Knights. A rectangular choir was added in 1240.

Since the Hospitallers already had a London base at Clerkenwell, they leased the Temple property to lawyers practicing at the King's Court, just through the gate between London and the city of Westminster. Because of its location, the gate was called the Barrière du Temple, or Temple Bar, and those lawyers going back and forth through the "Bar" became known as "barristers."

The property passed into Crown hands after the dissolution of the monasteries in 1534, but Henry VIII allowed the barristers to remain as sitting tenants. In 1608, King James I permitted the senior barristers of the Temple, the "Benchers," to purchase the property, on condition that they would also assume responsibility for the maintenance of the Temple Church. This they have done for nearly four centuries, even to the extent of rebuilding bomb damage sustained during the London blitz. Temple Church enjoys a unique status that is quite in keeping with its Templar ancestry. It belongs to no diocese; its Anglican canon, whose title is Master of the Temple, reports directly to the Crown.

And in 1917, when General Edmund Allenby led a column of British troops through the gates of Jerusalem—the first Christian army to do so since 1244—the barristers of the Inner and Middle Temple held a special service of thanksgiving in Temple Church, and processed into the round church to lay laurel wreaths upon the effigies of the Knights Templar in silent remembrance.

About the Authors

Poul Anderson was born in 1926 and grew up mostly in Texas and, later, on a Minnesota farm. He majored in physics at the University of Minnesota, graduating with honors, but having already sold a few stories while in college, went into free-lance writing. In 1953 he moved to California and married Karen Kruse, who has published work of her own, some of it in collaboration with him. They live in the San Francisco Bay Area. Their daughter Astrid is married to their colleague Greg Bear and has two children, both incomparable.

Although most active in the science fiction and fantasy fields, Anderson has also published mystery, historical, contemporary, and juvenile fiction, as well as nonfiction, poetry, and translations. Among his better-known books are *Brain Wave, The Broken Sword, Tau Zero, Operation Chaos, Harvest of Stars, The Stars Are Also Fire,* and *The Time Patrol,* in whose universe "Death and the Knight" is set. Honors include seven Hugos, three Nebulas, and investiture in the Baker Street Irregulars. He is a past president of Science Fiction Writers of America and a knight of the Society for Creative Anachronism.

Debra Doyle was born in Florida and educated in Florida, Texas, Arkansas, and Pennsylvania—the last at the University of Pennsylvania, where she earned her doctorate in English literature, concentrating on Old English poetry. While living and studying in Philadelphia, she met and married her collaborator, James D. Macdonald, and subsequently traveled with him to Virginia, California, and the Republic of Panamá. Various children, cats, and computers joined the household along the way.

James Douglas Macdonald was born in White Plains, New York, on February 22, 1954, the second of three children of W. Douglas Macdonald, a chemical engineer, and Margaret E. Macdonald, a professional artist. After leaving the University of Rochester, where he majored in medieval studies, he served in the U.S. Navy.

Doyle and Macdonald left the Navy and Panamá in 1988 in order to pursue writing full-time. They now live—still with various children, cats, and computers—in a big nineteenth-century house in Colebrook, New Hampshire, where they write science fiction and fantasy for children, teenagers, and adults.

Deborah Turner Harris was raised in Florida and gained a doctorate in English literature from FSU. As well as collaborating with Katherine Kurtz on the *Adept* series of novels, she is also the author of the *Mages of Garillon* trilogy. Her latest novel is *Caledon of the Mists,* a fantasy inspired by the legends and history of Scotland, which is soon to be followed by *The Queen of Ashes* and *The City of Exile.* She plays the guitar and Celtic harp and enjoys riding. She lives in St. Andrews, Scotland, with her husband Robert and their three sons.

A native Scot, **Robert J. Harris** has in his time been a classics scholar and a bartender, but is perhaps better known as the inventor of the world's best-selling fantasy board game *Talisman*. His hobbies include gaming, fencing and always backing the losing team in the Superbowl.

Tanya Huff lives with her partner and four cats in rural Canada. After spending three years in the Naval Reserve (she was a cook; no tattoos) she got a degree in radio and television arts that she's never used—although there are those who say it's responsible for a certain visual quality in her work. With *Blood Pact,* she thought she concluded the Vicki/Henry/Celluci books, her vampire series which definitely could use a series name. Her most recent book is *Sing the Four Quarters,* a heroic fantasy much like *The Fire's Stone* in feel, out from DAW in December 1994.

Katherine Kurtz is the best-selling author of the *Deryni* series, now comprising the *Deryni, Camber, Kelson,* and *Heirs of St. Camber Trilogies.* She is also the creator of the *Adept* series, coauthored with Deborah Turner Harris, in which she first began exploring the background of the Knights Templar. She lives in Ireland, where she and husband Scott MacMillan are restoring a gothic revival house that strongly resembles a castle.

Scott MacMillan is best known for his *Knights of the Blood* series—referred to among family and friends as "Nazi Vampires from Hell." He is a collector of vintage motorcars, antique edged weapons, old movies, orders of chivalry, and ghosts. He and wife Katherine Kurtz share their Irish country house with at least three of the latter.

Elizabeth Moon grew up in south Texas, on the Mexican border. Two universities share the responsibility for her warped imagination: Her history degree is from Rice University, and her biology degree is from University of Texas. She has had the usual writerly patchwork of occupations, including computer programmer (while in the Marine Corps), math tutor, sign painter, ambulance jockey, and city alderman. She lives on the edge of a small town in central Texas with her husband, son, horse, and piano.

Lawrence Schimel lives in Manhattan. He has sold short fiction to more than forty anthologies, including *Black Thorn, White Rose; Grails; Visitations of the Night; Excalibur;* and *Tales from the Great Turtle,* and his stories have been translated into Dutch, Finnish, Polish, German, and Mandarin. He played polo while attending Yale University, where he studied English, and is learning to dance flamenco.

Richard J. Woods was born and reared in New Mexico, works in Chicago, where he is on the graduate faculty of Loyola University, teaches and learns at Oxford University when he can, and lives mostly in Ireland. A Dominican friar with a particular interest in Meister Eckhart, he has published eight original nonfiction books, edited three anthologies, and authored a number of articles on spirituality, sexuality, and Celtic studies. Close friends include two cats and one dog who tolerate his efforts in art and music.

Bibliography

Baigent, Michael, and Richard Leigh. *The Temple and the Lodge.* London: Jonathan Cape, 1989.

Baigent, Michael, Richard Leigh, and Henry Lincoln. *Holy Blood, Holy Grail.* New York: Delacorte Press, 1982.

Barber, Malcolm. *The Trial of the Templars.* Cambridge, England: Cambridge University Press, 1978.

Berman, Edward. *The Templars: Knights of God.*

Currer-Briggs, Noel. *The Shroud and the Grail.* New York: St. Martin's Press, 1987.

Delaforge, Gaetan. *The Templar Tradition in the Age of Aquarius.* Putney, Vermont: Threshold Books, 1987.

Partner, Peter. *The Murdered Magicians.* (Also published as *The Knights Templar and Their Myth.*) Oxford University Press, 1981.

Robinson, John J. *Born in Blood.* New York: M. Evans, 1989.

Robinson, John J. *Dungeon, Fire, and Sword.* New York: M. Evans, 1991.

Simon, Edith. *The Piebald Standard: A Biography of the Knights Templar.* Boston: Little, Brown, 1959.

Upton-Ward, J. M. *The Rule of the Templars.* (Translated from the French of Henri de Curzon's 1886 edition of the French Rule, derived from the three extant medieval manuscripts.) New York: Boydell Press, 1992.

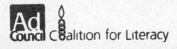